CHRISTMAS EVE

13 Stories

Books by Maeve Brennan

In and Out of Never-Never Land

Long-Winded Lady: Notes from The New Yorker

Christmas Eve: Stories

MAEVE BRENNAN

CHRISTMAS EVE

13 Stories

Charles Scribner's Sons
New York

Copyright © 1974 Maeve Brennan

Library of Congress Cataloging in Publication Data
Brennan, Maeve.
  Christmas Eve: stories.
  CONTENTS: The joker.—The view from the kitchen.
—The servants' dance. [etc.]
  I. Title.
PZ4.B8372Ch [PS3552.R38] 813'.5'4 73-1117
ISBN 0-684-13643-0

With the exception of "The Poor Men and Women" all the stories
in this book appeared originally in *The New Yorker*
"The Poor Men and Women" appeared originally in *Harper's Bazaar.*
Copyright 1952, 1953, 1954, 1955, ©1956, 1959, 1962, 1967,
1972, 1973 Maeve Brennan.
1 3 5 7 9 11 13 15 17 19 V|C 20 18 16 14 12 10 8 6 4 2
Printed in the United States of America

For Deirdre and Gilbert Jerrold

CONTENTS

CHRISTMAS EVE

13 Stories

The Joker

Waifs, Isobel Bailey called her Christmas Day guests. This year she had three coming, three waifs—a woman, an elderly man, and a young man—respectable people, well brought up, gentle-looking, neatly dressed, to all appearances the same as everybody else, but lost just the same. She had a private list of such people, not written down, and she drew on it every year as the holiday season descended. Her list of waifs did not grow shorter. Indeed, it seemed to lengthen as the years went by, and she was still young, only thirty-one. What makes a waif, she thought (most often as winter came on, always at Christmas); what begins it? When do people get that fatal separate look? Are waifs born?

Once she had thought that it was their lack of poise that marked them—because who ever saw a poised waif? You see them defiant, stiff, rude, silent, but aren't they always bewildered? Still, bewilderment was not a state reserved for waifs only. Neither was it, she decided, a matter of having no money, though money seemed to have a great deal to do with it. Sometimes you could actually see people change into waifs, right before your eyes. Girls suddenly became old maids, or at least they developed an incurably *single* look. Cheerful, bustling women became dazed widows. Men lost their grip and became unsure-looking. It wasn't any one thing that made a waif. Isobel was sure of that. It wasn't being crippled, or being in disgrace, or even not being married. It was a shameful thing to be a waif, but it was also mysterious. There was no accounting for it or defining it, and over and over again she was drawn back to her original idea— that waifs were simply people who had been squeezed off the train because there was no room for them. They had lost their tickets. Some of them never had owned a ticket. Perhaps their parents had failed to equip them with a ticket. Poor things, they were stranded. During ordinary days of the year, they could hide their plight. But at Christmas, when the train drew up for that hour of recollection and revelation, how the waifs stood out, burning in their solitude. Every Christmas Day (said Isobel to herself, smiling whimsically) was a station on the journey of life. There on the windy platform the waifs gathered in shame, to look in at the fortunate ones in the warm, lighted train. Not all of them stared in, she knew; some looked away. She, Isobel, looked them all over and decided which ones to invite into her own lighted carriage. She liked to think that she occupied a first-class carriage—their red brick house in Bronxville, solid, charming, waxed and polished, well heated, filled with flowers, stocked with glass and silver and clean towels.

Isobel believed implicitly in law, order, and organization. She believed strongly in organized charity. She gave regular donations to charity, and she served willingly and conscientiously on several committees. She felt it was only fair that she should help those less fortunate than herself, though there was a point where she drew the line. She never gave money casually on the street, and her maids had strict orders to shut the door to beggars. "There are places where these people can apply for help," she said.

It was different with the Christmas waifs. For one thing, they were not only outside society, they were outside organized charity. They were included in no one's plans. And it was in the spirit of Christmas that she invited them to her table. They were part of the tradition and ceremony of Christmas, which she loved. She enjoyed decking out the tree, and eating the turkey and plum pudding, and making quick, gay calls at the houses of friends, and going to big parties, and giving and receiving presents. She and Edwin usually accepted an invitation for Christmas night, and sometimes they sent out cards for a late, small supper, but the afternoon belonged to the waifs. She and Edwin had so much, she felt it was only right. She felt that it was beautifully appropriate that she should open her house to the homeless on Christmas Day, the most complete day of the year, when everything stopped swirling and the pattern became plain.

Isobel's friends were vaguely conscious of her custom of inviting waifs to spend Christmas afternoon. When they heard that she had entertained "poor Miss T." or "poor discouraged Mr. F." at her table, they shook their heads and reflected that Isobel's kindness was real. It wasn't assumed, they said wonderingly. She really was kind.

The first of this year's waifs to arrive was Miss Amy Ellis, who made blouses for Isobel and little silk smocks for Susan, Isobel's five-year-old daughter. Isobel had never seen Miss Ellis except in her workroom, where she wore, summer and winter, an airy, arty smock of natural-color pongee. Today, she wore a black silk dress that was draped into a cowl around her shoulders, leaving her arms bare. And Miss Ellis's arms, Isobel saw at once, with a lightning flash of intuition, were the key to Miss Ellis's character, and to her life. Thin, stringy, cold, and white, stretched stiff with emptiness—they were what made her look like a waif. Could it be that Miss Ellis was a waif *because* of her arms? It was a thought. Miss Ellis's legs matched her arms, certainly, and it was easy to see, through the thin stuff of her dress, that her shoulders were too high and pointed. Her neck crept disconsolately down into a hollow and discolored throat. Her greeny-gold hair was combed into a limp short cap, betraying the same arty spirit that inspired her to wear the pongee smock. Her earrings, which dangled, had been hammered out of some coal-like substance. Her deep, lashless eyes showed that she was all pride and no spirit. She was hopeless. But it had all started with her arms, surely. They gave her away.

Miss Ellis had brought violets for Isobel, a new detective story for Edwin, and a doll's smock for Susan. She sat down in a corner of the sofa, crossed her ankles, expressed pleasure at the sight of the fire, and accepted a Martini from Edwin. Edwin Bailey was thirty-seven and a successful corporation lawyer. His handshake was warm and firm, and his glance was alert. His blond hair was fine and straight, and his stomach looked as flat and hard as though he had a board thrust down inside his trousers. He was tall and temperate. The darkest feeling he acknowledged was contempt. Habitually he viewed the world —his own world and the world reflected in the newspapers—with tolerance. He was unaware of his wife's theories about Christmas waifs, but he would have accepted them unquestioningly, as he accepted everything about Isobel. "My wife is the most mature human

3

being I have ever met," he said sometimes. Then, too, Isobel was never jealous, because jealousy was childish. And she was never angry. "But if you understand, really understand, you simply cannot be angry with people," she would say, laughing.

Now she set about charming Miss Ellis, and Edwin had settled back lazily to watch them when the second waif, Vincent Lace, appeared in the doorway. He sprinted impetuously across the carpet and, without glancing to the right or to the left, fell on both knees before Susan, who was curled on the hearth rug, undressing her new doll.

"Ah, the grand little girl!" cried Vincent. "Sure she's the living image of her lovely mother! And what name have they put on you, love?"

"Susan," said the child coldly, and she got up and went to perch under the spreading branches of the splendid tree that blazed gorgeously from ceiling to floor between two tall windows. Beyond the windows, the narrow street lay chill and gray, except when the wind, blowing down the hill, swept before it a ragged leaf of Christmas tissue paper, red or green, or a streamer of colored ribbon.

Undisturbed by the child's desertion, Vincent rocked back on his plump behind, and wrapped his arms around his knees, and favored his host, then Miss Ellis, and, finally, Isobel with a dazzling view of his small, decaying teeth.

"Well, Isobel," he murmured, "little Isobel of the peat-brown eyes. You still have the lovely eyes, Isobel. But what am I thinking of at all!" he shouted, bounding to his feet. "Sure your husband will think me a terrible fellow entirely. Forgive me, Isobel, but the little girl took my breath away. She's yourself all over again."

"Edwin, this is our Irish poet," Isobel said. "Vincent Lace, a dear friend of Father's. I see you still wear the red bow tie, Vincent, your old trademark. I noticed it first thing when I ran into you the other day. As a matter of fact, it was the tie that caught my attention. You were never without it, were you."

"Ah, we all have our little conceits, Isobel," Vincent said, smiling disarmingly at Edwin.

Vincent's face appeared to have been vigorously stretched, either by

4

too much pain or by too much laughter, and when he was not smiling his expression was one of dignified truculence. He was more obviously combed and scrubbed than a sixty-three-year-old man should be, and his bright-blue eyes were anxious. Twenty years ago, he had come from Ireland to do a series of lectures on Irish literature at colleges and universities all over the United States. In his suitcase, he carried several copies of the two thin volumes of poetry that had won him his contract.

"My poems drive the fellows at home stark mad," Vincent had confided to Isobel's father, the first time he visited their house. "I pay no attention to the modern rubbish at all. All that crowd thinks of is making pretty-sounding imitations of Yeats and his bunch. Yeats, Yeats, Yeats, that's all they know. But my masters are long since dead. I go back in spirit to those grand eighteenth-century souls who wandered the bogs and hills of our unfortunate country, and who broke bread with the people, and who wrote out of the heart of the people."

At this point (for it was a speech Isobel and the others were often to hear), he would leap to his feet and intone in his native Irish tongue the names of the men he admired, and with every syllable his voice would grow more laden, until at the last it seemed that he would have to release a sob, but he never did, although his small blue eyes would be wet and angry. With his wild black hair, his red tie, and his sharp tongue, he quickly became a general favorite, and when his tour was over, he accepted an offer from one of the New York universities and settled down among his new and hospitable friends. Isobel's father, who had had an Irish grandmother, took to Vincent at once, and there had been a period, Isobel remembered, when her mother couldn't plan a dinner without being forced to include Vincent. At the age of fifty, he had lost his university post. Everyone knew it was because he drank too much, but Vincent blamed it on some intrigue in the department. He was stunned. He had never thought such a thing could happen to him. Isobel remembered him shouting at her father across the dinner table, "They'll get down on their knees to me! I'll go back on my own terms!" Then he had put his head in his hands and cried, and her mother had got up and left

5

the room in disgust. Isobel remembered that he had borrowed from everyone. After her father died, her family dropped Vincent. Everyone dropped him. He made too much of a nuisance of himself. Occasionally, someone would report having seen him in a bar. He was always shouting about his wrongs. He was no good, that was the sum of it. He never really had been any good, although his quick tongue and irreverent air had given him the appearance of brilliance.

A month before, Isobel had run into him on the street, their first meeting for many years. Vincent is a waif, she had thought, looking at him in astonishment. Vincent, the eloquent, romantic poet of her childhood, an unmistakable waif. It was written all over him. It was in every line of his seedy, imploring face. Two days before Christmas, she had invited him to dinner. He was delighted. He had arrived in what he imagined to be his best form—roguish, teasing, sly, and melancholy.

Edwin offered him a Martini, and he said fussily that he was on the wagon. "I will take a cigarette, though," he said, and selected one from the box on the table beside him. Isobel found with disagreeable surprise that she remembered his hands, which were small and stumpy, with long pared nails. Dreadful hands. She wondered what wretchedness they had brought him through in the years since she had known him. And the famous bow tie, she thought with amusement—how poorly it goes under that fat, disappointed face. Clinging to that distinctive tie, as though anyone connected him with the tie, or with anything any more.

The minute Jonathan Quin walked into the room, Isobel saw that she could expect nothing from him in the way of conversation. He will be no help at all, she thought, but this did not matter to her, because she never expected much from her Christmas guests. At a dinner party a few days before, she had been seated next to a newspaper editor and had asked him if there were any young people on his staff who might be at a loose end for Christmas. The next day, he had telephoned and given her Jonathan's name, explaining that he was a reporter who had come to New York from a little town in North Carolina and knew no one.

At first, entering the soft, enormous, firelit room, Jonathan took Miss Ellis to be his hostess, because of her black dress, and then, confused over his mistake, he stumbled around, looking for a chair to hide in. His feet were large. He wore loose, battered black shoes that had been polished until every break and scratch showed. He had put new laces in the shoes. Edwin asked him a few encouraging questions about his work on the newspaper, and he nodded and stammered and joggled his drink and finally told them that he was finding the newspaper a very interesting place.

Vincent said, "That's a magnificent scarlet in your dress, Isobel. It suits you. A triumphant, regal color it is."

Isobel, who was sitting in a yellow chair, with her back to the glittering tree, glanced down at her slim wool dress.

"Christmas red, Vincent. I think it is the exact red for Christmas, don't you? I wore it decorating the tree last night."

"And my pet Susan dressed up in the selfsame color, like a little red berry she is!" cried Vincent, throwing his intense glance upon the silent child, who ignored him. He was making a great effort to be the witty, rakish professor of her father's day, and at the same time deferring slyly to Edwin. He did not know that this was to be his only visit, no matter how polite he proved himself to be.

It was a frightful thing about Vincent, Isobel thought. But there was no use getting involved with him. He was too hard to put up with, and she knew what a deadly fixture he could become in a household. "Some of those ornaments used to be on the tree at home, Vincent," she said suddenly. "You might remember one or two of them. They must be almost as old as I am."

Vincent looked at the tree and then said amiably, "I can't remember what I did last year. Or perhaps I should say I prefer not to remember. But it was very kind of you to think of me, Isobel. Very kind." He covertly watched the drinks getting lower in the glasses.

Isobel began to think it had been a mistake to invite him. Old friends should never become waifs. It was easier to think about Miss Ellis, who was, after all, a stranger. Pitiful people, she thought. How they drag their wretched lives along with them. She allowed time for

7

Jonathan to drink one Martini—one would be more than enough for that confused head—before she stood up to shepherd them all in to dinner.

The warm pink dining room smelled of spice, of roasting turkey, and of roses. The tablecloth was of stiff, icy white damask, and the centerpiece—of holly and ivy and full-blown blood-red roses—bloomed and flamed and cast a hundred small shadows trembling among the crystal and the silver. In the fireplace a great log, not so exuberant as the one in the living room, glowed a powerful dark red.

Vincent startled them all with a loud cry of pleasure. "Isobel, Isobel, you remembered!" He grasped the back of the chair on which he was to sit and stared in exaggerated delight at the table.

"I knew you'd notice," Isobel said, pleased. "It's the centerpiece," she explained to the others. "My mother always had red roses and holly arranged just like that in the middle of our table at home at Christmas time. And Vincent always came to Christmas dinner, didn't you, Vincent?"

"Christmas dinner and many other dinners," Vincent said, when they were seated. "Those were the happiest evenings of my life. I often think of them."

"Even though my mother used to storm down in a rage at four in the morning and throw you out, so my father could get some sleep before going to court in the morning," Isobel said slyly.

"We had some splendid discussions, your father and I. And I wasn't always thrown out. Many a night I spent on your big red sofa. Poor old Matty used to find me there, surrounded by glasses and ashtrays and the books your father would drag down to prove me in the wrong, and the struggle *she* used to have getting me out before your mother discovered me! Poor Matty, she lived in fear that I'd fall asleep with a lighted cigarette going, and burn the house down around your ears. But I remember every thread in that sofa, every knot, I should say. Who has it now, Isobel? I hope you have it hidden away somewhere. In the attic, of course. That's where you smart young things would put a comfortable old piece of furniture like that. The most comfortable bed I ever lay on."

8

Delia, the bony Irish maid, was serving them so discreetly that every movement she made was an insertion. She fitted the dishes and plates onto the table as though they were going into narrow slots. Her thin hair was pressed into stiff waves under her white cap, and she appeared to hear nothing, but she already had given Alice, the cook, who was her aunt, a description of Vincent Lace that had her doubled up in evil mirth beside her hot stove. Sometimes Isobel, hearing the raucous, jeering laughter of these two out in the kitchen, would find time to wonder about all the reports she had ever heard about the soft voices of the Irish.

"Isobel tells me you've started a bookshop near the university, Mr. Lace," Edwin said cordially. "That must be interesting work."

"Well, now, I wouldn't exactly say I started it, Mr. Bailey," Vincent said. "It's only that they needed someone to advise them on certain phases of Irish writing, and I'm helping to build up that department in the store, although of course I help out wherever they need me. I like talking to the customers, and then I have plenty of time for my own writing, because I'm only obliged to be there half the day. Like all decent-minded gentlemen of leisure, I dabble in writing, Mr. Bailey. And speaking of that, I had a note the other day from an old student of mine who had through some highly unlikely chance come across my name in the Modern Encyclopaedia. An article on the history of house painting, Isobel. What do you think of that? Mr. Quin and Miss Ellis, Isobel and her father knew me as an accomplished and, if I may say so, a reasonably witty exponent of Irish letters. Students fought with tooth and with nail to hear my lecture on Irish writers. . . . 'Envy Is the Spur,' I called it. But to get back to my ink-stained ex-student, whose name escapes me. He wanted to know if I remembered a certain May morning when I led the entire student body, or as many as I could lure from the library and from the steps of the building, down to riot outside Quanley's—a low and splendid drinking establishment of that time, Mr. Quin—to riot, I repeat, for one hour, in protest against their failure to serve me, in the middle hours of the same morning, the final glass that I felt to be my due."

9

"Well, that must have been quite an occasion, Mr. Lace, I should imagine," Miss Ellis said.

Vincent turned his excited stare on Isobel. "You wouldn't remember that morning, Isobel."

"I couldn't honestly say if I remember it or not, Vincent. You had so many escapades. There seemed to be no end to your ingenuity."

"Oh, I was a low rascal. Miss Ellis, I was a scoundrelly fellow in those days. But when I lectured, they listened. They listened to me. Isobel, you attended one or two of my lectures. I flatter myself now that I captivated even you with my masterly command of the language. Isobel, tell your splendid husband, and this gracious lady, and this gracious youth, that I was not always the clown they see before them now. Justify your old friend, Isobel."

"Vincent, you haven't changed at all, have you?"

"Ah, that's where you're wrong, Isobel. For I have changed a great deal. Your father would see it. You were too young. You don't remember. You're all too young," he finished discontentedly.

Miss Ellis moved nervously and seemed about to speak, but she said nothing. Edwin asked her if she thought the vogue for mystery stories was as strong as ever, and Vincent looked as if he were about to laugh contemptuously—Isobel remembered him always laughing at everything anyone said—but he kept silent and allowed the discussion to go on.

Isobel reflected that she had always known Vincent to be talky but surely he couldn't have always been the windbag he was now. Again she wished she hadn't invited him to dinner, but then she noticed how eagerly he was enjoying the food, and she relented. She was glad that he should see what a pleasant house she had, and that he should have a good meal.

Isobel was listening dreamily to Vincent's story about a book thief who stole only on Tuesdays, and only books with yellow covers, and she was trying to imagine what color Miss Ellis's lank hair must originally have been, when she became aware of Delia, standing close at her side and rasping urgently into her ear about a man begging at the kitchen door.

"Edwin," Isobel interrupted gently, "there's a man begging at the back door, and I think, since it's Christmas, we should give him his dinner, don't you?"

"What did he ask you for, Delia?" Edwin asked.

"He asked us would we give him a dollar, sir, and then he said that for a dollar and a half he'd sing us our favorite hymn," Delia said, and began to giggle unbecomingly.

"Ask him if he knows 'The boy stood on the burning deck,' " Vincent said.

"Poor man, wandering around homeless on Christmas Day!" Miss Ellis said.

"Get an extra plate, so that Mr. Bailey can give the poor fellow some turkey, Delia!" Isobel cried excitedly. "I'm glad he came here! I'm glad we have the chance to see that he has a real Christmas dinner! Edwin, you're glad, too, although you're pretending to disapprove!"

"All right, Isobel, have it your own way," Edwin said, smiling.

He filled the stranger's plate, with Delia standing judiciously by his elbow. "Give him more dressing, Edwin," Isobel said. "And Delia, see that he has plenty of hot rolls. I want him to have everything we have."

"Nothing to drink, Isobel," Edwin said. "If he hasn't been drinking already today, I'm not going to be responsible for starting him off. I hope you people don't think I'm a mean man," he added, smiling around the table.

"Not at all, Mr. Bailey," Miss Ellis said stoutly. "We all have our views on these matters. That's what makes us different. What would the world be like if we were all the same?"

"My mother says," said Jonathan hoarsely, putting one hand into his trouser pocket, "that if a person is bad off enough to ask her for something, he's worse off than she is."

"Your mother must be a very nice lady, Mr. Quin," Miss Ellis said.

"It's a curious remark, of Mr. Quin's mother," Vincent said moodily.

"Oh, of course you'd have him in at the table here and give him the house, Vincent!" Isobel cried in great amusement. "I remember your reputation for standing treat and giving, Vincent."

"Mr. Lace has the look of a generous man," Miss Ellis said, with her thin, childlike smile. The heavy earrings hung like black weights against her thin jaw.

Vincent stared at her. "Isobel remarks that I would bid the man in and give him the house," he said bitterly. "But at the moment, dear lady, I am not in the position to give him the leg of a chair, so the question hardly arises. Do you know what I would do if I was in Mr. Bailey's position, Miss Ellis? Now this is no reflection on you, Mr. Bailey. When I think of him, and what is going on in his mind at this moment, as he gazes into the heaped platter that you have so generously provided—"

"Vincent, get back to the point. What would you do in Edwin's place?" asked Isobel good-naturedly.

Vincent closed his mouth and gazed at her. "You're quite right, my dear," he said. "I tend to sermonize. It's the strangled professor in me, still writhing for an audience. Well, to put it briefly, if I were in your husband's excellent black leather shoes, I would go out to the kitchen, and I would empty my wallet, which I trust for your sake is well filled, and I would tell that man to go in peace."

"And he would laugh at you for a fool," Edwin said sharply.

"And he would laugh at me for a fool," Vincent said, "and I would know it, and I would curse him, but I would have done the only thing I could do."

"I don't get it," Jonathan said, with more self-assurance than before.

"Oh, Mr. Quin, Vincent is an actor at heart," Isobel said. "You should have come to our home when my father was alive. It was a one-man performance every time, Vincent's performance."

"I used to make you laugh, Isobel."

"Of course you did," Isobel said soothingly.

She sat and watched them all eat their salad, wondering at the same time how the man in the kitchen must feel, to come from the cold and deserted winter street into her warm house. He must be speechless at his good fortune, she thought, and she had a wild impulse to go out into the kitchen and see him for herself. She stood up and said, "I want to see if our unexpected guest has enough of everything."

She hurried through the pantry and into the white glare of the kitchen, where it was very hot. She rigidly avoided looking at the table, but she was conscious of the strange man's dark bulk against her white muslin window curtains, and of the harsh smell of his cigar. She wanted him to see her, in her red dress, with her flushed face and her sweet, expensive perfume. She owned the house. He had the right to feast his eyes on her. This was the stranger, the classical figure of the season, who had come unbidden to her feast.

Fat-armed Alice was petting the round brown pudding where a part of it had broken away as she tumbled it out of its cloth into its silver dish. Delia stood watching intently, holding away to her side— as though it were a matador's cape—the stained and steaming cloth.

"Take your time, Alice," Isobel said in her clear, nicely tempered voice. "Everything is going splendidly. It couldn't be a more successful party."

"That's very considerate of you, Ma'am," Alice said, letting her eyes roll meaningfully in the direction of the stranger, as though she were tipping Isobel off.

As she turned to leave the kitchen, Isobel saw the man at the table. She did not mean to see him. She had no intention of looking at him, but she did look. She saw that he had hair and hands, and she knew that he had sight, because she felt his eyes on her, but she could not have given a description of him, because in that rapid, silent glance all she really saw was the thick, filthy stub in his smiling mouth.

His cigar, she thought, sitting down again in the dining room. She leaned forward and took a sip of wine. Miss Ellis's arms, Vincent's bow tie, this boy's broken shoes, and now the beggar's cigar.

"How is our other guest getting along out there, Delia?" Isobel asked when the salad plates were being cleared away.

"Ah, he's all right, Ma'am. He's sitting there and smiling to himself. He's very quiet, so he is."

"Has he said nothing at all, Delia?"

13

"Only when he took an old cigar butt he has out of his pocket. He said to Alice that he strained his back picking it up. He said he made a promise to his mother never to step down off the sidewalk to pick up a butt of a cigar or a cigarette, and he says this one was halfway out in the middle of the street."

"He must have hung on to a lamp-post!" Jonathan cried, delighted.

"Edwin, send a cigar to that poor fellow when Delia comes in again, will you?" Isobel said. "I'd like to feel he had something decent to smoke for once."

Delia came in, proudly bearing the flaming pudding, and Edwin told her to take a cigar for the man in the kitchen.

"And don't forget an extra plate for his pudding, Delia," Isobel said happily.

"Oh, your mother was a mighty woman, Isobel," Vincent said, "even though we didn't always see eye to eye."

"Well, I'm sure you agreed on the important things, Mr. Lace," Miss Ellis said warmly.

"I don't like to disappoint or disillusion you, Miss Ellis, but it was on the important things we disagreed. She thought they were unimportant."

A screech of surprise and rage was heard from the kitchen, which up to that time had sent to their ears only the subdued and pleasant tinkling of glasses and dishes and silver. They were therefore prepared for—indeed, they compelled, by their paralyzed silence—the immediate appearance of Delia, who materialized without her cap, and with her eyes aglow, looking as though she had been taken by the hair and dropped from a great height.

"That fellow out there in the kitchen!" she cried. "He's gone!"

"Did he take something?" asked Edwin keenly.

"No, sir. At least, now, I don't think he took anything. I'll look and see this minute."

"Delia, calm yourself," Isobel said. "What was all the noise about?"

"He flew off when I was in here with the pudding, Ma'am. I went out to give him the cigar Mr. Bailey gave me for him, and he was gone, clean out of sight. I ran over to the window, thinking to call him back for his cigar, as long as I had it in my hand, and there wasn't a sign of him anywhere. Alice didn't even know he was out of the chair till she heard the outside door bang after him."

"Now, Delia. It was rude of him to run off like that when you and Alice and all of us have been at such pains to be nice to him, but I'm sure there's no need for all this silly fuss," Isobel said, with an exasperated grimace at Edwin.

"But Mrs. Bailey, he didn't just go!" Delia said wildly.

"Well, what did he do, then?" Edwin asked.

"Oh, sir, didn't he go and leave his dirty old cigar butt stuck down in the hard sauce, sir!" Delia cried. She put her hands over her mouth and began to make rough noises of merriment and outrage while her eyes swooped incredulously around the table.

Edwin started to rise, but Isobel stopped him with a look. "Delia," she said, "tell Alice to whip up some kind of sauce for the pudding and bring it in at once."

"Oh dear, how could he do such a thing?" Miss Ellis whispered as the door swung to on Delia. "And after you'd been so kind to him." She leaned forward impulsively to pat Isobel's hand.

"A shocking thing!" Vincent exclaimed. "Shocking! It's a rotten class of fellow would do a thing like that."

"You mustn't let him spoil your lovely dinner, Mrs. Bailey," Miss Ellis said. Then she added, to Edwin, "Mrs. Bailey is such a *person!*"

"I never cared much for hard sauce anyway," Jonathan said.

"I don't know what you're all talking about!" Isobel cried.

"We wouldn't blame you if you were upset," Vincent said. "But just because some stupid clod insults you is no reason for you to *feel* insulted."

"I think that nasty man meant to spoil our nice day," Miss Ellis said contentedly. "And he hasn't at all, has he?"

"Let's all just forget about it," Edwin said. "Isn't that right, Miss Ellis?"

"Are you people sympathizing with me?" Isobel said. "Because if you are, please stop it. I am not in the least upset, I assure you." With hands that shook violently, she began to serve the pudding.

When they had all been served, she pushed her chair back and said, "Edwin, I have to run upstairs a minute to check on the heat in Susan's room before she goes for her nap. Delia will bring the coffee inside, and I'll be down in a second."

Upstairs, in the bedroom, she cooled her beleaguered forehead with eau de cologne. She heard the chairs moving in the dining room, and then the happy voices chorusing across the hall. A moment later, she imagined she could hear the chink of their coffee cups. She wished bitterly that it was time to send them all home. She was tired of them. They talked too much. It seemed twenty years since Edwin had carved the turkey.

The View from the Kitchen

Herbert's Retreat is a snug community of forty or more houses that cluster together on the east bank of the Hudson about thirty miles above New York City. Some of the houses are small and some are middle-sized. No two are alike, and because they are separated by trees, hedges, wooden fences, or untidy vestiges of ancient woods, and because of the vagaries of the terrain, they all seem to be on different levels. Some of the houses certainly reach much higher into the air than others, because a few roofs can be glimpsed from the highway, and in wintertime, when the trees are bare, an occasional stretch of wall is disclosed to passing motorists, but otherwise the community is secluded. One characteristic all the houses have in common: They all eye the river. This does not mean that they all face the river. Some of them face vaguely toward the highway, as though they were not sure exactly where it was. Some face the private roadway, hardly more than a path, that strings them all together. Some face each other, while keeping their distance, and a few seem to stand sideways to everything. But in every house the residents have contrived and plotted and schemed and paid to bring the river as intimately as possible into their lives. The people with houses directly on the river are in luck, of course. The most any of them had to do was to knock out a side wall, widen a window, or build a porch. Those fortunate enough to have houses facing directly on the river had no problem, since the view was theirs for the taking. It is among the people with houses set back from the river that the competition for its favors is keenest. The tallest of these houses have had square wooden balconies balanced on their roofs, where the host and hostess and their guests may perch and drink and admire the view. Occupants of the smaller houses have been very ingenious in devising ways to trap and hold their own particular glimpse of the water. Some have centipede-like porches creeping sideways from their houses to the nearest break in the wall of trees and buildings that cuts them off from the river, so that the vantage point gained, while not exactly natural to the house, is still part of the establishment. It is of no advantage to repair to a neighbor's house in order to see the water and show it off to visitors; each householder feels he must have a view of his own to offer. Several tree houses have been built. One man went so far as to erect a slender round tower of brick in his garden. Only one person can squeeze up the steep spiral staircase of the tower, and only one can stand in the tiny room that tops it, but sooner or later each guest, glass in hand, makes the solitary, claustrophobic ascent and returns to report on the merits of the view from the tower, and to compare it favorably with all other points of survey around.

All the people who live at Herbert's Retreat own their own houses. Newcomers can seldom get a foot in, except in the summertime, when a few residents let their places for two or three months. The tone and welfare of the community is guarded by a board of trustees. There are almost no restrictions on the behavior of children and animals belonging to the community, but there are iron restrictions against strange children and strange animals. The general atmosphere of the place is one of benevolent freedom. The life there is casual and informal, but gracious. A good deal of quiet entertaining is done. All the residents know each other very well or fairly well. There are no strangers. Living there is rather like living in a club.

Late one November afternoon, a splendid dinner for three was in the first stages of preparation in the kitchen of one of the houses at the Retreat. This house was long, low, and white. It was not large, but it was charming. It was the property of Mrs. George Harkey, who was generally said to be a very romantic-looking young woman, although her face was not pretty. In her kitchen, Bridie and Agnes, the maids, were taking their time about getting the dinner. They knew that the guest of the evening had only just arrived, that drinks had only started, and that they had plenty of time before they need bother with the dining room, where the table was already set with silver and glass and linen, and with candles ready for lighting.

Bridie belonged to the house. She lived in. Agnes worked and lived at the Gieglers', up the road, and had come to help out for the evening. Bridie, who liked heat, had planted her broad self on a chair beside the stove. Agnes, hovering inquisitively around the strange kitchen, was at a double disadvantage. Not only was she relegated, for the time being, to the position of helper but she was new to the community, having come out from New York City only the week before. She longed to stand at the kitchen window, to watch the antics of Mr. and Mrs. Harkey and their guest, whose voices she could hear outside, but the balance of amiability was still uncertain between her and Bridie, and she feared to put herself in a position that might prove embarrassing if Bridie chose to make it so. However, Bridie's unwavering, ironic stare finally drove her to drift with a show of unconcern to the window, where she saw enough to give her courage to make a remark.

"They're at the statue!" she cried.

Bridie rose from the chair as though it had burnt her, and made for the window.

"Don't let them see you looking," she said, and the two of them crowded together at the side of the window, behind the curtain, and stared out.

They could see the river, separated from them by a long, descending sweep of lawn as wide as the house and guarded on either side by a dense barricade of trees and hedges. The grass on the lawn had only recently been planted. It was still thin and tender, but the earth had been rigorously plowed, raked, dug, and rolled to receive it, and there was no doubt that eventually it would present a carpet of emerald-green velvet leading precisely to the edge of the river. A naked woman in white marble, her limbs modestly disposed, stood to the right of the lawn, not far from the house. Farther from the house, and on the left, a gray stone clown, dwarf-sized, bowed his head dejectedly. The clown wore baggy pants, a flowing tie, and a jacket too small for him. His gray stone wig hung dead from one of his hands, and his face, with its despairing grin, had just been freshly powdered, and painted with purple lipstick. It was the guest of the evening, Mr. Charles Runyon, who had decorated the clown, using tools from the handbag of his hostess, Leona Harkey. Now Charles stood with his arm around Leona, and they laughed together at his handiwork. A little apart from them, George Harkey stood alone, joining uncer-

19

tainly in their amusement, which was exaggerated and intimate and hard to live up to. It was evident he could think of nothing to say. At the start of the jest, Charles had handed him the handbag, asking him to hold it open for him. The handbag still dangled from his hand, and he glanced awkwardly down at it from time to time, and sipped uneasily from the glass he had carried out with him.

"That's the new husband?" Agnes whispered.

"That's him, all right," said Bridie. "Mr. Harkey. George, his name is."

"He's not bad-looking."

"Oh, he *looks* all right. How old would you say he was?"

"About thirty, I'd say, looking at him from here."

"That's what I thought. The same age as herself, then."

"The other fellow is older. Mr. Runyon."

"Mr. God Runyon," said Bridie emphatically. "Yes, he's a good bit older. He must be past fifty, that fellow."

"Why do you call him Mr. God?"

"Ah, the airs he puts on him, lording it around. And the way she kowtows to him. She'll make the new husband kowtow to him, too."

"How long are they married?"

"A month, it is."

"And how long was she a widow?"

"Four months," said Bridie, smiling grimly at Agnes's astonished face. "Finch, her name used to be."

"And he was killed in a car?"

"He was dead-drunk and ran himself into a young tree. Destroyed the tree and killed himself. She had to get a new car. He was all over the windshield when they found him, and the front seat, and bits of him on the hood—blood, hair, everything. Ugh. I often wonder did they get both his eyes to bury him. His face was just pulp, that's all—all mashed. The police were mystified, that he could do himself so much damage against such a small tree. He must have been going awful fast. She never turned a hair. I was here when she got the call. Not a feather out of her."

"She's hard."

"That rip hasn't got a nerve in her body. And there she is now, laughing away the same as ever with Mr. God, and Mr. Harkey standing there in place of Mr. Finch. You'd hardly know the difference, except that Mr. Finch was fair-headed and this fellow is black."

"Where does Mr. God come in?"

"He's her *admirerer*. He admires her, and she admires him. They *admire* each other. Oh, they talk a lot about their admiring, but you should have seen the way he hotfooted it out of the picture when Mr. Finch was killed. She was all up and ready to marry him, of course. She thought sure she was going to be *Mrs.* God. But Mr. God was a match for her. All of a sudden didn't he discover there were people all over the country he had to visit, Arizona and everywhere, and he ended up going to Italy. This is his first night back. This is the first time she's seen him since the summer. That's what all the fuss is about, getting you in to help with the dinner, and all. This is the first Mr. Harkey has seen of him, either. You can imagine what's going on in *his* mind. He never laid eyes on him before tonight."

"He has a great look of a greyhound. Mr. God, I mean."

"Oh, he's a very *elegant* gentleman. Did you notice the pointy shoes he's wearing. And the waistcoat with the little buttons on it. And the way he shapes around, imagining everybody is looking at him. He'd make you sick."

"They're coming in now. They'll be looking for more drinks, I suppose?"

"That crowd takes care of their own drinks. Out of shame, if nothing else, so we won't see how much they put down. As if I didn't have to carry the empty bottles out. It's a scandal. *He* makes the drinks. He stands up in front of the bar in there like a priest saying Mass, God forgive me, and mixes a Martini for himself, and one for her, and maybe an odd one for the husband. Mr. Finch used to like to make his own. He had a special big glass he used to drink out of. He had a little song he used to sing when he'd had a few. He used to go off by himself in a corner of the living room, and he'd sing, very low—it wouldn't bother you, except that he kept it up—he'd sing

"You're too nice, you're too nice,
You're too nice for me."

21

"Is that all the words there was to it?"

"That's all. Then he'd get up and make himself another drink in his big glass, and he'd stand and look at the two of them, and sing it all over again, and laugh and laugh."

"And wouldn't they say anything?"

"No, because if they paid any attention to him, he'd point his finger at Mr. God and sing the same thing, over and over, except he'd say '*He's* too nice, *he's* too nice.' It used to get on their nerves."

"Look at them now."

"What did I tell you. That's the way it always is."

Leona and Charles were strolling arm in arm toward the house, carrying their almost finished Martinis in their free hands. George, with the handbag, brought up the rear. George liked sweet Manhattans, and his glass was empty. Charles glanced over his shoulder at the river, and George stopped dead and looked over his shoulder, too.

"Leona, darling, it's exactly what I dreamed of for you," Charles said. "And of course you've done exactly what I would have done. Do you remember how we used to talk and *talk* about it. Who would ever have thought it would all come true?"

"Charles, darling, I hope it won't ever rain again," Leona cried in her dark, husky voice. "I want that poor dismal face to stay just as you painted it, to remind me that you are back at last, and to commemorate our first evening all three together."

Charles' reply was unheard in the kitchen, because the three celebrants had disappeared around the side of the house, and would by now be arranging themselves before the living-room fire.

Bridie turned away from the window. "I don't know where she thinks she's going to get the lawn from," she said, "if she's not going to let it rain. Would you ever think that only a month ago you couldn't see hardly an inch beyond that kitchen window there? The kitchen here was as dark as a cellar, even in the middle of the day. There was a hedge out there almost as high as the house."

"They cut the hedge?" Agnes said politely.

"Cut the *hedge.* God almighty, she couldn't get it down soon enough. I thought she was going to go after it with her nail scissors, the way she was carrying on. I tell you, Agnes, the poor fellow was hardly out of bed the first morning after they got back from the honeymoon when she started screaming about the hedge. 'The hedge must go!' she kept yelling. 'Down with the accursed hedge! I must have my view. Where is my wonderful, my promised view!' Did you ever hear the like of that?"

"Them and their view. You'd think it was a diamond necklace, the way they carry on about their *view*. Mrs. Giegler is just the same. The minute a person walks into the house, it's me view this and me view that, and come and look at me view, and dragging them over to the window and out on to the porch in every sort of weather. Damp, that's all I have to say about it. Damp."

"Oh, this one is a terror on the view. She's had her eye on that view ever since I've been here. She was bound and determined to get that view."

"Well, and now she has it."

"Two people had to die before she could get it. First the poor old daisy who owned the cottage that used to be down there died in her sleep one night, and then, not two weeks later, doesn't poor Mr. Finch go and smash himself up."

"And then she bought the cottage?"

"Not at all," said Bridie, rudely. "She couldn't afford to buy the cottage. There were dozens of them around here after it, but she got herself on the inside first. Mr. Harkey inherited the cottage from his aunt. That was the old one who died. Miss Harkey. An old maid. They were all after that cottage. That's why she married him in such a hurry, apart from the fact that she knew Mr. God would never show his face in the house till she had a new husband."

"Mr. Harkey got the cottage from his aunt, and then this one married him and made him pull it down."

"Pulled it down and carted it away as fast as I'm saying the words. Oh, she was in a terrible hurry about it. She had them out there marking the place for the lawn and planting the grass and putting up the statues before you could turn around. He never said a word, but I think he was sorry to see the cottage go. He said to her that it was the only thing he'd ever owned in his life."

"I would've thought he had money, from the looks of him."

23

"Not that fellow. Oh, he likes to look as if he was somebody, but he hasn't a penny except what he gets from his job. The old aunt didn't leave him any money, only the cottage. I don't think she had much else to leave. She kept very much to herself. She hadn't much patience with the crowd around here. Well, Mr. Harkey was all pleased. He came down here, just weekends, and began settling in, cooking little meals for himself and all, and the next thing you knew, there *she* was, charging down the road with little *housewarming* presents for him—little pots of patty de fwa, and raspberry jam *I'd* made, and a tin of green-turtle soup she paid a fortune for. She thought he might like the unusual flavor of it, she said. Oh, she'd never have looked at him, only for his view. It would have matched him better to have sold up the place and taken his money and run. She just took it out from under him. He never had a chance, once *she* took after him."

"The poor fellow."

"Oh, I'd waste no sympathy on that fellow, Agnes. Do you know what his job is? Well, now, I'll let you guess. The lowest thing, about the lowest thing you can think of. Go on, guess. I'll give you three guesses."

"An undertaker?"

"No."

"A pawnbroker?"

"No, but you're close."

"A summons server?"

"No. He's a credit manager."

Agnes emitted a low, prolonged shriek and sat down on Bridie's chair by the stove. Bridie smiled her satisfaction.

"A credit manager!" cried Agnes. "A credit manager. Oh, my God, the lowest of the low. A credit manager. And to think I'm going to have to put his dinner in front of him. Oh, the dirty thing."

"At Clancyhanger's," Bridie said.

"Clancyhanger's. The worst bunch of thieves and knaves in the country. The persecutors of the poor. Oh, the way they hop off you when you haven't got the money. Bridie, I've heard enough. I hope she cuts him up and eats him."

"Of course, *she* doesn't say he's a credit manager. That's not good enough for *her*. She makes out he's a junior vice-president, if you don't mind. But I heard him talking to her the first time he came in here for a drink, and that's what he told her. He's a credit manager, and that's all he is."

"One of the ones that does the dirty work. When our Blessed Lord was crucified, he was standing there holding the box of nails."

"That's the sort he is. No real good in him. Although to look at him you'd think butter wouldn't melt in his mouth. Oh, he was all full of himself that first day he came in here. He had a girl he brought with him."

"A girl?"

"She was staying with him in the cottage. And there was only the one bed in the place, because I saw the furniture when it was carted out. She was *staying* with him all right, in the full sense of the word."

"Imagine doing the like of that, and probably not engaged or married or anything. Isn't it disgusting?" Agnes said enviously.

"This one may not have been married, Agnes, but she had the *experience* of being married, I'll guarantee you that much. Oh, I think she thought he was going to marry her. She was all busy, making curtains and cushion covers and all, and cleaning up the weeds in the garden down there where the old one had let it go. She was a nice enough girl, too, I'll say that much for her. All excited about the cottage. But she didn't last long after the Madam got to work."

"Tell us, Bridie, what did she do to her?"

"She didn't have to *do* anything. Not that one. She was all nice to the girl. All advice on how this should go in the cottage, and how that should go, all over her, she was, sweet and nice as you please. But then one night he came up by himself, and the first thing you know, she was on the phone asking him over for a drink. 'I love your girl,' she says to him, 'a dear girl. What does she do?' she says—as if she didn't know, I heard her questioning the girl myself. 'She works in the advertising department in the store,' he says. 'Isn't that interesting,' she says. 'But isn't it a pity she's not more at ease here,' she says. 'We're such a select little group, you know. A lot of artists and writers, *creative* people. We see each other all the time,' she says. 'It's so important to fit in, as you do,' she says. 'I want to give a little party for you, and introduce you to everybody. And there's my friend Charles Runyon, the critic—you know his name, of course.' That's Mr. God. 'You must meet him the minute he gets back from Europe. He's so charming,' she says. 'I know you'll adore him, as we all do.' And then she invited him to a dinner party she was giving, not mentioning the girl, and he didn't mention the girl, either, and he never brought her near the place again. Of course, he didn't know what he was getting in for, with this one. He thought she was all interested in his cottage. And all she was thinking about was how fast she could get it out of the way so she could have her precious view."

"And now I suppose all she's thinking about is how fast she can get *him* out of the way."

"Ah, no, she doesn't mind him, as long as he behaves himself and doesn't cause her any trouble. He's not a bad-looking young fellow, you know. And now she has Mr. God coming around again, paying her compliments and inviting her in to New York to see the new plays, and all. You'll see—he'll be out here every weekend, just the way he used to be. He has his own room here, even. He told her the way he wanted it, and she had it all done up for him. He hasn't even got his own car, but they fall over themselves around here to see which one of them will give him a lift out from the city. They think it's an honor, having him around. He's supposed to be very *witty*. A wit, he is. He never opens that narrow little mouth of his but they all collapse laughing."

"The way they carry on, it's not decent."

"Oh, the things I could tell you about their carrying-on," Bridie said ominously. "It would curl your hair."

"You mean her and Mr. God."

"No, no, nothing like that there. He's the sort that just pays compliments. I heard him telling her she has a face on her that belongs to the ages. What do you make of that?"

"Is that a compliment? What sort of a compliment is that? Isn't that a queer thing to say to a woman!"

"She liked it. She says she's in love with his mind."

"In love with Mr. God's mind?"

"She's in love with Mr. God's mind."

"In love with his mind. Well, that's a new one. I never heard that one before."

"Neither did Mr. Harkey, by the look of him."

"There he is now," said Agnes, who had resumed her stand by the window. Bridie came to look over her shoulder.

Flashlight in hand, George was making his way timorously over the darkened lawn. He passed the naked woman, at whom he did not glance. Passing the clown, he turned the light briefly on the painted face, and proceeded on. He walked slowly over the place where his cottage had raised its walls, and reached at last the edge of the river, where he stood stabbing convulsively with the flashlight out into the blackness. The path he lighted across and around and over and above the water was ragged and wavering. His hand seemed to be shaking.

"What's he up to now, I wonder," said Bridie.

"Maybe he's looking for his view," Agnes said, and grimaced nervously at her own smartness.

"Well, he's not going to find much down there," Bridie said, and gave her a companionable nudge in the ribs.

Emboldened, Agnes thumbed her nose at the window, and immediately collapsed on the table in a heap of shuddering, feeble giggles, with her hands covering her face. After a second, she moved one finger aside and peered up to see how Bridie was taking this demonstration.

Bridie winked at her.

The Servants' Dance

On Saturday morning, Charles Runyon awoke in a mood of rapturous gaiety. This day, this evening, this weekend, promised—no, guaranteed—a triumph so complete, both in secret and in public, that it must surely, Charles felt, become one of the succession of platforms that marked his progress through life, each platform raising him higher, the better to survey the world and the men and women in it. My stage and my actors, he said to himself; my arena. Charles was a literary gentleman whose main interest was the theatre. He lived alone in a single room in an old and famous hotel in the Murray Hill district. He never entertained, having, as he laughingly explained, no facilities for doing so, but he went out a great deal, and had a reputation, undefined but definite, as a wit and an epigrammatist. His weekends were spent at Herbert's Retreat, thirty miles from New York on the east side of the Hudson, and always at Leona Harkey's, where one bedroom was sacred to him.

Now, lying in his narrow, canopied four-poster there, he stretched his stringy little arms and his long stringy neck, and yawned. Then he got out of bed, pattered over to his writing table, and snatched up a large notebook, in which, the night before, as every night, he had recorded his impressions of the evening. The notes had been very enjoyable to write. They were copious and would be memorable. Edward Tarnac, Charles' old enemy, the one member of this river community who had ever been able to get under his skin, had returned to the Retreat after five years' absence, and he had returned a ruined man. Ruined at thirty-eight, Charles thought, with a tender side glance for his own unmarred years, which numbered fifty-four.

He pulled open the curtains. Leona's lawn, starting immediately beneath this window, slanted smoothly down to the river's edge, two hundred yards away. It was a lovely view, a sunny day, a glorious prospect, and still only ten o'clock in the morning. Charles rang for his *café au lait* and sat down in the great chintz-covered armchair that Leona had thoughtfully placed near the window but not so near that Charles, thinking or reading, could be seen from the garden. He still had his notebook in his hand, and he glanced at a passage here and there.

Bridie (Charles liked to refer to her as "that splendid Irishwoman of Leona's") clumped in with the tray. The glare of pure hatred that was her characteristic expression descended in full force on Charles' silky gray head, but he was indifferent and she was silent, respectfully handing him his orange juice, pouring his coffee and his hot milk (Sye-mull-tane-eusssly, Bridie, she said to herself, the coffee and the milk sye-mull-tane-eusssly), and departing.

Sipping his coffee, he began to read over his notes, but very soon he set both coffee and notes aside and lay back in his chair, to savor— not the sweetness of this present triumph, because, after all, he had that now, but the bitterness of the long grudge he had cherished against Edward Tarnac. The grudge was partly inexplicable to him, and this intensified it. Edward had been well-to-do, free, charming, happy, handsome, attractive, and athletic, but still, when one came right down to it, how many did not have those qualities? It was the literate, cultured, aloof fellows like himself, the true gentlemen, who were the exception. Indeed, it was curious that Edward had always succeeded so in irritating him, at times beyond endurance.

And then Tarnac had always been so self-confident, so sure that everybody liked him. Why, quite often he had even spoken to Charles as a friend, chatted with him as a friend, completely forgetting the times he had slighted Charles, the gibes, the smart little mockeries that rankled in Charles' mind and glowed there, polished daily until they had the brilliance of jewels. No more, though. This weekend would wipe all that out. Last night was almost enough. Oh, Charles thought, the satisfaction of seeing someone brought down who has been riding high! Well, Tarnac had been thoroughly humiliated, somewhere, somehow, since leaving the Retreat. That much was obvious. The apologetic air of him now, where once he had been so— cocky was the only word for what he had been. He no longer took it for granted that people liked him. Quite the other way around now. Odd, to see him and Lewis Maitland together now. They were bosom friends in the old days, and so much alike that they might have been brothers, with Edward always shining just a little the brighter. Edward had always patronized Lewis—unconsciously, perhaps, but Lewis had felt it. Charles had seen to that. Now the shoe was on the other foot.

Oh, I'm not the only one enjoying this weekend, Charles thought. Whether Lewis knew it or not, he must have been waiting for the opportunity for years. And then to run into Edward on the street like that was sheer good luck. And apparently Edward was delighted to come up for the weekend. Thinking we'd all be glad to see him. The appalling nerve some people have.

I would never have done that, Charles thought, smiling a grim, happy little smile. I would never have come back. As long as he stayed away, we couldn't be sure what had become of him, no matter what reports we heard. But now! It's an object lesson, he thought, and, suddenly anxious for talk, for the delicious rehashing of last night's scene, he bounded to his feet, dashed into his shower, and emerged, clean and shiny, to select from his wardrobe a pair of brown Bermuda shorts, beautifully cut, and a beige wool shirt. He buttoned the cuffs of the shirt, knotted a beige-and-brown silk scarf carefully around his neck, put on a pair of knee-length beige socks and brown sandals, and, opening a door in the side wall of his room, stepped onto an outdoor staircase that curved to bring him, as he hopped lightly from the bottom step onto the grass, in face with the river.

There was Leona, coming out of the kitchen door, and talking animatedly to Bridie. Her Bermuda shorts were of red linen and her navy-blue wool shirt was open at the throat and rolled to her elbows. She paused to strap on her wristwatch, and then, seeing Charles, she smiled brilliantly and hurried to take his arm.

Leona's lawn was as wide as her house, and its green velvet expanse was unbroken except for two statues—one of a white marble woman, which stood far to the right and about a third of the way down, and another, much nearer the river and on the left, of a gray stone clown who raised his sad grin to the heavens. On each side, the lawn was bounded by a high, dense wall of old trees, old hedge, old thicket, all sorts of old greenery—uncared for now and growing wild but still putting forth fresh leaves and new shoots—that shielded Leona's domain from the view of the neighboring houses, although their white stone walls, glittering in the sunlight like her own, sometimes showed a flash of brightness through a break in the foliage. The house on the right belonged to Lewis and Dolly Maitland, Leona's closest friends—except, of course, for Charles, who, in addition to being her dearest companion, was her lion, her literary light, and also, although she did not say this, her claim to distinction in the community.

Leona was tall and slim, with a halo of cloudy black hair that swept becomingly around a face crowded with unformed features. Surely, one thought, the nose would grow larger, or the mouth would settle, or a bone would show itself on one cheek, at least. Even the eyes seemed to have been left unfinished. Brown, they should have been a shade lighter or a shade darker. "My mysterious Leona," Charles called her. "Mysterious, dreaming, romantic Leona."

Walking arm in arm to the river, they did not speak, Leona because she was always careful to discover Charles' mood before conversation, and Charles because he didn't want to get to the subject closest his heart before he was comfortably settled in a chair.

From the house, two pairs of eyes watched them. Through the kitchen window, the beady Irish eyes of Bridie followed their movements with malevolent attention, and from the window of the second-floor bedroom he shared with Leona, George Harkey, who had just got out of bed, watched his wife and Charles Runyon with a muffled brown gaze in which curiosity and resentment struggled for supremacy with a very bad hangover.

Charles walked rather stiffly, perhaps because he missed the comforting concealment of a jacket, and from the back his small, shapely figure wagged more than a little. Leona's shorts gave to her slow and sinuous prance a very curious effect, as though with every step she was on the verge of sitting down hard, but she continued fairly upright, flirting her cigarette, until they reached the lawn's edge. There, where the ground fell steeply to the river, Leona's latest improvement was now, after months of talk and effort, ready to be enjoyed. Just below the level of the lawn but well above water level she had built

31

a wooden deck, six feet wide and running the whole width of the lawn, with a low railing around it. This was not a jetty, for Leona disliked sailing. This was purely a deck. It was painted a very pale blue, and furnished for lounging, with red canvas sling chairs and tables of black wrought iron. It was a delightful spot, private, uncluttered, Leona's realization of the perfect boat, on which she could ride the restless waters of the river while remaining safely anchored not merely to the land but to her own lawn.

"The deck is really charming," Charles said, lowering himself into a chair, but his tone was perfunctory.

"Wasn't it clever of me to have it built so low, so that it doesn't interfere with the view from the house at all. Even from the upstairs windows you simply can't see it, unless you know it's here."

She would have gone on, for the house—the frame and expression of her personality—interested her endlessly, but Charles, with a brisk nod, stopped her. He lit a cigarette, threw away the match, snuggled back in his chair, and looked her straight in the eye. "Well, Leona," he said, "and what do you think of our friend Tarnac now? Quite a revealing evening we had last night, eh?"

They had already discussed the evening at length, and at double length, before they went to bed, but realizing that Charles wanted every detail of it recalled, and herself eager to savor it all again, Leona said, "Oh, Charles, isn't it appalling to see a man so shattered? And in such a short space of time. Why, you know, Charles, I walked into Dolly's living room last night and I simply didn't know him. I actually didn't recognize him. He was standing over by the fireplace with Lewis, and I looked at him, and I looked at Lewis, and I said, 'Where's Edward?' "

"I know, darling, we all heard you."

"And then, of course, I was so overcome when I saw who it was that I simply lost my head."

"I'm afraid you were very cruel, Leona."

"I didn't mean to be cruel. You know I'm never intentionally cruel. Besides, what you said was much, much worse, and you didn't even have my excuse of being flustered. No, you were perfectly cold-blooded. You waited till we were all settled with our drinks, and everything was all smooth and lovely, and then— Oh, Charles, it was perfectly killing. I'll never forget how funny you looked, peering around the room until Dolly was driven to ask you what was wrong, and you said, 'I'm looking for Edward's pretty girl. Isn't she coming down?' "

She paused to laugh at the recollection, and Charles neighed softly.

"And then Edward said, 'What pretty girl?' and you said, 'Why, surely you're not up here alone, Edward. Why, Edward Tarnac without a pretty girl is only half the picture.' "

"That stung," Charles said with satisfaction.

"You know, Charles, I was quite worried for you. If you'd said that to him five years ago he'd have thrown his drink at you."

"But that was five years ago, wasn't it? And instead of throwing his drink he swallowed it, didn't he? Oh, he's learned what's what, these last few years. He's learned his lesson, all right. And then, of course, your poor George had to put his foot in it."

"Oh, poor George is such a fool, Charles. Not a glimmer of social sense. Instead of letting it drop then, he had to pipe up, 'And why shouldn't he come up alone if he wants to?' And naturally that set you off again."

"Well, really, what could I do? George has such a sagging effect on conversation, don't you think? And of course, being a newcomer, he couldn't be expected to know how things were. Obviously I had to tell him what we all know—that Edward's appearance in solitary, as it were, showed how greatly he had changed."

"And Lewis enjoying it all hugely. Edward always made Lewis look rather dim. Not now, though. Edward's face is so ruined-looking, somehow."

"Positively raddled. Of course, Edward always looked much younger than his age. You know that, Leona. He kept those boyish looks of his a very long time."

"Oh, that was another thing, Charles. Did you have to keep on calling him Boy? Really, I was squirming."

"Don't be a hypocrite, Leona. You know you loved it all. And he

33

had it coming to him. Of course, when you consider how he was brought up, the youngest son, an adoring mother, a trust fund from that uncle of his——"

"Do you know, Charles, I don't believe he has a penny of that money left."

"Well, what would you expect? You remember how he threw money around. That boat, and those silly little racing cars, and that procession of vacant-faced girls, and that endless, exhausting masculinity, constantly being paraded before us—just a show, of course. The psychiatrists know about that. But so wearisome. And terribly bad manners, if you remember."

"Yes, Charles, you have a few scores to settle with him, haven't you, dear?" She stopped, afraid that she had gone too far. Charles would not tolerate familiarity. But he answered her calmly.

"Certainly not. His kind of schoolboy humor never affected me, except to bore me. I do know it used to be impossible to have any good conversation when he was around. Those insufferable interruptions, and— Do you remember his abominable habit of saying 'Now the question direct'?"

" 'Cutting through the grease,' he used to call it."

"Exactly. Exactly. A thoroughly uncivilized mind, if you call it a mind. A man who will express himself in such terms is capable of any gaucherie. No sensitivity, no character, no breeding, and of course, now that all that juvenile charm has been drowned in liquor, you can see what he is. It's pitiful, of course." He sat up and glanced, with impatience, toward the green wall of foliage that concealed the Maitlands' house. "Aren't Lewis and Dolly coming over," he asked, "and our beaming friend Edward, for lunch? Aren't they late? It must be after noon."

Leona laughed melodiously. "Charles, Charles," she said in affectionate reproval. "Are you so eager to sharpen your teeth on poor Edward again? They'll be here soon. Lewis is probably mixing his famous whiskey sours. He said he'd bring a jug over. He and Edward will probably need them."

"Dolly, too," Charles said, settling himself comfortably again. "I fancy she got quite a shock when she saw our returned hero last night. She used to have quite a thing about him, you remember."

"She's trying to forget it now," Leona said.

"Trying to forget what?" Dolly cried, jumping gaily down onto the deck. She was a short, bouncy girl with brown hair, which she had braided into pigtails. "This thing is divine, Leona. I'm going to lie down flat." She lay down flat on her back, sighing luxuriously in the sun's heat. "The others will be right along," she said. "Lewis is bringing the whiskey sours, or will bring them, after he's had a few himself."

"Where is Edward staying in town? He wouldn't tell me last night," Charles asked.

"That's just it," Dolly said. "He won't say where he's staying. He says he's looking for an apartment." She stopped a moment, then turned to them with a conspiratorial grimace. "Listen," she said. "Don't tell Lewis I told you, but he tried to borrow money last night. A hundred dollars."

"Did Lewis give it to him?" Charles asked sharply.

"Not he. You know Lewis. Lewis never lends money, to anyone."

"Well, Tarnac is down and out, then," Charles said.

"Oh dear. I hope he's not going to start borrowing all around," Leona said. "But I was quite cool with him last night. I doubt if he'd have the nerve to ask me."

"I hope he asks me," Charles said. "I'll give him short shrift. But then I was cool, too, to say the least."

"That's another strange thing," Dolly said. "You know, ordinarily he'd have struck out at you last night. You know how belligerent he used to be. But I got the feeling that everything you and Leona said to him just passed over his head. He didn't seem to care. It was Lewis he was looking to. I suppose he always knew you two disliked him, but apparently he thought of Lewis as a friend."

Charles nodded. "Everyone saw how Lewis felt about Edward— except Edward himself, of course. That blessed obtuseness of his saved him from a lot in those days."

"He tried to settle down to a heart-to-heart talk after you people left," Dolly said, "but he got to the borrowing part too soon, and Lewis cut him off short."

"Oh, why doesn't he get on the bus and go back to New York!" Leona cried impatiently. "He's ruining the whole weekend."

"Nonsense, my dear," Charles said. "Far from ruining the weekend, he's adding a certain excitement to it. Besides, he'll undoubtedly stick around now in the hope of retrieving himself. Not that he has a chance. He must see that he made a mistake in coming here. He should never have come, that's all."

"Oh, don't think he doesn't know that now!" Dolly cried. "You know how he was last night—almost apologetic. Today he's just morose. I don't think he's said two words all morning. Don't worry, though, Leona. I don't think he'll make any scenes. He's hardly in a position to, after all. And of course he doesn't want Lewis to tell about his attempt to borrow money."

"It's what we were talking about earlier, Leona," Charles said. "What used to pass as—uh, conversational dexterity in our friend would now be sheer bravado. He can no longer meet us on our own ground. He has to pretend not to notice. He's no longer an equal, after all."

"Really, Charles!" Dolly cried. "Aren't you carrying this a little too far? He's broke, of course, and obviously he's been on a long bender, but I think it's nonsense to talk about him not being an equal, and so on. I mean, I think that's silly."

Leona sat up straight. "Dolly," she said, with a nervous glance at Charles, "please remember to whom you are speaking."

Charles, whose face had grown small, dark, and closed, was silent for a moment, while Dolly, confused, cast about for words of apology.

"Don't apologize, Dolly," he said at last. "I may seem silly to you, and of course, you must say what you think. We won't discuss it."

"Yes, of course, Charles," Dolly said, on the verge of tears. "I only thought—"

"Don't think, dear," Charles said. "It does not become you."

"I can't tell you," Dolly said desperately, directing herself at Leona, who was still stiff with outrage, "how glad I was to get away from the house this morning. Susie woke up at six sharp, and screamed

36

continuously from six-thirty until after eight. I nearly lost my mind."

"Oh, yes, Susie. How old is she now?" Leona asked coldly.

"Four," Dolly said disconsolately. "That was her fourth birthday the other day, Leona. When I had the party."

"I detest children," Charles said. "They're so short."

"Here come Lewis and Edward with the whiskey sours!" Leona cried. "And not a minute too soon, either. We have the glasses all ready here, Lewis. Edward, what do you think of my new sun deck?"

"Great," Edward said with no enthusiasm. "Just great, Leona." He pulled a chair from the group around the table, turned it to face the river, and sat down apart from the company.

"Come now, Edward!" Leona cried, with a smile for the others. "I have to almost twist my neck off if I want to see you. Why don't you come in with the rest of us?"

"I'm all right, thanks," Edward said. He was wearing gray slacks and last night's shirt without a tie.

Edward and Lewis were both tall, both blond, and both strongly built. They both had the same kind of regular, clean-cut, blue-eyed good looks. Lewis's face, bland in his youth, had grown blander. The restlessness that had always characterized Edward had worn his face, and the self-confidence had gone, taking the shine with it. Also, he was suffering from a bad hangover, and looked, generally, perhaps more unhappy than he felt. Lewis at once started to pour the whiskey sours.

"I hear you're looking for an apartment, Edward," Charles said smoothly. "Perhaps I could help you. I hear of things—friends in the theatre going to Hollywood and Rome and such places. What have you in mind? I mean, what price have you in mind?"

Edward gulped the first drink and handed his glass back to Lewis for a refill. "I'm not going to hurry about the apartment," he said. "I want to look around a bit, find what I really want. I'm all right for the time being. And since I know what your next question is going to be, I'll save you the trouble of asking. I'm staying at the Tenley, on Washington Square. Now you know."

"The Tenley!" Dolly cried. "Oh, poor Edward, but that's a terrible old flea bag. Oh, I'm sorry, Edward, I didn't mean anything."

"It's all right, Dolly," Edward said. "It's a flea bag. You're absolutely right."

"I thought they'd torn the Tenley down years ago," Charles murmured. "It was one of the hangouts of my rather rowdy youth."

Lewis kicked impatiently at the table leg. "Not to change the subject, but isn't Bridie bringing the lunch down here? Edward and I were a little ahead on those whiskey sours."

"Which reminds me that I need a drink," Edward said, passing his glass over his shoulder.

"Oh, she's bringing a basket down any minute now," Leona said. "She's rattled, as all the maids are today. They can think of nothing but the ball."

"The ball!" Charles shrieked. "Great heavens, Leona, do you know that I completely forgot the ball. And I thought of nothing else all week. I even brought my embroidered French waistcoat along. I should look superb in the waltzes. I'm going to cut quite a figure, Leona."

"I'm sure you are, darling," Leona said, "and the girls will go wild over you, as usual. They adore waltzing with you, Charles." She turned to Edward. "I suppose you know the maids are having their ball this weekend?" she inquired, smiling. "Tonight's the big night. Or did you remember?"

"I remember the ball," Edward said. "I thought it was always on Saint Patrick's Day."

"It used to be," Dolly said, "but they had too much competition from New York, so they changed it."

"Charles puts us all in the shade," Lewis said, and gazed at them with the air of fascinated and respectful amusement that Charles always inspired in him.

"You did rather well yourself, Lewis," Charles said, pleased. "Last year, some of the policemen were quite jealous."

"Oh, I'll admit I have my little following," Lewis said, grinning.

"Well, of course some of the maids must cherish secret passions," Dolly said. "Poor things. How they must look forward to tonight."

"There's no secret about their collective passion for Charles," Leona said. "Charles maintains that only servants can dance the waltz really well, Edward. Female servants, that is. He says their souls are clad in caps and streamers. They hold their heads up to keep the caps on, whirl to make the streamers flutter, and so they achieve the perfect posture for the waltz. You see, Charles, how well I remember what you say?"

"Your memory is phenomenal, darling," Charles said, "and quite accurate, too. That is just how I imagine them when I dance. I keep my eyes shut tight, of course, and the hall seems filled with black and white dresses, the full black skirts, the frilly white aprons, and streamers—oh, it's a charming picture. My waistcoat provides the significant, necessary note of color. Can you see it all, as I do now?"

"You should have been a painter, Charles," Dolly said shyly.

"Dolly banal," Charles said, but kindly. "We can always count on you, can't we, dear."

"What are you wearing, Leona?" Dolly asked hastily. "I bought a pair of black net stockings with rhinestones on the insteps. After all, it is sort of a fancy-dress thing for us. And why not give those nice cops something to look at, I thought."

"Very generous of you, darling," Leona said. "I'm wearing the white crêpe, you know. That should get them."

"They were eager enough last year," Lewis said. "I was afraid they'd eat you girls up. The atmosphere got almost primitive."

Leona laughed throatily. "Well, I do think they like us to come," she said.

"I think it's a nice thing for us to do," Dolly said. "I think it's something we *ought* to do," she added virtuously.

"Well, of course, they're honored that we come to their little party," Charles said. "Why, it's positively feudal. And whether they know it or not, that's why they enjoy it."

"Feudal my foot," Edward said. He stood up suddenly, staggered, and was obliged to grab the handrail. "Feudal my foot," he repeated. "You're all itching to go. You wouldn't miss going for the world."

"Well, that's our old Edward," Lewis said unpleasantly.

"I always thought you were a friend of mine, Lewis. Did you know that?" Edward said.

39

Lewis looked first at Dolly and then into his glass. "Of course I'm your friend, Edward," he said.

"That's just it!" Edward shouted, ludicrous in rage. "You're not my friend! None of you are. You all hate me. I should never have come. I thought there was something here. I thought we were all friends here. Old friends." He seemed about to weep.

"Edward," Leona said. "Edward, darling, you've had quite a lot to drink, and you're sitting in the sun. Please go and lie down. Please, Edward. Do go into the house."

"That's right," Lewis said. "What you need is sleep. You can lie out on Leona's side porch. There's shade there. Can't he, Leona?"

"Of course he can!" Leona cried. "Do you want any of us to go with you, darling? Oh, poor Edward, you've been through such a lot, and—"

"Never mind about all that now, Leona. Never mind what I've been through. I know what you'd like. You've had your spectacle, and you want me to go away quietly, don't you? You'd like that, wouldn't you? You'd like me to get on the bus and go back to New York. But I'm not going back to New York, see? I'm going to stay here till I'm good and ready to go, and I'm going to make this weekend so miserable that you'll remember it for the rest of your days. I'm not leaving. I've no shame. I'll make everything you say about me true—you see if I don't. But don't get your hopes up. I'm not leaving." From the lawn, where he was standing now, he waved his arm at them. "I'll be back," he said, and started his unsteady progress toward the house.

Charles made a disgusted gesture. "I always knew it," he said. "The fellow is a peasant."

Lewis said, "I don't envy him his head when he wakes up about four o'clock this afternoon and remembers all this. Did you know he took a bottle up with him last night, Dolly? He must have been drinking all night."

"Really," Leona said, "I do wish he'd go. I've seen enough of him to last me a very long time."

Charles smiled. "Oh, we may as well see the finish," he said. "Mr. Tarnac seems to have gone through so many metamorphoses since his arrival. First, an almost touching friendliness. Then this morning, mo-

40

rose silence. Now, a futile aggressiveness that is more pathetic than anything. And tonight, I expect, painful penitence. We'll just have to be nice to him, my dears, but don't get so softhearted that you invite him down again, Lewis—for all our sakes."

They were distracted by a shout. Edward had retraced his steps and was standing only a short distance away from them, balancing himself against the stone clown. "Do you know what you people are?" he shouted. "I just thought—do you know what you are?"

"Oh, God, what now?" Leona whispered. "Charles, what will I do? The servants will hear him!"

Charles stared grimly at the floor of the deck, hoping that by avoiding Edward's eye he would also avoid his attention. The others, too, looked down, praying for silence.

"You're the people who never make mistakes, that's what you are!" Edward bellowed. "Do you hear me? You're the people who never make mistakes! Not a single mistake does a single one of you ever make in your whole lives! That's what I think of you." He turned back up the lawn, and disappeared in the direction of the Maitlands' house.

They all took exaggerated attitudes of relief.

"Goodness," Dolly said. "I couldn't imagine what he was going to say. I was petrified! Is that bad, never to make a mistake? Really, I think Edward must be losing his mind."

Charles smiled benignly at her, and then his gaze continued past her and across the wide river to the opposite side, where the green bank rose solid to the tranquil blue sky. "I must congratulate you again on your deck, Leona," he said. "An excellent idea. Such an educated view, my dear."

"And here at last is Bridie with the food," Lewis said. "I'm hungry enough to eat a horse."

"And poor George, bringing up the rear," Leona said. "As usual."

"I still cannot believe that you're actually married to a credit manager," Charles said. "Not that George isn't a dear, but it seems such an unlikely occupation. Almost exotic."

Leona, who always referred to George as a vice-president of the store where he was employed, turned almost purple with shame, but she understood that she was being punished for her earlier boldness, and didn't try to defend herself.

At five o'clock that afternoon, jaded with talking about the dance, anxious now only to get on with it, willing even to have it past, so that they could start enjoying the discussion of it, most of the maids at Herbert's Retreat lay down on their beds for an unaccustomed ceremonial nap before getting dressed for the evening. The fine white stone houses, those beside the river and those scattered a little distance from it, were silent—the families departed for cocktails and dinner, the maids, supine, for once acknowledged mistresses of the kingdom they regarded, in any case, as their own.

The kitchens were deserted, but from every kitchen ceiling a freshly pressed dress, a long dress, hung and shivered gently in the mild breeze that stole up at intervals from the river. The maids' dresses were of bright colors—pink, yellow, blue, violet, red, and green—because the girls liked to escape as thoroughly as they could from the grays and black-and-white of their daily uniforms.

Only in Bridie's kitchen was there a black dress to be seen, a matronly taffeta that hung with uncompromising stiffness from the center beam. Not far from the dress, Bridie herself, scorning sleep, sat at her table by the window, stirring one of her eternal cups of strong tea. She had commanded her friend Agnes, who worked for the Gieglers, to join her, and at this moment Agnes sat drooping, with her pale eyes fixed on Leona's lawn and her ears half attentive to Bridie's conversation, which consisted, as usual, of a series of declamatory, denunciatory, and entirely final remarks.

"Naps in the afternoon," she said fiercely, slamming her wet teaspoon on the table. "If they were in their beds at a decent hour at night, when they ought to be sleeping, they wouldn't be looking to lie down at this time of day. What do they want with naps, big strong lassies like them? Cocktails they'll be after next, I suppose. Cocktails with the family, I suppose."

She drew up with a jerk, intrigued by the last picture she had conjured up. Suppose now, she thought, Mr. Harkey, or Mrs. Harkey herself, were to come out here and invite me to sit down for a cocktail

42

with them. She glanced covertly at Agnes, who was still contemplating the grass.

Bridie went on with her meditations. Well, then, I would sit down with them, she thought—not on one of the comfortable chairs but on an ordinary chair, just to show them that I know as much about good manners as they do, and I'd take a drink, whatever they were having themselves, and I wouldn't be pushy, but neither would I be backward. "Mrs. Harkey," I'd say, "as one woman to another—" "Oh, go on, Bridie," she'd say, smiling a little bit. "Won't you call me Leona? It's ridiculous for us, living along here in the same house year after year, and not being real friends."

This pleasant scene was interrupted by Agnes, who spoke up suddenly in her thin, incurious voice. "Here's Josie. I would've thought she'd be lying down along with the rest of them. I wonder what she's after."

Bridie peered out the window. Josie, the newest maid at the Retreat, and one of the youngest, was crossing the lawn on quick fat legs, coming from the Maitlands' house, where she worked. She was a short, stocky girl, with a pretty face.

"She should have come round by the house," Bridie said. "Mrs. Harkey hates to see anybody using up that lawn of hers. . . . Well, and what brings you here this time of the day, Josie? I thought you'd be asleep like the rest of them."

"I couldn't sleep," Josie said. "I'm too nervous. And I'm all alone there, except for that Mr. Tarnac, and he's up in his room sleeping it off."

Bridie nodded heavily at Agnes. "What was I telling you?" she said. "And where are all the rest of them?" she asked Josie.

"They've all gone off driving somewhere. And then they're taking the child to her grandmother's, so they can go to the dance."

"And they didn't ask Mr. Tarnac to go with them?" Bridie asked.

"He wouldn't go. Sure, he's in no fit state to go anywhere. He's been falling-down drunk ever since they got in last night. And the rest of them all making fun of him and all. I don't know what sort of a fellow he is to put up with it. You should have heard them at dinner last night. You should have heard that little Mr. Runyon of yours.

43

The things he said, I couldn't begin to remember the half of them."

"It's a pity Mr. Tarnac couldn't stay where he was, and not give them the satisfaction of laughing at him," Bridie declared. "The men around here were always envious of him, with his money and his big boat and his racing cars and all. And the women, that used to be throwing themselves at him, are congratulating themselves now that they stayed clear of him. The one here was forever inviting him over. And that Maitland lassie was very sweet on him. Oh, I believe to this day that there was more went on there than anybody'll ever know about. But that little Mr. God—I hate to see him so set up. I hate to see him getting any kind of satisfaction. I heard him last night, himself and Mrs. Harkey talking after they came home. Laughing and carrying on about Mr. Tarnac's clothes and the way he's all broken up, and each of them repeating to the other what they'd said. And then this morning they couldn't wait to start in on it again."

Josie, who had been listening respectfully, turned to Agnes. "Did you know Mr. Tarnac, Agnes?"

"No, he was before my time," Agnes said regretfully. "But Bridie's been telling me all about the big house he had and how he sold it and all. And lost all his money. It's a terrible thing, a man to throw away a fortune like that."

"But still and all," Bridie said, "he's a decent sort of a man, and I always liked him." She almost believed she was telling the truth, but the fact was that when Edward Tarnac lived at the Retreat, he was no more to her than one of a group she hated; it was only in his new role that she liked him. She took the cups and saucers off the table and carried them over to the sink.

Agnes sighed. "What are you wearing to the dance tonight, Josie?" she asked.

"Me ballerina," Josie said. "And me ballerina-type sandals. And I've dyed a pair of stockings to match. Pink. Do you think it'll be all right?"

"Lovely," Agnes said. "Pink is lovely on you, Josie—lovely with your skin."

"That's another thing!" Bridie shouted, splashing noisily among the dishes. "There'll be Josie in her pink stockings, and you in that green getup of yours, Agnes, and that crew from here'll be there laughing at you behind their hands and making little of you. That's all they come for, to have something to laugh about. They make me sick."

Josie was red with indignation. "What's Mrs. Maitland going out and buying special black net stockings for, then, if she's only coming to laugh? Special stockings that she paid twelve dollars for. She's dying to come to the dance, so she is. She went and spent twelve dollars for special stockings to wear to the dance. What would she do that for if she's only coming to laugh? You're only making it up, Bridie, to stop us from enjoying ourselves."

Bridie, who had abandoned the sink, stared at her in astonishment. "What's that about stockings? Now, Josie, don't start crying. I wasn't trying to stop you from enjoying yourself. I was only thinking *they'd* be trying to stop you enjoying yourself. Now sit down and tell me and Agnes about the stockings Mrs. Maitland bought. Black, did you say they were?"

"Black net," Josie said, subsiding, "with a whole lot of rhinestones here—" She indicated her own chubby instep. "And she went all the way in to some special actresses' shop in New York to get them. I heard her talking to Mrs. Ffrench about them yesterday afternoon when I was waxing the hall. 'Aren't they the sexiest things you ever saw in your life?' Mrs. Maitland says. 'Do you think our visiting policemen will like them?' she says. 'Why, I should think they'd go berserk,' Mrs. Ffrench says, and they both laughed and laughed. 'I don't know why you bother,' Mrs. Ffrench says. 'I think they're a dull collection, myself.' 'Oh, I think they're sweet,' Mrs. Maitland says, 'and very attractive, some of them. Lewis was quite jealous last year. And you know, they're wonderful dancers. I wouldn't miss this for anything.' Well, I was curious, wanting to know what they were talking about, so I went into the living room on the excuse of asking them did they want anything, and there was Mrs. Maitland with the long shorts on her, y'know? And the stockings up against her leg. She put them away quick, but I found them in her drawer this morning,

45

and I looked at them. And the price was on them, twelve dollars. I'm telling you, wild horses wouldn't keep her from the dance. She's dying to go."

"Well, I declare to God," Bridie said. She sat down at the table again. "What else did they say, Josie?"

"Nothing, except Mrs. Ffrench asked Mrs. Maitland, 'What's Charles going to surprise us with this year?' she says. 'He had such an amusing outfit last year,' she says, 'and the girls made such a fuss over him,' she says. 'Oh, the girls adore Charles,' Mrs. Maitland says, 'and he's like a little child about the dance, he's so excited about it. He pretends not to be, of course,' she says, 'but you know it gets to be a bit of a bore, he can talk of nothing else all day afterwards. You know, Charles is a tiny bit conceited,' she says, 'and he rather fancies himself in the waltz.' And then they went on talking about the party Mrs. Ffrench is giving next Friday. That was in the afternoon, before Mr. Maitland and Mr. Tarnac got here."

" 'The girls adore Charles,' " Bridie repeated. " 'The girls adore Charles.' Sure they were all laughing their heads off at him, the way he was shaping around on the dance floor with his eyes closed and all. You never saw such a sketch in your life. We were all breaking our hearts laughing at him. And he brought those special little flat patent-leather shoes of his, too. I saw them when I was doing the room this morning. Well, I declare to God. And that one upstairs, Mrs. Harkey—I wonder what she's going to doll herself up in. I declare to God, all the parties and all they have to go to, and they have to take over our little party, too. Wouldn't you know it of them."

"And every time one of the fellows asks one of them to dance, one of us is left sitting!" Josie cried. "Oh, I know there's extra men, and all, but still I don't think it's fair. And all the money they have to spend on themselves and all, and us trying to struggle along on what we make— How can we put up an appearance against them? It's not fair, so it's not." She stood up. "Well," she said, "I'd better be getting home. I have to get ready for the dance, although I haven't much heart for it now."

Bridie folded her arms and leaned on the table. "Wait a minute

46

now, Josie," she said. "Maybe there's something we can do about all this. What do you say, Agnes?"

"Sure what could we do?" Agnes asked nervously. "You don't want to get into any trouble, now, Bridie."

"No need to get into any trouble," Bridie said. "We could just pass the word around. They only come around to look. That's what Mrs. Harkey said to me. 'We're only going to drop around for a little visit,' she says to me. 'Just for a look. It's such fun to sit and watch.' Well, then, let them look, if that's what they want. We'll boycott them. Very polite, of course, as though we thought they just came to look. As though we didn't think they wanted to dance. Who can make any trouble out of that?"

"I don't want to risk my job," Agnes said.

"No fear of that," Bridie said. "How can you risk your job when they won't know anything about it? They'll just think the fellows are shy, or something."

Josie sniggered. "Oh, God," she said, "there she'll be sitting up there with her black stockings on her, and nobody coming near her!"

Agnes smiled meanly, stood up, and brushed bread crumbs from the front of her skirt. "We'll have to make sure all the girls know about it, Bridie," she said.

The dance began at nine o'clock. At eleven, George Harkey still waited, surrounded by the empty chairs he was holding for Leona, on a dais at one end of the long village hall. His solitary dinner at the village bar-and-grill had been preceded by five very sweet Manhattans, and he was drowsy. He tried, with a monotonous lack of success but nonchalantly all the same, to count the eyelashes of his left eye with the fingers of his right hand and the eyelashes of his right eye with his other set of fingers. Head bent, eyes alternately glazing and wandering, he still could not entirely avoid seeing the feet of the dancers as they galloped past his perch. Underneath him, the dais, which had been built for some pageant, thudded industriously in time with the dancing, and around him the empty chairs rattled. Suddenly the hall darkened slightly. Someone had turned the lights down. To

47

George, who had just then been gazing intently into the palms of his locked hands, the change seemed tremendous. The music, the laughter, the pounding of feet, and the voices, that formerly had come at him in one bright, enveloping blast of exhausting but familiar sound, now seemed to deepen and at the same time to grow more shrill. It was an ominous alteration. Was he in the same room? Had he, perhaps, slept?

He raised his eyes fearfully and gazed down the length of the hall. Dimly, far away across the sea of jiggling heads, he perceived the glitter of instruments. There was the stage, there were the musicians. In front of the stage stood a bank of the same thick, stiff green shrubbery that sprouted at intervals in tubs along the side walls, separating into chummy groups the empty chairs that had been set aside for tired dancers. Were there any tired dancers? George couldn't tell. The nausea that had been caressing him at intervals all day embraced him without warning, and roughly. He closed his eyes tight and gripped the seat of his chair with both hands, but still, in his horrified vision, the dance floor swung right, swung left, with sickening precision, as though some giant pendulum had control of it, and the dancers, oblivious, whirled giddily on, and he was increasingly aware of the Manhattans and of the two tough pork chops that since suppertime had lain, almost forgotten, inside him.

The wave passed, leaving its victim trembling but not seriously impaired. He opened his eyes, put his hand to his hip pocket, and took out a large silver flask. He unscrewed the top, poured some whiskey into one of the two sticky glasses that some earlier Retreat visitors had left on the chair beside him, and drank. That was better. He hoped no had had noticed him, but it was too late to worry now, and he poured another drink, finished it off, and set the glass on the floor, so carelessly that it turned on its side and rolled dismally under one of the chairs.

He recorked the flask, crossed his legs, and sat back to survey the festivities, with the suave, aloof smile he had often seen Charles Runyon wear. On George's square, earnest face the smile sat awkwardly, but he knew only that he felt tired, and tried to solve the problem by leering on one side of his face while he rested the muscles of the other side.

At this moment, through the wide entrance door at the side of the hall, he saw Leona enter, pause, and raise her arms in greeting to the merrymakers. She was wearing a sleeveless white crêpe dress that clung to her tall, slender figure, and there were diamonds in her ears. She raised herself on tiptoe, waved to the band, and pranced gracefully to the dais and to George. Behind her, Charles, Dolly, and Lewis followed confidently, their smiles radiating pleasure, camaraderie, and, above all, approval.

Leona tripped up the steps and stood beside George, regarding him with a humorous *moue* that he found peculiarly repellent.

"Well, George, all alone? Poor George has been sitting here all alone," she said to Charles, who had already taken a chair and arranged himself in an attitude.

"Never mind the poor-George stuff," George muttered, but no one heard him.

Dolly plumped herself down beside him. "Where is everybody?" she demanded. "Are we the only people here?"

"The Gieglers were here," George said, "but they left. The Ffrenches left, too, and the Pearsons. Some of the others were here. The Allens, I think. Anyway, they're all gone. But now you're here," he added with an effort.

"George, how do you like my fancy dress?" Dolly asked.

She was wearing her favorite cocktail skirt, of black satin cut in a wide circle, and with it a tight, sleeveless, modestly low jerkin blouse of black-and-white striped satin, that laced at the back with red corset strings. There were towering red heels on her black satin sandals, and a small triangle of rhinestones glittered on each black net instep. Her hair was piled in curls on top of her head and decorated with a bright-red rose.

"You look fine, Dolly," George said. "What do you mean, fancy dress? It's just a dress, isn't it?"

"Well, it's a little costumy, don't you think? Lewis said I looked like a French doll."

49

"Dolly means it's not quite what one wears," Leona interrupted, leaning across George to twinkle brilliantly at Dolly. "You must excuse George, Dolly. I suspect he's not seeing quite clearly. Didn't you dance at all, George?"

"No one asked me to dance," George said. He stood up. "No one asked Nat Ffrench to dance, either," he said, "or Rita, or the Gieglers, or anybody. Nobody asked anybody to dance. So they left."

"Been to the bar, George?" Lewis asked boisterously. He was in great good humor, and looked large, solid, and secure in his well-cut dark-blue suit.

"I didn't go near the bar," George said. "It's in the room behind the stage. You have to walk right through the dance to get to it."

"That's where it always is," Leona said happily. "Go on, Lewis. You play waiter. I'll have a Scotch-and-water."

"I think I'll leave now," George said. "I'd like some fresh air. I'll go along home, I think."

"You'll do nothing of the sort, George," Leona said. "You're not going to march out the minute I come in. Did you see Bridie?"

"She has a chair down there near the stage, I think," George said. "I really think I'll go now, Leona."

"Sit down, George," Leona said.

"Oh, for heaven's sake, sit down and shut up, George," Charles said.

"All right," George said. "Didn't know I was so popular. But I'll sit at the back here. See, I'll sit here."

He tilted a chair back against the wall and sat down, sleepy but resigned to staying awake. He closed his eyes.

"Isn't this gay?" Leona said. "Well, for goodness' sake, will you look at Edward! I forgot all about him. He's dancing with the Ffrenchs' maid, Eileen something. He didn't come in with us, did he? I thought he stayed in the car."

"He woke up when I was getting out," Dolly said. "I took it for granted he'd gone to the bar."

"Well, I never," Charles said, two or three minutes later. "Our Edward is getting quite a whirl. There he is again, with a different girl."

"The Bennetts' cook," Leona said absently.

"Never you mind, Charles!" Dolly cried gaily. "Wait till the waltzes start. You'll put poor Edward completely in the shade."

"Really, Dolly!" Charles snapped. "This brawl means nothing to me. Be serious, my dear, even if you can't be intelligent. I'm here to observe, not to dance."

"Haw-haw," George said from the back. They all turned to stare at him. He had the flask in the open again.

"George, what on earth! What are you doing with that ridiculous flask?" Leona cried.

"My own flask." George, unperturbed, took another swallow, keeping his eyes fixed on Leona.

"Well, he's a pretty how-de-do," Charles whispered angrily. "You should have let him go home, Leona."

"He'll go in a minute," Leona whispered back. "Let's just ignore him."

"It's bedlam in the bar," Lewis said, returning with their drinks, "but I must say they gave me quick service. They're a nice bunch of fellows, those cops, or whatever they are." He put the loaded tray on the floor of the dais and began to hand drinks around.

"What are they, anyway, Leona?" Charles asked. "It really interests me. It is in the nature of a social phenomenon, you know, this gathering. Who are these imported stalwarts?"

"Policemen, mostly. Firemen, I suppose, too," Leona said. "Who cares, as long as they can dance?"

"The Department of Sanitation is represented, too," Dolly whispered, gazing at a red-faced young man in a white linen jacket, who was dancing with the Gieglers' long-faced Agnes.

"Complete with carnation in lapel," Charles remarked. "My, aren't we chic!"

Leona giggled. "You're both perfectly terrible," she said. "That's a very respectable-looking coat. And a very nice-looking young man, too. I think you should be ashamed of yourselves."

Dolly choked suddenly, and hid her face behind Leona's shoulder. "Leona!" she spluttered. "Will you look at our Josie in the dyed pink stockings. Did you ever see anything like it in your life?"

51

"Macabre, my dear," Leona murmured. "Poor thing, she must have slaved to get that color. It matches her ears, though."

Charles threw an arm casually over the back of his chair, and his black flannel coat slipped open to show more than a glimpse of the gray-and-rose brocade waistcoat he was wearing.

"This dais was a charming thought," he said expansively. "What do they use it for? May queens and things? I adore sitting here, being at once a member of the audience and a player. And yet, not really of either group. The critic's lot is a lonely one, my dears. I feel remote from the rollicking servants, and just as remote, in a different way, from you delightful people. The cold, uncompromising eyes give me no peace. I say it ruefully, I assure you." He sipped his ginger ale and smiled at them complacently.

Lewis made an impatient movement, and Dolly glanced at him warningly. "Well, I wish we'd start dancing," she said. "I'm getting restless, sitting here like this. How do they make chairs this hard?"

"There is something strange about it," Lewis said. "How long have we been here? Twenty minutes? Half an hour?"

"I suppose they're shy," Leona said. "George said none of the Retreat people who came danced."

George, who had been dozing, came to at the sound of his name and sat up, looking around blearily.

"Well, where's the rush, girls?" he inquired. "I thought we were going to be stampeded. What happened to the stag line?"

Leona shot him a venomous glance. Turning to Lewis, she said in a low voice, "Did you notice anything in the bar? I mean, were they friendly and everything?"

"Sure," Lewis said. "They went out of their way to help me get the drinks. They were—well, you know, the same as they always are."

"I'm afraid you girls outsmarted yourselves," Charles said, chortling faintly. "The poor creatures are paralyzed by the splendor of your attire."

Leona turned impulsively to Lewis. "Lewis, why don't you and Dolly start things off by dancing together. Not that I care that much about dancing, but if they're shy—"

52

"Nothing doing." Lewis said.

"Oh, Leona, we can't do that," Dolly said. "They have to ask us. We can't just jump right into the middle of their dance. After all, we don't really come here to dance. We just come—well, to be nice."

"You're stuck," George said. "It's a boycott. They're on to you, girls."

"That's ridiculous, George!" Leona cried indignantly. "They're dancing with Edward."

George shrugged.

"If it were a boycott," Charles interposed, "we'd know it by their demeanor. They'd giggle or point their fingers or something. These people can't control their emotions. They have to show what they feel. But I can see no evidence of hostility in this assemblage."

"Neither can I!" Leona cried. "Why, they're smiling and friendly and all. There's Bridie waving at me now. They're just shy, incredible though it may seem. Well, who ever would have thought it? It's too bad. Not that it matters, of course."

"I didn't know Edward could even stand up," Dolly said suddenly, "and look at him now. The life of the party."

"The parlormaids' Don Juan," Charles said. "The Scullery sheik."

George emitted a rude crow of mirth. "A rehearsal, by God!" he cried. "Is that what you're going to say to Tarnac tomorrow, Charles? I've always wanted to see you working on those witty sayings of yours. Try some more, Charles. We'll tell you the good ones."

Charles froze into a dark knot of rage. Leona turned pale.

"Shut up, you," Lewis said. "Do you hear me? Shut up. We know Tarnac; you don't."

George waggled a finger at him. "Now, now, Lewis. Just because Tarnac is dancing and you're not. No one asked me to dance, but you don't see me getting all red and angry."

Lewis crouched like a beast on his straight wooden chair. "Come outside," he said. "I'll break your neck for that."

"Break it here," George said with enthusiasm. "Come on, break it. Hit me. Come on, hit me."

"Oh, God!" Leona moaned. "Will you two stop it! Stop this at

53

once. The servants, Lewis! Have some sense! Oh, Charles, smile as though nothing had happened. Dolly, stop glaring at George that way. Lewis, pull yourself together, please."

Lewis squared around to face the dancers again. Behind him, George grinned.

"All right," Lewis said. "All right. But I won't forget this, Leona."

"How could you, dear?" Leona said soothingly. "And neither will George," she promised, in a different tone.

"Oh, let's go home. Let's get out of here, for heaven's sake!" Dolly said.

"You can't go home that fast," George said. "Maybe it *is* a boycott. Maybe they're not shy at all. Maybe they want to teach you a lesson. Us a lesson, I mean. Us a lesson."

"I couldn't care less!" Dolly cried. "It's all a great bore as far as I'm concerned. Let's you and me go anyway, Lewis."

"Little feelings hurt?" George inquired, and sniggered.

Lewis set his glass carefully on the floor, and then clenched his fist melodramatically. "Listen, little man," he said to George, "my wife's feelings are not hurt. My wife's feelings could never be hurt by a crew of drunken servants and street-sweepers and God knows what."

"Oh, Lewis, old man, *I* know that," George said, "but do *they* know that?"

"What do I care what they think!"

"Keep your voice down, Lewis," Leona said coldly. "For once, George is right. We have to stay a little while, I'm afraid, deadly though it is. We can't let them think they drove us out. We'll stay a reasonable time, and then go. I still don't think they're doing it on purpose. It would be too silly."

"We'll know tomorrow, anyway," Dolly said, sighing. "Edward will tell us."

"I must say he has a nerve," Leona said. "He hasn't come near us once. After all, Dolly, you are his hostess."

"Edward has reached his proper level, my dear," Charles said. "Look at the pathetic fellow, capering around."

"Utterly smug," Dolly said. "Oh, God," she added. "He heard us talking this morning on the deck, Leona. About the dance, I mean, and these damned stockings and all. Do you suppose he'll tell them? I really can't bear to think of them laughing at us."

"I don't think he'll say anything," Lewis said. "I don't think he'd go that far."

"I really think we've stayed long enough, don't you, Charles?" Leona said.

"We will not go home, children," Charles said. "I know you girls are disappointed you weren't asked to dance. Lewis and George, too, of course. But we mustn't let our little peeve show. This is much too interesting a scene to miss, and I intend to sit it out. Chins up, now. We're not leaving. Don't look so down, Dolly. There'll be other dances."

"What do you mean there'll be other dances?" Dolly cried furiously. "You're the one who's been making all the fuss about coming to this wretched thing. What about your special waistcoat and your waltzing slippers?"

Charles regarded her with cool amusement. "Leona knows all about that, Dolly," he said. "I have a severely infected foot, which obliges me to wear a pliable shoe. I never had the slightest intention of dancing tonight, but I didn't want to spoil your fun by refusing to come, and in any case the spectacle interests me, and you are making it even more interesting, my dear, with this childish display of temper because the little boys didn't notice your sexy new stockings. Isn't that so, my sweet? Leona, you remember my telling you about my wretched foot?"

"Of course, darling," Leona said. "You should apologize, Dolly."

"Haw, haw, HAW," George said. "He made that all up just now to save his face, such as it is."

"Leave the room at once, George," Leona said.

"Make me," George said. "Go ahead, make me. Make me."

"Make you what?" Charles asked in contempt.

Leona threw Charles a glance of anguish. "Oh, Charles, don't provoke him. Poor George is not himself this evening."

"Poor George," George said, apparently to himself. "Poor George," he said again. He stood up. "POOR GEORGE!" he roared. "POOR, POOR George!"

55

The nearest dancers hesitated and then went on. George smiled and sat down again.

"I'll kill you for this, George," Leona said.

"I'll do it again, and I'll do worse than that, Leona," George said, "unless you say after me now, 'Nice George.'"

Leona stared at him and then spoke quickly. "Nice George," she said.

"Keep smiling, children," Charles said brightly. "Remember, it's all just a little joke. Don't let them guess there's anything wrong."

"Now, Leona," George said, "say, 'Rich, handsome, *good* George.'"

"Rich, handsome, good George," Leona gabbled.

George looked pleased. "'Popular George'?" he suggested.

"Popular George."

"Good enough," George said. "Now Charlie—'Nice George,' please. If you don't say 'Nice George,' Charlie, I'm coming over there and twist your ears, one to the front, one to the back. 'Nice George.'"

"Nice George," Charles said, sneering. Leona, Lewis, and Dolly, all three turned their gaze uneasily from him.

"Stop making faces, Charlie," George said good-humoredly. "Now all together—'Rich, handsome, witty George, good George, nice George.'"

"Rich, handsome, witty George," they chorused feebly, "nice George, good George."

George took out his flask. "'Pleasant, popular, *able* George.'"

"Pleasant, popular, able George."

In the swollen peace that followed, Leona and Dolly smiled stiffly at one another. "I really never felt so much of a fool in my life," Dolly said.

"We can leave in about an hour, don't you think?" Charles said.

"An hour, Charles, yes, let's say an hour at the most," Leona agreed fervently.

They continued to sit, smiling. Behind them, having tasted heaven, George slept. Before them, the dance went on.

Next morning, Charles awoke as usual at nine-thirty, but he did not immediately open his eyes. He waited, lying very still, breathing calmly and deeply, until his first impression of uneasiness, of being on guard, had passed into a determined surge of good spirits, and then, to his delighted surprise, into a playful well-being that carried him out of bed and across to the table where his notebook lay. He lifted the book, admiring the neatness—that is, he thought, the dispassionateness—of last night's entries. He had stayed awake almost until dawn, sitting here in silence until his temper was cool enough to let him write as he knew he should write. Now it was all in hand. The day was full of promise. He was going into battle, and his adversaries, meagre enough in their normal state, would all have horrifying hangovers.

"George," he murmured, and read. It was disagreeable stuff, but he absorbed it bravely. George was easy game. George would learn his lesson well. Thinking of the awakening George must at this moment be enduring with Leona, Charles could almost find it in his heart to be sorry for the poor wretch. Edward would squirm, too. That would all be perhaps too easy.

But then came the difficult part, because already, at the memory of the evening, Charles was beginning to rage again. He was churning with rage. He could burn the memory of his own ludicrous part in the whole business from the minds of the others, by turning their derision back on them, but could he forget it himself? Because if he did not forget it, or destroy it, its damage would show, and the others would know for certain that he had been as vulnerable as they to the general humiliation. "They must not know," he said aloud. "It must not show," he said. "Today will prove what I am—a man above all this petty frenzy. I am different from all these people," he told himself angrily. He stood up and strode barefoot around the room.

Suddenly he stopped in the center of the woolly white rug and, gazing down at his untidy bed, clutched his head with both hands. "I simply must remember that I am an observer," he said. The image that had come to him again and again last night as he sat on the dais returned once more: He saw himself before leaving for the dance, posturing in front of this very pier glass, taking the attitudes of the waltz, actually dancing backward with the hand mirror, watching the swing of his coat and the curve of his trouser legs. "I cannot bear this!" Charles said wildly, and started to catalogue the shame of the others. Dolly's net stockings, he thought, and that absurd rose. Leona's open chagrin. Lewis's deathly embarrassment. And George with his sad little flash of courage. And Tarnac—why, he had enough gibes prepared to keep Tarnac reeling for a year.

Gradually Charles' head grew quiet. He opened the curtains. Another perfect day. It might be yesterday—but he thrust that thought quickly out of sight. He sat in the chintz chair and permitted himself an unusual indulgence: he smoked a cigarette before breaking his fast. Then he rang for Bridie, and when she appeared, he stared at her in amazement, for even he could not ignore the extraordinary violence she brought with her into the room.

She handed him his orange juice and poured the hot milk and coffee. He eyed her curiously as he sipped the orange juice. Her face was actually twitching with some emotion. Something must have upset her last night. He felt he could not bear it if she left the room before he knew what it was.

"A very pleasant party last night, Bridie," he said smoothly. "Very pleasant indeed. The girls looked so pretty in their little best dresses."

"I suppose they did, sir." Bridie hurled herself at the window curtains, and snatched them apart with such force that the whole inside window frame was left naked, ruining Leona's lovely draped effect. Charles frowned in surprise. More here than meets the eye, he thought, and wondered how best to approach this maddened woman.

"Poor dear Mr. Tarnac," he said tentatively. "Pathetic fellow, I'm afraid he's had a bad time these last few years. A pity, really."

"Mr. Tarnac is all right," Bridie said. She stared at him, and it seemed to Charles that for the first time that morning she remembered who he really was. "Oh, Mr. Tarnac's a lovely man," she said spitefully. "The girls all think he's God's gift to the women. They're all head over heels in love with him." She had rehearsed this speech the night before, as she sat watching the dance and watching the watchers on the dais. She got little satisfaction from it now. She wondered if anything would ever happen in the world again that would be awful enough to satisfy her.

Jealousy, Charles thought, with disgust. This laughable monolith fancies herself in love. He picked up his notes, dismissing her. "The girls' opinion is always of immense interest to me. I must tell poor Mr. Tarnac what you said when I see him at lunch."

"You won't see him at lunch, nor at dinner either," Bridie cried, "for he went off back to town with the rest of that crew. They were all mad to get back to the city. The way they drove off, I wouldn't be surprised if the half of them were found dead, and I wouldn't be sorry, either."

"Who went back to the city? What do you mean?"

"Mr. Tarnac went back with all the fellows that were up here for the dance, and a few of the young ones that are working here, too. A lot of use they'll be around here today, if they ever come back here at all."

Charles laughed. Really, it was too good, that sodden fool Tarnac dashing around with a carful of drunken servants.

"And where on earth did these wild young things go, Bridie? To some dance hall, perhaps?"

Bridie took a deep and unsteady breath. "Oh, great God," she said, "when I heard of it! I could have dropped dead, so I could. I could have killed them."

"What did they do, Bridie?"

"Oh, Mr. Runyon, wait till I tell you, I had a nice chair that I sat on the whole evening, between the door where you come into the hall and the door where you go into the bar. Near the stage, I was. A couple of us sat there, and then from time to time other girls would come along and sit with us a minute or two. You know the way it is. And you know the way you talk. The boys would bring me a little drink now and then. Not that I took much, but you know, Mr. Runyon, I'm not accustomed to it. Oh, Mr. Runyon, the things I said. Things I wouldn't want repeated. I won't have a friend in the place when it gets out. I don't know where to go or what to do. I'm nearly mad, thinking about it all night long, and praying to God the records would be broke by the time they got back to town."

"What records, Bridie?"

"The records they made at the dance. Didn't one of the young fellows in the band—a radio mechanic he is, bad luck to him—rig up one of them wire-recording things right behind where I was sitting. Every word I said. If they'd only have given me a hint. But of course nobody knew, only the young fellow himself, the young blackguard, and a couple of his friends that helped him fix it up. Things I wouldn't have repeated for the world—I—"

"And that was why they were in such a hurry to get back to town, to play the records over?"

"Why else. All laughing they were—"

"And Mr. Tarnac was with them, and some of the girls from here?"

"Josie next door, for one. Lazy young lump, she—"

"Bridie, please pay attention. Tell me, did they put recorders anywhere except behind your chair?"

"In the bar, they had one. I wouldn't have minded that, I wasn't in there. And one in the vestibule as you come in, but I hardly stopped there at all. And another one under the platform you and Mrs. Harkey and Mr. Harkey were on. I wasn't near there."

She stopped suddenly, astounded, listening to what she had just heard her own voice say. And to think that I missed that, she thought, and realized how far she had drifted from her moorings in these last few hours.

"Yes," she said, "that's right. There was one under where you were sitting, too, Mr. Runyon."

Staring greedily into his eyes, she saw and recognized what she had never hoped to see again—a chagrin as hot and as bitter as her own.

The Stone Hot-Water Bottle

Over the years, Leona Harkey had made many gifts to her friend and idol, Charles Runyon, the noted literary man and theatre critic, but of all the things she had given him, he liked best an old-fashioned stone hot-water bottle she had found one day, quite by accident, in a junk shop. Leona had wandered into the shop on the chance of finding something odd and funny that might please Charles, whose tastes were so unpredictable and yet so rigidly formed, and there, on a rickety table heaped with unmatched bits of china, the hot-water bottle lay, looking as though it had been waiting for her to come and find it. The minute her eyes fell on it, Leona remembered the story Charles had told her of one particularly terrible year during his lonely childhood, when a hot-water bottle just like this one was his dearest possession and his only consolation, because it was his only link with a dearly loved grandmother who had died, leaving him to the mercies of a crowd of cruder, less understanding relatives. Triumphant and excited, Leona knew she had made a find.

Charles was enraptured by his new possession, which before being presented to him had been purified and polished by Bridie, Leona's massive Irish maid, and encased, by Leona's dressmaker, in a tight, zippered jacket of olive-green quilted velvet. Furthermore—and this was another proof of Leona's imaginativeness—attached to one end of the velvet case was a lengthy loop of twisted velvet ribbon, so that when the bottle was not in use, it could hang decoratively from a brass hook near the head of Charles' bed. Charles had two beds. One belonged to the Murray Hill hotel where he had lived for over thirty years. The other belonged in Leona's beautiful house at Herbert's Retreat, forty miles outside New York on the right bank of the Hudson River, where Charles spent his weekends. It was understood, of course, that the stone hot-water bottle was intended for his room at Leona's.

Another happy thing about the hot-water bottle was that it was found in early October, just as the nights were getting cold; Charles was able to start using it immediately. Every night thereafter during his weekend visits, Bridie took the hot-water bottle to the kitchen, where she stripped it naked and filled it with boiling water. Then, covered again, it was returned to Charles' room and placed in his bed. Charles often claimed that the most blissful moment of his week came on Friday night, when his toes first touched the delicious velvety warmth of his hot-water bottle. After closing his book, but before turning out his bedside lamp, he hung his treasure back on its hook, where he could see it in the morning without being made aware of the chill that had come over it in the night. He couldn't bear to face the fact that the hot-water bottle grew cold in the night.

"One of the worst things about that terrible year when I was seven," he told Leona one Friday evening in November, "was waking up in the morning to find that my darling grandmother's hot-water bottle had died in the night. Because that is how it felt, you know—dead, cold and dead. Every morning, it was as though she had died again and left me. I used to cry myself to sleep with my arms wrapped around it—you know the way a child does. And then one of my aunts, Aunt Jane, the grimmest-faced one, decided I was making a fetish out of it (imagine, she used that word; where do you suppose she ever heard it?) and she took it away. She took it, Leona. Can you consider such cruelty? I never saw it again. Leona, darling, you know, this one looks exactly like it. Do you suppose it's the same one? Could it be?"

"Of course it could be. Of course it's the same one, Charles. Why, Charles, if you could see the little hole in the wall where I found it! The sort of place that ordinarily I'd never dream of entering. But I felt drawn in, and there was your hot-water bottle, in plain view. It must be the same, Charles. And don't you adore the little velvet coatee I had made for it?"

"I do adore it, Leona," Charles said, "and I adore you, my dear, sweet, romantic Leona. What ever would I do without you?"

Leona's eyes filled with tears, and she searched for an answer that would be pretty and responsive and yet light in its expression, because Charles detested any display of mawkishness, and Leona had suffered too many verbal trouncings to trust herself to speak impulsively.

"Dear Charles," she said cautiously, but for once she need not have feared. Charles was far away in memories she could not share except as a listener, and even then, although she did not know it, Charles edited himself carefully, because the truth of his background was too crowded and hearty to suit the slender, witty, cynical being he had become. They were in Leona's living room, and Charles, in narrow black slacks and saffron velvet jacket, was sitting in his favorite armchair, which was covered in a pale-blue linen. His silky gray head was inclined toward the firelight, and his sharp gray eyes glinted with thought.

Leona watched him respectfully from a chintz sofa. Charles must never be disturbed when he was musing, although he did not dislike having a witness to his silence, which was impressive, if studied. Leona, whose mind was uncomplicated, although her appearance was not, never ceased to be grateful that he allowed her the privilege of his friendship. Leona's fear of Charles, which was real, went in two directions. She was afraid of offending or disappointing him, having many times been obliterated by his scathing and horribly accurate tongue. She was also afraid of losing his favor, because his presence in the house every weekend gave her an unquestioned position among the women who lived at the Retreat, and their admiration, or envy, was the foundation on which Leona built up her importance. From the homage of her friends, Leona drew all the pleasure she got from her pretty, well-ordered house, her gracious life, and her distinguished wardrobe. Charles chose all her clothes, and she knew that without him she would never have attained her present perfection of chic and assurance. She was a tall, slender, shapeless girl with a pale face, vague features, and a head of thick, dark hair that she had always worn in a chignon low on her neck, just as she had habitually worn tweed skirts with sweaters in the daytime, and surplice dresses of dark wool at night. Always before she knew Charles, that is. Charles had changed her. He had started by taking her, on his first weekend at Herbert's Retreat, to the hairdresser, where under his intense supervision her present coiffure—a dark and cloudy halo that framed her face and shadowed it—came into being. Then he had insisted on a pale-mauve lipstick that defined her tiny mouth without emphasizing it, and, finally, he had taught her the several tricks that now gave her eyes their startled, yet languorous and enormously mysterious, gaze.

"Marie Laurencin!" he shouted gleefully that day when the miracle was accomplished and Leona sat transformed in her Early American living room. "But a sly, malicious Marie Laurencin. What fun, darling."

And they had both shrieked with laughter, Charles because he knew that Leona's near stupidity had no slyness in it and that her malice would always be, at its sharpest, a vapid reflection of his own, and Leona because she was pleased and excited.

"But your clothes, darling," he said severely when the little paroxysm of mirth had evaporated. "Your clothes are frightful. Now, let me see. No velvet, Leona—not even in a skirt. You are definitely not a velvet girl. I, on the other hand, am absolutely velvet—in moderation, of course. Velvet is immoderate stuff, Leona, and must be strictly disciplined. Always remember that, my dear. No, don't remember it. Forget it. Forget velvet altogether. Tweed, yes, but only in its thinnest, most gossamer interpretations. That thing you're wearing looks like tree-trunk bark. Thin, soft tweeds in divine colors: mauve, of course; periwinkle, of course; olive, apricot, cerise, maybe. And do bear in mind, my love, that a suit or a dress—anything you wear— is meant to illuminate you. You look positively surrounded in that thing you have on. That suit has conquered you, Leona. See the brazen independence of those grisly tweed shoulders. Why, they must be several inches above your own dear little shoulders. Clothes may be impertinent, Leona, and delightfully so, but they must never be domineering. Do run upstairs and take that thing off at once, Leona. It affronts me."

When Leona returned, in a dress that Charles also disapproved of, although not so violently, he smiled at her and said, "What an exciting day we've spent, Leona. We've turned you into a beauty. We'll spend this weekend deep in plans, and by next Friday you'll have at least two or three really splendid things. To begin with, a tremendous fireside skirt with a hem that measures at least a mile around. Now, let's see. For the skirt? Let me think."

"Taffeta?" Leona said timidly, for in those early days she was still unguarded enough to express her uninvited opinion.

Charles covered his face with his hands for a moment, and when he spoke, it was with mighty patience. "Taffeta," he whispered. "Taffeta. Taffeta? The first refuge of the fat young wallflower, who hopes vainly that the crisp rustle of the electric-blue skirt—it's always electric blue at that age, Leona—will drive the bepimpled stagline mad with desire. And the last refuge of the thin and fading wallflower, who depends on the vulgar shimmer of this execrable fabric—baby blue in the later stages, Leona—to avert the attention of prospective partners from her worried and disappointed countenance and to encourage them to perambulate her at least once around the badly waxed surface of the country-club floor. Tafetta? Leona, how *could* you?"

"I'm very sorry, Charles," Leona said breathlessly. "I just didn't know. You see, I just don't know anything. I won't make a single other suggestion. You'll see."

"Leona," Charles said seriously, "I'm beginning to think I came into your life just in time to save it. Do you realize the sort of woman you were about to turn into? Taffeta! And that sinister tweed. Two years—no, a year—from now, it would have been too late. I could have done nothing for you. I'll unswaddle your personality, Leona, and I'll dress you as it deserves to be dressed. Oh, you may not always like what I do, my dear, but I can promise you one thing. We'll have an awful lot of fun."

"Oh, I'll love it, Charles. I'll love it!" Leona said fervently.

"You are a creature of flame and smoke, Leona. I see it all now. I won't have to think any more. Flame red, flame yellow, flame orange, and all the magical blues and grays you see in smoke. Oh, Leona, my mind is brimming with ideas. Do fetch some paper, lots of paper, and boxes and boxes of pencils. We must start our list, beginning with the fireside skirt, which will, I think, be made of awning canvas, striped in mauve and the very clearest yellow, and quilted, and lined with thin black cotton. You're going to look divine, darling. Do you know that?"

Two weeks later, when Leona, wearing the fireside skirt for the first time, confronted Charles as he arrived from the city, he was already an indispensable part of her life.

So long ago all that was, Leona thought affectionately now, gazing at Charles' bent, musing head. Eight whole years ago. Poor Tommy—how furious it used to make him, having to drive Charles out every Friday. And George gets just as furious now, although he's not as quick to show it as poor Tommy was. George is such a fool.

Tommy Finch, Leona's first husband, who had brought her as a bride into his family's pleasant old home at Herbert's Retreat, was dead, having run his car into a tree one night. George Harkey, to whom Leona was now married, was a stolid young man who spent his days at Clancyhangers, one of the less celebrated New York department stores, where he was credit manager. Leona had married George chiefly for the sake of the tiny riverside cottage he owned, which cut her house off from the view, so highly prized by all Retreat dwellers, of the broad waters of the Hudson. Now Leona had her view, the cottage having been demolished without delay after her marriage to George. Unfortunately, she also had George. But a husband—even a dull, embarrassing husband like George—was better for Leona's purposes than no husband at all. She ignored George as completely as possible, and, so powerful was her pride in her house and in her position at Herbert's Retreat, she had almost forgotten that George's cottage ever existed. Her living room was no longer Early American. Charles had seen to that. Now it was a witty, sophisticated, and dashing melange of bright linens and chintzes, and reflected, as Charles said, the marriage of an informed eye with a wayward and original fancy. A wonderful room for a party, people always said when they saw it for the first time.

Leona loved to entertain, and her parties, which were always expertly planned and very successful, owed a good deal not only to Charles' advice but also to his presence. He was the only celebrated representative of the world of arts and letters who was familiar to the residents of the Retreat, and since most of them commuted daily to the comparatively unexciting circles of business and finance, they respected him immediately for his reputation, and learned to respect even more keenly his talent for withering with a look or drawing blood with a word. Charles treasured Leona's house for its comfort and for the verve with which he had endowed it. He treasured Leona for her subservience and for her appearance. "I invented you, my darling," he liked to say.

"I know, Charles. I know you did. Oh, I remember," Leona always answered, and at such times she would gaze anxiously into his eyes, as though she feared that by closing them he would dismiss her back into the nothingness from which he had rescued her.

Tired of musing, Charles suddenly sat straight up in the pale-blue armchair and laughed impishly at Leona's startled face. Leona, whose expression was not entirely spontaneous, was glad to be able to talk again.

"Charles," she said, "I have wonderful news. I just can't keep it to myself any longer. The most wonderful surprise. You'll never guess what it is. All right, Charles, I know you hate to guess. I'll tell you." She drew a deep breath and smiled tremulously. This was really too good. "Aunt Amelia is coming next weekend," she said. "Lady Ailesbury-Rhode, Charles. Can you believe it?"

"*Tommy's* aunt, wasn't she?"

"And my aunt by marriage. I always call her Aunt Amelia.

"Always? You only met her once, didn't you, when you dragged Tommy to visit her in Ottawa during your honeymoon?"

"Oh, Charles, you sound so cross. I can't help showing off just a little. She's going back to London to live, and she'll be in New York for two weeks, staying with friends. She called me this morning and said she'd like to come here next weekend. Well, I feel quite deflated. I thought you'd be pleased. I'm planning a marvellous party, Charles. Don't you want to hear about it?"

"Of course I want to hear about it. I'm always interested in your little dos, Leona. I simply wanted to say that titles are not so uncommon as you seem to imagine, my dear. I don't think you should permit yourself to be quite so fluttery about this Lady Ailesbury-Rhode. You're being quite girlish, my love. You're flapping. It isn't altogether becoming, Leona."

"Oh, Charles, I'm sorry. Don't scold me. I'm afraid I got carried away. I'm such a fool. But do let's talk about the party. Imagine how jealous Dolly and Laura—and, oh, all of them—are going to be. Why, if you think *I'm* bad, you should hear *them*. I mean they're simply slavish about titles. Of course, I don't care a bit, one way or another, but it is fun to have the only titled relative at the Retreat. Don't you see, Charles?"

"Of course I see, Leona. Rather, I understand your excitement, although I deplore it. I rather hoped you had matured beyond that kind of behavior. But the other girls will indeed be green with envy. Pea green. You say the old lady—she is *quite* old, isn't she?—telephoned you this morning. Had she written you from Ottawa?"

"Well, no, Charles. Why should she?"

Charles smiled disagreeably. "I hope you won't find her difficult. Bridie is a very precious servant, you know. You don't want Bridie flouncing out in a rage because some titled Englishwoman steps on her toes. You'd better be on guard, my dear. House guests are a very touchy proposition, especially when they happen to be people you don't know awfully well."

"Oh, Charles," Leona said reproachfully.

There was a nervous silence.

"After all, this was Tommy's house," Leona went on, "and it's only right that his aunt should come out here for a visit, probably the only visit she'll ever have a chance to make here. And think how she'll enjoy you, Charles! She's no doubt expecting to meet a lot of dull little husbands and wives. You'll be a revelation to her."

"All right. But don't say you weren't warned. Let's talk about the party. Whom did you think of asking?"

"Everyone!" Leona cried. "Just everyone in the Retreat, Charles, darling. Cocktails, a buffet supper, the works. We'll probably go on all night. It's going to be *the* best party. It'll be the last really big party before Christmas."

Aloof, even frigid, frowning a little to show he still harbored misgivings, Charles began to plan the party for Lady Ailesbury-Rhode.

The gratitude Leona felt toward Charles blinded her to the possibility that he might be jealous, and ordinarily she would have taken his disparaging remarks about her relative as an indication that he was in a bad mood; that is to say, annoyed with her. For Leona, a consistent worshipper, could imagine and could perceive only two moods in her god. Either Charles was mercifully disposed to her or he was not. Out of favor with him, she felt painfully bewildered and could hardly endure herself while she waited for him to approve of her again, and then, when the change came and he smiled on her and called her darling caressingly instead of with sarcasm, the pain went out of her bewilderment, and she found its absence pleasant and called herself happy. Charles' pronouncements on Lady Ailesbury-Rhode shocked her, but only for a moment. Her anticipation of her coming social triumph had already swelled into an airy, lightheaded satisfaction that could be punctured by no one—not even Charles.

On the following Friday afternoon at three o'clock, Lady Ailesbury-Rhode had not yet arrived, and Leona ran upstairs to take another last look at her guest's bedroom. There was nothing there that she could improve, and she descended nervously into her large, square center hall just as the doorbell rang. It seemed to Leona later that the uniformed chauffeur was already in the hall, and had deposited Lady Ailesbury-Rhode's suitcase there, before Bridie answered the door, but that, she knew, was only because she had become so confused. Lady Ailesbury-Rhode advanced on Leona, shook her hand briskly, and demanded, in clear, high-pitched tones, to be taken to her room. She was a short, round woman with a complacent, bad-tempered face and discolored blue eyes, and at the sight of her Leona felt so great an awe that she almost curtsied. Instead, she led the way upstairs. Bridie followed with the suitcase.

"I'm going to take a nap," Lady Ailesbury-Rhode announced. Then, to Bridie, "I'll have my tea in here. You can bring it up at four-thirty—and, mind you, I'll know instantly if the water is not boiling. You don't use those disgusting tea bags, I presume."

Before Bridie could answer, Leona spoke for her: "Of course not,

Aunt Amelia. Why, Bridie would no more consider using a tea bag than—than I would. Would you like some toast with your tea?"

"One slice of very thin bread, lightly buttered, please. Nothing else. Well, this all looks very nice, Leona. Charming house—I was out here once or twice when poor Tommy's mother was alive. We must have a long chat after I've had my nap. Now, there's just one thing, my dear. I see you've put no hot-water bottle in my bed. Perhaps you forgot. But I really would like it. Would you have your maid bring it here as soon as possible? I shudder to think of those icy sheets."

There were several hot-water bottles in Leona's house, but her thoughts flew naturally in the direction of only one.

"Bridie will fill it at once, Aunt Amelia," she said penitently. "How thoughtless of me. Bridie, fill the olive-green velvet bottle. Aunt Amelia, Bridie will have it here in just a minute. How careless of me to forget it."

"An olive-green velvet bottle? My dear girl, haven't you anything else? It sounds unsafe."

"It's a rather special hot-water bottle, Aunt Amelia, I'm sure you'll approve of it when you see it."

The old lady's words of pleased surprise when she saw and felt the pretty object sent Leona into a daze of pleasure that still possessed her when Charles arrived at the house at five-thirty. Leona met him at the door. George was putting the car away.

"A drink and news before you go up to change or afterward, Charles?" she asked.

"Afterward, if you don't mind," Charles said crisply. "Did Lady Ailesbury-Rhode arrive?"

"She's in her room, taking a nap. She had tea at four-thirty, so she should be down quite soon now. Do hurry, Charles, darling, so that we can have a little moment together before she comes. I've so much to tell you, darling."

Half an hour later, Charles came downstairs and joined Leona, who was sitting in front of the living-room fire, waiting to pour the first Martinis of the evening. The Martinis were in a tall crystal shaker, and on the tray beside them stood two tiny glasses, frosted from their sojourn in the refrigerator. Leona's air of anxiety as she poured the Martinis was genuine. Charles had been known to make an ugly scene over an inferior Martini. He sat down and sipped his drink before he spoke.

"Leona," he said suddenly, setting his glass on the table beside him, "where is my hot-water bottle?"

The shock, the violent realization of what she had done, cleared Leona's brain miraculously, and in one instant she saw her dreadful mistake and began, almost calmly, to think of a way to recover herself.

"Why, it's in the kitchen, Charles," she said. "Bridie noticed a loose thread in the quilting yesterday, and she actually offered to repair it herself. Now, there's proof that she really adores you. She never offered to mend anything for me. Quite the opposite."

Charles sighed, smiled, lay back in his chair, and took his glass in his hand. "Wonderful Bridie," he said. "And wonderful Leona. This Martini is perfection, darling."

"The Maitlands are coming for dinner," Leona said. "And Tom and Liza. I didn't ask anyone to come in afterward. I thought we'd better have an early night tonight. I don't want to wear Aunt Amelia out. After all, she's not so terribly young."

"Stop worrying about this evening. I'll shoo them all home myself, if I have to. Now, tell me about your aunt. What was she wearing? I want to hear all about her."

Leona wondered how she could go on talking so calmly. She was horrified at what she had done, and more horrified because of the stupid, useless lie. Why could she not have said honestly that she had lent the hot-water bottle, knowing he would understand? But he would never understand. And now I'm going to have to tell him before he goes to bed tonight, she said to herself, and how am I going to do that? Watching Charles' familiar gestures, seeing his mocking *moues,* his narrow, malicious smile, and his sharp eyes, which she knew could turn in an instant from tolerance to a destructive rage, she was terrified. How am I going to tell him, she wondered. How in God's name am I going to tell him?

But it never occurred to her not to give the velvet-covered hot-water bottle to Lady Ailesbury-Rhode again at bedtime.

71

Leona had been working as a secretary in a bank when she met Tommy Finch, and she had never really recovered from the incredulous elation she felt when he married her. Secretly, she was still as impressed by Herbert's Retreat now as she had been the day he brought her out to show her the house, just before their wedding. She had never forgotten her first sight of the Retreat, when Tommy turned in to the narrow private road that meandered from the highway in toward the river. The forty beautiful houses it connected had been built here and there at random, two hundred years ago, in a fine, thickly wooded glade that remained wild and green except for the smooth grass lawns and rims of grass that the householders claimed for themselves. Leona had never even heard of Herbert's Retreat until she met Tommy, but from the first she became fiercely attached to it. She loved the fact that it was a restricted, protected, rigidly exclusive community. During her first days there, she was timorously happy that Tommy's neighbors so easily accepted her. As she settled down, her pride stiffened. She began to take her own presence in the Retreat for granted and to feel she belonged naturally, not just by acceptance. Still, at the bottom of her heart, deeper even than her dependence on Charles, lay an irresponsible, unreasonable fear, carefully smothered most of the time, that someday some distant relative of Tommy's would turn up and take the house from her. It couldn't happen, she knew; she had her rights. But the rights, as she held and counted them, seemed slippery in her hands. She was not really very sure of herself, and Lady Ailesbury-Rhode's title only intensified her desire to get down on both knees and say to the old lady, "See? I'm the same sort of person, really, that you are. I belong here. See how naturally I fit in? See what a good job I do? Isn't the house charming? And beautifully appointed? No one else could do things so well. There can't possibly be any question that I belong here. Please say that you approve of me."

All during the familiar, laughing flurry of the Maitlands' and the Fryes' arrival, and during the decorous, excited interval that marked Lady Ailesbury-Rhode's descent into the company, and while poor George, who came downstairs very late, was fumbling at the bar for one of the warm, sweet Manhattans he loved, Leona's thoughts were with her titled guest. Even while her head seethed with distress over her predicament with Charles, she was judging the effect on the old lady of the room, the service, and the other guests. Charles was doing splendidly. Suave, humorous, attentive, he was showing quite plainly that he and Lady Ailesbury-Rhode belonged to the same world and that they were at home together. Lewis Maitland, tall, blond, and with a heavy, conventional handsomeness, spoke very little. Dolly, his thirty-year-old baby-girl wife, bubbled mutely, holding her cocktail glass carefully and casting inquisitive, delighted glances in all directions. Willowy Liza Frye was silent, too, her graceful, high-held head immobile in a halo of conscious poise. Tom Frye's plump face swelled with diffidence as he recounted some affectionate anecdotes of days spent in London as a schoolboy and as a young man. Lady Ailesbury-Rhode's clear, clipped voice dominated the cocktail hour and the dinner table, and after dinner she invited Charles to sit next to her on the sofa, where they engaged in a companionable, witty exchange of views on the deterioration of polite society since the beginning of the First World War.

Before meeting Leona, Charles had been the prey of any woman with a guest room for an extra man who would pay for his weekend in smiles and talk. Now he told a few reminiscences of those days, transfiguring the women, the houses, and the occasions until Leona was sick with the thought that she might lose him. Lady Ailesbury-Rhode's descriptions of the old, leisurely days in England entranced her hearers, and they all murmured protestingly when, at ten-thirty sharp, she stood up to go to bed. Leona offered to see her to her room, but the offer was refused, and after walking with her pleased, flushed guest to the foot of the stairs she slipped out to the kitchen, where Bridie, bathed in a blinding white light from the ceiling, was sitting on a chair that was all but invisible under her great, starched bulk. A cup of tea steamed on the table beside her. At her back, the window was uncurtained against the night. She was holding her spectacles against her eyes with one hard red hand, and reading the morning obituaries. Seeing Leona, she lowered the spectacles.

"The dinner was perfect, Bridie," Leona said. "The other maids went home, I suppose. You must be very tired."

73

"Ah, I'm used to that, Mrs. Harkey. You have to get used to being tired when you're in service. I was wanting to ask you—I put Her Ladyship's hot-water bottle in her bed at a quarter past ten, just like she said. Now, which hot-water bottle do you want me to leave up for Mr. Runyon? Or maybe he won't want one at all now, since the one he likes is in use."

Bridie had been waiting for this interview since the afternoon. You're on the spot now, Ma'am, she thought, watching Leona's distress. Let's see you wriggle out of this.

Leona said nothing, and Bridie continued, "He never had one before, Ma'am. Before you got him the stone one, I mean. Maybe he won't miss it."

Leona looked at her helplessly. "Frankly, Bridie," she said, laughing in the way she knew a maid would understand—not being too friendly but showing that she understood perfectly well that Bridie was human, too, and that this domestic emergency must involve them both—"Frankly, I don't know what to do. Lady Ailesbury-Rhode would have thought it odd if we'd given her an ordinary hot-water bottle tonight. You heard what she said about the velvet one this afternoon."

Bridie emitted a short, barking laugh. "If you'll excuse me for saying so, Ma'am, I think we'd all have heard about it if she hadn't found that same bottle in her bed when she went up tonight. All over it, she was, when I took the tea up in the afternoon. She had it hanging on the bedpost right beside her head. 'Where did Mrs. Harkey find it?' she asked me when I was fixing the bed tray. Well, I told her about how you had the little cover made for it and all, but sure she knew all that. You told her yourself this afternoon. She just wanted to talk about it. It's the sort of thing an old lady would fancy, you know, Mrs. Harkey. She took a fancy to it, right enough."

"She hung it on the bedpost, Bridie?"

"Yes, Ma'am. Where she could see it. Now, about Mr. Runyon—"

"Wait a minute, Bridie. Let me think."

Trembling, Leona sat down and patted her face nervously until her glance caught her own dim, ghostly reflection in the dark glass of the window. Then she put her hands in her lap and turned to Bridie and said, "I want you to help me. No, wait a minute, this is going to be difficult. You're going to have to be very, very careful."

This is the best yet, Bridie thought as she listened to Leona's instructions. Wait till I tell the girls about this. Oh, Lord above, this is the best yet!

When Leona returned to her living room, she was greeted with a flurry of excited cries from Dolly, who was evidently determined to make up for her evening of silence. Charles was back in his own chair by the fire, and a glass of brandy stood at his elbow. He winked at Leona. Oh, how wonderful he is, Leona thought. I must not let this terrible thing come between us. In spite of their pleasure in Lady Ailesbury-Rhode, her presence had been a strain on all of them, and now they subsided easily into the comfortable, companionable idle chat that was familiar to them. Even Charles seemed less guarded than usual. Leona's mouth was dry, and she sipped her brandy, waiting till Bridie should judge the time had come to go upstairs. After half an hour, Leona heard her slow, heavy tread, and the pause as she reached the landing. Then there was no sound from upstairs. Bridie must be waiting for the chance to get into Lady Ailesbury-Rhode's room. Leona threw Charles a glance of tremulous appeal, which he misinterpreted.

He stood up and clapped his hands gaily. "All right, boys and girls. Leona is much too polite and much too fond of you all to tell you so, but she has a big day tomorrow. And I want to go to bed."

A minute later, she stood in the doorway with him, waving goodbye and nodding with frantic enthusiasm at Dolly's repeated promises to see her tomorrow, to call her up first thing, to run right around if she needed anything at all.

Charles closed the door and leaned against it, making a comical face. "My God," he said, "I thought they'd never go. You don't think I was too abrupt with them? I don't think so."

"Of course you weren't abrupt, Charles, darling."

"Dear child, you're positively tottering," Charles said. "Come and sit down, and we'll have one little nightcap before we go up. I'll get it, darling; you look all in."

Leona wondered what in the name of heaven was keeping Bridie upstairs so long. Surely the old lady was asleep by now. All Bridie had to do was walk to the bedpost, take the hot-water bottle, take it to the kitchen, refill it, and have it in Charles' bed by the time he got upstairs. I'd better keep him here a few minutes longer, she thought.

George said good night and went upstairs to bed. Charles stood on the hearthrug, gazing into the mirror that hung over Leona's mantelpiece. He swirled his brandy gently in his glass and stared at his reflection.

"Your Aunt Amelia was quite taken with me," he said. "In fact, we flirted a little, there toward the end of the evening. She must have been quite a belle in her day. What is it you women see in me, Leona?" He turned his head and glanced sidewise at her, teasing her. "Tell me, Leona, darling, what do you see in me? Let's talk about it. . . . Oh, well, if you won't talk— No, you've had your chance. I'll puzzle it out myself. Mirror, mirror— No, that's too boring. But they do say the eyes are the windows of the soul." He leaned forward, smiling into his own eyes.

A dreadful squawk reached them from upstairs.

Charles leaped back from the mirror. "What was that?" he cried.

But Leona was already halfway up the stairs. She switched the landing light on as she reached the top, and saw Bridie, hair in disarray, eyes glittering, come out of Lady Ailesbury-Rhode's bedroom with the velvet hot-water bottle hugged to her bosom. Then Lady Ailesbury-Rhode appeared, wearing a camel's hair dressing gown, slippers of maroon leather, and a hair net.

"Leona, what is the meaning of this?" she asked. "I awoke from a sound sleep to find this woman clutching my foot."

"She had it in the bed with her, Ma'am," Bridie said.

"I'm dreadfully sorry, Aunt Amelia," Leona said, and started to cry.

Lady Ailesbury-Rhode blinked with embarrassment. "Oh, don't take on so, child. I appreciate your thoughtfulness, although I don't usually need the hot-water bottle refilled in the night. Oh, Mr. Runyon, there you are. What a pickle you find us in."

Leona realized that Charles had run upstairs after her, and was standing behind her. She moved to lean against the wall.

76

George's bedroom door opened, and he came out, knotting his dressing gown and blinking. "Anything wrong?" he asked. "I thought I heard voices."

"A little misunderstanding, George," Lady Ailesbury-Rhode said. "Leona, dear, if your maid will take the hot-water bottle to the kitchen and refill it now, I shall be delighted. So kind of you. Good night, my dear."

She withdrew into her room and closed the door. George disappeared into his room. Bridie rustled past Leona and Charles, and went downstairs. She tried to catch Leona's eye as she went past, but Leona no longer cared for plots or signals. She felt Charles standing near her, and longed for him to speak to her, but he walked down the hall to his own room and went in, shutting the door. Leona ran after him, and, receiving no response to her knock, she opened the door and stepped into the room. Charles was sitting in his great easy chair by the window, smoking. He looked coolly at her.

"Well?" he said.

"Oh, Charles," Leona sobbed, "what can I say? How can you ever forgive me? But I was so confused when she arrived, and I wanted everything to be just right. And then I was frightened and I didn't know what to do. Please try to understand, Charles! Here we're going to have this lovely party tomorrow night, and don't let's spoil everything. I'll make it up to you, Charles, I promise I will. I promise, Charles!"

"Sorry, my dear. I won't be at your party tomorrow," Charles said.

Leona stopped crying and stared at him. "Not be at the party, Charles?"

"I shall be leaving first thing in the morning, Leona. I can call a taxi from the village to take me to the station, I presume."

Leona watched him take a puff of his cigarette. She thought of Lady Ailesbury-Rhode's domineering voice, and of Bridie's imperfectly hidden derision, and of Dolly's inane laughter, and of the olive-green velvet hot-water bottle, and of the eternity she had spent this evening, alone and frightened, trying to make everything go right for everybody.

"All right, Charles," she said wretchedly. "Bridie will call your taxi whenever you want it."

She closed the door and walked, weeping, down the hall to her own room, where she threw her clothes on the nearest chair and fell into bed, and, strangely enough, dropped off at once into a deep sleep.

When she awoke, it was ten o'clock. She had meant to be up at eight, because of the party. There was so much still to be done. And then she remembered that although Lady Ailesbury-Rhode was still under her roof, Charles had gone. Forever, Leona thought. Tears rolled down her face. I can't go through with this day, she thought. Not without him.

There was a tap at the door, and Bridie came in, bearing a tray of coffee and toast.

"When you didn't come down for breakfast, Ma'am, I thought I'd let you sleep. You looked that tired last night." She gazed avidly at Leona, who sat up and reached for her robe, which was not in its accustomed place beside her bed. "I'll get it, Ma'am," Bridie said, and took it from the closet.

Leona ignored her glance at the untidy heap of clothes on the chair. She had no more favors to ask of Bridie, and she wasn't going to stand any nonsense from her.

"Has Lady Ailesbury-Rhode had her breakfast, Bridie?" she asked, lighting a cigarette.

"She had tea in her room at eight, Mrs. Harkey. And she came down to breakfast at nine. And now she's out walking with Mr. Runyon. He's showing her around the place."

"Mr. Runyon?"

"Yes, Ma'am. He gave me a note to give you. He was all worried for fear I'd wake you up with it. Here it is. He gave it to me when I brought him up his coffee, but I promised him I wouldn't give it to you till I thought you were ready to get up."

"All right, Bridie," Leona said. "Never mind those clothes. You can pick them up later. I'll be down in an hour."

Bridie left reluctantly. As soon as the door closed, Leona tore the note open. "Dear Leona," it said, "I was joking, of course. I was punishing you a little. You have been a bad girl, you know. What a delicious day for our party. My big oak turned quite gold in the night, and threw two of his leaves right through my window and onto my table, where they are still resting, the darlings. See you at lunch. Or sooner?"

Oh, Charles, Leona thought. Oh, thank you, Charles!

Light with joy and anxious for a complete reconciliation, she dressed quickly. As she came from her bedroom into the hall, she saw that his door, at the far end, stood open. She peered in. The room was empty, and it had not yet been tidied. She walked to the writing desk and touched the oak leaves gently. Dear Charles . . . She looked at the chair in which he had sat last night, so hurt, so cruel, and so unforgiving. Dear Charles, she thought gratefully, I'll make amends somehow. She glanced at his pier glass and saw herself wearing a dress of thin red wool, artfully fitted to her long figure. The clear, bright color made her skin glow and deepened the dark haze of her hair. A flame, she thought. Dear, dear Charles. She rested her elbow on his white mantelpiece and thought of him. Then, in surprise, she saw that his fireplace was scattered with ashes, although the logs had not been charred and the kindling under them was whole. She reached down. Charles had been burning paper, but not enough to start a blaze. A letter or something, she thought idly, and would have turned away, but her eye was caught by a tiny white ball that had rolled away from the grate and was caught by the floor boards. She picked it up and smoothed it out. "Dearest Leona," she read. "Of course you have realized by now that I was jesting. I was, you know. I was hurt and I tried to hurt you. I'll be here for the party. And I'll be here next weekend and next weekend and next weekend. What times we are going to have together. And do you know, that splendid oak outside my window (the one I call *my* oak, darling) blazed"

The note was unfinished. Leona put it in her pocket and looked at the ashes in the grate. There must have been several notes. She grew thoughtful. Why, Charles was *anxious* to stay. He was just as anxious to stay as she was to have him here.

Before leaving the room, she cast one last glance around it. It was, after all, a very nice room. It was an enchanting room. Any man would be glad to have such a room.

79

That night, Leona gave the best party she had ever given. Everyone said so. Lady Ailesbury-Rhode was charming, and Charles Runyon was in top form. Leona looked radiant, in a clinging dress of wood-smoke-blue silk that left her sloping white shoulders bare. She was really a marvellous hostess. She seemed to be everywhere at once, and yet she never seemed worried or abstracted. Her confidence was superb, and as she wandered, smiling, from group to group, and from room to room, the eyes of her friends followed her with admiration and envy. Curiously enough, no one noticed that she did not exchange one word with Charles all evening. Only Charles noticed.

This was a new game for Leona, and she loved it. She could feel Charles' tension as she moved lightly through the rooms. She knew that he was watching her, however entertained and entertaining he might seem to the others. She knew it by the turn of his head as she came near his chair, which she passed quickly, laughing to someone at the far side of the room. She knew it by the set of his back as he stood talking near the buffet table and heard her voice calling to someone at his side. She had first felt her power as they met in the living room before lunch, and she challenged his amused, ironical gaze with an amused, ironical gaze of her own, and saw his puzzled frown. How long, Leona thought, pushing open a window to let the cold night air into the loud, warm rooms—how long will I punish him? Will I forgive him tonight, when they've all gone home and he wants that last little nightcap by the fire? Or will I go straight to bed and let him spend the night wondering? I might forgive him before lunch tomorrow. Or wait until Aunt Amelia leaves. That might be best—to wait till she leaves. He'll really be worried by then. But I would like to talk over the party tonight. Oh, well, I have hours yet before they go. And she closed the window (a little of that air was enough) and wandered idly toward the spot where Charles stood, the center of a delighted group, fascinating everyone, as always. Everyone but me, Leona thought, and ignored his hopeful eyes and passed casually by to watch for another opportunity to ignore him. Leona thought she had never had such fun in her life as she was having ignoring Charles.

The Gentleman in the
Pink-and-White Striped Shirt

At one minute before nine on a May morning, Charles Runyon opened drowsy eyes to the high-walled, sunless reaches of the Murray Hill hotel room that had been his home for nearly thirty years. Always, awakening in that room, Charles thought with satisfaction of the legend that had grown up around it. Charles' room was a mystery to the world. None of his friends—his present friends or those of former years—had ever entered it. There had been a period when columnists had conjectured almost weekly about its shape (it was long and narrow) and about its color (its walls, once pearl gray, had hardened to stone gray and chipped during Charles' tenancy, but he refused to allow it to be repainted) and its furnishings. The furniture, massive and shabby, contrasted curiously with the almost dainty elegance of Charles' personal appointments—his silver-backed brushes and hand mirror, his gold-topped bottle of sandalwood cologne, his leopard-skin slippers. His desk held a large pad of thick white paper, a crystal inkwell, and a feathered pen. It also held the porcelain tumbler from which he drank his morning coffee. His bookcase contained twelve copies of each of his own six books, the latest of which was ten years old, and on the lowest, deepest shelf he kept issues of magazines and newspapers in which articles by him had appeared.

Charles was a critic of the theatre and of literature. He confined his efforts, these days, to a weekly column for a string of Midwestern newspapers. He said that this was the only regular writing he wanted to do, since the so-called novelists and so-called playwrights working today had made serious criticism impossible. Let the so-called critics have their little day, Charles said contemptuously. But he read the theatre and book-review pages of the daily papers with fierce attention, and held secret weekly sessions with *Variety* at the Quill and Brush Club, of which he was a member.

Charles' room had one tall, deep window, shrouded in ancient red brocade, which looked out on an air shaft. In his youth, Charles had been too much ashamed of his room to allow his friends to visit him there. In those years, it angered him that he had to be content with a cheap room hidden away in the back of the hotel, instead of being able to afford one of the splendid apartments in front. But his friends' curiosity, which at first made him uneasy, with time became flattering, and he grew fond of the room, and increased its mysteriousness by his reticence about it, and then by his arch evasiveness, and finally just by continuing to live there.

The years passed, and the old hotel changed hands and lost heart and dignity. The big front apartments were cut up into cubicles, the fine, long marble entrance hall grew dingy and was cluttered with soft-drink dispensers and a water cooler. The noble oak desk, discreetly placed at the rear of the lobby, was handed over to a cigarette vender, who also dealt in razor blades and penny candy, and its functions were transferred to a sort of bathing box of varnished pine, built almost at the mouth of the elevator, in a position that flaunted the new managers' distrust of their guests. Run down and shabby though the hotel was, it nevertheless suited Charles very well. And it was very cheap. He never thought of moving.

Besides, during the past few years Charles had spent nearly as much time away from New York as he had spent in it. He had formed a habit of going every weekend to Leona Harkey's charming house at Herbert's Retreat, thirty miles above the city, on the east bank of the Hudson. Charles occupied a unique and privileged position at the Retreat. Leona and her friends regarded him as their infallible authority on the rules of gracious living and on the shadowy and constantly changing dimensions of good taste. They were all a little in awe of him. Leona admitted, laughing, that she was afraid of him—but she adored him, too, she always added quickly, and she did not know how she had ever existed before she met him.

Lying in bed, waiting for Leona to telephone, Charles smiled. She really was a dear child, although he sometimes wished she could have been a little less wholehearted and a tiny bit more intelligent. Today was the eighth anniversary of their meeting, and they had a delightful celebration planned, for just the two of them.

At nine o'clock exactly, the phone rang. Charles laughed softly into the mouthpiece.

"Is this the gentleman in the pink-and-white striped shirt?" Leona sang. "Oh, is this the—"

"Not quite yet, my dear," Charles said. "The pink-and-white striped shirt is still nestling in its birthday tissue in a box on my dressing table, with its five little brother shirts."

"He *did* deliver them, then!" Leona cried. "Oh, Charles, I am so glad. I was so afraid that man would disappoint you. Oh, what a relief."

"My shirtmaker has never failed me yet, Leona," Charles said coldly.

Really, it was a task keeping Leona in check.

"Of course he hasn't, Charles. He wouldn't dare, would he, darling? But Charles, I want to tell you about my suit. It's divine, and almost exactly like yours. It was so sweet of you to let your tailor make it for me. And from your special cloth, too. We're going to look quite alike today, aren't we? Almost like twins."

"Almost like twins," Charles echoed generously, because it did promise to be a very pleasant day. "You know, Leona, this is quite an event in my life. I've grown very fond of you in the last eight years, my dear." He giggled gently. "How is the good George, by the way?"

"Oh, Charles, you know George. He trundled off an hour ago, just like a good little businessman. He's probably sitting behind his desk already, telling some wretched creature to bring back the dinette set or be sued, or something. What a job for a man to have."

George Harkey, Leona's husband, was credit manager of one of New York's larger and less fashionable department stores.

"Well, we all must work," Charles said briskly, sitting up in bed. "And I should have been at my scribbling an hour ago. We meet at the Plaza, then. At twelve-fifteen. That will leave us ample time to lunch and still get to the theatre by curtain time. All right, my dear?"

83

"Twelve-fifteen," Leona said. "And Charles, I have a most amusing surprise for you."

"Splendid, Leona. I adore surprises. Now I really must go, Leona. Goodbye."

He replaced the phone, slid out of bed, wrapped himself in a dressing gown of thin gold wool—a gift from Leona—and plugged in his electric kettle, after assuring himself that it held enough water to make two cups of coffee. Leona and her friends would have been astonished at the absence of grace and charm in Charles' domestic arrangements. They might even have been outraged, considering the stringent demands he made on their establishments. He puttered about, fetching a bottle of cream from his window sill, measuring powdered instant coffee into his porcelain tumbler, and unwrapping a large, sticky delicatessen bun. Then he looked around for his morning newspapers. They were nowhere to be seen. He searched the room carefully, and at last, growing peevish, he even peered under his armchair, shook the window curtains, and pawed through his bed coverings. No sign of the papers. He was in the habit of buying the *Times* and the *Tribune* on his way home every night, and leaving them unopened, to read while he breakfasted.

Mike, the undersized, bespectacled elevator boy, who doubled as bellboy and porter, delivered the morning editions of the newspapers to the doors of other tenants in the hotel, but Charles was frugal, and refused to pay the small fee that this extra service cost. Now he was paperless, and his coffee was cooling. He gazed gloomily at the bun that had caused this disorder in his life—for there was no doubt in his mind that he had left the papers on the delicatessen counter the night before. His breakfast was ruined. Well, he wouldn't *let* it be ruined.

Knotting the sash of his robe firmly around his small middle, he unlocked his door, opened it, and looked out into the hall. There, in front of the opposite door, were the *Times* and the *Tribune.*

Charles paused, looked, listened, dived across the hall, grabbed the papers, and bounded backward to his own door, which resisted him. Gently and treacherously, his door had locked itself. No use to wring the handle, no use to push, no use to peer in the keyhole. The door was locked. A faint sound issued from inside the room whose tenant he had just robbed. He sprinted for the elevator and rang. Mike would have a passkey. Mike would let him into his room, and he would be safe again. With horror, he realized that he was still clutching the newspapers in his arms, and that the elevator, shuddering with age and unwillingness, was climbing up to his floor. He rammed both papers down the front of his robe, wrapped his arms about himself as though he were cold, and, when Mike threw back the elevator door, said, "I seem to have locked myself out of my room, Mike—of all foolish things. Would you bring your passkey?"

"How come you got locked out?" Mike inquired loudly as he sauntered along behind Charles, swinging the keys on their large brass ring.

"I was looking for the maid. She forgot to leave me any soap. The inefficiency of that woman is quite monstrous."

"You could of called the desk for your soap," Mike said.

Oh, yes, Charles thought. I could have called the desk for my soap. And you could have brought my soap up. And I could have given you a tip. None of that, my lad. "Will you hurry with that door, please?" he said sharply. "I could catch my death of cold standing out here."

Mike unlocked the door and pushed it open. Charles slipped past him, and turned to shoulder the door shut, but Mike, with one foot over the threshold, stood holding it open. He removed his spectacles, hawed breathily on them, and began to polish them on the section of his jacket that lay between his breast pocket and his dingy brass buttons. "You want I should bring you some soap?" he asked, and squinted into his spectacles before replacing them on his nose.

"Later," Charles cried, seeing the door across the way begin to open.

Across the hall, a flannel-clad arm appeared and began to feel confidently around on the floor. Hypnotized, Charles watched the disembodied hand pluck blindly at the worn edge of the carpet. Above the arm, a tousled black head appeared, turned downward to the floor at first, and then turned up to reveal a pinched face full of sleep and bad temper.

"Why, good morning, Miss Carmichael!" Mike cried.

"Where the hell are my papers, Mike?" Miss Carmichael demanded, and, standing up, showed a tiny, spare figure enveloped in maroon flannel.

"Why, aren't they there, Miss Carmichael? I left them there," Mike said.

"Really," Charles said, "you must excuse me."

There was a second's silence.

"Would you mind removing your body from my door?" he said, and saw the suspicion in Mike's face turn to certainty.

"Why, certainly, Mr. Runyon," Mike said. "I'll do that little thing."

Charles kicked the door shut, locked it, hurled the papers onto his bed, dashed into the bathroom, and turned the shower on full, to save his ears from the altercation that he knew must be taking place outside.

When he emerged from the bathroom, he was calmer. He wasted no time in regrets. What had been done had been done. The question was how to survive the morning's absurd disaster with dignity.

He stepped into his shorts, which were of the same pink-and-white silk broadcloth as his new shirts. Then he lifted the papers from his bed to his desk and set about erasing Miss Carmichael's name. No use. Mike evidently wrote with an iron nail dipped in ink. The name had soaked through to the second page, and partly to the third. Charles sat down, lit a cigarette, and thought. He couldn't leave the papers here in the room, obviously. Mechanically, he put the bottle of cream out on the window sill. Then, suddenly inspired, he returned to the desk and picked up the papers. Of course. What could be simpler than to drop the wretched things down into the limbo of broken beer bottles, rusty hairpins, and odd shoes that lay eight floors below his window? In that mess, they would never be noticed, if anyone ever looked out there.

He raised the window an inch or two, and then, just as he was preparing to slide the papers out, there was a flurry and a thump on the fire escape across from him, and he stared straight into the dark and warlike countenance of Diamond, the floor maid, who was beating a tattoo on the rail of the fire escape with her dust mop, setting free a disgusting gray cloud that struggled a moment on the air before beginning to drift back into the rooms from which it had been taken.

The papers were still out of sight, and Charles let them drop to the floor. Raising the window a few inches higher, he gestured gracefully through the aperture, as though he were testing the quality of the air. His nonchalance undid him, for he upset the bottle of cream, which dropped from view with a soundless inexorability that was more alarming to Charles than anything that had yet happened that morning. A long, ascending skirl of wicked glee issued from the throat of Diamond, and her mop beats accelerated. From far below came the noise of a small crash, followed by swearing.

Charles plunged his head out the window and stared down. The square floor of the shaft was wet, and in the middle of it, brandishing a sputtering hose, stood a man whose upturned face looked, even at this distance, unpleasantly contorted. As Charles stared (Should he throw down some money? Or try to say something calming?), the man threw down the hose and vanished through a doorway.

Charles glanced up at Diamond, who was now resting herself comfortably against the rail.

"Gone to tell Mr. Dowd," she said. Mr. Dowd was the current manager.

Charles banged down the window and scurried to the middle of the room, where he stood chattering to himself with dismay. Deny it, of course, he said. Deny the whole thing. Knew nothing about it. Never saw a cream bottle. Heard nothing. Window was shut tight all morning . . .

He wrenched one of his new shirts out of its wrappings, dragged his new suit of slate-gray English flannel from its hanger, and began to dress himself. As, with trembling fingers, he tied his bow tie, which was also of the pink-and-white striped silk broadcloth, there was a knocking on his door. He stood still and waited.

"Got your soap here, Mr. Runyon!" Mike cried.

"Knock again," said Diamond's voice. "Knock good this time."

Mike dealt the door a mighty wallop. "I know he's in there," he said to Diamond.

"Maybe he's reading the paper," Diamond whispered, and the two tormentors moved off down the hall. Charles waited till he heard the elevator door close before he finished tying his tie. Then he dropped his hands to his dressing table and stared listlessly at himself in the mirror.

The phone rang. He picked it up and heard the intimate, confidential voice of Miss Knight, the telephone operator, who was very sensitive, and always smiled conspiratorially at Charles, because she knew that he was sensitive, too.

"Mr. Runyon," she whispered. "I wish you had confided in me about keeping food on your window sill. The management is very strict about cooking in the rooms, Mr. Runyon, but some of the tenants have their little ways, so that they won't be found out. Oh, I know how it is. I like my cup of coffee in the morning, and maybe an egg, but—"

"Your feeding habits are even less interesting than I would have imagined them to be, Miss Knight," Charles said, and hung up.

Miss Knight was probably the only friend he had in the hotel, but he didn't care. He wanted to get out, to see Leona, to sit at luncheon in the Plaza, to be treated with the deference he expected and deserved. But there were still the papers to deal with. His topcoat went poorly with his new suit, but he would just have to wear it, and carry the papers out underneath. . . . But no. In a burst of optimism brought on by yesterday afternoon's brilliant sunshine, he had sent the topcoat to the cleaner's, and his winter coat was already in storage. Grimly, he began to unbutton his new jacket.

A little later, Charles stood at the elevator, ringing the bell, for the second time that morning. His form no longer expressed the slender and fluid, yet snug, line that had given his tailor so much trouble and pleasure. From his neck to below his waist, he showed a solid, curving, birdlike bulge. He stood stiffly, and breasted his way warily into the elevator, turning an aloof and thoughtful profile to Mike's glances.

As Charles stepped from the elevator, the manager pounced from his place of concealment behind the desk. His round white face shone with the brimming contentment of the hotel man about to deal successfully with a tricky situation involving a guest. Miss Knight swivelled around to watch, ignoring frenzied appeals from her switchboard, and Mike let the elevator buzz.

"Mr. Runyon," the manager said. "That regrettable incident this morning—I'm terribly sorry but we can't permit light housekeeping in the rooms. Sanitary regulations, you know. I'm sure you understand, Mr. Runyon."

"Really, Mr. Dowd, I haven't the faintest idea what you're talking about," Charles cried.

"Then that's understood, Mr. Runyon," the manager said, and vanished behind the key slots. Miss Knight placed consoling hands on her switchboard. Her voice was soft and amused. Whistling, Mike entered his elevator and crashed the door to with the air of one who wields cymbals. Like a ghost, Charles passed through the lobby, through the entrance doors, and down the stone steps to the street. Only the hateful paper padding that was suffocating him seemed alive. He stood transfixed in the clean, clear spring sunshine and thought, I must not think, I must not remember. . . . A taxi loitered near him, and he plunged into it, and found he had to recline sidewise on the seat, because he could not sit. He directed the driver to the Altamont, a large commercial hotel on Eighth Avenue, where he could be fairly certain of not running into anyone he knew.

As he was getting into the taxi, a button popped from his jacket and dropped into the gutter. He felt it pop and saw it fall, but he let it go. Even had he wanted to leave the shelter of the taxi, he could not have bent to retrieve the button. A pity; the buttons for his suit had been specially ordered from Italy. Leona had the same buttons on her suit. Now he would have to go through the whole afternoon watching Leona preen herself in a complete set of his buttons, in a gigantic travesty of his suit—for she was taller than he, and her arms were very long. What a complete fool he had been to allow her to go to his tailor.

The men's room at the Altamont was at the foot of a curving flight of stairs immediately to the left of the main entrance. It was a dank, white-tiled vault, occupied, when Charles walked in, only by the attendant, who was sorting the brushes and rags in his shoeshine kit.

Charles took off his coat and unbuttoned his shirt, and pulled the papers out and threw them into the wastebasket. Turning his back on them and on his memories of the morning, he sprinkled a few drops of cold water on his chest and rubbed himself dry with his palms, averting his eyes from the paper towels over the washbasin. The attendant, a lanky man whose eyes were so blinded by boredom that he no longer troubled to focus them, raised his head at the sound of the running water and then lowered it again.

Refreshed, Charles stepped back from the washbasin and slipped his arms into his shirt. He buttoned the middle buttons first and moved swiftly up to the top. Really, he looked remarkably *soigné*, considering what he'd been through. The habit of poise, he thought contentedly. He had fastened the top button and was reaching for his tie when he saw that his fingers were smudged with newsprint and had left a track all the way up his front. He snatched a paper towel, dampened it, and rubbed at the smudges, making them worse. Leaning closer to the mirror, he saw that the damage was complete. Now his shirt looked like a used rag. He turned incredulously from the mirror to find the attendant standing behind him.

"Them marks'll never come out," he said.

Charles tore the shirt off and flung it into the wastebasket, on top of the papers. "Here is ten dollars," he said. "Go upstairs and get me a plain white shirt, size 14½. You can get it at that shop in the lobby. And hurry."

The sleeves of the new shirt were much too long, and the collar would have been more appropriate on a second-hand-car salesman, Charles thought. He let the cuffs slip down around his knuckles, just to see how awful they looked, and then pushed them back to his wrists. His pink-and-white striped tie looked like a little ribbon against the sturdy cloth of the new shirt.

Out in the street again, he hailed a taxi. It was not yet noon. He had just time to get to the Plaza ahead of Leona. He would catch her before she entered the hotel, and tell her of his new plan, which was to drive out into the country and have lunch at some secluded inn. Leona would have no audience to perform for today, he thought with satisfaction.

As he entered the lobby of the Plaza, he glanced furtively around, putting his hand to his throat as though to adjust his tie. Leona had not yet arrived. He took up his stand by a window and waited to see her come down the street.

Leona had arrived at the Plaza a few seconds before Charles, and had gone straight through the lobby and down the hall to the flower shop, where she bought two of the glowing, black-red carnations that he loved. One of these she pinned on her lapel, smiling at her own reflection as she did so. Perhaps it was a little naughty of her to have copied his shirt without asking his permission. But after all she had the suit; why not the shirt, too? Charles liked women to look absolutely perfect. How amused and pleased he would be when he saw her. Perhaps even a little flattered. She touched the narrow bow tie lightly, then took the second carnation and walked back to the lobby. There he was, waiting by the window. She called a bellboy and handed him the carnation and a dollar bill, and pointed to Charles, and whispered for a minute.

Crossing the busy lobby, the bellboy, who was very serious about his work, repeated to himself what he had been instructed to do and say. "First I say, 'Is this the gentleman in the pink-and-white striped shirt?' Then I give him the flower. Then I say, 'The lady in the pink-and-white striped shirt awaits your pleasure, sir.' " He held the carnation very carefully, fearful that the stem would snap.

Watching the boy approach Charles, Leona laughed excitedly. Dear Charles, she thought. I just can't wait to see his face when he turns around.

The Divine Fireplace

Thirty miles above New York, on the east bank of the Hudson River, there is a green, shadowy, densely wooded glade known as Herbert's Retreat. In the glade, still standing in it, many of them after two hundred years, are thirty-nine elegant white houses. A single narrow road, capricious, twisting, and unpredictable, meanders through the dark labyrinth of trees to make the only visible link between the houses, which are isolated and almost hidden, each one from the next. The road is strictly private, in keeping with the spirit of the Retreat, which is solemn, exclusive, and shaped by restrictions that are as steely as they are vague. The most important fact, not vague at all, about Herbert's Retreat is that only the right people live there.

One rainy Sunday morning early in April, an olive-green bus, very smart, with "Herbert's Retreat" printed in small capitals on its door, made its way slowly through the Retreat, stopping at every house, and from each doorway, in turn, a female figure, wearing a flowered hat and sheltered under a large umbrella, flew forward and climbed aboard. The Irish maids were going to Mass in town, eleven miles away. The maids looked forward to these Sunday-morning rides, which gave them the chance of a great gossip. And the ride gave them a chance to escape from the monotony of their uniforms. Their positive, coaxing voices rose and fell, but rose, mostly, in an orgy of sympathy, astonishment, indignation, furious satisfaction, and derision. Not one of them was calm, or thinking about saying her prayers, and every time the bus stopped they all peered eagerly through the streaming windows to see who was getting in next, as if they didn't know.

The Tillbrights—wild Harry Tillbright and his pretty second wife—owned the last house the bus stopped at before it swung out onto the public highway, so Stasia, the Tillbrights' maid, was the last to be picked up. This Sunday, as Stasia, dressed and ready, with her gloves on and her prayer book in her hand, waited in the Tillbrights' hall, she was in a painful state of mind, half wishing the bus would hurry and half wishing it wouldn't come at all. She wanted to be in her seat telling the girls about all that had gone on in her house last night, and at the same time she hated to leave, for fear something further would happen while she was away. She didn't want to miss one minute of this day, which was going to be about the worst the Tillbrights had ever known. It was terrible to Stasia to think she might miss the fearful, glorious moment when their two lady guests started to wake up and realize the condition they were in. Not to speak of the condition the house, the adored, cherished house, was in. And all their own fault. There will be murder here today, Stasia thought happily. No, no, I'm wrong, she thought—not murder today; the murder was last night. Today is when they pay the price. She could have danced with excitement, except that she was suffocating with it. She wanted to howl with laughter, but she dared not make a sound, for fear of rousing them too soon. What pleasure it would have been to run upstairs and gallop in and out of their bedrooms, shouting "Haw haw haw," giving them worse headaches than they already had. To charge into Mr. and Mrs. Tillbright's room and bend right down over the pillows they shared and roar into their defenseless ears, "Come on down and see what you did to your grand kitchen! And your living room! Wait till you see the carpet in the living room!" To keep after them, tormenting them till they howled for mercy. Except that they won't have the strength to howl this morning, Stasia thought. It was too good a story to believe, almost; too rich. The girls would be carried away. If I get any more carried away than I am, thought Stasia, I won't be able to talk at all.

To calm herself, she admired her reflection in the mirror on the wall. The beige gabardine suit was a nice fit. The copper-colored straw hat was nearly a match for her bushy hair, and the crimson poppies she had tacked around the crown did away with any danger of sameness. Her slippery nylon gloves were about the same green as the stems of the poppies, and she had a shiny green plastic bag hanging from her arm, and matching green sandals with delicate straps that wound twice around her bony ankles.

Stasia was forty-seven, with a pointed white face and very large ears. Somebody had once complimented her on her merry Irish eyes, and she had endeavored to live up to the remark ever since, rolling her eyes enthusiastically until it became a habit, and showing that she, at any rate, knew what was going on in the room and behind the scenes, even when there was nothing going on at all. Stasia's merry, knowing looks frightened some of her employers and irritated others. Stasia didn't care. "Some people have no sense of humor," she would say when she lost a job. She always got very good references, and then, too, as she said herself, she had the real Irish sense of humor, and there were very few could stand up against it. Stasia was famous for her sense of humor, which she brandished like a tomahawk. And she was a great storyteller. All the maids were agreed on that. Nobody could tell a story like Stasia. And the funny faces she made. Stasia was a scream.

Stasia didn't exactly tire of admiring herself in the mirror, but the silence in the house began to get on her nerves. Still no sound from upstairs, but they might start stirring around at any minute. Stasia tiptoed across the hall and, for the eighth time that morning, she opened the living-room door a crack and peered in. There on the sofa, stretched out flat with her shoes still on her feet, lay Miss Phoebe Carter, in sleep so deep that it might have been coma. Poor, pretty, high-voiced Miss Carter, so snippy and sure of herself when she first waltzed into the house last night on Mr. Tillbright's arm, so to speak. Stasia's smile as she regarded Miss Carter was not entirely without sympathy. Uninvited guests must expect what they get, of course, but this was a hard lesson. That rustly cocktail dress isn't going to be worth much when you get up off that sofa, Stasia thought, and removed her gaze to the steak that lay on the carpet, some distance from the fireplace. It was a huge steak, and thick, and it had been juicy. The carpet showed darkly how full of juice the steak had been before being rudely tumbled from its platter, which lay, right side up, well within the island of grease, which seemed to Stasia to have spread since the last time she looked. And how could I have gone in there to start cleaning up, with the young lady asleep on the sofa there, she thought, rehearsing for Mrs. Tillbright. Pretty, sweet, fluffy Mrs. Tillbright, she wouldn't be feeling so pleased with herself this morning. Stasia closed the door carefully, shutting Miss Carter in, saving her, with any luck, until the rest of them roused themselves to come downstairs and find her.

The bus should be here now, even allowing for a minute or so's delay on account of the rain. Stasia opened the front door and peered out. No sign of the bus, and the rain was coming down heavier. A pity about the rain. The old umbrella would be a nuisance. She turned back into the hall and saw Mr. Tillbright on the stairs. The shock of seeing him suddenly like that made Stasia think she was perhaps imagining things. But it was Mr. Tillbright, all right, dressed in the same pin-stripe suit he had worn to town yesterday, but without a tie. He was carrying his shoes in his hand, and bringing himself downstairs very tenderly, one step at a time. He hadn't seen Stasia.

"Good morning, Mr. Tillbright," Stasia said cheerily. "Isn't it a terrible day?"

Mr. Tillbright did not speak until he was safely on the hall floor.

"I have to get back to town," he said then. "Very urgent. Call just came through. Tell Mrs. Tillbright, will you? I'll stay in town overnight. Tell her I'll call her from the hotel."

"And what hotel will I say?" Stasia asked.

"I said *I'll* call *her*," Mr. Tillbright snarled.

Trying to run away, eh, Stasia thought, and she watched him fumble with the quaint little wall cupboard in which the car keys were kept. She said nothing, and after a minute or so he spoke, without turning around to look at her. No manners, none of them have any manners, Stasia thought good-humoredly.

"Have you any idea where the keys of my car might be?" he asked.

"Well, don't you remember, Mr. Tillbright? Mrs. Tillbright collected up all the car keys last night and said she was going to put them in a safe place. Your car's keys and her car's keys, and I believe she got hold of Mrs. Lamb's car's keys. While she was at it, you know. She thought all the keys ought to be together, she said. She said as long as none of you were going out last night, the keys ought to be out of harm's way. Of course she didn't know then that you'd be having to go to the office so early on a Sunday morning."

Mr. Tillbright said, "Since you know so much, perhaps you know where Mrs. Tillbright put the keys."

"I don't know where she put them," Stasia responded, with dignity, "but I think they should be someplace in the bedroom. She was going to the bedroom when I saw her with them in her hand."

Mr. Tillbright sat down suddenly on the bottom step of the stairs. "I've simply got to get out of this house today," he said, into his long, well-kept hands. "I've got to get in to town."

He stood up as suddenly as he had sat down, and turned around and started back up the stairs. He was still in his stocking feet. Well, you're in a bad way, all right, Stasia said to herself, and heard the bus pull up outside.

She clambered into the bus backward and bent, because she was trying to shut her umbrella and save her hat and get her heels on solid board all at the same time. She plumped herself down beside Delia Murphy, who smiled and nodded, under a platter of blue corn-flowers.

"Delia, Delia," said Stasia, "do you know what happened?"

"What happened, Stasia?" Delia asked, and the other maids stopped talking for the moment and began to listen, on the chance that Stasia had something worth hearing.

"Oh, you'll never in your life guess what that crowd did last night!" Stasia said, all of a sudden unwilling to part with her precious story. But she had to go on. Thirty-eight Irish noses were pointed at her in implacable demand. There was no stopping now. With a shrill crow of joy, Stasia plunged.

"They uncovered a fireplace in the kitchen!" she cried. "A bricked-up fireplace. Behind the stove. Behind the *stove.* They tore out the stove, and there's a hole as big as a coffin in the wall, with bricks falling out of it, and wires hanging out of it, miles of wires—you never saw the like of it. And the floor all covered with dirt and dust and bits of plaster and lumps of mortar. If a bomb had hit it, it couldn't look worse."

The maids exchanged glances of incredulous pleasure. They never ceased to marvel at the interest their employers took in their old houses and their old windows and walls and floor boards and doors and cupboards, and in their old fireplaces, of which there could never be too many, apparently, dirty and troublesome as they were, and unnecessary, too, with the central heating.

"Are they out of their minds, or what," Delia asked, "destroying the kitchen like that?"

Stasia looked mischievous. "Didn't Mrs. Tillbright find out that his first wife, the first Mrs. Tillbright, had the fireplace in the kitchen blocked up, and he never said a word to *her* about it when *she* came to move in, and when she found out about it last night she flew into a rage and insisted that he tear out the side of the kitchen. 'Me fireplace!' she kept screeching. 'I want me fireplace in me kitchen and I want it now, do you hear me, *now.*' "

"Of course they were— having something to drink?" said Alice Flaherty, leaning forward in her seat, which was behind Stasia's.

"Drinking like horses," Stasia said. "They'd been at it all day, too. Well, I know Mrs. Tillbright and that Mrs. Lamb had been at it from five o'clock on, because I was there in the house with them. Mr. Tillbright and this Miss Carter didn't turn up till seven, and a child could see they'd had a few—more than a few—by the look of them."

"You're driving us mad, Stasia," Delia said. "Will you go back and begin at the beginning? How did Mrs. Tillbright find out about the fireplace being in the kitchen? *He* didn't tell her, did he?"

"Not *he,*" Stasia said. "It all started when Mr. Tillbright brought this Miss Carter home for dinner—walked into the house with her, bold as brass, and not after telephoning to say could she come or anything. Well, Mrs. Tillbright was as mad as a hatter. She had invited this Mrs. Lamb out to spend the night, Saturday night, last night, and Mr. Tillbright knew that. Mrs. Tillbright would have been provoked enough if she'd been there by herself when he landed in with the girl, but to have this Mrs. Lamb see it, Mrs. Tillbright was fit to be tied. She doesn't really *like* Mrs. Lamb. It seems, or so I gather, Mrs. Lamb used to be a great *friend* of Mr. Tillbright. I don't know when. Since this one married him, for all I know. Anyway, Mrs. Lamb knew Mr. Tillbright's first wife. And Mrs. Tillbright only invited her out for the weekend to show her all the changes she'd made in the house, and what a fine place it is now, and all, and how happy herself and

Mr. Tillbright are together. Oh, Lord—" Stasia was overcome with amusement. "How happy they are, and all!" she cried, and the maids nodded and laughed along with her.

"This Mrs. Lamb just got a divorce, you see," Stasia went on, in a lower voice, "and Mrs. Tillbright said to him, 'Oh, we must have poor dear Norma out for the weekend and cheer her up.' Cheer her up, is it, I thought to meself. Of course, what she was thinking was Kill two birds with the one stone, have her out here and show off in front of her, and at the same time discourage him from any notion he might have of cheering Mrs. Lamb up on his own. Well, Mrs. Lamb arrived out yesterday evening around five, in this little bright-blue convertible, the sort of car a kid would have, but certainly not at all suitable for a woman her age. 'A parting gift from Leo, darling,' she says, patting the car, and she and Mrs. Tillbright give each other a kiss.

" 'Darling Norma,' says Mrs. Tillbright, 'how does it feel to be free?' 'Divine, simply heaven, so it is,' says Mrs. Lamb. 'You must try it sometime, Debbie. But then you and Harry are so comfy together, aren't you, dear? So—well, domesticated. I do hope you don't find it dull.' 'Oh no, we don't find it dull at all,' Mrs. Tillbright says, very soft, with one of them little secret smiles. Mrs. Lamb gave her a *look*, and I gave a little secret smile meself, thinking about the racket they kicked up the other night—Wednesday night it was—over Mr. Tillbright leaving his clothes strewn all over the bedroom and the bathroom, awful untidy habits he has, I can't blame her.

"Well, the next thing, Mrs. Lamb flounces into the house as if she owns it. You can see that every stitch she has on her is brand-new, just bought for the weekend—a little pointed yellow hat and pointed yellow bootees, and she's no spring chicken, you know.

"Well, she stood stock-still in the hall. 'Where's Harry?' she says. Mrs. Tillbright gives a nasty little laugh. 'Don't sound so disappointed, darling,' she says. 'Harry'll be here, don't worry. He had to run into town to see a client.' 'On a Saturday?' says Mrs. Lamb. 'That's not the Harry I knew. Or is it? Dear Harry. He's such a darling. But so unreliable, isn't he? You must be careful not to hold him on too tight a rein, Debbie darling. Just be patient. He'll grow up. It just takes some men longer than others, that's all.' 'Let's go upstairs, shall we?' says Mrs. Tillbright. 'I want to show you your room,' she says.

"Up the stairs we go, me bringing up the rear and carrying the bag Mrs. Lamb had brought along, heavy as lead it was. 'Oh, our bedroom door is open,' says Mrs. Tillbright when she got to the top of the stairs, and she goes across the landing and stands looking into her own bedroom as if she'd never set eyes on it before. And how else would it be but open, I thought, and you breaking your neck upstairs to open it when you heard the car coming.

" 'Wouldn't you like to see our little nest, darling?' she says, all quaint like. 'Harry adores this view,' she says, running into the room and across to the window. 'Come see,' she says, dragging Mrs. Lamb after her by main force. 'We had the bed made special,' she says. 'And this is Harry's very own armchair,' she says, 'for, you know, I'm dreadfully lazy. I'm ashamed to say it, but I am. And best of anything in the world I like to lie in bed on Sunday morning,' she says, shy, you know. 'And Harry must keep me company at breakfast, he won't have it any other way. I just have a cup of black coffee without sugar,' she says, 'and Stasia brings his big breakfast up, kippers or bacon and eggs, finnan haddie, lamb chops, whatever he fancies— Stasia and I like to pamper him a little, he always had such a barren sort of life, poor baby—and he sits there in his chair by the window and glances at the paper and reads me little bits out of it. And we chat—oh, you know,' she says. 'Sometimes we don't even get downstairs till lunchtime,' she says. 'It's scandalous, really.' And she gives a great laugh.

"Indeed so, I thought. That's the first I ever heard of any of that, and the last, I hope. Breakfast in bed, indeed! And I went off down the hall and left the bag, and then I went downstairs, and I filled the ice bucket and put it in the living room, and then *she* came down, all smiles.

" 'Will you be wanting tea, Mrs. Tillbright?' I asked her. 'Ooh, I don't know, Stasia,' she says. 'I'll let you know. You left ice, didn't you? That's all right, then. Mr. Tillbright will be home at six sharp, and when you hear him come in, bring up more ice, will you?' I said I would, and I went off down to the kitchen, and I heard Mrs. Lamb coming down the stairs and going into the living room, and then I heard no more out of them, and it got to be six, and it got to be seven, and at half past seven didn't I hear His Lordship's voice in the hall. So I got out the fresh ice and I hurried along to see what was what. No sign of him, he'd gone upstairs, but his *girl* friend was there, large as life, making herself at home. Miss Carter, she is, and a bold-looking piece of work if I ever saw one. Not more than twenty-two or so, I'd say, and all done up in a tight cocktail dress that showed her chest.

"Over she goes and stands in front of the fire. 'Mmm,' she says. 'Delicious! Harry and I nearly froze in that open car. I'm afraid I'm not dressed for the *country*,' she says, and she looks at what the other two have on, and you can see she's right satisfied with herself. Mrs. Lamb has blossomed out in a pair of light-gray velveteen slacks and a yellow pullover like a boy's pullover, and Mrs. Tillbright is wearing the same as she was wearing before—that great big skirt she has, her fireside skirt, she calls it, and a little white baby blouse. That Miss Carter doesn't know when to shut up, or she doesn't want to shut up, I don't know which. 'I'd let myself go terribly if I lived in the country,' she says, looking at the other two. 'I don't wonder that people go to pieces out here. I mean the whole thing is to keep warm, isn't it? It must be so demoralizing—for women, especially.' 'I don't live in the country,' Mrs. Lamb says, very sharp altogether. 'Oh, I know that,' says Miss Carter. 'Even if Harry hadn't told me all about you on the way up here, I'd know by your clothes. They have that wonderfully *considered* look, as though you'd really thought about what would look best on you. I bet I know why you chose that particular pullover,' she says, with a big nod. 'Why did I choose it, pray tell?' says Mrs. Lamb getting all red.

"Mrs. Tillbright speaks up, trying to be a hostess. 'I hope you have a ride back to the city tonight,' she says to Miss Carter. 'I hope Mr. Tillbright—Harry—explained to you that Mrs. Lamb is staying with us, and we have only one guest room.' Miss Carter gives a great squawk, as if she had a pain. 'Heavens, Mrs. Tillbright!' she says. 'It's too sweet of you, but you know, I wouldn't spend a night in the country to save my life. I can't *stand* the country! I simply can't imagine how you live out here, although I think your house is just as sweet as can be. I mean I can see you've worked over it. Goodness, no, I'm not staying. I have to be at a party at eleven, for one thing. Harry and I were having a drink, and he suggested that I run out here for dinner and see the house, and all. And of course I jumped at the chance to meet you and see where Harry lives. He's told me so much about it I feel as though I knew every room. What did you decide about the new furniture for the patio? Harry says you want rough, woodsy stuff, but I think wrought iron has so much more chic, don't you?'

" 'Where the hell *is* Harry?' says Mrs. Lamb, and just at that exact moment Mr. Tillbright comes running down the stairs, two at a time, with a big white woollen shirt on him and a red scarf tucked in at the neck. Miss Carter lets out another squawk. 'Harry,' she shouts, 'you look scrumptious!' And she looks at Mrs. Tillbright. 'If you don't get that outfit copied,' she says, 'I will. Harry darling, you look so chic. Honestly, men have *the* most wonderful clothes. If all the men out here dress like that, I think I'll take your sweet wife up on her week-end invitation.' 'Oh, that would be fine, fine,' says Harry, and you can see he's beginning to wonder what he's got himself in to. 'Not this weekend, darling,' Mrs. Tillbright says to him. 'We're full up this weekend. And in any case Miss Carter says she has to get back to town to some party. I hope you've arranged a ride for her.' 'Somebody's bound to be driving in,' Harry says, and makes himself a drink and one for Miss Carter. 'Who?' says Mrs. Tillbright. 'I don't know of anyone who's driving in. The weekend people won't be leaving till tomorrow or Monday. I don't know of anyone who's driving in tonight who would be willing to take Miss Carter.' 'Oh, hell,' says Mr. Tillbright, 'I'll drive her in myself, get her to her party, and be back before you can count to a hundred. Nothing to it.' 'Oh, grand,' says Miss Carter. 'That's settled then.' 'It's not settled at all,' says Mrs. Tillbright. 'Stasia, what on earth do you want?'

" 'I wanted to know what time you wanted the dinner, Ma'am,' I said, all quiet and polite—which she was *not* being. 'It's all ready, Ma'am, only to put on the steak.' 'Steak!' says Miss Carter. 'Oh, goody, I'm starved!'

" 'Oh, we're not in a hurry,' says Mrs. Tillbright. 'Take your time,

Stasia.' 'Harry, aren't you going to take me down to see your kitchen?' says Miss Carter. 'I hear you have the most divine old-fashioned kitchen,' she says then, to Mrs. Tillbright. 'Take the little girl to see the kitchen, Harry,' says Mrs. Tillbright. 'But see that she doesn't burn her little fingers,' says Mrs. Lamb. 'You should know about burnt fingers, Norma dear,' says Mrs. Tillbright, very nasty. 'Oh, poor sweet!' says Mrs. Lamb. 'It's just the same old dreary story, isn't it? And you put up such a brave front all evening, positively gallant. I do admire you so, dear.' 'Oh, cut it out, you two,' says Mr. Tillbright. 'Mind your own business,' says Mrs. Tillbright. 'Your pants are too tight, Norma,' she says. 'You look perfectly awful, and the reason is you *are* awful. Not interesting awful,' she says, 'just dreary, sad, pathetic awful. Do you know what? I feel *sorry* for you.' And she gives a great giggle.

"Mr. Tillbright is getting to look very sorry for himself. 'Debbie,' he says, 'why don't you go upstairs and lie down a while? Get a little rest, why don't you?' 'Some women just cannot drink,' says Mrs. Lamb, and tosses off her own Martini, trying to hold in her stomach at the same time.

" 'I'll let you know when to put the steak on, Stasia,' says Mrs. Tillbright, and I march off to the kitchen, wondering what'll happen next, since it's plain they're all well over the edge. Well, they all come after me, Mr. Tillbright and Miss Carter and the other two. Miss Carter is singing a little song, whispering like, and Mrs. Lamb said, 'Your kitchen used to be divine, Harry. We had such happy times here in the old days, you and Berenice and I. I hope you haven't changed it much.'

" 'Well, it looks just like any other kitchen,' says Miss Carter, when they're inside the door. 'I mean it's bigger, and there are the beams in the ceiling and all, but it's not really so terribly unusual, is it?' 'What did you expect—a wishing well?' says Mrs. Lamb. 'Well, a fireplace, anyway,' said Miss Carter. 'I mean the whole point of having a kitchen in the country is that you have a fireplace, isn't it? I mean why live in the country at all when you can live in the city.' 'But, Harry, where *is* the fireplace?' says Mrs. Lamb, all astonished. 'Let's get back to the drinks and leave Stasia in peace,' says Mr. Tillbright, very sudden and nervous. 'But, Harry, tell me,' says Mrs. Lamb, 'what *happened* to the fireplace? There used to be a divine fireplace right there,' she says to Mrs. Tillbright. 'Didn't Harry even tell you it was there? Harry, you *are* naughty.' 'You're out of your mind, Norma,' says Harry. 'You're thinking of some of the other kitchens around here. Some of them have fireplaces. Come on, let's go have a drink. What are we standing here for?' 'Oh, I suppose you and Berenice had it bricked up, Harry,' Mrs. Lamb said, 'but I do think it was mean of you not to tell Debbie about it. You know how she adores fireplaces.'

" 'Harry,' says Mrs. Tillbright, 'if there's a fireplace there, I want it.' 'Damn it all,' says Mr. Tillbright, 'I had it bricked up— Berenice and I had to have it bricked up, because we needed that wall for space when we were breaking that door through to the patio. Stop being a silly little fool, Debbie.' 'But it used to be so cozy, Harry,' says Mrs. Lamb. 'Silly to have a kitchen without a fireplace,' says Miss Carter.

" 'Harry,' says Mrs. Tillbright, 'I want that fireplace, and I want it now.' 'Oh, come on, now, Debbie,' he says. 'Come on yourself,' she says. 'Get moving. Where is it?' 'Now, honey,' he says, 'let's all go get a nice fresh Martini and talk it over.' 'I'm not moving out of this spot,' she says. 'All right,' he says, 'I'll bring the drinks down here.' And he goes off, and when he comes back with the Martini shaker, she's got the hammer and she's tapping all along the wall, above the stove and the sink, and all.

" 'Oh, for God's sake, Debbie,' he says, 'will you stop it. It's behind the stove, if you want to know.' 'That's what I thought,' says Mrs. Lamb. Miss Carter sat down by the kitchen table and started to cry. 'Oh,' she says, 'men are so awful! Imagine hiding the fireplace. Harry, how could you be so mean to your dear sweet little wife?' 'Move the stove, Harry,' says Mrs. Tillbright. 'I'll do nothing of the sort,' he says. 'All right, then, I'll move it,' she says. 'I'd better turn the oven off, so,' I said, and I went over and turned it off and took off the kettle I always keep hot there. Mrs. Tillbright goes over and starts pushing and pulling, trying to move the stove.

"Miss Carter gave another of her screeches. 'Harry,' she says, 'she'll strain herself trying to move that thing. You do it for her.' 'Oh, don't you do it, Harry,' says Mrs. Lamb. 'You know what might happen. Harry isn't as strong as he looks,' she says to Miss Carter. Well, Mr. Tillbright gave Mrs. Lamb a look, I can tell you.

" 'I'm going to have another drink,' he says, and they all have a drink—Miss Carter and Mrs. Lamb all excited, and Mrs. Tillbright just boiling with temper.

" 'I hope you're not going to regret this, Debbie,' says Mr. Tillbright when he's finished his drink, but by that time he doesn't care much about anything. He goes over and gives the stove a wrench, and it comes away and stands lopsided and rocking—you know those old crooked floors, one leg of the stove had been made short to fit against the wall. And there's a terrible clatter from inside the oven.

" 'Aw, Mr. Tillbright,' I said, 'I wish you'd told me you were going to do that, and I could have taken the dinner out.' He grabbed open the door, and the eggplant casserole and the cherry pie and all that I was keeping hot all come tumbling out, and the good dinner plates and the little bit of chicken I was keeping for meself—I was mortified that they saw it. All that good food.

" 'Well, there goes your dinner,' says Mr. Tillbright to Mrs. Tillbright. 'Oh, damn the dinner,' she says. 'Let's get the wall opened up.'

"Well, girls, they got every sharp thing in the house—chisels and screwdrivers and shears, all the carpentry stuff out of the basement, even the good poker out of the living room—and they began to loosen the bricks. Well, that's all, except a bit of the ceiling came down—not very much. And every bit of electricity in the house is dead, of course, and who can put it back together again I don't know, or what will be done. When the hole was big enough to suit them, they took the steak and carried it up to the living room, holding it up over their heads as if it was a football player. They said they were going to cook it in the fireplace—"

"All the electricity gone," said big Bridie, the bully, sprawled in her usual seat, which ran all the way across the back of the bus.

"Oh, they don't know that yet," Stasia said.

"Wait till he starts to shave himself," Delia said.

104

"He won't even be able to take a bath," Stasia said. "None of them will. The pump works by electricity."

"The radio!" Molly Ronan said, with horror.

"And the dishwasher," said Josie, the youngest maid.

"And the toaster and the rotisserie and the— everything," Delia said. "And with no water at all in the house."

"Not to mention the deep freeze," Bridie said.

The deep freeze. They had all forgotten the deep freeze.

"Trust you to think of that, Bridie," Stasia said, awed.

"All that reindeer meat," Bridie said. "All the reindeer meat, all gone, unless they finish it up today."

"And the pheasants, and all," Lily Rooney said. "Remember how pleased they all were, coming back with their pheasants and their trout and their salmon, and all."

"But the deer meat," Stasia said pleasurably. "Mr. Tillbright was so set up with that little red hunting hat of his."

"Oh, they're all great hunters," Delia said. "A rabbit would put the fear of God into any one of them, if they weren't carrying their gun."

"Aw, Lord, I forgot to tell you about the steak on the rug!" Stasia cried, seeing that the bus was stopping in front of the church. "And Mrs. Tillbright hiding the car keys, and Mr. Tillbright trying to sneak out this morning."

"We're late," Delia said. "The bell has stopped ringing. We'll hear it all on the way back, Stasia."

"And Miss Carter on the sofa," Stasia wailed. "I forgot all the best parts."

She would never get their attention all the way back again. They'd be crowding around and chattering and interrupting her, getting the story all wrong.

A Snowy Night on
West Forty - Ninth Street

It snowed all night last night and the dawn, which came not as a
brightening but as a gray and silent awakening, showed the city
vague and passive as a convalescent under light fields of snow that
fell quickly and steadily from an expressionless heaven. This Broadway section where I live is all heights of roofs and all shapes of walls
all going in different directions and reaching different heights, and
there are times when the whole area seems to be a gigantic store-
house of stage flats and stage props that are stacked together as eco-
nomically as possible and being put to use until something more sub-
stantial can be built, something that will last. At night, when the big
Broadway lights go on, when the lights begin to run around high in
the sky and up and down the sides of buildings, when rivers of lights
start flowing along the edges of roofs, and wreaths and diadems begin
sparkling from dark corners, and the windows of empty downtown offices begin streaming with watery reflections of brilliance, at that
time, when Broadway lights up to make a nighttime empire out of
the tumble-down, makeshift daytime world, a powdery pink glow
rises up and spreads over the whole area, a cloudy pink, an emana-
tion, like a tent made of air and color. Broadway lights and Broadway
nighttime color make a glittering spectacle that throws all around it
into darkness. The little side streets that live off Broadway also live in
the shadow of Broadway, and there are times, looking from the windows of the hotel where I live at present, on West Forty-ninth Street,
when I think that my hotel and all of us here on this street are behind the world instead of in it. But tonight when I looked out of
these windows just before going to dinner I saw a kaleidoscope out
there, snow and lights whirling sky-high in a furious wind that
seemed to have blown the Empire State Building clear out of the city,
because it was not to be seen, although I had my usual good view of
it this morning. It was a gray morning and the afternoon was gray,

but tonight is very dark, and when I walked out of the hotel into the withering cold of this black-and-white night, West Forty-ninth Street seemed more than ever like an outpost, or a frontier street, or a one-street town that has been thrown together in excitement—a gold rush or an oil gush—and that will tumble into ruin when the excitement ends. This block, between Sixth and Seventh Avenues, exists only as a thoroughfare to Broadway, a small, narrow thoroughfare furnished with what was at hand—architectural remnants, architectural mistakes, and architectural experiments. The people who decided to put this street to use for the time that remains to it have behaved with the freedom of children playing in a junk yard. The houses and buildings are of all sizes, some thin and some fat, some ponderous and some small and humble, some that were built for grandeur at the turn of the century, like my hotel, that now has a neon sign hanging all down its fine, many-windowed front, and some that never could have been more than sheds, even if they are built out of cement. In the daytime and especially in the early morning the street has a travel-stained look and an air of hardship, and then the two rows of ill-matched, ill-assorted, houses make me think of a team of worn-out horses, collected from everywhere, that are being worked for all the life that is left in them and that will have to keep going until their legs give out. Nobody will care when this street comes down because nobody really lives here. It is a street of restaurants, bars, cheap hotels, rooming houses, garages, all-night coffee shops, quick-lunch counters, delicatessens, short-lived travel agencies, and sightseeing buses, and there are a quick dry-cleaning place, a liquor store, a Chinese laundry, a record shop, a dubious movie house, a young, imperturbable gypsy who shifts her fortune-telling parlor from one doorway to another up and down the street, and a souvenir shop. The people who work here have their homes as far away from the street as they can possibly get, and the hotels and rooming houses are simply hotels and rooming houses, with tenants for a night or a week or a month or an hour, although there are a few old faithfuls who moved in for a little while and stayed on and on until the years turned them into permanent transients. The oldest houses on the street are four thin, retiring brownstones that still stand together on the north side, all of them with restaurants or bars on their ground floor. It was to one of these brownstone houses that I went for dinner tonight, to the Étoile de France. Above the restaurant all the floors of the house are abandoned, the windows staring blankly and the wall scarred, but the falling snow curtained the windows and shaped the roof so that the old house appeared once again as it did in its first snowstorm, when the street was new. I had walked along from the hotel, and I waited to cross over to the Étoile, but the cars were going wild, confined as they were to one uncertain lane by the mountains of snow piled up on both sides, and while I waited I looked back the length of the street. The bewildering snow gave the shabby street an air of melancholy that made it ageless, as it will some day appear in an old photograph. But it will have to be a very old photograph. The inquisitive and sympathetic eyes that will see this street again as I saw it tonight have not yet opened to look at anything in this world. It will have to be a very old photograph, deepened by time and by a regret that will have its source in the loss of all of New York as we know it now. Many trial cities, facsimiles of cities, will have been raised and torn down on Manhattan island before anybody begins to regret this version of West Forty-ninth Street, and perhaps the photograph will never be taken. But on the street level, Forty-ninth Street defied the snow, and business was garish as usual. The Étoile was very bright and cheerful when I walked in, but there were very few customers. There was only one man sitting, lounging sideways at the bar—an old Frenchman who comes in often at night, after having had his dinner at the Automat. Only three of the tables in the bar were occupied, and the big back room, the dining room, was dim and deserted. The Étoile is a very plain place, with plain wooden chairs, very hard chairs, red-and-white checked tablecloths, a stamped tin ceiling painted cream, and wallpaper decorated with pale romantic nineteenth-century scenes. I sat at a table across from the bar, which has a long mirror behind it to reflect the bottles and glasses and the back of the bartender's head and the faces of the customers and the romantic wallpaper on the wall behind me. One waiter was still on duty—Robert—and he brought me a Martini and took my order and went off to the kitchen in a hurry. I think the chef must have been making a fuss about getting away early on this stormy night when there were almost no customers and he was going to have trouble getting home. He lives in Long Island City. Mme. Jacquin, who owns the restaurant, had gone home, and her daughter, Mees Katie, was in charge, together with Leo, the bartender. Leo has been working here about fifteen years. He is Dutch, and I think he is in his late fifties, a few years younger than Mme. Jacquin. Mees Katie is about thirty. She has a singularly detached manner, as though she was only working at the Étoile while she waited for her chance to go to some place where she really wants to be, but she spends more and more time here, while her mother, who used to almost live in the place, often does not come in for days at a time. Mees Katie began coming in about five years ago, to help during the luncheon hour, but now she is here every night as well. She leaves at ten o'clock, when the chef goes home, and after that Leo manages by himself. On good nights the bar is open until two in the morning, or even later.

Mees Katie was sitting as she always sits, facing toward the door, so that she could jump up when the customers came in. She often sits alone at the table for one by the street window, a huge window partly curtained in colorless gauze, and when there is a rush on, she stands in the arch that leads from the front room to the back and watches both rooms. She never sits at the bar. Tonight she was sitting beside a lady I have never seen at the Étoile before, a very wide stout elderly lady whose elaborate makeup—eyes, complexion, and mouth—looked as though it had been applied several days ago and then repaired here and there as patches of it wore off. Her hair was dyed gold and curled in tiny rings all over her head, and her face and neck were covered with a dark beige powder. Her face had spread so that it was very big, but her nose and mouth were quite small, and she had enormous brown eyes that had no light in them. She had put on a great deal of black mascara, and blue eyeshadow. The shadow had melted down into the corners of her eyes and settled into the wrinkles. She was all covered up in a closely fitted dark blue velvet dress that was cut into a ring around her neck and had long tight sleeves that strained at her arms every time she lifted her spoon to her mouth. She was eating pears in wine, and she ate very carefully, looking into the dish as she chose each morsel. When she wasn't at-tending to the pears, she watched the man sitting opposite Mees Katie, and she listened to him, and Mees Katie listened to him, and he listened to himself. His name is Michel, and he never stops talk-ing. He has something to do with importing foreign movies, or with promoting them, and he is always busy. He is always on the run, going in all directions. He never finishes his dinner without jumping up from his chair at least once to dash into the back room where the telephone is, to make a call and it is always an urgent call. If the phone is busy, if there is someone ahead of him, he stands waiting im-patiently in the arch between the two rooms, looking importantly about him, and when he has finally got into the telephone booth and put his call through, he keeps the door open until he is halfway through his conversation. His voice can be heard all over the restau-rant until suddenly there is a little clatter as he shuts himself away with his secrets. He has a very high, harsh voice, and he twists each word so that only half of it sounds like English. Leo makes fun of him. Once, when Michel had pulled the phone booth door shut on himself, Leo called from the bar to Mees Katie, who was sitting at a table with some people just as she was tonight, "Michel is talking with the weatherman again," and Mees Katie looked annoyed, al-though she smiled. She gets impatient with the Étoile, and with the people there, and especially with Michel, because he pesters her, but she has a kind heart, and she is always polite.

Michel always comes into the restaurant alone, looking for com-pany, and once in a while when there is no acquaintance he can join for dinner he sits by himself. When he is alone, all his animation dies away and he looks old and tired. He has a very broad dark face, with loose wrinkles, furrows, running up and down it and overlapping its outline. His forehead is high, and he has kinky coal black hair and a neat, thin mouth. When he sits at his table with nobody to talk to or to pay any attention to him, he looks deserted, as though he had been brought to the restaurant and left there by someone who had no in-tention of coming back to claim him. Alone, he is morose and digni-fied, as though humiliation had taken him unawares but had not found him unprepared. On nights like that, when he knows he is doomed to solitude, he stands at the bar with his drink, sweet vermouth, until his dinner is brought, and then he goes to his table and sits down very deliberately and shakes out his napkin, very fussily. He places the napkin across his lap and folds it closely around him so that his jacket hangs free of it. He always wears a double-breasted suit, and a waistcoat. [Q.A. "vast"]. When the napkin is safely in place, he picks up his knife and fork and sounds all the food on his plate and looks severely at his green salad. Then he cuts off a piece of meat and places it in his mouth and begins to chew it. While he is chewing, his knife and fork lie in his plate, and his wrists rest against the edge of the table, with his hands limp, and he chews patiently, looking as proud and as indifferent as though he was facing a firing squad.

I think he must have had dinner alone tonight before I came in, and after dinner moved over to join Mees Katie and her acquaintance, the elderly painted lady. There was nothing, not even a glass of water, in front of Mees Katie, and nothing in front of Michel, but the elderly lady's part of the tablecloth looked as though it had been thoroughly occupied by several different dishes before her pears in wine were brought. Mees Katie looked very tired. She has a lot of acquaintances, most of them inherited from her mother, and I suppose the elderly lady was one of them. Mees Katie has an attitude she falls into, when she is being officially companionable. She sits with both elbows on the table, with her right hand placed flat against the side of her head and her left hand, with the fingers curled under, and turned down, supporting her chin. The right hand always holds her head up, while the left hand is ready to rise against her mouth, as though the polite attention she wants to give to people calls for modesty from her, and for as complete a concealment of her own personality as she can manage. Tonight, as she listened wearily to Michel, her hand hid her mouth and her eyes were fixed on Michel's face. She is often bored but as a rule she can escape from her entanglements by jumping up to greet a customer or to give an order to the waiter. There was no easy escape for her tonight—the Étoile might as well have been snowbound for all the coming and going there was. It was very quiet. Three men sitting at the last table in the bar were talking quietly, but the only voice really to be heard belonged to Michel, and Mees Katie kept her eyes fixed on him as though she feared she might fall asleep if she stopped watching him. She has extraordinary eyes, small slanted brown eyes that are filled with light, brilliant eyes of a transparent brown in which the color recedes, not growing darker but growing more intense, so that the point of truest color, the source of all that light, seems very far away, and perhaps it is for that reason that Mees Katie's expression always seems distant no matter how close her face is as she bends down to answer a question or to whisper to some customer she knows well.

Suddenly the elderly lady finished her pears, and she laid down her spoon and smiled, a small, mild, accustomed smile of pleasure, and she turned to look at Mees Katie, and Mees Katie yawned, and was shocked at herself.

"Oh, I am sorry, Michel!" she cried. "Excuse me, Mrs. Dolan, but I am so tired tonight."

Michel emerged from his monologue to see that he was in danger of losing his audience, and he looked over at Leo and called excitedly for cognac, cognac all round.

"Oh, no no no, thank you, Michel," Mees Katie said. "No cognac for me, thank you very much."

But Mrs. Dolan was delighted. She removed her lips from the edge of her coffee cup, which she was holding with both hands, and for a minute she looked like the perky little person she must once have been, who knew that at the mention of a drink a girl brightens up. "Well, thank you very much," she said to Michel, who had begun to stare at her with alarm. "I believe I will." She had a very loud, rusty voice, and after regarding Michel with approval she turned to Mees Katie. "Have a drink," she said. "A little cognac will settle your stomach."

Mees Katie laughed in a horrified way. "Oh, my stomach is all right," she cried, and she called to Leo. "M. Leo, *deux cognacs, si'l vous plaît.*"

Mees Katie is tall and slender, and she moves very easily and quickly. She went to the bar and took the little tray with the two cognacs from Leo and handed it to Robert, who had come running from

113

the end of the bar. Then she walked quickly away, through the bar and through the dim dining room, and pushed open one of the doors leading to the kitchen and went in there and stayed a few minutes. When she returned she was very brisk in her beaver hat and her beaver-lined coat. She said goodnight to Michel, who had become very glum, and to Mrs. Dolan, and to the old Frenchman at the bar, and to me, and she motioned Leo to the end of the bar and spoke a few words privately to him as she pulled on her gloves, and off she went. As she talked with Leo she stood sideways to the bar, and looked through the window, and a minute later, watching through the window, I saw her go past, walking carefully on the dangerous sidewalk, with her hand up to hold her hat against the wind. She and her mother have an apartment where they have lived for many years, far over on the west side, near Tenth Avenue. Leo also watched her through the window, and when she disappeared he stayed where he was and continued to watch. There is a big open garage across the street that has pushed itself through the buildings and now is open at each end, making an arcade and therefore a vista—you can see a little section of the Forty-eighth Street scene from this window here, and the people walking along there, who almost never turn their heads to look over in this direction, seem very far away, and they seem to be walking faster and with more sense of direction than the passersby immediately outside the window. Tonight was so blurred and wild you could see nothing much except movements of struggle out there, but Leo continued to watch. The back of Leo's head is perfectly flat, and his skin is putty-colored, but more white than gray or beige. His features are thick and fleshy and very clearly defined, the nose a wide triangle, the upper lip a sharp bow. His eyes are small and blue, and his half smile, for he never smiles right out, is always accompanied by a deliberate glance in which suspicion and interest are equally mixed. Sometimes the interest becomes dislike. He is vain. He is slow-witted and not handsome, and he is past sixty and a bit fat, and yet he wears the pleased, secretive expression of a man who has always got along very well with women. After a while he abandoned his survey of the window and moved along to speak with the old Frenchman. They spoke in French. The Frenchman objects to hearing English spoken at the Étoile, and he becomes very irritable when English-speaking strangers try to strike up an acquaintance with him. The three men at the end of the room left their table and moved across to that end of the bar and called for drinks. They were irresolute. They were marooned in the city for the night, and they had taken rooms at the Plymouth Hotel along the street, and they wanted to be entertained without becoming involved, and the evening was going flat on them. They had come to the Étoile for dinner because they often have lunch there and always imagined it to be a place where interesting people came at night—show people, artists and writers, people like that, or at least French people who would sit and stand around and talk excitedly as they did in the movies—but there was no one worth watching or listening to, and tomorrow night they will drive home to Larchmont with a disappointed feeling which they will translate as knowledge—New York City is just as dull as anywhere else when you have nothing to do.

Michel was still talking, but warily. The last thing he wanted was to be left alone with a strange woman, and he felt it was no compliment to him to be seen drinking with a Mrs. Dolan. He hadn't touched his cognac. She took a businesslike sip from hers and set the glass back on the table. She had stopped listening to him, and now she was sizing him up. A smile kept coming and going on her face— it was her contribution to the conversation and her acknowledgment of it. But she was considering, or ruminating, and a little trick occurred to her. She smiled and put her finger against her lips as though Michel were a child who was talking too much. Michel stopped talking.

"Do you come here much?" Mrs. Dolan asked him. It wasn't much of a question but it was too personal for poor Michel. He began to answer her, and then instead he jumped up and clapped his hands to the sides of his head. It is the gesture he makes when he remembers an urgent phone call, or when he has to run out of the restaurant on an urgent errand. Mrs. Dolan stopped smiling, but she showed no surprise, or embarrassment. She simply looked at him. He had to run out on an urgent errand, he said, but he would be back in ten minutes.

He always returns to the Étoile after these errands but Mrs. Dolan didn't know that, and it was clear she didn't believe him. She went on looking at him. In his excitement he knocked his chair back, and it fell against the edge of my table. He turned ungracefully and caught the chair and straightened it, using both his hands. "Pardon, Madame," he said to me, gaily. He looked me in the eye and smiled at me. He was triumphant, or at least relieved, because he was managing to break away from Mrs. Dolan, and he was glad of the diversion, of the fallen chair, because it made his getaway easier, but he would have smiled anyway, challenging me or challenging anyone to ignore him. When he smiles, his dark, even teeth remain tightly closed because he must always remain on guard and must always show that he does not fear the snub he watches for. I said quickly, "It doesn't matter at all," and I was glad I did, because, although he had already begun speaking to Mrs. Dolan again, he turned and nodded to me, and I knew I was forgiven for the sin I had not committed, of not recognizing him.

Then he bustled to the coat rack, beside where I was sitting, and began wrapping himself up in his warm clothes—his warm fur collared overcoat and his fur hat and his big gloves. Mrs. Dolan watched him as indifferently as though he was a stranger who had chanced to share her table on a train journey, and, as she might in a train, she turned her head from him to look at the view, in this case the bar, Leo, the old Frenchman, and the three exiles from Larchmont. Leo had a dour expression on his face as he watched Michel, who looked happily back at him, and then looked at Mrs. Dolan and saw he had lost her attention. He called to her, "You will wait? You will be here? You will not run away?"

She looked at him stupidly, and I was surprised when she answered him. "I'm not going anywhere," she said in her dreadful voice.

Leo spoke up. "It is snowing out, Michel," he said.

Michel grinned at him. "Ten minutes!" he cried, and vanished.

"That Michel is a great joker, he thinks," Leo said.

"You call him a joker?" Mrs. Dolan said loudly. "Some joker, I'll say." But Leo ignored her, and she began rummaging in the huge leather handbag that was on the table beside her, propped against the wall. She took out a mirror and moved it about while she examined herself, her eyes, her mouth, and her earrings, and then she took out a dark red lipstick and smeared it thickly back and forth on her mouth, and afterward, while she was putting the lipstick away, she pressed her lips closely together. With her little finger, she rubbed the lipstick smooth, and tidied the corners of her mouth, and when she had finished she cleaned the color from her finger with her dinner napkin and took a tiny sip of her brandy, and glanced at Michel's brandy, which he had not touched. After that she sat gazing at the stained tablecloth, and from time to time she pursed her lips thoughtfully at something she saw there.

There are three young girls who have been coming to the Étoile for their Sunday dinner the last few months. They share an apartment on Forty-seventh and they all work as secretaries. Lately one of them, Betty, has been dropping in alone, early in the evening, before ten o'clock. She never comes for dinner, and she never stays after Mees Katie has gone home. Betty is about five foot two, a brown-haired, blue-eyed, round-faced girl with a pretty figure and a pretty smile, who obviously enjoys being a friendly little child among the grown-ups. Her winter coat is dark green imitation fur, and she wears sweaters and skirts most of the time, schoolgirl clothes. She walks in timidly, as though she was not quite sure of her welcome, and then she sits up at the end of the bar and asks for a Perrier water and drinks it very slowly, making it last. She dreams of being an actress, but I think the part she dreams of playing is the part she plays as she sits up at the bar of the Étoile and sips her Perrier and stares wonderingly all about her. The Étoile reminds her of a waterfront café she saw once in a movie that starred Jean Gabin, and that I think has now been remade to include a very young unknown actress named Betty who sits at the bar with a Perrier stealing the show, although she has nothing to say and nothing to do except be herself, poor and alone and very young. She always puts down a dollar to pay for her Perrier, but Leo seldom takes the money, and if he does take it he gives her another Perrier on the house. Once or twice Betty has sat at Mees Katie's table and helped her listen to Michel. She finds Michel very entertaining. Tonight she walked in shortly after Michel ran out. She came in expectantly, almost laughing, walking out of the snowstorm as though she was walking into a party. She pulled off her scarf, shaking the snow from it, and as she began to unbutton her coat she looked around for Mees Katie. Leo had come to the end of the bar and was watching her, smiling.

"Where is everybody?" she cried. "Where's Mees Katie?" She sat up at the bar and Leo poured a Perrier for her.

"I'm celebrating, Leo," she said. "This is my very first snowstorm. The office let us off at three o'clock, and I walked round and round and round, all by myself, celebrating all by myself, and then I went home and made dinner, but I got so excited thinking about the snow I just had to come out again and thought I'd come here and see Mees Katie. I thought there'd be thousands of people here. Oh, I wish it would snow for weeks and weeks. I just can't bear for it to end. But after today I'm beginning to think New Yorkers never really enjoy themselves. Nobody seemed to be really enjoying the snow. I never saw such people. All they could think about was getting home. Wouldn't you think a storm like this would wake everybody up? But all it does is put them to sleep. Such *people.*"

"It does not put me to sleep, Betty," Leo said in his deliberate way.

"I wish it would snow for a year," Betty said.

"It will take something warmer than a snowstorm to put me to sleep, Betty," Leo said.

Betty laughed self-consciously and looked at Mrs. Dolan.

"Michel is a bad boy tonight, Betty," Leo said, and he also looked at Mrs. Dolan. "He told this lady he'd be back in ten minutes and it has been twenty."

"Nearly half an hour," Mrs. Dolan said disgustedly. "Nearly half an hour."

"He'll be back," Betty said. "Michel always comes back, doesn't he, Leo?"

"Oh, yes, Michel comes back," Leo said, and he put his hand on Betty's arm and leaned far across the bar and began whispering in her ear, or tried to begin whispering in her ear, because at the touch of his face against her hair she pulled roughly away and looked at him with such distaste that he stepped back. Then he went to the cash register and opened the drawer and began looking in at the money and pretending to count it. He was furious. If she had spent ten years pondering a way to express disgust, she could not have found a better way. Even if they had been alone, Leo would never have forgiven her, but the three lingering men were watching, and so was the old Frenchman, and so was Mrs. Dolan.

Betty sat alone for a minute, and then she took her Perrier and slipped down from her stool and walked over to Mrs. Dolan. Betty looked flustered but she was smiling.

"May I sit down?" she asked Mrs. Dolan.

"Oh, please do," Mrs. Dolan said.

Betty sat down in Michel's chair, diagonally across from Mrs. Dolan. "Michel will be back soon," she said. "He always comes back."

"He left me sitting here like this," Mrs. Dolan said.

"Michel is really a sweet kind person when you get to know him," Betty said. "He's a darling, really."

Leo called out, "Miss Betty, you owe me sixty cents."

Betty looked over at him in surprise.

"You forgot to pay for your drink, little girl," he said, smiling, and he waved at Robert the waiter. Robert took Betty's dollar to the bar and brought her back her change. She had got very red.

"He needn't have shouted at me," she said to Mrs. Dolan. Mrs. Dolan said nothing.

Betty began talking. "This is the first big snow I've ever seen," she said. "I thought it would be like New Year's Eve here tonight, or something. When they first told us we were getting off early from the office I felt it was like a party or something, but then after I walked around a bit it seemed more like a disaster, and I kept wanting to get into the spirit of the thing. I felt very left out all day. I kept walking around."

When she fell silent Mrs. Dolan still continued to watch her, but she said nothing. She had nothing to say, and nothing to give except her silence, and so she said nothing, and made no reply, and they sat without speaking until the silence they shared strengthened and expanded to enclose them both.

Not long ago I saw a photograph in the evening paper of a crowd of circus elephants gathered around a dying elephant, "Flora," who had fallen and was lying on her side on the ground. The elephant closest to Flora was trying to revive her by blowing air into her open mouth with his trunk. The newspaper story said that all the elephants in the troupe took turns trying to save their dying comrade, and the story finished by saying "This practice is instinctive among pachyderms."

But that practice, instinctive among pachyderms, that determination to win even a respite from death, is no more instinctive than the silence was which grew and turned into a lifeline between Betty and Mrs. Dolan, because their silence arose from a shame so deep that it was peace for them to sit in its silence, and to listen to this silence which was only the silence of their own nature, of all they had in common. Mrs. Dolan's face grew ruminative, and Betty's profile suggested she was lost in recollections that were not unhappy.

Michel walked in, a snowman. He must have been standing out in the open, or walking, ever since he left the restaurant. He stood still just inside the door and banged the palms of his gloves together and sent a fond glance at Mrs. Dolan and at Betty, who had turned to watch him. Michel was very pleased with the entrance he had made, and he looked as though he would like to go out and come back in again.

"Don Juan, he thinks he is," Mrs. Dolan growled.

Michel moved to the coat rack and began unwrapping himself. He was very slow about it, and all the time he was pulling off his gloves, and unwinding his scarf, and shaking his fur hat, he faced the room as though he faced a full-length mirror, and he smiled, watching all of us, but not as he would watch the mirror. At last he stood revealed in his navy blue and brown striped suit, and his rings, and his crinkly black hair and his bow tie, and he strolled back to his table and sat down beside Mrs. Dolan, and smiled sweetly at Betty, and picked up the cognac that had been waiting for him. When I left they were all ordering more drinks, and Mrs. Dolan had decided to switch to crème de menthe. The old Frenchman came out of his reverie and began looking unpleasantly at the three men who were chattering in English at the end of the bar, and I knew he was becoming happier. I paid my bill and left.

The self-service elevator at my hotel shivered piteously when I stepped into it, and hesitated before starting its painful ascent to the high floor where I live. That is as usual. The tiny, boxy elevator is as alien to this elegantly made hotel as the blue neon sign that winks on and off in front. A marble staircase winds all the way up through the heart of the building, and decorated windows over every stairwell still filter and color the light as they have done for more than sixty years. The fireplaces have all been blocked up long ago, but the rooms are very big and the ceilings are high and the walls shut out all sound. I looked again through the windows that give me my view of Broadway. Just below me, on Forty-eighth Street, on both sides of the street, a few small houses huddle together in the shadows, and from their low level other newer walls rise higher and higher to the south and east but tonight the big buildings, the giants that carry Manhattan's monumental broken skyline, were lost in fog. I could see only the little roofs below me and their neighbors immediately beyond, all of them under smooth snow that shaped them in the dark into separate triangles and squares and rectangles and slopes. The snow on Forty-eighth Street was rumpled but there was no one in the street and the open parking lot was empty. To the right, Broadway was still lighted up as high as the sky but the lights shone weakly, smothered in fog, except for the dazzling band of color that runs around the Latin Quarter, a few houses away from me. I pushed open the window. The cold air rushed in, but no noise. What sound there was was drugged, as though I was a hundred floors above the street instead of only eleven floors. The wind had died down, and the snow fell thickly, falling in large calm flakes.

Christmas Eve

The fireplace in the children's bedroom had to be swept out and dusted so that Father Christmas would have a place to put his feet when he came down the chimney. Lily and Margaret Bagot watched their mother, who knelt close in to the grate, brushing the last few flecks of ash out of the corners. Lily was eight and Margaret was six, and the long white nightgowns they wore fell in a rumpled line to their ankles. They wore no dressing gowns although the room was cold—they would be getting into bed in a minute. It was a square room, the back bedroom, with faded garlanded wallpaper in blue and pink and green, and it was lighted by a single bulb that hung from the middle of the ceiling. One large window looked out onto the garden and the adjoining gardens. Mrs. Bagot had pulled the blind down all the way to the sill. She wanted the children to have their privacy and, beyond that, she wanted them to be safe. She didn't really know what she meant by safe—respectable, maybe, or successful in some way that she had no vision of. She wanted the world for them, or else she wanted them to have the kind of place that was represented to her by lawyers and doctors and people like that. She wanted them to go on believing in Father Christmas and, more than that, she wanted to go on believing in Father Christmas herself. She would have liked to think there was someone big and kind outside the house who knew about the children, someone who knew their names and their ages, and that Lily might go out into the world and make something of herself, because she was always reading, but that Margaret was very defenseless and unsure of herself. Lily was maybe a bit too sure of herself, but at the same time she was very soft, very nice to people who maybe wouldn't understand that it was her nature and that she wasn't the fool she seemed to be. Father Christmas knew that Lily was clever, always getting good marks at school. No matter where the presents came from, Father Christmas came down the chimney, Mrs. Bagot was sure of that. He was probably hovering over Dublin now, seeing how the city had changed since last year. The children were all older, that was the great change. It was always the great change, every day, not just once a year. She placed her dusting brush across the paper in the scuttle and stood up.

"Now Father Christmas will have a place to put his feet," Lily said.

"He wears big red boots," Margaret whispered.

"Time to go to bed now," Mrs. Bagot said. "Come on now, into bed, both of you. Margaret is nearly asleep as it is." She had left them up long past their usual bedtime and Margaret was drooping. Lily was as wide awake as ever; she'd be awake all night if this kept up. But it was Christmas Eve, and Martin was home early from work. He was downstairs now, reading the paper and waiting to come up and say good night to them. Because Martin was home, the two cats and Bennie, the dog, were all shut up in the kitchen. He hated to see the animals around the house, and the animals seemed to know it—they had all settled themselves very comfortably around the stove the minute she told them to stay. They were all stray animals that had found their way to the house at one time or another, and they had never lost their watchfulness. They knew where their welcome was. Bennie was Mrs. Bagot's special pet. He was a rough-haired white terrier with bits of black here and there. Mrs. Bagot had rescued him years before from a gang of small boys who were tormenting him, and since then she had seldom been out of his sight. He slept on her bed at night. Martin Bagot didn't know that. Martin had his own room at the back of the house. He generally got home from work very late, after Mrs. Bagot and the children and Bennie and the cats were all asleep. He didn't like to have Mrs. Bagot wait up for him, she had to get up so early in the morning to get the children off to school. He thought the animals all slept in the little woodshed behind the house.

Daisy, the thin black cat, belonged to Lily, but Rupert was Margaret's. Rupert was a fat orange cat who was so good-natured that he purred even the time his tail was caught in the kitchen door. Martin knew the names of the animals and sometimes he asked the children, "How is Daisy?" or "How is Rupert?" but he liked them kept out of the house. He half believed the animals carried disease and that the children would suffer from having them around.

Downstairs in the front sitting room Martin was watching the flames in the grate. He had thrown the evening paper aside. There was nothing in it. He was thinking it was nice to be home at the time other men got home at night. Nice for once, anyway. He wouldn't want to have to get home on time every night the way other men did, walking into a squalling household, with the children trying to do their homework on the same table where their mother was trying to set the tea. But, of course, he was different from other men. He wasn't the least bit domesticated. Nobody could call him a domestic animal. How many other men in Dublin had their own room with their own books in it, and their own routine going in the house—an unbreakable, independent routine that was perfectly justified because it depended on his job and his job depended on it. Delia had her house and the children and he had his own life and yet they were all together. They were a united family all right. Nobody could deny that. Delia was a very good mother. He had nothing to worry about on that score. Ordinary men might want to be lord and master in the house, always throwing their weight around, but not Martin. A bit more money would have come in handy, but you couldn't have everything.

The room was decorated for Christmas. He and the children had worked all afternoon on it, with Delia running up and down from the kitchen to see how they were getting along. They had all had a great time. Even Margaret had come out of herself and made suggestions. There were swags of red and green paper chain across the ceiling and he had put a sprig of holly behind every picture. The mistletoe was over the door going out into the hall. At one point Delia had come hurrying up to say they must save a bit of holly to stick in the Christmas pudding and he had caught her under the mistletoe and given her a kiss. Her skin was very soft. She looked like her old self as she put her hand up against his chest and pretended to push him away. Then the children came running over and wanted to be kissed too. First he kissed them and then Delia kissed them. They were all bundled together for a minute and then the children began screaming, "Daddy, kiss Mummy again! Daddy, kiss Mummy again!" and Delia said, "Oh, I have to get back to the kitchen. All this playacting isn't going to get my work done." Lily said, "Women's work is never done." Lily was always coming out with something like that. You never knew what she'd say next. Margaret said, "I want to kiss little Jesus," and she went over to the window where the crèche was all set up, with imitation snow around it and on its roof.

The window was quite big, a bow window that bulged out into the street. Delia had filled it with her fern collection. They were mostly maidenhair ferns, some of them very tall, and she had them arranged on small tables of varying heights. Sometimes Martin felt the ferns were a bit overpowering and that they darkened the room, but to-night they made a wonderful background for the crèche, making it seem that the stable and the Holy Family and the shepherds and their animals were all enclosed and protected by a benign forest where they would always be safe and where snow could fall without making them cold. The Three Wise Men stood outside the stable as though they were just arriving. Lily had carefully sprinkled snow on their shoulders. Some of the snow had sifted down onto the carpet, where it lay glittering in the firelight.

On his way home today, Martin had bought two small gold-colored pencils for the children. Each pencil was in its own box, and the girl in the shop had wrapped the boxes in white tissue paper and tied them with red ribbon. They were out in his coat pocket in the hall now, together with a special present he had bought for Delia in the same shop, and he wanted to get them and put them on the kitchen table so that they wouldn't be forgotten. He knew Delia had the rest of the children's presents hidden in the kitchen. He'd better do it now, while he was thinking about it. He went out into the hall, shutting the door quickly after him to keep the heat in the sitting room, and as he fumbled in his pocket for the pencils he heard Delia talking to the children in the room upstairs. Her voice was low, but it was very calm and definite, as though she was explaining something to them, or even laying down the law about something. He had the pencils now and he stood very still. He couldn't hear what she was saying, only her voice, and once or twice he thought he heard the children whispering to her. It was very peaceful standing there in the hall, very peaceful and comfortable, although the hall was a bit cold after the warmth of the sitting room. But he felt very comfortable, very content. All of a sudden he felt at peace with the world and with the future. It was as though the weight of the world had fallen from his shoulders, and he hadn't known the weight of the world was on his shoulders, or even that he was worried. In a few years he would be making a bit more money, and then things would be easier. He had no desire to know what Delia was saying, or to go up there and join in. That was all between her and the children. He would only upset her if he went up there now—he would wait till she called him. It was dark in the hall except for the faint light filtering through the glass panels in the front door from the street lamp outside. He listened to Delia's voice, so quiet and authoritative, and he had the feeling he was spying on them. Well, what if he was. He didn't often have the chance to watch them like this, in the gloaming, as it were. How big this little house was, that it could contain them all separately. He might have been a thousand miles away, for all they knew of him. They thought he was in there in the room reading the evening paper, when in fact he was a thousand miles above them, watching them and watching over them. Where would they all be if it wasn't for him. Ah, but they held him to earth. He had to laugh when he thought of the might-have-been. He might have travelled. There was very little chance now that he would see the capitals of the world. He never knew for sure whether Delia and the children were his anchor or his burden and at the moment he didn't much care. He had seldom felt as much at peace with himself as he did now. It would be nice to fall asleep like this, happy like this, and then wake up in the morning to find that the world was easy. He had often thought the house cramped, and imagined it held him down, but to-night he knew that he could stretch his arms up through this hall ceiling and on up through the roof and do no damage and that no one would reproach him. There was plenty of room. He was as free as any man, or at least as free as anybody could be in this day and age. Now he would run down to the kitchen with the pencils. Delia would be calling him any minute. But the light was switched on on the landing above, and Delia appeared at the head of the stairs and saw him.

"Oh, Martin, I was just coming down to get you," she said.

"I was just coming up," he said, and he started up the stairs, two steps at a time.

The closer it came to their bedtime the more excited the children were, although they stayed very quiet. Delia was afraid they wouldn't sleep, or that if they did sleep they'd wake up in time to find herself and Martin creeping into their room with their presents. She stood by their bed, talking to them to calm them down, and she found that the sleepier they became the more apprehensive she herself was. She was getting what she called "nervous" and she couldn't understand it, because she had been looking forward to Christmas. She didn't know what was the matter with her. She was as fearful tonight as she used to be long ago at home when she lay in bed listening to the wind blowing around and around the house. The fear was the same in this house, exactly the same, except that this house was attached on both sides to other houses and so the wind couldn't blow around it but only across it. But the fear was the same. She hated the wind. In the daytime she was able to keep busy, but at night as she lay alone in the dark her mind went back, and instead of going back into dreaming, like daydreaming, it went back into conjecture and from there into confusion. Instead of rebuilding the past to her own design and making things happen as they should have happened, she was blown by the noise of the wind against bitter obstacles that she was able to avoid when the weather was steady. Words like "why" and "when" and "how" rose up against the dreaming that rested her, and she was forced back on herself, so that instead of rearranging things she had to face them. The past led to the present—that was the trouble. She couldn't see any connection at all between herself as she used to be and herself as she was now, and she couldn't understand how with a husband and two children in the house she was lonely and afraid. She stood there talking to the children about what a lovely day they were all going to have tomorrow, and she was well aware that she was falling into a morbid frame of mind. And there was no excuse for

128

her. She had nothing to worry about, not tonight anyway. There wasn't even any wind, although it had rained earlier and would probably rain again before morning. There was really nothing to worry about at the moment, except, of course, how to get Bennie up out of the kitchen and into her room without Martin knowing about it. It would be terrible, awful, if Martin found out that Bennie slept every night on her bed, but she couldn't leave him out in the shed in the cold. The cats always slept on the children's bed, but they'd be all right in the shed for the one night. She had a basket out there for them. They could curl up together. But Bennie couldn't go out there—she'd miss him too much. She wished she could talk to Martin and explain to him that Bennie was important, but she knew there was no use hoping for that. It was time now to go down and call him to come up and say good night to Lily and Margaret, but when she walked out on the landing she saw him standing in the hall below.

The hall was quite narrow, and was covered with linoleum, and it served its purpose very well, both as an entrance to the house and as a vantage point from which the house could be viewed and seen for what it was—a small, plain, family place that had a compartmented look now in winter because of all the doors being closed to keep whatever heat there was inside the rooms. In the hall there was a rack with hooks on it for coats, and there was an umbrella stand, and a chair nobody ever sat on. Nobody ever sat on the chair and nobody ever stood long in the hall. It was a passageway—not to fame and not to fortune but only to the common practices of family life, those practices, habits, and ordinary customs that are the only true realities most of us ever know, and that in some of us form a memory strong enough to give us something to hold on to to the end of our days. It is a matter of love, and whether the love finds daily, hourly expression in warm embraces and in the instinctive kind of attentiveness animals give to their young or whether it is largely unexpressed, as it was among the Bagots, does not really matter very much in the very long run. It is the solid existence of love that gives life and strength to memory, and if, in some cases, childhood memories lack the soft and tender colors given by demonstrativeness, the child grown old and in the dark knows only that what is under his hand is a rock that will never give way.

In the big bed in the back room upstairs, Lily Bagot lay sleeping beside her sister, and if they dreamed nobody knew about it, because they never remembered their dreams in the morning. On the morning of Christmas Day they woke very early, much earlier than usual, and it was as though the parcels piled beside their bed sent out a magic breath to bring them out of their sleep while the world was still dark. They moved very slowly at first, putting their hands down beside the bed and down at the end of the bed to feel what was there, to feel what had been left for them. They went over each parcel with their hands, getting the outline and trying to make out from the shape what was inside. Then they couldn't wait any longer, and Lily got out of bed and put on the light so that they could see what they had been given.

The Springs of Affection

Delia Bagot died suddenly and quietly, alone in her bed, with the door shut, and six years later, after eight months of being bedridden, Martin, her husband, died, attended by a nursing nun and his eighty-seven-year-old twin sister, Min. And at last Min was released from the duty she had imposed on herself, to remain with him as long as he needed her. She could go home now, back to her flat in Wexford, and settle into the peace and quiet she had enjoyed before Delia's death summoned her to the suburbs of Dublin. To the suburbs of Dublin and the freedom of that house where she had wandered so often in her fancy. For fifty years she had wandered in their private lives, ever since Delia appeared out of the blue and fascinated Martin, the born bachelor, into marrying her. Min wasn't likely to forget that wedding day, the misery of it, the anguish of it, the abomination of deprivation as she and her mother stood together and looked at him, the happy bridegroom, standing there grinning his head off as though he had ascended into Heaven. She and her mother and her two sisters, all three of them gone now, and Martin, too, gone. Min thought of the neat graves, one by one—a sister's grave, a sister's grave, a mother's grave, a brother's grave—all gone, all present, like medals on the earth. And she thought it was fitting that she should be the one to remain alive, because out of them all she was the one who was always faithful to the family. She was the only one of the lot of them who hadn't gone off and got married. She had never wanted to assert herself like that, never needed to. She had wondered at their lack of shame as they exhibited themselves, Clare and Polly with their husbands and Martin with poor Delia, the poor thing. They didn't seem to care what anybody thought of them when they got caught up in that excitement, like animals. It was disgusting, and they seemed to know it, the way they pretended their only concern was with the new clothes they'd have and the flowers they'd grow in their very own gardens. And now it was over for them, and they might just as well have controlled themselves, for all the good they had of it. And she, standing alone as always, had lived to sum them all up. It was a great satisfaction to see finality rising up like the sun. Min thought not many people knew that satisfaction. To watch the end of all was not much different from watching the beginning of things, and if you weren't ever going to take part anyway, then to watch the end was far and away better. You could be jealous of people who were starting out, but you could hardly be jealous of the dead.

Not that I was ever jealous, Min thought. God forbid that I should encourage small thoughts in myself, but I couldn't help but despise Delia that day, the way she stood looking up at Martin as though she was ready to fall down on her knees before him. She made a show of herself that day. We were late getting out for the wedding. We were late getting started, and then, we were all late getting there and they were all waiting for us. And after it was over and they were married and we were all in the garden, she came running up to my mother and she said, "Oh, I was afraid you weren't coming. I began to imagine Martin had changed his mind about me. I thought I would burst with impatience and longing. I had such a longing to see his face, and then, when I saw you driving up, I still had a great fear something might come between us. I'll never forget how impatient I was—I see it would be easy to go mad with love." She said that to my mother. "Mad with love," she said. My mother just looked at her, and when she flew off, all full of herself as she was that day, my mother turned and looked at me, and said to me, "Min, I am an old woman, but never in my life have I spoken like that. Never in my life have I said the like of that. All the years I've lived, and I've never, never allowed myself to feel like that about anybody, let alone be that open about it. That girl has something the matter with her. My heart goes out to Martin, I can tell you. There's something lacking in her."

Min remembered that Martin's wedding day was a very long day, with many different views and scenes, country roads, country lanes, gardens and orchards and fields and streams, and a house with rooms that multiplied in recollection, because she only visited them that one time, and they attracted her very much—dim, old rooms that maintained an air of simple, implacable formality. She envied the way the rooms were able to remain unknown even when you were standing in them. It was the same with the people out there in the country—even when they were most friendly and open they kept a lot of themselves hidden. Min thought they were like a strange tribe that only shows up in force on festival days.

The days before the wedding were a great strain, and Min always said she never understood how they got themselves out of the house the morning of the wedding. If it had not been that Markey was standing outside with the horse and car they had hired, they might all have stayed in the house and let Martin find his way out to Oylegate as best he could. He might have changed his mind then, and remained at home where he belonged. Driving out of the town of Wexford, they crossed the bridge at Ferrycarrig and there was the Slaney pouring away under them, flowing straight for the harbor as unconcernedly as though it was any old day. And then the long drive out to Oylegate. And when they got to Oylegate the chapel yard was waiting for them, looking more like an arena than a religious place. And the chapel itself, all solemn and hedged in with flowers so full in bloom that they seemed to be overflowing their petals, color flowing freely through the air. Min drew deep breaths, filling her lungs with fright. The fright built up inside her chest—she could feel it beginning to smother her. There was no air in the place. She said to her mother later, "I nearly got a headache in the chapel. I thought I might have to walk outside. It was too close in there. I began to feel weak. I thought we'd never get away out of the place." Polly was listening. Polly always seemed to be listening in time to turn your own words against you.

Polly said, "You always tell everybody you never had a headache in your life. You always say you never had time to have a headache. You leave the headaches to the rest of us. Clare and Polly have time for all that kind of nonsense, imagining themselves to be delicate— that's what you always say. And then in the next breath, every time anything goes against you, you tell us you *almost* got a headache. If you almost got a headache it would show on your face. You're overcome by your own bad humor—that's all that's the matter with you."

"In the name of God," their mother said, "this is not the time for the two of you to start fighting. Do you want to make a show of us all, have them all laughing at us more than they're laughing already?"

They were walking through the chapel yard after the wedding and Min went ahead, looking hurried, as though she had left something outside in the road and wanted to look for it. In Polly's voice she heard the enmity that had been oppressing her all day, enmity that came at her out of the streets of the town as they started to drive out here, distant, incomprehensible enmity that rose up at her from the bridge at Ferrycarrig, and from the road itself, and from the fields and trees and cottages they passed, and even from the sky itself, blue and white and summery though it was. Even the faraway sky looked satisfied to see her in the condition she was in. Min didn't know what condition she was in. She knew that she couldn't say a word without being misunderstood. She knew that something had happened that deprived her of an approbation so natural that she had always taken it for granted. She only noticed it now that she missed it—it was as though the whole world had turned against her. Polly must have rehearsed that speech—Polly was very spiteful. But where had Polly found that tone of voice, so hard and condescending? She's very sure of herself all of a sudden, Min thought. I must have given myself away, somehow. But what was there to give away—Min knew she had done nothing to earn that tone of contempt from a younger sister. She had an awful feeling of being in disgrace with somebody she had never seen and who had never liked her very much, never, not even when she was a little mite trying to help her mother with the younger children. No, wherever it came from, this impersonal dislike had been lying in wait for her all her life. And it was clear from the way people were looking at her that everybody knew about it. She couldn't even say a word to her mother about a headache without being attacked as though she was a scoundrel. All the good marks she had won at school were forgotten. Nothing was known about her now except that she had presumed to a place far above her station in life. She had believed she could fly sky-high, with her brains for wings. Nobody notices me as I am, Min thought; all they can see is the failure. I was done out of my right, but they'd rather say, She got too big for her boots, and, Pride must have a fall. She had to face up to it. There was nothing she could say in her own defense, and she condemned herself if she remained silent. It is impossible to prove you are not a disappointed old maid.

Min remembered Martin's wedding day as the day when everything changed in their lives at home. My mother was never the same after Martin married, she thought, and it was then, too, that Clare and Polly became restless and hard to get along with, and stopped joining in the conversation we always had about the family fortunes and talked instead about what they were going to do with their own lives. *Their* lives—and what about sticking together as a family, as we had been brought up to do? They got very selfish all of a sudden, and the house seemed very empty, as though he had died. After the wedding he never came back again except as a visitor. They lived only around the corner but it wasn't the same, knowing he was not sleeping in his own bed.

There was eight years between Delia and Martin, and then, since he lived six years after her, there was fourteen years between them, and now that they were both gone none of it mattered at all. They might have been born hundreds of years apart, Min thought with satisfaction. But it was not likely that Martin would ever have belonged to any family except his own, or that he would ever have had sisters who were not Min and Clare and Polly, or that he would ever have had another woman for his mother than their own mother, who had sacrificed everything for them and asked in return only that they stick together as a family, and build themselves up, and make a wall around themselves that nobody could see through, let alone climb. What she had in mind was a fort, a fortress, where they could build themselves up in private and strengthen their hold on the earth, because in the long run that is what matters—a firm foothold and a roof over your head. But all that hope ended and all their hard work was mocked when Delia Kelly walked into their lives. She smashed us up, Min thought, and got us all out into the open where blood didn't count anymore, and where blood wasn't thicker than water, and where the only mystery was, what did he see in her. It was like the end of the world, knowing he was at the mercy of somebody outside the family. A farmer's daughter is all she was, even if she had attended the Loreto convent and owned certificates to show what a good education she had.

Min sat beside her own gas fire in her own flat in Wexford and considered life and crime and punishment according to the laws of arithmetic. She counted up and down the years, and added and subtracted the questions and answers, and found that she came out with a very tidy balance in her favor. She glanced over to the old brown chest that now held those certificates, still in the big brown paper envelope that Delia had kept them in. Min intended to do away with the certificates, but not yet. She liked looking at them—especially at the one given for violin playing. It was strange that in spite of her good memory she had quite forgotten that Delia had a little reputation as a musician when she first met Martin. A *very* little reputation, and she had come by it easily, because she had been given every chance. All the chances in Min's own family had gone to Martin, because he was the boy, and he took all their chances with him when he left. And spoiled his own chances for good, because he did nothing for the rest of his life, tied down as he was, slaving to support a wife and children, turning himself into a nobody. After all that promise and all that talk and all those plans he made nothing of himself. A few pounds in the bank, a few sticks of furniture, a few books, and a garden that still bloomed although it had gone untended for six years—that was the sum of his life, all he had to show for himself. He would have done better to think of his mother, and stay at home, and benefit from the encouragement of his own family, all of them pushing for him in everything he did. With his ability and his brains and the nice way he had about him, he could have done anything. He could have risen to any height, a natural leader like him, able to be at ease anywhere with anybody. As it was, he died friendless. How could he have friends when he was ashamed to invite anybody to the house? He was ashamed of Delia and ashamed of the house, and more than anything else, he was unwilling to let people know of his unhappiness. He was like all of us in that, Min thought, proud and sensitive and fond of our privacy. Delia came from another class of people altogether. They were a different breed, more coarse-grained than we are, country people, accustomed to being out in all weathers, plowing, and gathering in the hay, and dealing with animals. They had no thoughts in their heads beyond saving the corn. They tried to be friendly; Min gave them that much. She wanted to be fair. But she didn't trust them, and in any case they were rejoicing over herself and her mother, because Martin made himself such an easy catch. Min didn't like to see mother being made a fool of, and Martin too being made a fool of, because he didn't know what he was doing when he turned around and got married. He went out of his head about that girl, mad with longing, all decency gone. He was like somebody in a delirium. Min couldn't help feeling a bit contemptuous of him, to see him so helpless. And then the same thing overcame Clare and Polly, Clare marrying a dirty shabby fellow nearly old enough to be her father, and Polly marrying a commercial traveller and having one child after another until she nearly had her mother and Min out in the street with the expense she put on them. But Martin started it all, vanishing out of their lives as casually as though he had never been more than a lodger in the house.

It was a shame, what happened, all their plans gone for nothing. By that time they were all out working—Polly in the knitting factory, Clare in the news agent's, Martin in the County Surveyor's office, and Min in the dressmaking business. She was a dressmaker from the beginning, through no choice of her own, and she made a good job of it. Everybody said she was very reliable and that she had good style. As soon as she could manage it she moved the sewing machine out of her mother's front parlor and into the rooms on the Main Street, where she now lived. One way and another, she had had a title to these rooms for almost sixty years. The house changed owners, but Min remained on. She had no intention of giving up her flat, especially since her rent included the three little atticky rooms on the third floor, the top floor of the house. She showed great foresight when she had those top-floor rooms included in her original arrangement, all those many years ago. Now she had made the top floor into a little flat, makeshift but very nice. She found young couples liked it for the first years or so of their married lives. And she still had the lease of the little house at the corner of Georges Street and Oliver Plunkett Street, where her mother had taken them all to live when they were still babies. That little house Min had turned, in her informal way, into two flats, and she had the rent from them. And she had her old-age pension, and something in the bank—nobody knew how much, although there were many guesses. Some said she was too clever, too sharp altogether. The butcher downstairs under her flat hated her. She didn't care. She had the last laugh. He could stand in the doorway of his shop and watch her coming up the street, and give her all the black looks he liked—she didn't care. She couldn't help laughing when she thought of how sure he was when he bought the house that he would be able to get rid of her simply by telling her she wasn't wanted, and that he needed the whole house for his growing family. She wasn't going to die to suit him and she didn't care whether he wanted her or not. It was presumptuous of him to imagine she would care whether he wanted her there or didn't want her there. He even had the impertinence to tell her that he and his wife had the greatest respect for her. Min didn't know the wife but she knew the people the wife came from. No need to see people of that class to know what they were, and what their "respect" was worth. She told the butcher to his face that he might as well leave her alone. She wasn't going to budge. Of course, it would be very nice and convenient for him only to have to walk upstairs to his tea at night after he shut up the shop, but he was going to have to wait for his convenience. A narrow gate alongside his shop entrance led into a covered passage, and there was her downstairs front door at the side of the house, as private as you please. She was very well off there. The place was nicely fixed up. She liked being there in the flat alone, with the downstairs door locked and the door of her flat locked and the fire going and the electric reading lamp at her shoulder and an interesting book to read and the day's paper to hand, in case she felt like going over it again. And she had Delia's little footstool to keep her feet off the floor. She thought it was like a miracle the way things had evened out in the end. She had gone around and around and up and down for all those years, doing her duty and observing the rules

138

of life as far as she knew them, and her feet had stopped walking on the exact spot where her road ended—here in this room, with everything gathered around her, and everything in its right place. Her mother had always said that Min was the one who would keep the flag flying no matter what. Min had never in her life been content to sit down and do nothing, but now she was quite content to sit idle. What she saw about her in the room was a job well done. She had not known until now that a job well done creates an eminence that you can rest on.

The room where she sat beside the fire, and where she spent nearly all of her time, had been her workroom in the old days. It was the front room, running the whole width of the narrow old house, and it had a high ceiling and three tall windows. The windows were curtained in thin blue stuff that showed gaps of darkness outside when she pulled them together at night. Min didn't care. Often she didn't bother to pull them but just left them open. The house opposite was all given over to offices, dead at night, and in any case, she told herself, she had nothing to hide. . . . It was only a manner of speaking with her, that she had nothing to hide: she meant that she wasn't afraid to be alone at night with the windows wide open to the night.

There were three doors in the wall that faced the three windows. Two of the doors led into the two smaller rooms of the flat, and the middle door led out into the hall. One of the smaller rooms used to be her fitting room, and the tall gilt mirror was still attached to the wall there. It was Min's bedroom now, although more and more she slept on the narrow studio couch against the wall in her big room. The gas fire was on so much, the big room was always warm. She craved the warmth. She believed the climate in Wexford to be warmer than in Dublin, and she blamed the six years she had spent living with her brother for the colds that plagued her life now. She wore two cardigans and sometimes a shawl as well, over her woollen pullover. She buttoned only the top button of the outer cardigan. The inner cardigan she buttoned from top to bottom. Her pullover had long sleeves, and so she appeared with thick stuffed arms that ended at the wrist in three worn edges—green of the pullover, beige of the inner cardigan, and mottled brown of the outer cardigan, which was of very heavy wool, an Aran knit, Min called it. Her hands were mottled too, brown on pink, and she had very small yellow nails that were always cut short. She was very small and thin, and only a little stooped, and in the street she walked quickly, with no hesitation. She went out every day to buy a newspaper, and she bought food. Bread, milk, sometimes a slice of cooked ham or a tomato. She liked hard-boiled eggs. She nodded to very few people as she went along, and very few people spoke to her. She was a tiny old woman, dressed in black, wearing a scrap of a hat that she had made herself and decorated with an eye veil.

She read a good deal, leaning attentively back toward the weak light given by the lamp she had taken from Delia's bedside table. Before getting the lamp she had relied on a naked bulb screwed into a socket in the middle of the ceiling. She was very saving in her ways— she had never lost the habit of rigid economy, and in fact she enjoyed pinching her pennies. She hadn't amassed a great fortune, but it was the amassing she enjoyed as she watched her wealth grow. She looked at people with calculation not for what she might get from them but for what they might take from her if she gave them their chance. She wasn't inclined to gossip. She admitted to disliking or hating people only to the degree in which they reminded her of a certain type or class. "Oh I *hates* that class of person," she would say, or "Oh that's not a nice class of person at all." Grimaces, winks, nods, and gestures indicating mock alarm, mock shyness, mock anger, and mock piety were her repertoire, together with a collection of sarcastic or humorous phrases she had found useful in her youth. But she saw few people.

In the days when this was her workroom, the furniture had been sewing machines, ironing boards, storage shelves, and, down the center of the room, the huge cutting table that was always having to be cleared of its litter of fashion books and paper patterns, and cups of tea, and scissors, and scraps and ribbons of cloth. Underfoot there was always a field of thread and straight pins. Mountains of color and acres of texture were submerged in that room under the flat, tideless peace of Min's old age. The gas fire glowed red and orange—it was her only extravagance. On the floor was a flowered carpet that had once been the pride of Delia's front sitting room in Dublin, and the room was furnished with Min's souvenirs—Delia's books, Martin's books, Delia's low chair, Martin's armchair. She had Delia's sewing basket, and Martin's framed map of Dublin. On the fourth finger of her left hand she wore Martin's wedding ring. She had slipped it from his dead hand. She told herself she wanted to save it from grave robbers.

If she lifted her eyes from her book she could see, down a length of narrow side street, the sky over the harbor, and if she stood up and walked to the window she could see the water. Below her windows there was the Main Street. The streets in Wexford are very narrow, and crooked rather than winding. At some points the Main Street is only wide enough to allow one car to pass, and the side path for pedestrians shrinks to the width of a plank. There are always children bobbing along with one foot in the street and one on the path, and children dodging and running, making intricacies among the slowly moving bicycles and cars. It is a small, worn, angular town with plain unmatched houses that are dried into color by the sun and washed into color by the rain. There is nothing dark about Wexford. The sun comes up very close to the town, and sometimes seems to be rising from among the houses. The wind scatters seeds against the walls and along the edges of the roofs, so that you can look up and see marigolds blooming between you and the sky.

Min's father had been a good deal older than her mother, Bridget, and he could neither read nor write. He was silent with his vivacious, quick-tempered wife, who read Dickens and Scott and Maria Edgeworth with her children, and he worked at odd jobs, when he could get them. It was the dream of his life to make money exporting pigs to the English market, and to everyone's surprise he succeeded on one occasion in getting hold of enough money to buy a few pigs and rent a pen to keep them in. He discovered at once that possession of the pigs brought him automatically into the company of a little crowd of amateurs like himself, who gathered together in serious discussion of their animals, their ambitions, their hopes, and their chances. The pigs were young and trim and pink and healthy, and they were very greedy. He found he very much enjoyed giving them their food and that he didn't mind cleaning up after them. He began talking about how clean they were, and how well mannered, and how friendly. He marvelled at the way they opened and shut their mouths, and he thought their big round nostrils were very natural-looking, not pig-like at all. He liked to see them lift their heads and look up at him with their tiny, blind-looking eyes. He said a lot of lies had been told about pigs. He interpreted their grunts and squeals as words of affection for him, and after a day or two Bridget told the children their father had gone off to live with the pigs. "He likes the pigs better than he likes his own children," she said. He did like the pigs. He liked having a place of his own to go to, outside the house. He liked being a man of affairs. He began smiling around at his children, as though he was keeping a little secret from them. Martin kept his accounts for him, writing down the number of pigs, the price he had paid for them, and the price he expected to get for them. Once Martin visited the pen and saw the pigs. He was forbidden to go a second time. Bridget said that one lunatic in the family was enough. Martin cried and said he wanted a dog of his own. He knew better than that. There was never a dog or a cat in that house. Bridget said she had enough to do, keeping their own mouths fed.

The great day dawned when the pigs were to be sold. Their father was gone before any of them were awake, and he didn't come home until long after the hour when they were supposed to be in bed. They weren't in bed. They all waited up for him. When he came in they were all sitting around the stove in the kitchen waiting for him. They heard him coming along the passage from the door at the Georges Street side of the house and, as their mother had instructed them to do, they remained very quiet, so that he thought there was nobody up. At the doorway he saw them all and he looked surprised and not very pleased. Then he put his hand in his top pocket and took out the money, which he had wrapped in brown paper, and he walked over to the kitchen table and put it down.

"There's the money," he said to Bridget. "Blood money."

He looked very cold, but instead of getting near the stove to warm himself he sat down at the table and put his elbows on the table and his head in his hands.

"What sort of acting is this?" Bridget asked. "What ails you now, talking about blood money in front of the children. Will you answer me?"

"I'm no better than a murderer," he said. "I'll never forget the look in their eyes till the day I die. I shouldn't have sold them. I lay awake all last night thinking of ways to keep them, and all day today after I sold them I kept thinking of ways I could have kept them in hiding someplace where nobody would know about them—I got that fond of them. They knew me when they saw me."

Bridget stood up and walked to the table and picked up the money and put it into her apron pocket. She was a very small, stout, vigorous woman with round blue eyes and straight black hair, and she was proud of the reputation she had for speaking her mind. She was proud, cunning, suspicious, and resourceful, and where her slow, stumbling husband was concerned she was pitiless. She didn't want the children to grow up to be like him. She didn't want them to be seen with him. She told them she didn't want them dragging around after him. She had long ago grown tired of trying to understand what it was that was holding him back, and so, impeding them all. But tonight, for once, it was clear to her that he was going to make an excuse of the pigs for doing nothing at all about anything for weeks or even months to come. It would be laughable if it wasn't for the bad effect his laziness might have on the children. But he was useful to her around the house, as a bad example. The children were half afraid of him, because they were afraid of being drawn into his bad luck. They were ashamed of him. Min thought anybody could tell by the way her father spoke that he couldn't read or write. Maybe that was the great attraction between him and the pigs. He always seemed to be begging for time until his speech could catch up with his memory, and he never seemed to have come to any kind of an understanding with himself. He always seemed to be looking around as though somebody might arrange that understanding for him, and tell him about it.

On the night he came back so late after having sold the pigs, he was so distressed that he forgot to take off his hat. It was a hat he had worn so long as any of the children could remember, and Bridget told them he had been wearing it the first time she ever set eyes on him. She said she was so impressed by the hat that she hardly noticed him at first. It was a big, wide-brimmed black hat, a very distinguished-looking hat, although it was conspicuous now for its shabbiness. It was green with age, and the greenness showed up very much in the lamplight that night as he sat by the table with his face in his hands, grieving for his pigs. He never went out without first putting his hat on. He was never without it. He depended on it, and the children depended on being able to spot it in time to avoid meeting him outside on the street someplace. When the money was safe in Bridget's deep pocket she reached out and snatched the hat off her husband's head. "Haven't I told you never to wear that hat in the house?" she said.

He looked up at her in bewilderment and then he stood up and reached out his hand for the hat. "Give me back my hat," he said, looking at her as though he was ready to smile.

Min hated her father's weak, foolish smile. Sometimes Martin smiled like that, when he was trying to prove he understood something he couldn't understand. She thought Martin and her father were both like cowards alongside her mother. She wished her mother would throw the hat in her father's face and make him go away. She wished everything could be different—no pigs, no old hat, no struggling and scheming. She wished her mother hadn't snatched the hat off her father's head. She didn't like it when her mother started fighting, and sometimes it seemed she was always fighting. She even went out of the house sometimes and went into the house of somebody who had annoyed her and started fighting there. Then she would come home and tell the children what she'd said and what had been said to her.

One time Bridget's sister Mary came storming into the house. Bridget and Mary hated one another. They began fighting, and then they began hitting one another. Bridget hit the hardest and Mary ran out of the house with her children screaming at her heels. Martin and

Min saw it all and they told their mother she was very brave, but they were frightened. Afterward, when Bridget told the story of the battle, she always ended by saying, "And there was my sister Mary with her precious blood running down her face." Min despised her father, but she hoped her mother wouldn't hit him. She didn't want to see his precious blood running down his face. She began to cry, and when Clare and Polly saw their formidable older sister crying they began crying along with her. Martin stood up and begged, "Give him the hat, Mam, give him his hat!" And then he began crying and lifting his feet up and down as though he was getting ready to run a race.

"You'll frighten the wits out of the children," their father said, and for once in his life he sounded as though he knew what he was saying. "Give me that hat this minute. I'm going out. I'm getting out of here." And he made a grab for the hat, which Bridget was holding behind her back.

She struck out at him. "Don't defy me, I'm warning you!" she screamed. But he dodged her hand and reached behind her to snatch the hat away, and then he hurried out of the kitchen, and they heard the Georges Street door bang after him.

He didn't come home again that night, but he was there in the morning, sitting at the kitchen table, and Bridget gave him his tea as usual. The children looked around for the hat. It was in its usual place, where he always left it, on top of a cupboard that stood to one side of the door that led out into the yard. He used to lift the hat from his head and toss it up on top of the cupboard in one gesture. Always, when he walked in from outside, he threw the hat up, as though he was saluting the wall of the house. And when he was going out, in one gesture he lifted his arm to reach the hat and put it on his head, often without even looking at it. One afternoon, when they were all in the kitchen after school, Bridget decided to play a little trick on their father, a joke. She said he needed a new hat anyway, and that a cap would suit him better. A cap would be better for keeping out the rain—a nice dark-blue or dark-grey cap. He looked a sketch in the old hat, and it was time he got rid of it. Once he was rid of it, he would be glad, and he would thank them all, but there was no use trying to persuade him to get rid of it himself—he would only say no. He could feel loyalty for anything, even an old hat. Look at the way he had gone on about those pigs. He wasn't able to deal with his own feelings, that was his weakness. There are only certain things a person can be true to, but he didn't know that. Once the hat was gone he'd soon forget about it, and it was a shame to see him going around with that monstrosity on his head. She had an idea. They would take the hat down and cut the crown away from the brim and then put the whole hat back on the top of the cupboard and see what happened when he lifted it down the next time he was going out. They got the hat down and Bridget cut the brim away, but she left a thin strip of the velours—hardly more than a thread—to hold the two parts of the hat together when their father lifted it down onto his head. It all happened just as they expected—the brim tumbled down around their father's face and hung around his neck. He put his hands up and felt around his face and neck to see what had happened, and then he took the hat off and looked at it.

"Which of you did this?" he said.

"We all did it," Bridget said.

He held the hat up and looked at it. "It's done for," he said, but he didn't seem angry—just puzzled. Then he went out, carrying the hat in his hand, and they heard no more about it.

Not long after that, Bridget went to see a man she knew who worked in Vernon's on the Main Street, and he arranged for her to buy a sewing machine on the installment plan, and she set about teaching herself to make dresses. Min was the one who helped her mother, so Min was sentenced to a lifetime of sewing, when she had her heart set on going to a college and becoming a teacher. Min wanted to teach. She wanted to have a dignified position in the town, to be appointed secretary to different committees, to meet important people who came to Wexford, and to have numbers of mothers and fathers deferring to her because she had their children under her thumb. But she learned to cut a pattern and run a sewing machine, and the only committee she ever sat on was the Committee of One she established in her own place on the Main Street. She always thought if her father had gone ahead with the pigs, and learned to control his feelings, and if he had cared anything about her, she would have had a better chance. But all the chances in the family had to go to Martin, because he was the boy, and because he had the best brains, and because he was the only hope they had of struggling up out of the poverty they lived in. He was doing very well and turning out to have a good business head when he threw it all away to get married. The best part of their lives ended the day Martin met Delia. Min remembered the nights they all used to sit around talking, sometimes till past midnight. They were happy in those years, when they were all out working, and at night they had so much to talk about that they didn't know where to start or when to stop. Clare used to bring all the new books and papers and weeklies home from the news agent's on the sly for them to read. Polly and Martin had joined the Amateur Dramatics and they were always off at rehearsals and recitations, and they began to talk knowledgeably about scenery and costumes and dialogue and backgrounds. They talked about nothing but plays and acting, and they knew everything that was going to happen—they had all the information about concerts and performances and competitions that were coming off, not merely in Wexford but in Dublin. Min thought the future was much more interesting when you knew at least a few of the things that were going to happen. There was something going on every minute, and it was really very nice being in the swim. People went out of their way to say hello to the Bagots in the street. They had a piano now, second-hand but very good. It was the same shape as their tiny parlor and it took up half the space there. They took turns picking out tunes, but Clare had the advantage over all, because she had had a few lessons from the daughter of a German family that lived in the street for a short time. The Germans knew their music—you had to admit that. Clare felt that with a few more lessons she might have made a good accompanist. They all liked to sing—they got that from Bridget. Martin went off by himself to Dublin once in a while, just for the night, and he always brought back something new—a song sheet, or a book. He always went to a concert, or a play, or to hear a lecture.

Martin and Polly liked to act out scenes, and Min used to get behind them and imitate their gestures until her mother said that she'd rather watch Min than the real thing any day. Min was glad she had found a way to join in the fun. She hadn't as much voice as the others and serious acting was beyond her.

In one way it was a pity their father wasn't there to witness their prosperity, but in another way it was just as well, because he would have done something to spoil things—not meaning any harm but because he couldn't help himself. Min remembered how irritating it used to be to have him hanging around, like a skeleton at the feast. And he got on their mother's nerves, because they all knew he didn't understand a word of what they talked about. And he had a peaceful death. He must have been glad to go. He was never more than a burden to himself and to everybody else.

Min always remembered how stalwart and kind Martin was, comforting her mother after their father's death, and she never could understand how he could be so thoughtful, and make the promises he made, and pretend the way he did, and then run off and leave them all the first chance he got. She always said, "I can get along without the menfolk. They are more trouble and annoyance than they're worth." But she had liked very much having Martin in her life. She liked it very much when he crept upstairs to her workroom in the Main Street and stood outside the door and called out, "There's a man in the house. Will you let me in, Min?" And he would stand outside making jokes while all the women scurried about pretending to be alarmed and making themselves decent. The women used to tease her about having such a handsome brother, and ask her if she wasn't afraid some girl would steal him away. And Min always replied that Martin thought far too much of his mother ever to leave home.

"He's devoted to my mother," she always said, lowering her eyes to her work in a way that showed Martin's devotion to be of such magnitude that it was almost sacred, so that the mere mention of it made her want silence in the room. Silence or an end to that kind of careless, meddlesome talk.

"Martin has no time to spend gadding around," she said to a customer who teased her too pointedly.

148

"Oh, Min, you're a real old maid," the customer said. "Martin's going to surprise you all one of these days. Some girl will come along and sweep him off his feet. Wait and see."

Min told her mother about that remark. "Pay no attention to her, Min," Bridget said. "Martin's no fool. He knows when he's well off. He's too comfortable ever to want to leave home. He's as set in his ways as a man of forty. Martin's a born bachelor."

And of course, the next thing they knew, Martin was married and gone. And then Polly ran off with the commercial traveller, a Protestant, and it turned out he was tired of travelling and wanted to settle down. Being settled didn't suit him either; he was never able to make a go of anything. And Clare married another Protestant, an old fellow who made a sort of living catching rabbits, and he used to walk into the house as if he owned it, with the rabbits hanging from his hand, dripping blood all over Bridget's clean floor.

Min never understood how things could come to an end so fast and so quietly. It was as though a bad trick had been played on them all. There was an end to order and thrift and books and singing, and the house seemed to fill up with detestable confusion and noise. Everywhere you turned, there was Clare's husband or Polly's children, he with his dead rabbits and his smelly pipe and the children always wanting a bag of sweets or wanting to go to the lavatory or falling down and having to be picked up screaming. She couldn't stick any of them, couldn't stand the sight of them. And then Martin moved off to Dublin in anger, telling them that his mother wouldn't let Delia have a minute's peace, that Delia had no life at all in this place, and that there was no future in Wexford anyway. Bridget always said that Delia had ruined Martin's life, and Min agreed with her, except that Min said Delia ruined all their lives. They were a good team before Delia arrived on the scene. The saying was that when a couple got married they went off by themselves and closed the door on the world, but Min thought that in her family what they did was to get married and let the whole world into the house so that there wasn't a quiet minute or a sensible thought left in this life for anybody. Such a din those marriages made, such racket and confusion and expense and quarrelling. She thought it was awful that brothers and sisters could shape your whole life with doings that had nothing at all to do with you. She felt they were all tugging at her, and that her mother was on their side.

When Min got back to Wexford after Martin's death, and got her flat all cleared out and arranged with her new acquisitions—Delia's things, Martin's things, their set of wedding furniture and their books and pictures and lamps—she suddenly realized that she was at home for good. There was nobody left who mattered to her, nobody to disturb her. The family circle was closed. She was the only one left of them. She could only think of them as the crowd in the kitchen at home long ago, and she felt it was they who had finally died, not the men and women they had turned into, who had been such an aggravation to her. She dismissed Delia. Delia was just a long interlude that had separated Martin from his twin, but the twins were joined at the end as they had been at the beginning. Min was Martin's family now.

It was hard to believe that only nine years had elapsed between her father's death and Martin's marriage. Those were the best years. She remembered the day her father died, giving them all a great fright. None of them really missed him. It was a relief not to have to worry about him—an old man not able to write his name, going around looking for work, or pretending to look for work. He couldn't stay in the house. He was gone before any of them got up in the morning, but he was always there to spoil their dinnertime, and to spoil their teatime. And often in the evening he was there listening to them, although they all knew he couldn't understand a word they said. What was most annoying to Min was that he took it for granted he had a right to come in and join them and sit down in the corner and settle himself as though he had something to offer. He had nothing to offer except his restlessness. He always seemed to be on the point of leaving. He even interrupted their conversations to describe long journeys he might take, but he never went anywhere in particular. He just wandered. The restlessness that brought him to Wexford afflicted him till the day he died.

Maybe if he'd learned to read he would have been more content.

He could have learned if he'd wanted to. Bridget would have taught him to read when they were first married, but he said no, he'd wait till the children were big enough and then learn when they were learning. But the children weren't pleased to have him sit down with them when they were doing their homework, and he said himself that he felt in the way. Bridget felt that he was indeed in the way, and that he was depriving the children of a part of something they needed a good deal more than he needed it. Bridget was surprised at how strongly she felt that he should not look into their books. She was afraid he might hold the children back. She despised him, the way he went on talking about his dream of being a sailor, when everybody knew he was afraid of water. Oh, he was a great trial to them all, and toward the end of his life people got to be a bit fearful of him, and even the children seemed to know there was something not quite right about him.

It was probably the same restlessness that made their father queer that drove Martin to go off and get married on impulse, the way he did. He made up his mind in two seconds, and there was no arguing with him. Min would never forget that wedding day, the struggle they had to get Bridget dressed. She was dressed in black from head to toe, as though she was going to a funeral. She generally wore black, very suitable for a middle-aged woman who was a widow, but that day the black seemed blacker than usual. Min made her a new bonnet for the wedding, of black satin with jet beads, and a shoulder cape of black satin, with jet beads around the neck. It made a very fetching outfit, but Bridget spoiled the effect by carrying her old prayer book stuffed with holy pictures and leaflets and memory cards, and she wound her black rosary beads around the prayer book so that the big metal crucifx dangled free. She looked very smart, quite the Parisienne, until she got the prayer book in her hand. Her iron-grey hair was pulled up into a tight knot on top of her head, the same as every day, and the bonnet, skewered with long hatpins, crowned the knot and gave her a few more inches extra height. Min and her sisters wore stiff-brimmed white hats and white blouses with their grey costumes, and Min felt they gave the country wedding a cosmopolitan touch. But of course Clare had to spoil it all by saying to anybody who would listen to her, "We're Martin's sisters. We have the name of being short on beauty but long on brains." Clare always said the wrong thing at the wrong time. It was her way of trying to get on the right side of people. It didn't matter whether she liked a person or not, Clare had to curry favor. She couldn't help herself. You could trust her to make a fool not only of herself but of you. And Polly got fed up and said, "Oh, it's well known that Martin's the beauty of the family." And naturally there was no one at the wedding but friends and relatives of Delia and her family; Bridget invited nobody, because it wasn't at all certain, she said, that Martin would go through with it.

It was true that Martin, with his glossy black curls and his bright-blue eyes, was the beauty of the family. On him the features that were angular in Clare and lumpy in Polly and pinched in Min became regular and harmonious. Before he got married, when they all used to go around together, the three girls took lustre from Martin's face, and that was fair enough, because their faces reflected his so faithfully that one could say, "He shows what they really look like." But after he left them the likeness between them became one they did not want attention for. Instead of being reflections of Martin they became copies of one another, or three not very fortunate copies of a face that was gone. It was as though Martin was the family silver. They all went down in value when he went out of their lives.

Martin's wedding day always opened up in Min's memory as though it had started as an explosion. It was because they had been so full of dread driving out in the car they'd hired, and then, when they arrived in Oylegate, there was everybody ready and waiting, the priests and all the strangers, and candles and flowers, and the terrible sense of being caught up in the ceremony and of having to go on and on and on, knowing all the time that you had no voice in the matter and that it didn't matter what you did now. That was a terrible drive out to Oylegate that day. When they finally succeeded in getting their mother out of the house and into the car, she closed her eyes and kept them closed until she got out at the chapel gates. Up to the last minute she had been hoping Martin would change his mind.

"Martin, I'm asking you for your own good," she said. "Couldn't you put it off till tomorrow? I'll never get used to losing my little son, but I might feel stronger tomorrow." She even offered Martin the fare to go to Dublin and start up on his own, away from all of them, at least until any fuss there was blew over.

"Ah, what's the use of this, Mother?" Min said. "Come on, now, and we'll all go out together with big smiles on our faces, not to let everybody in the town know how cut up you are."

Min was angling for a grateful look from Martin, and she got it. She thought how easily swayed he was, for all his brains. Oh, she could have kept him and given me his chances, she thought. But Min could not really have been accused of holding a grudge against Martin. She could be angry with him, but she couldn't hate him or even dislike him. He was her twin. There should have been only one of us, she thought, in despair, and saw Delia Kelly making free with a part of Min Bagot, who had known more about hard work when she was ten years old than Delia Kelly could ever know. She wondered what Delia really saw when she looked at Martin. She wondered what Delia saw and how much she noticed with those queer, cloud green eyes. All the Bagots had bright-blue eyes, very keen eyes, and they all had coal-black hair, but only Martin's was curly. The Kellys were much fairer in coloring; they didn't look Irish at all, Bridget said. And except for Delia they were all bigger than the Bagots, big and strong-looking, country people. Min felt defeated by them, and she didn't know why. She felt that what mattered to her could never matter a bit to them, and she didn't know what mattered to them. They were friendly enough, and why wouldn't they be, with Martin taking one of the girls off their hands. They're not our sort at all, she thought. East is East and West is West. In a way, it was worse than if Martin had married a girl from a foreign country.

On the way out to the wedding Bridget made Markey go slow. They jogged along, and they were late already; they were late leaving the house. The horse kept flicking his tail as though he was impatient with them. Markey was irritated, because he'd had such a long wait outside the house, but he tried to put a good face on it with philo-sophical chat about weddings and marriages and young men, and on and on. Bridget lost patience with him and asked him whether he charged extra for the conversational accompaniment. Markey was so insulted he started to stand up, which shook the car and made the horse try to turn his head to look back at them, and Polly squealed with fear and asked her mother if she was out to have them all killed with a runaway horse. Bridget replied, "I wouldn't mind."

It was an inside car, and they sat three on each seat, Markey and Clare on one side with Min in between, and, facing them, Bridget and Polly with Martin in the middle. Markey looked at Polly when she spoke, and then he winked at her and sat down without saying a word, and they continued on at the same slow rate until they got to the chapel gate.

Entering Oylegate, they passed the top of the lane that led with ups and downs and various curves to the house where Delia lived. The lane was on their left and on their right there was a prosperous-looking grocery with a public house attached to it. There was a gap between the grocery and a row of whitewashed cottages with thatched roofs. Outside one of these an old white-haired woman sat crouched on a short wooden bench. The narrow door of her cottage stood open behind her, showing how much darkness can gather in a small room on a bright day in June. She had a piece of sacking tied around her waist for an apron, and on her head she wore a man's cloth cap. She smoked a clay pipe and regarded the carful of Bagots with an amusement that was as empty of malice as it was of innocence. Markey touched his hat to her and said, "Fine day, Ma'am." The others didn't notice her—their eyes were ahead to the little knot of people at the chapel gates. Min knew Delia must be waiting, and she thought, One good thing, we've given her a few anxious minutes. Martin looked as if he had felt a twinge of doubt about what he was doing. He said, "I feel like a great stranger all of a sudden."

"There's time yet, Martin," Min said. "We can hurry the horse and go on past them all and go to Enniscorthy and take the train back to Wexford and never see any of them again."

Bridget turned her head and opened her eyes and looked at Martin. "Come on home with us, darling," she said, "and you'll never hear another word about it."

Markey pulled the horse up and said to Martin, "Here you are, now."

Martin stood up, making the little car suddenly flimsy, and he pushed his way between their skirts and jumped out onto the road. It was at that moment, when she heard his feet land on the ground, that the day began whirling in Min's memory. She had known perfectly well that the day would be hateful, but she had not known that it would all be so unnatural, or that she herself would feel worn and dry and unable to manage, because the only thing she wanted was to escape from it all, and she couldn't leave her mother's side. Min had never felt trapped before that day. She felt like a prisoner. She longed to be back in her workroom, where she was monarch of all she surveyed. She didn't like the voices of the people out here in the country. They were hard to understand. She knew they were discussing her behind her back and she tried to let them know she was on to them by the knowing way she looked at them. Martin behaved as though he had forgotten she was alive. She thought it was strange that the world lit up in moments of joy but that everything remained exactly the same when disaster struck. Martin turned into a different person when he jumped out of the car at the chapel gate. From now on there would be nothing more between her and him than running into each other in the street once in a while.

After the wedding ceremony was over, they all drove out a very long way along the road to Enniscorthy, and then off that road onto a rough country road that took them to the Slaney River. Delia's mother's family, her old brother and her three old sisters, lived by the Slaney in a very big farmhouse, whitewashed, with a towering thatched roof. The size of the house and the prosperous appearance of the place impressed Min. Delia's aunts and her uncle were all unmarried, and they had all been born here. Min heard the house was very old, and that the family had been in this lovely spot beside the Slaney for centuries. She and her mother were amazed by the furniture they saw in the parlor and in the rooms beyond the parlor. It was grandeur to have furniture like this.

"This house must have a great upstairs," Bridget whispered to Min, and Min felt very sorry for her mother. The best her mother had been able to do was to struggle out of a district where the people were down and out and into a street where the poor lived—self-respecting people, but poor. And here they were, at Martin's wedding, surrounded by women who were mistresses of farms, some of them owning more than one house, all of them in possession of so many acres, and even the least of them with a firm hold on the house she lived in, even if it was only a cottage, or even a half acre.

Min glanced about. These people out here in the country all belonged to one another and they were related to one another from the distant past. These families went a long way back in time, and they remembered marriages that had taken place a hundred years before. They didn't talk, as Min understood talk. Here in the country they wove webs with names and dates and places. The dead were mentioned in the same voice with the living, so that fathers and sisters and cousins who had been gone for decades could have trooped through the house and through the orchards and gardens and found themselves at home, the same as always, and they could even have counted on finding their own names and their own faces registered faithfully somewhere among the generations that had succeeded them. Min thought of all the dead who had been familiar here, and she wished her name could have been woven into talk somehow. She noticed there were no children in sight—they must have been sent off to play by themselves. There was plenty of room for children here—the farm was big, a hundred acres.

She thought many acres seemed to have been given to the orchard—there was no end to it, and from where she stood the view was more like a forest than like a field of fruit trees, which is what she understood an orchard to be. The ground was uneven, for one thing, slanting this way and that. In her reading, she had always imagined an orchard to be a geometrical place, square or oblong, with the trees spaced evenly. This orchard was wild and looked unknown, as though it had been laid out and cultivated long ago and then forgotten until this wedding day. Min thought of the town of Wexford, of the trees and houses and shops, and she thought of the harbor. Even in the dead of night when people were asleep, the town remained alive and occupied, waiting to be reclaimed in the morning, and the harbor was always restless. The town was always the same, very old and always on the go, with people around every corner, and no matter who they were you knew you had as much right there as they had. Min knew every inch of Wexford and every lift of the water in the harbor, and she thought that even if everybody belonging to her was dead and gone she would never feel lost or out of place as long as she could walk about in the streets she had known all her life. Out here in the country, things were different. You had to own your place—not merely the house but some of the land. And the houses were miles apart from one another, and the families lived according to laws of succession that were known only to them, and people had to depend for recognition on a loose web of relationships, a complicated geneal- ogy that they kept in their heads and reinforced by repetition on days like today when they were all gathered together. Min thought it would be pleasant to walk around the orchard once in a while when the weather was fine, but for a nice interesting walk she would take the streets of Wexford any time.

Min stood on a narrow path that led from the orchard's entrance to nowhere—it seemed to pause and fade under grass somewhere among the trees. There were rounded grassy banks on either side of the path, but they disappeared into high ground beyond the point where the path gave out. Near the edge of the bank, which was not very high, Min's mother sat talking with two of Delia's aunts— Aunt Mag and Aunt Annie. Some of the lads had carried out three kitchen chairs so that the ladies could rest themselves while they looked at the orchard. The ladies talked comfortably, all of them glad to have something to divert them from the marriage that had brought them together. Bridget lost something of her ediginess and made complimentary remarks about the house, and said it was a treat to get out into the country on a day like this. The day grew in beauty, coming in like the tide, minute by minute. There were a lot of butterflies. Min saw a bronze-and-gold one she would have liked for a dress, except that she was not likely to have occasion to wear such colors, and it would be hard to find a design like that anyway, even in the best silk.

157

"Oh, Min has good sense. She is a born old maid. I can always depend on Min," she heard her mother say, but she kept her eyes on the ground as though she was deep in thought. She didn't care what they said and she wasn't going to be drawn into their talk. She thought of wandering off toward the garden. Most of the younger people were there, and she supposed Martin was there too, with Delia at his side. She wondered when Martin and Delia would be leaving for the station. They were taking the train to Dublin. They were going to a hotel there. Well, she wasn't going to the station to see them off. She would get out of that little demonstration, even if it meant she had to walk back to Wexford. She would go on toward the garden now, not to have to listen to her mother talking nonsense to these strangers. There were times when her mother was as bad as Clare.

There was a stone wall around the garden and inside the wall a rich green box hedge that grew very tall and was clipped into a round arch over the narrow gate at the garden entrance. A similar green box arch showed the way into the orchard, but the orchard had no gate. When Min and her mother walked into the orchard earlier, Min had the impression, just for a second, that she was coming out of a dark tunnel, the green box was so thick at her sides and over her head—so dense, you might say—and that they were walking into an unfamiliar, brilliantly illuminated place full of shadows and green caves and a floor of broken sunlight that seemed to undulate before their dazzled eyes. The boys who carried the chairs out from the kitchen were going to put them in an open space where the ground dipped—a very suitable-looking grassy sward, Min thought it. But Delia's Aunt Mag wanted to sit close to a particular tree she said was her favorite, and that is where her chair was placed, with the two other chairs nearby. The boys couldn't get the chair close enough to the tree to suit Delia's Aunt Mag, and when she sat down she moved her body sideways in a very adroit quick way, and then she put her arm around the tree and her face up against the trunk as though she was cuddling it. "I love my old tree," she said. She looked up into the tree, stretching her head back, and she began laughing. "The best parts of the sky show through this tree. Now you know my secret." Min thought she was a bit queer.

She told them the tree bore cooking apples that were as big as your head and too sour to eat. Delia's Aunt Mag and her three sisters, including Delia's mother, all wore long-sleeved, high-necked black dresses cut to show the rigidity of their busts and waists, and the straightness of their backs. They were big women, and the sweeping motion of their long heavy skirts gave them the appearance of nuns. Yes, they looked like women belonging to a religious order. Min thought them very forbidding, all four of them, and she was surprised at the change in Aunt Mag once she got her arm around the tree. Her face got much younger and she looked a bit mischievous. She was a strange, wayward old woman, and Min wondered if Delia took after her. There was something dreamy about Delia that Min didn't really trust.

Thirty years later, when Min was obliged to have Clare locked up in the Enniscorthy lunatic asylum, she remembered Delia's Aunt Mag, and she wondered how many people were abroad in the world who should by rights be locked up out of harm's way. By then, of course, Bridget was dead. Bridget had always said that their father would have ended up in the poorhouse if he had been left to himself. Min thought he might have been very well off in the poorhouse. Maybe that was where his place was. There were people who couldn't manage in the world. But Bridget would never have let Clare go into the lunatic asylum. She always said, "Poor Clare, she takes after her father." Min couldn't see that at all. Their father had been very silent. But Clare never shut up, and all she did was pray for them all. It got on Min's nerves to hear the rosary going day and night. Clare's rabbit-chasing husband was no help at all. He just laughed, probably pleased in his heart to hear the prayers mocked. Min finally lost patience when she found out that Clare had given away every piece but one of the blue-and-white German china their mother had treasured. Only the soup tureen remained, with its heavy lid. Min never got over the loss of that china. She would have gone and demanded it back, but Clare wouldn't tell her who had it. It was gone for good, no hope of ever seeing it again. Clare claimed the china was hers, and that where it went was none of Min's business. Min knew otherwise. Clare didn't live many years after being shut up, and Min brought her

159

body back to Wexford and buried her there where they would all be buried. All but Martin. Martin and Delia were buried together in St. Jerome's in Dublin.

During the years she lived with him after Delia died, Min found Martin very changed. Fifty years with Delia had left their mark on him. He wasn't the brother she remembered. She had seen other men like that—so buried in habit that their lives were worth nothing to them when the wife was gone. Martin would begin to read, and then his hand would sink down, with the book in it, and he would stare over to the side of his chair, as though he was trying to remember something. More likely he was trying to understand something, Min thought. He had had a habit like that when he was young, of staring away at the wall, or at nothing, when things were going against him. He didn't want her in the house with him—that was obvious— but he had to put up with her. She didn't care. She was being loyal to their mother, that was the main thing. He continued to take his walk every day till his legs gave out. He never went out in the garden, never, but every once in a while he would go to the big window that looked out on the garden and he would stand there staring and always turn away saying, "The garden misses her."

Min got tired of that, and one day she burst out, "Oh, she was a good gardener. That is what she had a talent for. She was good at gardening." He turned from the window and he said to her, "What did you say? What was that you said?" She repeated what she had said. She wasn't afraid of him. "I said, she was a good gardener. That is what she was good at, I said." Min was shocked at what he said to her then. "And what were you ever good at, may we ask?" he said. Martin of all people ought to know she had always been good at anything she chose to put her hand to. All the times she came here to visit them, he used to hold her up as an example to Delia. He used to tell Delia that Min could have done wonders if she hadn't been tied to the sewing machine. Martin ought to be ashamed of himself, but she said nothing to defend herself now. He was an old man, wandering in his mind like their father.

160

Martin was restless too, and the more feeble he became, the less he wanted to stay in the house. He said he wanted to see the water again. He wanted to go to the sea. He wanted to walk on the strand. He even talked about paying a last visit to the west of Ireland. He wanted to walk by the Atlantic Ocean once again. He said the air there would put new life into him. Once he began talking about Connemara and Kerry there was no stopping him. He liked to recall the adventures he'd had on the holidays he used to take by himself in Connemara and Kerry long ago. He used to go on long walking tours by himself. He'd stay away for a week at a time. He liked to recall those days when he was on his own. He seemed proud of having gone off on his own, away from this house and from Delia and the children, away from all he knew. He sounded like a conjurer describing some magical rope trick when he talked about how he left the house at such and such an hour, and what So-and-So had said to him on the train, and how he carried nothing with him but his knapsack and his blackthorn stick. Min didn't like hearing about it. She knew his adventures, and she had no sympathy with him. If he was all that anxious to have a change from Delia—and nobody could blame him for that—why hadn't he come to Wexford to see his mother, and to see his sisters, and to go about the town and have a word with all the old crowd? Most of them were still there at that time.

He could have taken a walk about the town with me, Min thought. It would have set me up, in those days, to be seen with him, show off a bit. Many a time he could have come down to see us, but no, he was off to Connemara, or to Kerry, to enjoy another holiday by himself with the Atlantic Ocean. The Irish Sea wasn't good enough for him anymore, and Wexford Harbour was nothing compared with the beauties of Galway Bay. He talked about the wild Mayo coast as though wildness was a sort of virtue, and one you didn't find in the scenery in Wexford. She reminded him that he had once been in love with their own strand at Rosslare, and she described to him how he used to spend half his life out there, riding out on his bicycle every chance he got. Every free minute he could get he spent at Rosslare. He listened to her, but as though he was being patient with her. "I'd be very glad to see Rosslare again," he said when she had finished talking.

Then he gave up talking about Connemara and Kerry, and he began to wish for a day out at Dun Laoghaire. And he said he'd like to have a day at Greystones. And he wanted to go out to Killiney for a day. Which would Min like best? Maybe they could manage it. Min didn't see how they were going to manage it. A whole day out of the house, and no guarantee of what the weather might be like. They might not be able to find shelter so easy in case of a sudden shower. If he got his feet wet there'd be the devil to pay. They had no car, even if they could drive, and it was an awful drag out to Killiney and back on the bus, or on the train, if they took the train. It would be foolish to go to the expense of hiring a car. She didn't see how they were going to do it.

He seemed to let go of the idea, and then one day he said, "Min, do you remember the lovely view of the Slaney from the garden that day? Do you remember how the Slaney looked that day, flowing past us into Wexford? And we all stood looking at it? I thought of the passage of time. I stood there, and I thought for a minute that the garden was moving along with the river. And then later on when Delia and I were at Edermine station waiting for the train to Dublin, there were all the flowers in the station, and the stationmaster laughing at us and talking to us, and the white stones spelling out the name of the station. Delia said an expert gardener must have planted the bed of flowers beside the station house, and the stationmaster said he'd done it all himself, getting the place ready for her. But the garden they had there by the Slaney—that was magnificent. Wasn't it, Min?"

Min remembered standing in the garden, surrounded by roses with big heavy heads, and hearing her mother say that she would like very much to have a bunch of flowers to take back to Wexford with her. They all got bunches of flowers to take home. And there was a bunch of flowers for Markey to take to his wife. The car was filled with flowers, and still the garden looked as though it hadn't been touched.

"That was a grand place they had there," Min said, and she was glad to know that the garden was in ruins now, and that the house stood empty with the roof falling in and that the door there stood open to display the vacant rooms and the cold hearth in the kitchen. "It's all gone now," she said.

"It was a marvellous day," Martin said. "I never forgot what Delia's Aunt Mag said to me. Do you remember—she said the air was like mother o' pearl. Wasn't that a funny thing for an old country woman to say? I wonder what put a thought like that in her head. 'The air is like mother o' pearl today,' she said, looking at me as though we were the same age and had known one another all our lives."

"She didn't look at me that way," Min said. "But I remember her saying that. She was a bit affected, I think—inclined to talk above herself. I didn't care for her. Something about her made me very uneasy."

"Ah, no," Martin said. "Delia was very fond of her."

"Oh, Delia," Min said impatiently. "Delia said the first thing that came into her head. You told her so often enough, to her face, with me sitting here in this room listening to you barging at her. She couldn't open her mouth to suit you. There was no harm in Delia, but she never knew what she said. Half the time she made no sense. There was nothing to Delia."

The minute she finished speaking, she was sorry. She didn't want to start a row. But Martin was silent, and then he said, "Nothing to Delia. That's true. I never thought that. But as Shakespeare says, It's true. It's true, it's a pity, and pity 'tis it's true. Nothing to Delia. Shakespeare was right that time."

"Shakespeare didn't say it. I said it," Min cried furiously.

"You or Shakespeare, what matter now. It's true, there was nothing to Delia. Wasn't she a lovely girl, though."

"Are you going to make a song out of it?" Min said. "What's got into you, Martin?"

She looked at him sitting across the hearth from her. His snow-white curls floated on his head. His narrow face was the same shape as her own face. His blue eyes watched her through his rimless spectacles, and he smiled easily, as though they were discussing something pleasant from the past. She thought of Clare singing "You stick to the

163

boats, lads . . ." that morning when she was being driven off in the car that took her to the asylum. They told Min later that Clare stopped singing quick enough when she saw where she was going. Min wondered if the queer strain that was in Clare had touched Martin and she was glad that she herself was free of it. Martin seemed to follow her thoughts.

"You put poor Clare into the asylum," he said gently.

"She was off her head, driving us all to distraction, trying to give the house away!" Min said indignantly. "What help were you, up here in Dublin, away from all the unpleasantness?"

"Clare was mad," Martin said. "There was nothing to Delia. That's a weight off my mind. I know where I am now. I always knew where I was with her, even though I didn't know what she was, and now I still don't know what she was, and God knows I don't know where I am without her. But there was nothing to her."

"My mother said Delia didn't amount to much," Min said spitefully. "Right from the beginning, she said that."

"Nothing to her. You said it yourself," Martin said. "I'll show you a picture of her, taken when she was sixteen years old."

He pulled himself slowly to his feet, and made his way across the room to the cupboard, which had glass doors on top and solid wooden doors underneath. Behind the glass doors Delia's Waterford glass bowls and her Waterford glass jug shimmered dimly. They had a shelf to themselves. Another shelf held her good Arklow china. Martin bent painfully to open the lower doors, and when they were open wide he reached in and took out a large brown envelope. He pushed the doors shut and made his way back to where Min sat in Delia's chair on Delia's side of the fire. He unfastened the envelope and slid the photograph out carefully, holding it as though it was thin glass. His hands are trembling more these days, Min thought. When the photograph was free, he held it up for Min to see.

"There she is," he said. "That's what she looked like. Look at the hair she had. Who ever had hair like that, that color? Nobody else in that family had hair like that. They said she took after her father. He died young. Look at that, Min."

"That photograph glorifies her," Min said.

"She was very good," Martin said. "I remember that day we got married, I was standing off to myself, looking at the Slaney. I was lost in admiration. I was looking through a gap in the hedge—one of the children had pulled open a place there, to look through. The river seemed very close up to the garden, under my feet. It was very close. Even then the water was eating in under the garden, and the little strand they told me they had there at one time was gone, or nearly gone. I remember I was there by myself—the water was dazzling. I didn't know where I was. I was inside a dream, and everything was safe, I know. The Slaney was very broad that day, and powerful, sure and strong—you know the way it used to be. An Irish river of great importance, the inspector said the day he visited the school. But I felt grand, looking at the Slaney that day. To know it was my own native river and was so, long before I was born. I was standing there like that, when Delia's Aunt Mag came up alongside me. 'I was looking for you,' she said. My God, how well I remember her voice, as if it was five minutes ago. We might still be there. 'I was looking for you,' she said. She saw the break in the hedge. 'Ah, you found a spy hole,' she said. And do you know what she did? She put her arm around my shoulders. She was taller than me—they were big women in that family—and she stuck her face out past me so that she could see what I was looking at. I started to move to the side, to give her room, but she held on to me. 'Stay where you are,' she said. I said, 'I'm in your way.' 'You're not in my way, child,' she said. 'Haven't you more right to stand here than anybody? I only want to have a little look before Willie comes along and finds this hole and starts to patch it up. "The lads have been up to mischief again"— that's what Willie will say. He says they're tearing down the hedge, helping the garden into the river. The river is eating up the garden, you know—if it wasn't for Willie always on guard, we'd be swallowed up.' I said, 'It's great to see the Slaney like this.' 'I have a great fondness for the water,' she said. 'I couldn't be content any place but here where I was born and brought up. I've never spent a night away from this house in my life, do you know that? It's a blessing the day turned out so grand. And nobody was sick or anything. Everybody was able to come see Delia married. The Slaney is in full flood, and the springs of affection are rising around us.' She spoke the truth. The Slaney was in full flood that day."

"That's sheer nonsense," Min said. "How could the Slaney be in full flood on a fine day in June? The Slaney was the same as any other day."

Martin went to his own chair and sat down. "My legs aren't getting any better," he said. "I can't stand on my own feet these days."

"You've tired yourself out making speeches," Min said.

Martin still held the photograph of Delia. He lifted it, to see it better. He's trembling too much, Min thought. She wondered if she could get him to go to his room and lie down. "You're wearing yourself out," she said.

Martin gazed at the shaking photograph. "It's very like her," he said. Then he fitted it back into its envelope, pressing his lips together and frowning, like a foolish old man making an effort to do something that was beyond him.

"I'll do that for you," she said, getting ready to stand up and go over to him.

"You stay where you are," he said, and when he had the photograph safe he placed the envelope on the low shelf under his table. "I shouldn't have stood up so long," he said, and then he took his book from the table and began reading, but after a minute he got up and went out of the room, carrying the book with him. "I'm going to my room," he said without looking at her. "I might lie down for a bit."

Min was glad to see him go. There would be peace now, for a while. She didn't like to see him getting into these states where he talked so much. All that raking up of the past was a bad sign. She would have asked the priest to come in and talk to him, but she knew Martin would fight the priest's coming until he could fight no more. Martin didn't want the priest in the house. His mind was made up to that, and there was no use arguing with him. Min only hoped she would be able to get the priest in time, when the time came. She didn't want her brother dying without the Last Sacraments. She didn't understand Martin's bitter attitude toward the Church. Polly went very much the same way, of course. Min would never forget Polly's blasphemous language when the third-eldest child died, the little one they called Mary. Min was trying to comfort Polly by telling her the baby would be well taken care of in Heaven, when Polly burst out laughing and crying and saying she could take care of her own child better than God and His Blessed Mother and all the saints and angels put together. "They might have left poor little Mary with her own Mammy!" Polly said. "They must have seen the way she was holding on to my hand, wanting to stay with me. They have very hard hearts up there, if you ask me." Martin had never gone that far in his talk against the Church. At least, as far as Min knew he'd never gone that far, but she knew she was going to have to do a bit of scheming to get the priest into the house. "The springs of affection are rising." She didn't like to hear him talking like that. What Min remembered of that day in the garden by the Slaney was that she felt worn out and dried up, and trapped, crushed in by people who were determined to see only the bright surface of the occasion. They could call it a wedding or anything they liked, but she knew it was a holocaust and that she was the victim, although nobody would ever admit that.

She thought they were all very clumsy. It wasn't that she wanted to be noticed. But she knew that any notice she got was pity, or derision. Nothing she could say was right. She was out of it, and nothing could convince those people that she wanted to be out of it. She would ten times rather have been back in Wexford working as usual, but she had to go to the wedding or cause a scandal. Now here they were. Bridget was giving every evidence of enjoying herself, and so were Polly and Clare, and in Min's opinion they were letting the side down. She had been dragged out here like a victim of war at the back of a chariot, and all to bolster Martin up, and he didn't need bolstering up.

She stood outside the garden gate. The children had all vanished and she imagined they had gone to play somewhere by themselves, but suddenly the place was full of children running around, and she thought they must have been having their dinner. Children always had to be fed, no matter what. These children were a healthy-looking lot, fair-haired or red-headed, most of them. Min remembered how black she and Martin had been as children, Martin with his black curls and she with her straight black plait. They were a skinny pair, very different from these children. A little boy ran up to her so suddenly that she thought he was going to crash into her, but he stopped just in time and stared up at her. He was about five years old, a very solid-looking little fellow. His eyes were so blue that it was like two flowers looking at you, and he had a very short nose, and there was sweat on his forehead. His hair was nearly white. He wore a little suit of clothes, a little coat and trousers and a white shirt, and black stockings pulled up on his legs under the trousers. He opened his mouth, but he said nothing, just stared at her. Min gave him no encouragement. She didn't dislike children, but she had no great fondness for them, and she didn't want a whole crowd of them trooping along after him and asking her questions and making her conspicuous. He turned red, and he threw his arm up over his eyes, and peered up at her from under his sleeve, and began to smile. She smiled at him. He was a nice little fellow. She ought to say something to him.

"Are you a good boy?" she asked him. He turned and ran off, flapping his arms at his sides like a farmyard bird, and when he was a little distance away he turned and looked back to see if she was watching him. Then he ran off out of the garden. She didn't see him again.

The next thing she remembered was a moment of terrible unhappiness—it gave her a shock. What happened was that Martin and one of Delia's brothers and a woman she didn't even know came up to her and began talking about the train. They kept saying that it wouldn't do for Delia and Martin to miss the train. Min never knew the woman's name, but she remembered that she made a great fuss, as though she imagined that the day depended on her. There were always people like that everywhere, trying to boss things. She wanted to tell that woman to mind her own business. All these strangers were taking Martin over. They thought they owned him now.

"The springs of affection are rising." It would be those people who would say a thing like that, including everybody in their inspirations, everybody, even people who didn't want to be included. Min thought of that garden. She thought of the green box hedge and the monkey-puzzle tree and the pink and white roses and all the big dark and white star-shaped flowers, and she thought of Delia's Aunt Mag on the kitchen chair under the cooking-apple tree, and she remembered Delia's brothers and sisters and Delia's mother, and the white-haired child. She had forgotten nothing of that glittering day, and she saw it all enclosed in a radiant fountain that rushed up through a rain of sunlight to meet with and rejoice with whatever was up there— Heaven, God the Father, the Good Shepherd, everything everybody ever wanted, wonderful prizes, happiness.

Min knew it was only the transfiguration of memory. She was no fool and she was not likely to mistake herself for a visionary. The lovely fountain was like a mirage, except that in a mirage people saw what they wanted and were starving for, and in the fountain Min saw what she did not want and never had wanted. Why was it nobody ever believed her when she told them she wanted nothing to do with all that hullabaloo? The fortunes of war condemned her to a silence that misrepresented her as thoroughly as the words she was too proud to speak would have done, and she knew all that. Martin's lightmindedness had changed the course of her life, and there wasn't one single thing she could do about it. He turned all their lives around. He cared no more about his mother and sisters and what happened to them than if he had been a stranger passing through the house on his way to a far better place, where the people were more interesting.

He made his mother cry. For a wedding present, Bridget wanted to give Martin the good dining-room set that she had paid for penny by penny at a time when she couldn't afford it. A big round mahogany table and four matching chairs that must have had pride of place in some great house at one time. She kept that furniture up to the nines, polished and waxed till you could see to do your hair in it. But Martin turned up his nose at it. No second-hand stuff for him and Delia, and the mahogany was too big and heavy anyway. He didn't want it. He and Delia went and ordered furniture made just for them; new furniture, all walnut—a bed, a chest of drawers, a wardrobe, a washstand, and two sitting-room chairs so that Delia could hold court in style when they had visitors. Those were Martin's very words. "Now Delia can hold court in style," he said, and never noticed the look on his mother's face. Min noticed the bed had vanished out of the house in Dublin and she was never able to find out what happened to it. But the other things were still there. Above all, the two sitting-room chairs were still there—Martin sat in his own, and she sat in Delia's. She would take the whole lot back to Wexford when the time came. She would bring the furniture back where it belonged. It was never too late to make things right.

In Wexford, in her own flat, she sat in Delia's chair, and sometimes for a change sat propped up with pillows in Martin's big chair, his armchair. It was nice to have the two chairs. The wardrobe and the chest of drawers went into her bedroom, and the washstand into the room she used for a kitchen. Delia's old sitting-room carpet was threadbare, but the colors held up well, and it looked nice on the floor, almost like an antique carpet. And the hearthrug from the house in Dublin looked very suitable in front of Min's old fireplace, where so many girls and ladies had warmed themselves when they came in to be measured for a dress, or to have a fitting.

Against the end wall, facing down the room to the fireplace, Delia's bookshelves were ranged along, filled with Delia's books, and with some of Martin's books. Some of Martin's books Min wouldn't have in the house, and she had sold them. She was glad now that she had never spent money on books; these had been waiting for her. The room looked very distinguished, very literary. It was what she should always have had. She wished they could all see it. There was room for them, and a welcome. There was even a deep, dim corner there between the end wall and the far window where her father could steal in and sit down and listen to them with his silence, as he used to do. There was a place here for all of them—a place for Polly, a place for poor Clare. A place in the middle for Bridget. A place for Martin in his own chair. They could come in any time and feel right at home, although the room was warmer and the furniture a bit better than anything they had been used to in the old days.

The Poor Men and Women

The priest's mother was distracted with herself, wakeful, impenitent, heated in every part by a wearisome discontent that had begun in her spirit very young. She wore herself out cleaning her house, going over her rooms with her dry violent hands, scraping and plucking and picking and rubbing the walls and floors and furniture, and stopping in the middle to clench her fingers tight, tight, tight, but not tight enough, never enough for her, there was no tightness hard and fast enough to satisfy her. Therefore she continued in want.

She was forty-seven, with a gaunt body and a long soft face. Her hair, brown, was done up at the back into a kind of bun or loaf. Her hands were large and hard, like a boy's. By comparison her husband's hands seemed small, because although about the same size they were narrower and better shaped, with soft scrubbed tips. He, Hubert, was an accountant and wore a hard black hat to work. His mouth, smiling and placid in youth, still smiled, but it had withered and darkened, and he wore no mustache over it.

Every Friday morning he gave her the housekeeping money. She would waylay him as he came down the stairs buttoning his waistcoat, ready to leave for the office, and ask him for the money. She would hurry up the three steps from the kitchen, where the dirty breakfast things were, to catch him on the way out. One morning she closed the kitchen door and waited behind it to see what he would do. He put on his hat and took his umbrella and went out of the house without a pause. She thought he might have left the money on the hall table but he had not done that, and she had to ask him for it point-blank in the evening. He smiled pleasantly and took it out of an inner pocket where he had it all folded and ready.

"I thought maybe you didn't need any money this week," he said. "You weren't in the hall this morning."

"I was in the back hanging out the clothes and I mistook the time."

173

She would not give him the satisfaction of knowing he had scored. Still, her spite broke out.

"I might have run short," she cried. "For all you cared there might not have been a penny in the house."

He was sitting reading the evening paper and he bent it backward to look at her.

"Always the martyr, Rose," he said, and she knew he had seen through her trick.

"Is that the only word you know!" she cried. "Martyr, martyr."

"Wife and martyr," he said, without interest. It was an old joke of his.

They were Mr. and Mrs. Derdon, and they had been married to each other for twenty-eight years. He was the senior by five years. They slept in the back bedroom upstairs, and their window looked over their little walled garden, not much different from the other gardens in the terrace, and beyond that over a strip, gray and corrugated, of garage roofs. Beyond the garage yard and off to one side of it were the velvety, emerald green courts of a private tennis club, that were shaded on their most distant side by a dense, irregularly placed wall of strong old trees.

Mr. and Mrs. Derdon shared a double bed made of brass and fitted with a long bolster and a heavy patchwork quilt. The quilt she had made during her school days. The foot of their bed was to the window, which had a cream-colored pulldown blind and white net curtains.

Hubert went to bed about ten every night, she a little later. She got up at seven, he at seven-thirty. On Sundays she got up and went to eight Mass, and came back and got the breakfast in time for him to be at the chapel door by ten.

In bed he wore flannel pajamas, and she wore a flannel nightgown. Their bodies were about the same length, lying down. Neither of them snored, but they both breathed heavily. He huddled himself up into his shoulders and slept on his right side, with his face to the wall. She slept on her back. He slept calmly. She slept desperately, looking as exhausted in sleep as though she had been very sick. Sometimes he would turn the blankets down off him in the night. Then her neck and shoulders would be uncovered, and she would wake up stiff in the morning and frown painfully, first thing. At bedtime she let her hair down into a loose plait. In the morning she pinned it up into its bun without ever looking in the mirror.

She liked to see the changing daytime sky. The night sky had less interest for her; she wanted no mystery, no blackness, no stars, no soft darkness, no curtains, no comfort, no promise of rest. The daytime sky, impassive gray, impassive blue, had won her. That endless off-hand gaze occupied her, and when she raised her eyes and met it, it was in contention, returning stare for stare. She felt she was proud.

The gathering of the clouds enthralled her, whether they were lumped together in little balls or rolls, or separated into great soft masses, or dragged out in streaks. She relished the black congestion of the rain clouds, as they sank helplessly down on their swollen stomachs before bursting. The water poured over her roof, over her soft grass and over the spindly frame of her laburnum tree. It could not touch her. She stayed inside, near a closed window, and watched the glass run down. She said the rain had a smell. To prove it, she opened her kitchen door after a storm and tasted without pleasure the cool steam rising up from her relaxed garden earth. She raised her eyes at the same time to see how the sky drew back relieved and clean.

As long as the light of day lasted, she kept looking up as often as she got the chance. She was ashamed to be seen standing in her garden or in the street looking up. She thought the others might think her queer.

At times, more when she was a young woman than later on, she took a bus out to the country, where she could sit on a wall or lie down on the grass and give herself up to her stare. More often she took a ride on the top of an open tram, and watched the sky slyly from under the brim of her hat, and imagined that she was ploughing a soft furrow in it with the top of her head as the tram rushed her along.

She could see the clouds easily from the windows of her house, but then she considered the neighbors. It disgusted her to think they might see her standing looking out, and perhaps imagine she had some interest in what they did, so she kept away from the windows except when she had to clean them.

One time she was recovering from the flu. She got out of bed for the first time on a Sunday afternoon, and Hubert brought up a comfortable chair from downstairs and put it near the bedroom window, with a low stool before it for her feet. She lay back in the cushions there, lying low in her shawl and in her loose black hair, and passively watched the sky. The next day she felt strong enough to go downstairs, and she never sat there like that again; but years later, all the same, she could recall every line of the sky on that evening when she lay there weak from her sickness.

That evening the clouds met and parted and rose and descended in a way that she never forgot. Their deliberations were delightful, as they touched back to back and front to front, and slid alongside each other, and melted slowly into each other and slowly drew apart, and folded each other with blind white stretchings and opened themselves freely into long uneasy yawns. At last the light behind them grew very strong and seemed about to break through, but to her satisfaction, because she did not trust the brash pure light, it began its final retreat, a long slow fading, until she realized with surprise that she had witnessed the full twilight and that night had arrived before her eyes.

She roused herself unwillingly in the silent room, and a moment later Hubert came in with a tray of tea and toast, and exclaimed to find her awake there in the darkness, with the blind up.

"I should have come sooner," he said reproachfully.

When he snapped on the light, balancing the tray awkwardly on his arm, crouching over it as though anxiety would save it from falling to the floor, she gazed at him with such heavy eyes that he was startled, thinking she had a return of her fever, but it was luxury that lay on her eyelids and wetted her eyes, and she pressed her untidy invalid's hair back with her flat hands and tried to say something; but then her joy, too vague, too large, unshared and already lost, turned to weak tears, and he shook his head in despair and put the tray down on her knees.

"Don't cry till you've tasted it anyway," he said, watching her for a sign of a smile. "Maybe it's not as bad as you think."

"Oh, it's not the tea," she said. "Thanks very much, Hubert. The tray looks lovely."

He pulled the shawl up around her shoulders and sat down on the side of the bed, watching her to encourage her, with his hands between his knees. She touched the teapot with the point of her finger, feeling the hotness of it, and could find nothing to say to him.

He said reluctantly, "What are you worrying about now, honey? You shouldn't be worrying your head about things that don't matter."

"The things that matter to me might not be the things that matter to you. Has that ever crossed your mind?" she cried at once.

The tears ran slowly down her cheeks. She might cry like that for an hour, he knew.

He sighed and got up.

"Well, is the tea all right, at least?" he asked.

"Oh yes. The tea is all right, thanks. You shouldn't have gone to the trouble. I hate to put you to any trouble."

She turned her eyes to the window and looked resentfully out at the darkness, putting her hand against her mouth as though she were appalled.

"In the name of God, Rose, why don't you make an effort to pull yourself together. Come on now, and I'll wrap you up and you can sit downstairs all comfortable till it's time to get back into bed. It'll be a change for you, to get out of this old room."

"You're very nice all of a sudden, Hubert. All concerned about me."

When she looked directly at him her eyes were wild and afraid with malice.

"What ails you? Now what's ailing you?" he cried.

"Nothing ails me, except that I'm sick and tired of being made an excuse of. I hate a hypocrite. If you want to go back downstairs, go on."

"Are you gone mad, or what?"

"Oh yes. The first minute I go against you, I'm gone mad. All I want is to be left in peace."

"Look, bang on the floor if you want anything. I'll be down there if you want anything. I declare to God, I don't know who'd have patience with you."

"I won't want anything," she said dispiritedly.

She was lying back as passive and stricken as though she had not spoken for hours. She did not look up when he went out of the room, but she listened to his steps going down the stairs, and knew a moment later, by a stealthy settling of the house, that he was buried in his armchair by the fire again, with his pipe and the Sunday crossword. She drew a difficult breath of relief and exhaustion and eagerly poured herself a cup of tea.

It was not often that she was sick. She had a strong constitution. She was originally from a country district. She liked to work around in her little back garden, keeping the grass bright and whole, and growing lupins, London pride, wallflowers, freesia, snowdrops, lilies of the valley, forget-me-nots, pansies, nasturtiums, marigolds and roses. She had other flowers, too. In one corner she had grown ambitious, and made a rock garden. In front of the house, in the tiny plot of ground, hardly bigger than a tablecloth, she had peonies, poppies and crocuses, and a diamond of frail new grass. In the window of her front sitting room she had an array of ferns, and in the spring hyacinths and tulips in red pots.

She was drawn to the poor. There was a constant stream of poor men and women, beggars, coming to her door to ask for food or money. She had never been known to refuse anybody at the door. This annoyed Hubert. He said too many came begging, and that they had got to know her, and that they took advantage. He was often known to give money himself, but he protested that with her it was too much of a good thing. She continued to give to whoever came to the door. Two or three came regularly, some came once in a while, and there were some who only came once. There were some who offered needles, pins, shoelaces or pencils for sale. One man brought his wife and a large family of young children, and stood in the street singing heartily before he came to the door. His wife carried a baby in her arms. She took up her stand, glanced at her husband, and murmured timidly along with him as he sang, while the children gazed hopefully about at the blank windows up and down the terrace.

There was one man who had been coming to the door longer than any of the others. This was the man with the crooked hand. He always came at a certain time on Thursday afternoon. Mrs. Derdon took an interest in this poor man because she suspected that like herself he came from the country. He wore a countryman's soft cloth cap and a navy blue serge suit, with the collar of the coat turned up around a scarf in the winter, and in the summer around a shirt that was not clean and that had neither collar nor tie. His left hand hung down at his side. It was sound. His right hand he carried high against his chest, like a treasure, with the shoulder hunched protectively behind it. This hand was deformed, or rather it had been maimed, crushed into a hard veiny lump, the skin of it cured a tender red, a boiled color, very sore-looking. Only the stumps of the fingers were left, and the thumb had folded over into the palm. His eyes, blue, seemed weary enough to die, but still the poor natural mouth, obedient to its end, a mouth so lonely it appeared to have no tongue, opened itself to her in a thin, bashful smile of recognition and supplication. Never mind, never mind, never mind, no blame to you nor to me nor to anybody, the mouth said, only fill me.

This man's humanity, the sin he got with it and its daily punishment, lay so plain on his cheeks that he looked hammered and chilly, like a corpse. From the very beginning he looked to be on his last legs. Once Hubert, glimpsing him from behind the sitting room curtains, said "God help us, if he doesn't look like every poor unfortunate man you ever saw."

There must have been a time when he knocked on all the doors of the terrace, to find out who was open to him, but for years now he had come straight to her. His feet slapped the pavement inoffensively as he went along. He begged in silence. She kept thinking he might say something to her, but he never did. One time she threw a friendly remark after him, and he turned back so confused that she was ashamed. It was a long time before she tried to speak to him again. No matter what the weather was like, he appeared at the door on the dot. Even on the worst days of winter he did not spare her, but stood before her, shivering, dripping, shrinking and smiling, with his cap and his shoulders black from the rain, and his upraised hand turned to flaming glass by the wet and cold.

She often thought of asking him for a cup of tea, but she had not the courage. Besides, if by an odd chance he accepted, and came down into the kitchen, what would they talk about? Of course she could give him the tea and leave him to drink it, there were plenty of little jobs she could find to do to keep her busy, but that would be uncivil, and in any case she knew very well that what she wanted was to talk to him. What she did not know, and could not imagine, was what in the name of God they would talk *about.* She could not be sure of more than a *yes* or a *no* out of him, and the idea of asking him in for a cup of tea and then firing a list of questions at him was even more uncivil than to keep herself silent and busy while he drank it. And she wanted to hear what he had to say. She was curious about what had happened to him in his life, but over and above the ordinary recounting of events and changes, there were things she wanted to hear him talk about that she could not accurately put a name to. There was a lot went through her mind while she worked around the house and garden, alone all day.

Mr. and Mrs. Derdon had one son. Father John Derdon, the priest. He never let her know when he was coming to see her, because he said she made too much fuss getting ready for him. As a rule he came to the house when both his father and his mother would be likely to be at home, but one afternoon he dropped in and found her alone, it being the middle of the week. She shouted joyfully at the sight of him, and began to unbutton his raincoat with her accustomed rough anxiety. He let her pull him out of it, and he struck lightly at her, laughing. She still had not grown accustomed to the black priest's clothes on him. The black cloth gave him a bad air, as though he had stolen in from another century, or out of a bad dream. He was not the same.

He was fair-haired and fair-skinned. His head was long, and he brushed his limp fair hair very smooth around it, making a point of the high square forehead he had. His eyes were light blue, troubled, even aghast light blue. His clothes were the clothes of any priest, and yet there was something thin and jaunty about him, in the tilt of his head, or in one of the conscious, unnecessary gestures he was always making, that belonged more to an actor than to a priest.

"It's long enough since you came near us," she said. "I'll get something for you to eat. Thanks be to God, I have a nice little bit of chicken down there."

He went upstairs to wash his hands and look about his old room. He had the front bedroom, the best. There was everything just the same as ever. There were photographs of him, alone, and with other boys, and other seminarians, and on his ordination day. His mother had got frames for them and placed them on the chest of drawers, on the desk, on the mantelpiece, and around the walls. He heard her come into the room, and he turned, rolling up his shirt sleeves, to smile at her. He turned from her eyes to the gardens outside.

"Look at all the flowers," he said foolishly.

She was close behind him and had taken his hand. She had strong, dry hands; it was impossible to forget their grasp. She captured his limp hand and fell down on her knees to kiss it and force it with her mouth. She petted it along her cheeks, along the hard curve of her jaw, and into her neck, so that he could feel that warm hair springing stiff and strong above it, and the soft hollow of her flesh below. Out of this dream he snatched away and hurled on her, half in laughter.

"Mother, Mother, how often must I caution you. My hands. Mother, my hands."

"Ah, Glory be to God, the consecrated hands," she cried, covering her mouth with her fingers, mocking him with her dismay. She screamed with laughter, squaring back on the floor with her knees spread out and her eyes staring up from under a scalding water of pain and rage.

"I forgot about your hands, son. Wasn't it naughty of me. Wasn't it *naughty*. Such impertinence, touching the almighty hands of a priest. I know you dislike me to touch your precious hands. Oh, I know it very well."

"Not only you, Mother. Anyone, you know very well. A priest's hands, as you know very well—"

"Oh, I know, I know. I knew it before you were born. Don't harp on it now. All I wanted was your blessing, John. That's all, that's all I wanted."

She snapped at him pettishly, scrambling to her feet, very much exerted, brushing off her dress.

"I'll give you my blessing, Mother, a hundred blessings. There's nothing I wouldn't give you, if I had it to give. Do you want me to give you a blessing?"

She straightened like a housekeeper, with her hands under her chest.

"Never mind about that, now," she said sharply. "But hurry yourself and come on down to the table."

She came a step toward him.

She said, "Oh, love, what's the matter with me. I'm all nerves. Don't mind what I say."

"I'm all to blame, Mother," he said hurriedly. "I'll be down before you have the cloth on the table."

From the dining-room window she saw, as she had earlier in the day, that the laburnum tree in the back garden had come to full bloom. She smiled hardly to see it, the generous little tree, a furious yellow, a million blossoms, lifting itself as near to glory as color could bring it. That spindly trunk, thin as a leg, was glorious for them every summer, boiling in the sun with smell and color. She had to smile, knowing the look of the shapely little blossoms, each one as yellow as the next, the petals of them unusually smooth, to see and to rub. Her finger tips tingled, and she caressed the complicated lace of her best cloth spread on the table for John.

She could remember years ago, sitting in this room with John, or sitting above in his own room, talking to him for hours, deriding his father to him, and repeating tales about the shopkeepers she had to deal with, and about the neighbors. Night after night she had followed him upstairs when he went to do his homework. She was constantly being insulted by shopkeepers and hawkers at the door, and by people she came up against in the street, or in the park when she went for a walk. She couldn't measure up to them, she often said, but she wouldn't let them have the satisfaction of getting away with it. Hubert had grown weary of listening and said she would do better to forget these things. Hubert said there was no sense dredging things up, and that if a person as much as looked crooked at her, she felt she had been dealt a mortal injury. He said she was only punishing herself, and that if she wanted to, all right, but she could leave him out of it.

But John was a very sympathetic little boy, always. From his earliest years there had been an understanding between him and her. They used to go together to the park, and they would sit on a bench and stare the people down. If a woman they didn't like looked at them, he would pipe up and ask the woman what she thought she was staring at. That was when he was a child. Later, when he got to be twelve or so, he became very conscious of his dignity, and he used to like to go off and spend long hours in the library. On the day he left to study for the priesthood, she went to the parish church and posted a slip of paper in the petition box, and on the paper she had scribbled with her indelible grocery list pencil, *I want my own back, I want my own back.*

The seasons of the year made little difference to the poor men and women. They came winter and summer, but in the cold weather they looked worse off. A young woman came knocking at the door, a day that was very cold. She had a child with her, a little girl. The woman was bedraggled, servile, and not far from witless. The little girl was eight, very small for her age, with a sly, worn face that had great spirit in it. She wore heavy boy's boots on her little feet, and no stockings. When the door was opened she smiled ingratiatingly, chin out like a monkey. She jumped up and down and rubbed her knees together for warmth. She examined Mrs. Derdon's dress with bright envious eyes, and tried to see past her into the hall.

"What's up there?" she asked rudely, pointing straight up to the bow window that belonged to Father Derdon's room. "Is that a room up there?"

Her mother turned and slapped her sharply in the face.

"She's too forward altogether, ma'am," she said, with an anxious smile. She gave the child a shake.

"Tell the lady you're sorry," she demanded.

The child, whose face was blotched with the marks of her mother's hand, grinned and waved her arms. She seemed to be daring her mother to give her another slap. Mrs. Derdon stepped back into the hall.

"It's my son's room up there," she said. "I'll let you see into it, but you have to come down to the kitchen first of all and let your mother have a cup of tea."

The child refused milk and drank tea with the two women. When she had eaten everything on the table, she got up and began to wander around the kitchen.

"This is mine," she said, touching the chair on which she had been sitting.

She touched the gas stove. "This is mine," she said.

"She's always acting around," her mother said indifferently, keeping a tight grip on the handle of her teacup as it sat in the saucer. "I'm grateful for the tea, ma'am," she added. Since sitting down at the table she had gone sleepy, basking in the warmth of the range.

"This is mine," said the little girl, putting her hand up to the checked curtain at the window.

"Now," said Mrs. Derdon, seeing that the tea was all finished, "would you like to see the room upstairs?"

"I want to see in there," the child said pertly, as they ascended the three steps to the hall. She pointed at the sitting-room door and darted to open it.

"This is mine," she shrieked. "This is mine, this is mine."

She touched the sofa, and the two upholstered chairs, and the table of ferns, and the mantelpiece vases, and the china figures standing neatly spaced on the piano, where they were safe since it was never opened.

"This is mine," she screeched, squatting on the carpet like a big bedraggled frog.

"A lovely place you have, ma'am," the mother said.

"Now we'll go upstairs and see what's there," said Mrs. Derdon, with an awkward, encouraging smile. The child slipped adroitly past her, dodging her hand, and streaked up the stairs as though she knew the house.

When they reached Father Derdon's room, she was standing at the window with her face pressed to the glass and the white curtain bunched out of her way.

"There's the gate we came in at," she cried to her mother, beckoning excitedly. She tugged at her mother's hand. "And there we are, Mam, coming up the street. Look at us out there."

A little girl with long shining ringlets and a pink coat walked up the terrace, and with her a lady wearing a fur scarf on her shoulders.

The child took her eyes from the window to stare at her mother. "The lady there is you, Mam, and that's me with the coat and the curly hair."

The mother gave her a derisive push.

"Go on with you," she said, smiling sheepishly at Mrs. Derdon.

The child pulled violently and cried out with temper.

"There we are!" she screamed. "Look at us out there."

"Shut up your mouth. I'm getting sick and tired of your lies," the mother cried, giving her a hard slap. The child grinned quickly up at them before the tears had gone back into her eyes.

"You slap her too often altogether," Mrs. Derdon protested.

"Ah, you know yourself it's the only way to get any sense into them, ma'am. This one's got into the habit of telling lies, and trying to show off every minute. She's got too impudent."

The child left the window and bounced on the bed.

"This is mine," she said, a trifle subdued, winding her long dirty fingers over the end rail. Her fingers were like twigs, her eyes were sharp as thorns; there was neither love nor shame in her smile. She lay back on the bed and stretched her ragged arms across the white quilt.

"That's a brooch you have on you," she said inquisitively.

Mrs. Derdon was wearing an elaborate brooch of gold and blue enamel. She put her hand up and touched it.

"I'll tell you what I'll do. I'll give it to you for a present," she said quickly, and she leaned over the end of the bed and pinned the brooch to the child's dress, where it lay heavily among the rags as though it had been thrown away. The child glanced triumphantly at her mother who, observing Mrs. Derdon for the first time, wore a startled and distrustful air. The poor woman grew jumpy, fearful that the gift might be regretted before they had time to get out of the house. She urged the child to get up off the clean quilt, and to stop annoying the lady, and to say thanks for the lovely brooch. The child, an experienced conspirator, hopped obediently off the bed and was downstairs in the hall before her mother had finished blessing their benefactor.

Mrs. Derdon regretted her brooch before she had the door well shut on the two hastening backs. It was a brooch that had come to her at her mother's death. Her mother had worn it day and night, and used to leave it lying among her hairpins when she went to bed. It had been familiar to the eyes of her long-dead father. Some of her own earliest memories depended on it, and now she had set it adrift. The only thing remaining to her out of the past was the patchwork quilt on the bed above.

It was not the first time she had given in haste like that, and regretted it. John's baptismal shawl, that she had spent long months making, had gone the same way, to a poor woman at the door, and a pair of new gloves of her own, another time. Sometimes she wondered if she hadn't spent her whole life giving away the things she valued the most, and never getting any thanks for them. There seemed to be no limit to what people would take. She had often said to John that if you gave people an inch they'd take an ell. Hubert, hearing her, remarked that she had only herself to blame since she forced the ell down people's necks. Hubert then asked John if he could tell him what an ell was, and they both laughed.

Out of all the poor men and women who had come to the door all the years she had been living in the house, there was not one she had ever run across in the street up to the time she met the man with the crooked hand on O'Connell Street bridge, on her way to buy new sheets.

The suburb in which she lived was about a twenty-minute bus ride from the center of the city, but she seldom made the journey except for a special reason. The bus run came to an end at the near side of the Liffey, and she was glad of that, because it gave her an excuse to walk across the bridge and get a look at the river. There were crowds of people about. Mrs. Derdon was wearing black-laced shoes that she had polished before leaving the house, and the soles were so thin that she was made aware of the hard pavement at every step. Being still a countrywoman, she was accustomed to clearer streams, but she still was anxious for a sight of the dark forceful Liffey in her high bed. As she walked across, feeling the cold push of the wind on her face, she spotted the man with the crooked hand, stealing along near the parapet, guarding his hand before him. As they came face to face, he raised his eyes and saw her. At the sight of her his face expressed such surprise and welcome that she put out her hand and began to speak to him, but he recovered himself and touched his cap and passed her by. She continued on, and a few seconds later turned to look for his back in the crowd, but he had disappeared. She stepped out of the stream of people, and looked searchingly all the length of the bridge, but he had really gone. She thought he must have been in an extraordinary hurry, to get out of sight so fast.

Going home on the bus, she thought with satisfaction that the encounter on the bridge would give her the chance she had been looking for, to strike up a conversation with him. She made up a dialogue between them:

SHE: I saw you on the bridge the other day.

HE: Yes. I saw you, too. I would have spoken, but you seemed to be in a hurry. How strange that we should meet.

SHE: Not at all. It's a small world.

Or she might say:

"You've been coming to the door a good many years now."

No, that would never do. He might think it was a hint to stay away. She might take a joking tone, asking him what was the great hurry he was in on the bridge. Well, the words would present themselves when the time came.

That Thursday, when he did not turn up at the door at the usual time, she became uneasy and spent the rest of the afternoon waiting for him in the front sitting room. At five-past-six Hubert turned the corner of the terrace and walked slowly up to the house, as he did every night. When she saw Hubert she realized that the man with the crooked hand would not be coming at all. She went and took his money off the hall table, where she had left it early in the day, and put it into a cup on the kitchen dresser. Hubert let himself in with his key, and finding the tea not ready, not even started, he inquired in surprise if he was early. He compared his watch with the clock on the sitting-room mantelpiece, and called cheerfully down to the kitchen that he would like a boiled egg.

When they were sitting at the table having their tea she told him about meeting the poor man on the bridge, and about him not turning up at the door.

"You probably frightened the life out of him," Hubert said placidly. "Running up to him like that with your hand out, especially since there was nothing in it."

"But I was only going to say a word to him; there's no harm in that."

"All you have to do is look at that man's face, for God's sake. A man like that has no use for your fuss and talk, Rose. Give him whatever you want to give him, but let him alone."

"But he looked so glad to see me, Hubert. I never saw anybody in my life so glad to see me."

"He'll know better next time. How was he to know you'd want to embrace him."

"Hubert, the way you always put me in the wrong."

"Rose, honey, you bring it on yourself. You will not get it through your head that in this life you have to learn to leave well enough alone."

After a moment of silence, to give him time to take the top off his egg, he said consolingly that he was sure the man with the crooked hand would be back, as soon as he got over his fright. He added that if the man *didn't* come back, it might be just as well, since it would save them a little money. He was only joking, saying that. He meant no harm.

On the following Thursday the man with the crooked hand appeared at the door as he always had, in the middle of the afternoon. As soon as she saw him she knew that he would not say anything. She had made up her mind that she would leave him alone unless he said something of his own accord. He held up his sore hand and gazed at her without a sign of the radiance that she had seen in his face on the bridge. If he felt ashamed that he had given himself away, there was no sign of that either. He was too far gone in want. He was gone out of reach. It gave her great comfort to see him at the door again. She never afterward thought of getting him into conversation, and after a while she forgot the curiosity that had devoured her concerning him, although she continued to watch for him, and for the others who came.

The Rose Garden

Mary Lambert, an Irish shopkeeper, was left a widow at the age of thirty-nine, after almost ten years of marriage. She was left with two children—Rose, seven, and Jimmy, two. As far as money was concerned, she was no worse off than she had been, since it was she who supported the family, out of the little general shop she kept.

Her husband, Dom, first showed his illness plainly in the month of October, but he lingered on, seeming to grow stronger at Christmas time, and died early in February, at about seven in the morning. Mary and a young priest of the parish, Father Mathews, were in the room with him when he died. Mary had Dom's comb in her hand, because he had asked her, one time during the night, to comb the hair back off his forehead. The comb was broken in half. She was accustomed to use the coarse-toothed half for her own hair, which was long and black. The fine-toothed half had been suitable for his lifeless invalid's hair. Even in health his hair had been fine and lifeless, but now it just looked dusty against the pillow. Father Mathews, who was anxious to get away, asked Mary if she would like him to send the woman next door up to see her, but she shook her head violently, and said that she'd be forced to make an exhibition of herself soon enough, at the wake and the funeral, and that for the time being she'd just as soon be left alone.

She sat down beside the bed, on the chair she had carried up from the parlor the morning she first had to send for the doctor. It was a straight-backed mahogany chair with a black horsehair seat. Ordinarily there would be no chair in the bedroom. She had expected the doctor to sit on it, but instead he had put his black bag down on it. She stared at the room. The room, its walls, its dull color, its scarce furniture, its dust, its faded holy pictures, its bad, sick aspect, disgusted her, and the body on the bed was a burden she could not bear. The seat of the little parlor chair was hard under her. There was no rest in the room. Her legs were tired. One leg was shorter than the other, so that she had to walk crookedly, leaning forward and sideways. The exertion she had to make gave her great power in her right leg. She wore long skirts, and tall black boots laced tightly in but leaving her knees free. The laced boots were very solid and hard-looking, as though the feet inside them were made of wood. The feet inside were not made of wood. She had a great feeling in them, and in all parts of her body.

She was big, with a narrow nose, and a narrow-lipped mouth too small for the width of her face. She was well aware that she was ugly and awkward, especially from the back. She said that the crookedness in her legs came from climbing up and down the twisted stairs of this house, in which she was born. The house was really two corner houses that had been knocked into one. The houses had been thrown together, and the staircase twisted determinedly from one house up into the other, although it was impossible to tell whether it had been built from the first floor up or from the second floor down, the construction of it was so ungainly and uneasy. The stairs thrust its way, crooked and hard, up through the house, and some of its steps were so narrow it was difficult to find a foothold on them, and some started wide and narrowed to nothing at the other side, so that they could not be depended on going down as they could going up. It was a treacherous stairs, but no one had ever been known to slip on it, because it forced respect and attention, and people guarded themselves on it.

Mary knew it very well. She knew where the hollows were, and the worn places, and where it turned, and where it thinned off. It changed appearance as the hours of the day went by, and looked entirely different at night, in lamplight or candlelight. In the wintertime the bottom step was always slippery with wet feet in from the street. In the summertime the top step was warmed by sun from a stray window, and when Mary was a child she often sat there for hours, because her father spent all his time in the shop downstairs. Her mother had died at Mary's birth. Her father, a retired policeman, was sixty when she was born. In his shop, in what had once been the parlor of one of the houses, he sold bread, sugar, milk, tea, cigarettes, apples, penny sweets, and flour. The milk stood in a big tin can on the counter, with a dipper hanging from the side of it, to measure out the customers' pints. The same farmer who brought the milk brought eggs and butter. There was a sack of potatoes slumped open against the wall in one corner.

From the time she could walk, Mary hung around the shop. Because of her crippled leg, she often was allowed to miss school. Sometimes her father would sit her up at the window, which was filled with sweets, pencils, and cigarettes, and she would play with the sweets, and eat them, and look at the other children playing in the street or looking in at her. She grew fat, and by the time she was twenty she had settled into a wide, solid fatness. She developed a habit, in the street, of whirling around suddenly to discover who was looking at her ungainly back, and often she stood and stared angrily at people until they looked away, or turned away. Her rancor was all in her harsh, lurching walk, in her eyes, and in the pitch of her voice. She seldom upbraided anybody, but her voice was so ugly that she sounded rough no matter what she said.

She was silent from having no one to talk to, but she was very noisy in her ways. When she was left in charge of the shop, she would push restlessly around behind the counter, and move her hands and feet so carelessly that by the time her father got back, half the stock would be on the floor. There would be cigarettes, spilt sugar, toffees, splashes of milk, and even money down there by her boots. Her father would get down on his knees and scramble around, picking up what could be picked up, and cursing at her. She cared nothing for what he said. She had no fear of him, and he was not afraid of her, either. He had forgotten her mother, and she had no curiosity about her mother.

The counter in the shop was movable, and when she took charge, she made her father help her shove it forward from where she sat, to give her legs plenty of room. She always went to early Mass, when the streets were deserted, so that no one would have a chance to see her awful-looking back and perhaps laugh at her. During the whole year, there was only one occasion, apart from Mass time, when she willingly went outside the door, and that was in June, on the Feast of the Sacred Heart, when the nuns of the Holy Passion, who occupied a convent on a hill over the town, opened their famous rose garden to the public.

These nuns lived and had their boarding school in a stately stone building surrounded by smooth green lawns and spiky boxwood hedges, and hidden from the world by towering walls and massive iron gates. Except for the one day of the year when they threw open their garden, they had very little to do with the daily life of the town. Their rose garden was very old. An illustrious family had once owned these grounds, and it was they who had marked out the garden, and dug it, and planted it, and enjoyed it, long ago, years before the nuns came. Surrounded by its own particular wall, and sealed by a narrow wooden door, the garden lay and flourished some distance behind the convent, and it could only be reached by a fenced-in path that led directly out of the back door of the convent chapel. Only the nuns walked there. It was their private place of meditation, and because of its remoteness, and also because of the ancient, wild-armed trees that dominated the old estate, it could not be viewed from any window of the convent.

All during the year the nuns walked privately in their garden, and only opened it to ordinary people the one day. It is a pity that everyone in the world could not be admitted at one time or another to walk in that garden, best of all to walk there alone, it was so beautiful in the sun. The nuns walked there undisturbed, apparently, and still it was altogether a stirring place, warm red, even burning red, the way it filled the nostrils and left a sweet red taste in the lips, red with too many roses, red as all the passionate instruments of worship, red as the tongue, red as the heart, red and dark, in the slow-gathering summertime, as the treacherous parting in the nuns' flesh, where they feared, and said they feared, the Devil yet might enter in.

Even if there wasn't much of a summer, even if the sun was thin, what heat there was somehow collected itself inside the high stone walls of the garden. The walls should have been covered by a creeper, a red leaf or a green leaf, but instead they were bare and clean, warm under the hands. The tall walls of the garden were uncovered and stony under the sun, except for one, the end wall, that was covered by forsythia, yellow at its blooming time, on or about Christmas Day. Then the forsythia wall would stand up overnight in a brilliant tracery of true yellow, a spidery pattern of yellow, more like a lace shawl than a blanket, but none the less wonderful for that. Of course, the forsythia showed to great advantage then, with the rest of the garden a graveyard.

When word came of the yellow blooming, the nuns would come out together in twos and threes, with their black wool shawls around their shoulders, to witness the miracle. It was a great pleasure to them, confused in their minds with the other joys of Christmas, and they compared the delicate golden flowers to "baby stars in the canopy of heaven" and "tiny candles lighted to honor the coming of Our Lord." All of their images were gentle and diminutive, and they spoke in gentle excited voices, crying to each other across the frosty air, "Sister, Sister, did you hear what Sister just said?" "Sister, have you noticed how clear and silent the air is this morning?"

But with the coming of June the roses arrived in their hundreds and thousands, some so rich and red that they were called black, and some so pale that they might have been white, and all the depths between—carmine, crimson, blush, rose, scarlet, wine, purple, pink, and blood—and they opened themselves and spread themselves out, arching and dancing their long strong stems, and lay with lips loose and curling under the sun's heat, so that the perfume steamed up out of them, and the air thickened with it, and stopped moving under the weight of it.

Mary loved that burning garden. From one summer to the next, she never saw the nuns, nor did she think of them. She had no interest in them, and there was not one among them who as much as knew her name. It was their urgent garden she wanted. She craved for her sight of the roses. Every year she made her way up the hill, alone, and went into the garden, and sat down on a stone bench, covering the bench with her skirt so that no one would offer to share it with her. She would have liked to go in the early morning, when few people would be there and she would have a better look at the garden, but she was afraid she would be too much noticed in the emptiness, and so she went in the middle of the afternoon, when the crowd was thickest.

Once she had seen the garden in the rain. That was the year she remembered with most pleasure, because the loitering, strolling crowd that usually jammed the narrow paths between the rose beds was discouraged by the weather. She had the garden almost to herself, that time. Wet, the roses were more brilliant than they ever had been. Under the steady fine rain the clay in the beds turned black and rich, and the little green leaves shone, and the roses were washed into such brightness that it seemed as though a great heart had begun to beat under the earth, and was sending living blood up to darken the red roses, and make the pink roses purer.

Another year, the day turned out cold, and all the roses stood distinctly away from each other, and each one looked so delicate and confident in the sharp air that Mary thought she could never forget one of their faces as long as she lived. She had no desire to grow roses herself, or even to have a garden. It was this red garden, walled, secret, and lost to her, that she wanted. She loved the garden more than anyone had ever loved it, but she did not know about the forsythia that came in December to light up the end wall. No one had ever told her that the forsythia bloomed, or how it looked. She would have liked the forsythia very much, although it could not have enveloped her as the roses did. All during the year, she thought backward to her hour in the garden, and forward to it. It was terrible to her, to think that the garden was open to the nuns and closed to her. She spoke to no one about her longing. This was not her only secret, but it was her happiest one.

Mary's father used to take in lodgers—one lodger at a time because they only had one room to spare. The lodgers were men who visited the town from time to time, commercial travellers. Sometimes a man would take a job in the town, and stay with them for a few months or so. Once they had a commercial traveller who made a habit of staying with them every time he came to town, and then he got a job selling shoes in a local shop, and stayed almost a year. When he left for good, to take a better-paid job with a brother-in-law who had a business in Dublin, Dom Lambert came, and moved into the lodger's room.

Dom was a meek and mild little draper's assistant, with wide-open, anxious blue eyes and a wavering smile. He was accustomed to watch his customers vacillate between two or more rolls of cloth, and his smile vacillated from habit. He had small, stained teeth that were going bad. When they ached, he would sit very quietly with his hands clenched together and ask for hot milk. He told Mary that his skull was very thin. He said it was as thin as a new baby's, and that a good crack on it would be the finish of him. He was always stroking his skull, searching for fissures. He was afraid a roll of cloth might tumble down on him off a shelf and he would die with customers in the shop. Even a spool of thread, he said, might do considerable damage.

Dom dressed neatly, in dark draper's suits. He was most particular about the knot of his tie, and he wore a modest stickpin. He was proud of his small feet, and polished his shoes in the kitchen every morning, assuming various athletic positions according to whether he was wielding the polish brush, the polishing cloth, or the soft finishing brush. He brushed his suits, too, and did his nails with a finicky metal implement he carried in his pocket. He tidied his own room, and made his bed in the morning. Every morning he left the house at eight-thirty, and he returned at six-thirty. He liked to read the paper at night, or play a few games of patience, or go for a stroll. He went to bed early, and in the morning descended looking brisk and ready to do his day's work. Still, his color was bad, and he often had to hammer his chest to dislodge a cough that stuck there.

When Dom had been living nine years in the house, Mary's father died very suddenly, one night. Mary was lying awake in the dark, and she heard her father's voice calling loudly. She found him hanging half out of bed, holding the little white stone holy-water font, that he had dragged off its nail in the wall.

"The font is dry," he cried to her. "Get me the priest."

He waved his dry fingertips at her, that he had been feeling in the font with, and died. Dom helped her to raise him back against the bolster. She lifted the dry font from the floor and upended it over her father's forehead.

"There might be a drop left in it," she said, but there was nothing.

The font was sticky and black on the inside, and when she put it to her nose it smelled like the room, but more strongly.

"He went very quick," Dom said. "Are you going to call the priest?"

"I don't know what I'm going to do," she said. "I meant to fill the font with holy water this coming Sunday."

"Are you going to shut his eyes?" Dom asked, pressing his hands painfully together, as though he already felt the cold man's lids resisting him.

"No," she said. "They'll be closed soon enough."

She took up her candle and walked back to her room, her white flannel nightdress curved and plunging around her large body. She got into bed and pulled the clothes up around her.

"Good night now," she said to Dom. "There's no more to be done till morning."

She raised herself on her elbow to blow out the candle.

Dom said, "Are you not afraid to be in here by yourself, with him dead in there like that?"

"He can't do anybody any harm now," she said. "What ails you, Dom? Are you trying to tell me you're afraid of a poor dead man?"

"I'm afraid of my life," Dom said. His shirt, which was all he had on, shivered in the leaping candlelight.

"Let me stay in here a minute," he said.

"Are you afraid he'll come after you, or what?"

"Let me kneel up here against the bed till it gets light!" he begged. "I'm not able to go back into that room by myself, and pass his door. Or put on your clothes, and we'll go together to call the priest."

"I'll do nothing of the sort," said Mary. "If you won't go back to bed, throw that skirt there around your shoulders, or you'll catch your death."

She dragged her great black skirt from where it hung over the end rail of the bed, and flung it to him. Then she blew out the candle and fell asleep, although she had intended to stay awake. As the room grew light, she woke up, to find Dom huddled against her in sleep. He was lying outside the covers, with his nose pressed against her shoulder, and her skirt almost concealing his head. As she watched him, he opened his eyes and gazed fearfully into her face. He started to close his eyes again, to pretend he was asleep, but thought better of it.

"I only wanted to get in out of the cold," he said.

"That's all very fine," said Mary, "but don't go trying to get on top of me."

"Oh, God, I wouldn't do the like of that!" Dom said.

"I don't know, now, there was a man lodged here before you came. He weighed a ton, it seemed like."

"A great big man!" said Dom, who was shocked.

"The same size as yourself. Maybe not even as big, but he was like lead. He came in here two nights running, just before he went off for good. The first night he came in, it was black dark. I thought for a minute it was my father getting in the bed with me, and then didn't I realize it was the commercial traveller. The next night, in he came again. I let on in the morning nothing had happened, and so did he."

"And did you not tell your father?"

"Why would I tell him?"

"Maybe it was your father all the time."

"It wasn't him. It was the commercial traveller, all right. If nothing else, I'd have known him by the feel of the shirt he had on him. Anyway, my father hadn't that much interest in me."

"Lord have mercy on him—your poor father, I mean," said Dom, who was growing uncomfortable and ashamed as the increasing light disclosed them to each other.

Mary had run out of small talk, but because she wanted him not to go, and because she had as much ordinary courage as any other human being, she spoke up. "I'll move over," she said, "and you lie in here beside me. As long as you're here, you may as well settle yourself."

The bed in which they lay, like all the beds in that house, was made with only one sheet, the undersheet. There was no top sheet— only the rough warm blanket, and then another blanket, a thinner one, and on top of all a heavy patchwork quilt. The beds were high up off the floor, and made of brass, and all the mattresses sagged. The floors sagged, too, some sliding off to the side, and some sinking gently in the middle, and all of the rooms were on different levels, because of the way in which the two houses had been flung together. There were no carpets on the floors, and no little mats or rugs. The bare old boards groaned disagreeably under the beds, and under Mary's feet, and under Dom's feet.

Mary and Dom got married as quickly as they could, because they were afraid the priest might come around and lecture them, or maybe even denounce them publicly from the pulpit. They settled down to live much as they had lived before Mary's father died. Most of their life was spent in the kitchen. This was a large, dark, crowded room set in the angle where the two houses joined, and irregular because it took part of itself from one house and part from the other. The only window in the kitchen was small and high up, and set deep in the thick old wall. It looked out on a tiny, dark yard, not more than a few feet square, in which there was an outhouse. In this window recess Dom kept his own possessions—his playing cards, a pencil, a bottle of blue-black ink, a straight pen, a jotter, a package of writing paper with matching envelopes, and the newspapers. After Rose got big enough to be with him, he began to keep a tin box of toffees there, and he liked to play a game of coaxing with her, with a toffee for a prize. The toffees were not of a kind sold in Mary's shop, which offered only cheap loose sweets, sold five for a penny, or even eight or ten for a penny. Rose liked those sweets, too, but she liked the tin-box toffees in the bright twists of paper best of all.

Rose was her father's girl. Everyone said so. Mary said so, more often than anyone else. She said it bitterly to Dom, and mockingly to Rose, but once she had said it she shut up, because it was not to start a quarrel that she said it but only to let them know that she knew.

Jimmy, the little baby, was Rose's pet. Dom liked him, but Rose clung to him, and when he fretted she would hang over the side of his cradle and talk to him, and dangle toys in front of him, and try to make him laugh.

Mary and Dom were not long married when Mary began to nag at him to give up his job at the draper's. Her reason for doing this, which she could not reveal to him, was that she could not bear to let people see him smile. She was unsmiling herself, as her father had been, and she believed that people only smiled in order to curry favor. People like herself, at any rate. "People like us," she was always saying, "people like us," but she did not know what she meant, unless it was that the rest of the people in the world were better off, or that they had some fortunate secret, or were engaged in a conspiracy in which she was not included.

Dom's smile did not disturb her until one afternoon she went over to the draper's to buy the makings of a dress for herself. She did not want him to wait on her, because she was ashamed to let him know how many yards it took to go around her, but she watched him with a customer, and it was then, against his own background of trying to sell and trying to please strangers, that she saw the history of his hopeful, uncertain smile, as he eagerly hauled down rolls of cloth and spread them out for inspection. After that day she gave him no peace till she got him out of his job. She told him that he could take over the running of her shop, and Dom liked that idea, because he had always wanted to be his own man, but he was just as anxious-faced behind her counter as he had ever been, and she gradually edged him back into the kitchen, out of sight.

She only wanted to take care of him, and protect him from people. She had known from a child that if she asked she would get, because of her deformity. She had always seen people getting ready to be nice to her because they pitied her and looked down on her. Everyone was inclined to pity her. How could they help themselves? She was an object for pity. The dead weight of her body, that she felt at every step, was visible to all the world. She almost had to kneel to walk. Even her hair was heavy, a dense black rug down her back. She was always afraid people might think she was asking for something. She always tried to get away from people as quickly as she could, before they got it into their heads that she was waiting for something. What smile could she give that would not be interpreted as a smile for help? In fact, that is what she thought, herself—that if she smiled at them it would only be to ingratiate herself, because she had no other reason to smile, since she hated them all. If she had said out loud why she hated them, she would have said it was because they were too well

200

off, and stuck up, and too full of themselves. But she never would give them an opening for their smiles and greetings, and she came to feel that she had defeated them, and shut them all out. To have rescued Dom's weakness from their sight, and from their scornful pity—that was a triumph, although she was unable to share it with him, since she did not know how to explain to him that while she thought he was good enough, other people would never think him good enough, and therefore she had to save him from them, and hide him behind herself.

To pass the time, Dom began to do odd jobs around the house. Once in a while he took a broom and swept the upstairs rooms. Sometimes he got a hammer and some nails and wandered around, trying to tighten the floor boards or the stair boards, but the rigid, overstrained joints and joinings of the house rejected the new nails and spat them back out again before the tinny glitter had even worn off their heads. He often spent the whole day at a game of patience, and when Mary came back out of the shop to see about their middle-of-the-day meal, he would be sitting hunched over the kitchen table, with the cards spread out in front of him and a full cup of cold tea, left over from his breakfast, at his elbow. When Rose got to be big enough, he liked to tell her about the days when he was a draper, and he collected a few reels of thread, and some needles and pins, and bound some pieces of scrap cloth into neat rolls, and the two of them would play shop for hours.

Before Rose was born, Dom scrubbed out the old cradle in the kitchen, and polished it till it shone. The cradle had been there for Mary, and after she grew out of it it was used as a receptacle for old and useless things of the house. Before Dom scrubbed it, Mary cleared it out. It was a huge wooden cradle, dark brown and almost as big as a coffin, but seeming more roomy than a coffin, and it had a great curved wooden hood half covering it, that made the interior very gloomy. It stood on clumsy wooden rockers. There was no handle to rock it by. Mary remembered her father's hand on the side of it, and the shape of his nails. She had slept in the cradle, in the kitchen, until she was four, or nearly five. Her father had looked after her himself, so the cradle was left within easy distance of the shop. She could well remember her father looking in at her. Sometimes a woman would look in at her, but her father did not encourage visitors. He had the idea that all women were trying to marry him, or to get him to marry again, and he kept them out.

If Mary made a sudden movement, or jumped around, the cradle would rock far to the left and far to the right on its thick, curved rockers, and she knew that no power on earth could stop it until in the course of time it stopped itself. If she tried to clamber out, the cradle would start its deliberate plunging, right, left, right, left, and she would cower down with her face hidden in the bottom until the cradle was still under her again. She was always afraid alone in the dark bottom of the house. Her father slept upstairs. At night she would see his face, darkened by the candle he held aloft, and then the very last thing she would see was his shadow falling against the shallow, twisting staircase.

In the cradle, when she set about emptying it, Mary found a dark-red rubber ball with pieces torn, or rotted, out of it, and some folded, wrinkled bills, and a new mousetrap, never used, and a pipe of her father's, and two empty medicine bottles with the color of the medicines still on the bottoms of them, and a lot of corks, big and little, and a man's cloth cap, and a stiff, dusty wreath of artificial white flowers from her own First Communion veil, and a child's prayer book, her own, with the covers torn off.

When they were first married, Dom used to walk to early Mass with Mary on Sunday, but after a while he began making excuses, and they got into the habit of attending different Masses. She continued to go to the early Mass, and he would go later. When Rose started to walk, he took her with him. He would wash her, and do her hair, and see that her shoes were polished, and then she would give Mary a kiss goodbye and run off down the street after him.

One weekday morning, about a year before he died, Dom gave Mary the shock of her life. Instead of lying on in bed, as he usually did, he got up at seven-thirty, and shaved himself, and did himself up the way he used to in the days when he was at the draper's. When she saw him go out, she said nothing, but after a few minutes she locked the shop door, and went back and sat down at the kitchen table. People came knocking, but Mary paid no attention, and when Rose came to stand beside her she pushed her gently away. At three in the afternoon, she told Rose to mind the baby, and she put on her hat, and her Sunday coat, and went out looking for Dom. There was no sign of him on any street. At the draper's she stood and looked in, but he was not there. The man who had taken his place was only a youngster, very polite and sure of himself, she could see that. It occurred to her that even if she met Dom, she'd hardly know what to say, so she turned around and went home.

"Oh, I thought I would never see you again!" Mary cried.

Dom did not look up, but Rose looked up from her bead box.

Dom asked, "What put that idea in your head?"

"I thought you'd gone off on me."

"Can't a man even go for a walk now, without the house being brought down around him?"

"I was full sure you were gone for good, when I saw you walking out of the door this morning. I didn't know what to do. I didn't know what I was going to do."

"Where would I go, will you tell me that?"

"Is that all you have to say to me, after the fright you've given me—that you have no place to go to? Is that the only reason you came back?"

"Rose," he said, turning from the stove. "Give us a look at the little necklace you're making there."

Mary got the tea ready. When they were all sitting at the table, she said loudly, "I suppose it was on Rose's account you came back. You were afraid I wouldn't take good enough care of her, I suppose?"

"That's a nice thing to say in front of the child," he said.

"You take her part against me."

"Somebody has to take her part."

"And who's to take my part?"

"Aren't you able to look after yourself?"

"I wish to God she'd been born crooked the way I was. There'd have been no pet child then."

"God forgive you for saying the like of that!" he shouted, and he jumped up out of his chair and made for the stairs.

"God has never forgiven me for anything!" she screamed after him, and she put her head down against the edge of the table.

Rose slipped around the table and put her arm around Mary's neck. "I'll mind you, Mammy," she said.

Mary looked at her. Rose had her father's uncertain smile, but on her face it was more eager. Mary saw the smile, and saw the champion spirit already shining out of Rose's eyes.

"Who asked you to mind me?" she said. "Go on and run after your father. You're the little pet. We all know that. Only get out of my sight and stay out."

Rose got very red and ran upstairs. Mary got to her feet and lumbered up after her. Dom was lying on the bed with Rose alongside him.

Mary said, "Nobody's asking you to stay here! Nobody's keeping you. What's stopping you from going off—and take her with you. Go on off, the two of you."

"I wish to God I could," Dom said. "I declare to God I wish I could, and I'd take her with me, never fear."

That night, as they lay in bed, Dom said, "Mary, I'm terrible sorry about what I said to you today. I don't know what got into me."

"Oh, Dom, never mind about it," she said. "I gave you good reason."

Encouraged by these words, she put her arms around him. With his body in her arms, she was comforted. That is what she wanted—to be allowed to hold him. She thought it was all she wanted—to be allowed to hold a person in her arms. Out of all the world, only he would allow her. No one else would allow her. No one else could bear to let her come near them. The children would allow her, but their meagre bodies would not fill her arms, and she would be left empty anyway.

As Dom fell into sleep, his body grew larger and heavier against her. Holding him, she felt herself filled with strength. Now if she took her arms from him and stretched herself out, she would touch not the bed, and not even the floor or the walls of the room, but the roofs of the houses surrounding her, and other roofs beyond them, far out to the outer reaches of the town. She felt strong and able enough to encircle the whole town, a hundred men and women. She could feel their foreheads and their shoulders under her hands, and she could even imagine that she saw their hands reaching out for her, as though they wanted her.

In all her life, there was no one had ever wanted her. All the want was hers. She never knew, or wondered, if she loved or hoped or despaired. It was all the one thing to her, all want. She said every day, "I love God," because that is what she had been taught to say, but the want came up out of herself, and she knew what she meant by it. She said, "I want the rose garden. I want it," she said, "I want to see it, I want to touch it, I want it for my own." She could not have said if it was her hope or her despair that was contained in the garden, or about the difference between them, or if there was a difference between them. All she knew was what she felt. All she felt was dreadful longing.

When Father Mathews found that Mary wouldn't allow him to get one of the neighbors up to take his place at the bedside, he didn't know what to do. It seemed unchristian and unfeeling to leave her alone, but he was dying to stretch his legs and get a breath of fresh air, and above all he wanted to get away out of the room. He decided that the most likely thing would be to talk his way out, and so he said again what he had said before—that Dom's fortitude was an example to the whole parish, and that he had left his children a priceless legacy of faith and humility, that the priest and the teachers at the school would have a special interest in the bereaved little ones, and that Dom's soul was perhaps even at this instant interceding for them all before the throne of the Almighty.

"What about me, Father?" Mary asked.

"What was that?" asked Father Mathews.

"What about me, Father? That's all I'm asking you."

"Oh, Mrs. Lambert, your heart is heavy now, but have no fear. God will comfort you in His own time and in His own way."

"I might have known you wouldn't give me a straight answer, Father."

"Mrs. Lambert, Our Blessed Lord enjoins us to have *faith*," Father Mathews said gently.

He was developing a headache out of the endless talk, in this airless room, with no sleep all night, and he was beginning to wonder if he hadn't already done more than his duty.

Mary stared indifferently at him, and he hesitated to speak for fear of provoking her into some further rigmarole. After a few seconds the rising silence in the room pushed him to his feet almost in spite of himself, but at the door he turned and whispered that he would speak to Father Dodd immediately about the arrangements for the funeral, which would probably be on Thursday. He then said that he would call back later in the day to see how she and the children were getting along, and he added that Father Dodd himself might even find time to come—just for a few minutes, of course, because he was greatly taken up at this time of the year, between Christmas and Easter.

As he felt his precarious way downstairs, he couldn't help rehearsing a question that he knew he would never ask, because it would seem uncharitable. The question was what sort of a woman is it could sit beside her husband's body, with her unfortunate children in the next room, and think only about herself?

An Attack of Hunger

Mrs. Derdon had the face of a woman who had a good deal to put up with. At this moment, she was in the kitchen, putting up with getting the tea ready for herself and her husband. Her husband's name was Hubert. She was putting up with setting out the two cups and the two plates and the two saucers and so on, two of everything. There was no need now to set the table for more than two people. The third place was empty, and the third face was missing. John, her son, had left the house and he would not be back, because he had vanished forever into the commonest crevasse in Irish family life—the priesthood. John had gone away to become a priest.

The thought that Mrs. Derdon was not putting up with (because she had never faced it) was Oh, if only Hubert had died, John would never have left me, never, never, never. He would never have left me alone. . . . But she was putting up with the secret presence of this thought in her spirit, where it lived hidden, nourishing itself on her energy and on her will and on her dwindling capacity for hope.

She had never made up her mind about anything. Decision was unknown to her. Her decisions, the decisions she made about the food she put on the table and about various matters about the house, were dictated by habit and by the amount of housekeeping money Hubert allowed her. Hubert was a frugal man. It was not that he meant to be unkind, but he was careful. He had calculated that the household could be run on such and such a sum, and that was the sum he produced every Friday morning. He always had it ready in his hand, counted out to the penny, when he came downstairs on his way to work. Every Friday morning she waited at the foot of the stairs and he handed her the money without a comment.

Before, when John was still at home, he would sometimes be there when Hubert gave her the money and then the two of them, she and John, would exchange a look. On her part the look said, "You see the way he treats me." And John's look said, "I see. I see." They agreed that Hubert knew no better than to behave the way he behaved. This knowledge, that Hubert *knew no better,* formed the foundation and framework of the conspiracy between them that made their days so interesting and that gave a warm start to most of their conversations. They were always talking about Hubert. There was no need for Hubert to do anything unusual to get himself talked about—not that he ever did do anything unusual or out of the ordinary. All he had to do was go about in his habitual way, coming in after work and sitting down with the paper and then sitting down to his tea and going to bed and getting up in the morning and doing all the things he always did in his routine that never varied and that at the same time never became monotonous. There was something insistent about Hubert's daily procedure that called attention to itself, as though he was behaving as he did on purpose, and as though at any moment he might drop the charade and turn and show them the face they both suspected him of possessing, his true face, the face of a *villain,* the face of a man of violence, capable of saying and doing the most passionate and awful things, shocking things. He kept them in a constant state of suspense, and they were always exchanging looks when he was in the house, even when they only heard him walking about upstairs. But Hubert maintained his accustomed countenance, mild, amiable, complacent, burnished with his natural distrust of everyone and of every word anyone said, and held in firm focus by his consciousness of the worth of his own judgment.

Now, with John gone, there was no one for Mrs. Derdon to exchange glances with. There was no one for her to look at, except Hubert, and Hubert could turn into a raving lunatic, frothing and cursing, and there would be no one to see him except herself. There was no one to look at her, and she felt that she had become invisible, and at the same time she felt that in her solitude she followed herself about the house all day, up and down stairs, and she could hardly bear to look in the mirror, because the face she saw there was not the one that was sympathetic to her but her own face, her own strong defenseless face, the face of one whose courage has long ago been petrified into mere endurance in the anguish of truly helpless self-pity. There was no hope for her. That is what she said to herself.

There was no hope for her inside the house. Her entire life was in the house. She only left it to do her shopping, or to go to Mass. She went to the early Mass on Sundays (she and John had always gone together) and Hubert went to the late Mass by himself. It had been many years before John left since the three of them had gone for a walk together, and she and Hubert never went anywhere or visited anyone. He never brought anybody from the shop to his house, to spend an evening or to see the garden in the summertime or anything like that. From the time they were married, Hubert had shown that he distrusted her with money—he said she had no head for money—and as the years went by he had come to distrust her presence everywhere except in the house. In moments of nervousness— with the priests at John's school or at occasional gatherings they had attended in the early days of their marriage—Hubert had noticed that his wife turned into a different person. In the presence of strangers, she sometimes took to smiling. One minute she would produce a smile of trembling timidity, as though she had been told she would be beaten unless she looked pleasant, and then again, a minute later, there would be a grimace of absurd condescension on her face. And before anyone knew it, she would be standing or sitting in stony silence, without a word to say, causing everybody to look at her, and wonder about her. And if she did speak, she would try to cover her country accent with a genteel enunciation, very precise and thin, that Hubert, from his observation of the world, knew to be vulgar. He felt it was better to leave her where she felt at ease, at home. Somehow she wasn't up to the mark. She wasn't able to learn how things were done or what to say. She had no self-confidence, and then, too, her feelings were very easily hurt. If you tried to tell her anything she took it as an insult. Hubert thought it was very hard for a man in his position to have to be ashamed of his wife, but there it was, he was ashamed of her. And he was sorry for her, because her failure was not her fault. She had been born the way she was. There was nothing to be done about it.

When Mrs. Derdon turned away from the mirror that reflected her hopelessness, she saw the walls of her house, and its furniture, the pictures and chairs and the little rugs and ornaments, and the sight of all these things hurt her, because she had tried hard to keep the house as it had been when John left it, and the house was getting away from her and away from the way it had been when John lived in it, when she and John lived in it together. There seemed to be no way of controlling the change that was taking place in the house. Two of the cups from the good set had slipped out of her hands for no reason at all, when she was taking them with the rest of the good china to wash, and now her arrangement of glass and china in the glass-fronted cupboard in the back sitting room looked incomplete. There was a big stain on one of the sofa cushions in the front sitting room and she did not know how it had got there. One of the children from the neighboring houses threw a ball into the front garden and crippled a rose tree that had grown in safety for years there. She herself in a fit of despair removed a little pile of newspapers and magazines and pamphlets that John had left on his desk in his bedroom. She had not thrown them out, they were on the bottom shelf of the cupboard in the kitchen, but even if she carried them back up to his room they would not be exactly as he had left them, and they would never again look just as they had when he had last seen them. And she bitterly regretted pulling out the rusty little wad of newspaper that he had been accustomed to stuff underneath the door of his wardrobe to keep it tightly shut. She had thrown it into the fire and fitted a new bit of newspaper under the door. Nothing would ever be the same.

There were worn patches in the stair carpet that had appeared suddenly after all these years, and the wallpaper around the hall door had begun to peel badly and something would have to be done about it. Even the dust seemed to have found new places to settle, or to be settling in different places, and it seemed to her that in sweeping up the dust, day in and day out, all she was doing was sweeping up the time since John had left—more dust every day, more time every day—and she began to think that all she would do for the rest of her life was sweep up the time since John left. The dust got on her nerves. It made her feel sick to see the way it was there every day, new dust, but looking just as old and dirty as the old dust her mother used to be always sweeping up and throwing away, long ago in the country town where she had been born and brought up. As surely as the clock ticked and had to be wound up again, the dust made its way around the house, and it got on her hands. It got on her hands and on her wrists, and no matter how hard she scrubbed her nails, there always seemed to be some of it left there under her nails. She told herself that she had the hands of a servant. Hubert's hands were soft and neat but hers were big and rough, as though she were a person who worked with her hands. She had often caught Hubert looking at her hands when she was dealing with the food on her plate and looking at her when she put food into her mouth. She always ate a lot of bread and she thought he must sometimes wonder how she could eat so much bread or why she ate it so fast. She couldn't help it—she felt there was something shameful about eating so much of bread or of any food, but she wanted it and she ate it quickly and there were times when she felt her face getting red with defiance and longing when she reached for the loaf to cut another slice. One thing, she had stopped putting jam on the table since John left. She and John both loved jam but Hubert had no taste for it at all. When John was at home, she used to make jam—raspberry, damson, and gooseberry—but what they both liked best was the thick expensive jam that came in jars from England. It was best not to put the jar on the table. Hubert never questioned the expense, but he would sometimes take the jar in his hand and turn it around and read the label very slowly and then put the jar back again. Even if the jar was nearly full he would tip it and look into it. One time he had said, "It's a good idea, having something to read on the table." John had laughed out loud, and she had thought it heartless of him to laugh when he knew that his father was only looking for another way to make little of her.

Every day of the six months that had passed since John left to become a priest, Mrs. Derdon realized that he was gone and that he was not coming back, and every day she thought she was only realizing it for the first time. The realization was alive and it possessed her completely and directed all her actions, one minute telling her to sit down and the next minute telling her to stand up immediately without delay and without reason—except that the power of the realization was reason enough, because it directed her every minute now, and controlled her and kept her going and gave its own mysterious organization to everything she did. If it had not been for this realization, keeping at her all day, she would not have known what to do next and she would have done what she really wanted to do, which was to crawl in under the bed and put her face down on the floor and sleep. She kept wanting to lie down on the floor. The realization that John was gone and would not be back took different shapes inside her, but it always stayed in the same place, just under her chest, in the center, between her ribs. Sometimes it went away altogether and she felt empty, and then, at these moments, she would go and get herself something to eat, but almost always when she had the food before her, the realization would come back again and she would feel sick at the thought of eating. At times the realization would go away altogether, or seem to go away, and she would become terribly excited and run to the front windows *knowing* that John was coming home, that he was at this exact moment walking along the street carrying his suitcase, and that she would have to wait only a minute or so to get her first sight of him, coming around the corner from the main road. But of course he wasn't coming, and he wouldn't be coming, and the excitement inside her would flatten out and stupefy her with its weight, and her disappointment and humiliation at being made a fool of would be as cruel as though what she had felt had really been hope and not what it was, the delirium of loss.

Out of this recurrent delirium two daydreams had grown, long, peaceful, pleasant dreams, always expanding, always increasing in their progress and in their detail, alike in only two respects—in their soothing monotony and in their endings. Both dreams ended at the moment when John became her own again, only hers.

In the first dream, John came back. In this dream, she was watching for him at the front window, and when he turned the corner she went to open the front door for him, but then she wanted him to have his first glimpse of her framed in the window and she went back and stood in the window (holding the net curtain aside with her hand) until he saw her and smiled. When he got to the low gate that opened backwards into her tiny front garden, she hurried into the hall to open the front door wide so that he could walk straight in and put his suitcase down in the hall, to get rid of the weight of it—he had never been very strong. Then they would look at each other and she would say, "I knew you'd be back, John." Or she might put it this way: "I knew you'd come back to me, John." And he would say, "You always knew what was best for me, Mother." They would go down to the kitchen, where she would have the table set and ready, everything he liked on the table. He would eat something, and then he wouldn't be able to hold it in any longer, what was bothering him, and he would say, "But Mother, didn't you mind when I went away? Didn't you miss me at all? You never said one word, not a word." Those words would tell her what she wanted to know— that he had noticed her heroic silence, how she hadn't said a word when she realized he was going off and leaving her, how she had kept back all the reminders and reproaches that she had been longing to let loose at him, and that he understood how brave and unselfish she had been, letting him go off free as she had done. There would be no end to the amount they would have to say to each other, once that point in their reunion had been reached. They would drink an awful lot of tea. She would tell him that she had missed him terribly. She would say that she had been dead lonely, even crying with the need of him (she would remind him that his father wasn't much company), but that she had been only thinking of his own good, and only wanting the same thing that she had always wanted—what was best for him. And that she had never imagined not letting him go in peace, as long as his heart was set on it.

But it was all a dream. He wasn't coming back at all, and she bitterly regretted having let him go as easily as she had done. She had been so sure he would come back that she hadn't said a word, getting her sacrifice ready for him to admire. There were many things she could have said to him, the evening when he finally spoke to her, telling her that it was all settled and that his mind was made up and he was going. At that point, his mind wasn't made up at all. She could have stopped him with a word. She could have reminded him that he was an only child and that his duty was to his father and mother. And he had no faith at all in himself; it was only because of her prayers and encouragement that he had got through his examinations his last year in school. She had carried him all his life, and now he imagined he was going to be able to get along without her. And how did he think he was going to be able to get along in a house full of men—priests and students—all better ready for the priesthood than he was, and all better up on the world than he would ever be. They would look down on him. He would be very glad to get away out of that place and come back to her.

But he wasn't coming back, there was the realization of *that* stirring in her again, and it would start giving her orders again, taking charge, and she would obey it, getting up and sitting down and walking, here and there and never easy anywhere, because the only ease that could come to her would come if she could just get down on the floor and put her face in the corner and let her mind wander away into sleep, but into a different, roomy kind of sleep, very deep and distant, where there was no worry and where her mind would not be confined in dreams but could float and become vague and might even break free and sail off up like a child's balloon, taking her burden of memory with it.

There was not only nothing nice, there was nothing definite at all to remember, only a great many years that had passed along and were now finished, leaving only the remnants of themselves—herself, Hubert, the furniture; even the plants in the garden only seemed to hold their position in order to mark the shabbiness of time. All the things that she had collected together and arranged about the house could blow away, or fall into a pitiful heap, if it were not that the walls of the house were attached on both sides to the walls of the neighboring houses. There was nothing in sight that rested her eyes and nothing in her mind except the realization that John was gone, and the necessity of obeying the dictates of that realization in order to continue, even for a little while longer, her flight from it. The realization badgered her and she had to obey it and at the same time pretend she didn't notice it. There was only one time of day when she ignored it, when it was weakest and she was strongest, when they first woke up in the mroning, she and it, and it barely stirred, and what it told her then was that she should go back to sleep at once and not wake up at all. But she ignored it then, because it was a mat-

214

ter of pride with her to be up and dressed and downstairs before Hubert opened his eyes, and to have his breakfast ready and waiting for him and part of her housework done by the time he came down to the kitchen.

It was terrible having nobody to complain to; not that she had anything actual to complain about, but it was terrible having no one to talk to. John had always been a great confidant, and the Blessed Virgin had been a great consolation to Mrs. Derdon all her life, the One she had always turned to for help and advice and understanding, but she could hardly turn to the Blessed Virgin now, when it was the Blessed Virgin who had taken John away. It was not the Blessed Virgin herself who had taken John away but his own devotion to the Blessed Virgin, but it all amounted to the same thing in the end, and between the two of them she felt she was left out and left behind.

John had always been a very holy little boy. He was always going over his collection of holy pictures and sorting them out and looking at the holy medals he had and strewing his little saints' relics all over the house. He had a habit when he was small of wandering into the kitchen with a holy picture in his hand and standing looking at it until she asked him to tell her what he was thinking, and it was always some holy thought, surprising in such a young child. Sometimes he would prop a holy picture in front of his father's place at tea, prop it against the sugar bowl or the milk jug so that his father would see it when he was sitting down to the table. But Hubert put a stop to that one evening by putting the holy picture—it was of St. Sebastian being tortured—on his bread and smoothing it with his knife as though it was butter and then biting it. He tore off a corner of it, along with some bread, and he sat there chewing it and smiling what he called his happy-family-man smile. John cried and Hubert pretended he didn't know what he had done wrong and she said, "Hubert, I'm scandalized at you." Then she cried, too, because Hubert said, "I'm fed up with the two of you."

The second dream she had of John was a very simple one. It was more a vision than a daydream, and all that really happened in it was that she saw his grave. In the second dream, he had not gone away at all, he had died. It had not been his fault, after all. He had not wanted to leave her. In the second dream she visited his grave every day, and sat beside it for hours, and wore black, like a widow. When she cried everybody sympathized with her, because who has a better right to cry than a woman who has lost her only son. Everyone marvelled at her devotion when they saw her going to the grave every day, rain, hail, sleet, or snow, no matter how she felt, bringing flowers and leaves and ferns according to the season of the year. She would mourn John constantly, and even Hubert would hardly have the heart to reproach her for her long face.

This evening, getting the tea for herself and Hubert, she was arranging Christmas holly and ivy on John's grave when she heard Hubert's key in the lock, and then the closing of the front door. Now Hubert would go into the back sitting room and light the fire there and sit beside it until she called him to tea. Sometimes she lighted the fire in the back sitting room and sat there herself. This afternoon she had hardly left the kitchen. They burned coal. They kept the coal and the firewood, together with her garden things, in a small wooden shed that was attached to the back of the house. Every day she carried in two scuttles of coal, one made of iron, for the kitchen stove, and one made of brass, for the sitting room. She sometimes wondered, when she lifted the coal, if Hubert had any idea how heavy it was. Now, crossing the kitchen to turn the gas from low to high under the kettle, she saw the brass scuttle standing alongside the stove, filled and ready. She had carried it in and then forgotten to carry it up to the sitting room. She was irritated with herself for forgetting to bring it up and leave it ready for him when he came in. It was a bad sign— to start to be forgetful, to start forgetting things that ought to be done. Well, she wouldn't give him the chance to come down and ask for it, or to watch her clamber with it up the three steps that led to the hall and the sitting room. He said his heart was bad and that that was why he couldn't do much of anything that would exert him. But it had been the same when he was forty and thirty and younger. He loved to be waited on.

She took the handle of the brass scuttle in both hands and carried it with difficulty across the kitchen and up the stairs and into the back sitting room. She found that Hubert had already put a match to the fire, which she had laid ready with paper and wood and a few bits of coal that she had dotted across the top of it. He was fanning the small blaze with his open newspaper, his evening paper. He turned when she came in, and the newspaper billowed toward the fire and then blazed up. Hubert dropped the newspaper in his fright. Mrs. Derdon ran and got the poker and pushed the newspaper into the grate. Scraps of the blazing newspaper floated out and around the room. While she was stamping them out, Hubert raced off to the kitchen shouting, "That's all right, that's all right. I'll get some watter!," and then he came dashing in with the hot kettle that he had snatched off the stove and poured a stream of water all over the fireplace. The fire, already tamed, gave up at once and turned into black soup, which streamed out between the bars of the grate and down onto the tiles of the hearth, where it settled into puddles of various sizes and shapes.

Mrs. Derdon sat down in a chair and began to cry helplessly. She hid her face behind her hands and then she pushed her hands into her hair and pushed her hair about and then she wrapped her arms about herself and rocked in grief. Disorder had finally prevailed against her and there was nothing further she could do. She could kill herself over this room now and it would never look the same. This was the worst thing Hubert had ever done, and John had not been here to see it, and she would never be able to find the words to describe it to him. She glared at Hubert, who was watching her with dislike and alarm.

"Oh, what will I do!" she cried.

"Oh, for God's sake, pull yourself together," Hubert cried. "What ails you? No harm done."

"What ails *me?*" she cried. "It's what ails *you,* coming in here and setting fire to the grate with nothing in it but paper. You couldn't come down to the kitchen and ask me for the coal. Oh, no, not you. You'll wait till it's brought up to you and burn down the house in the meantime."

"You shut up!" Hubert shouted. "Do you hear me? Shut up before I say something you won't want to hear."

"First you drive my son out of the house and then you try to burn the place down around my ears, around my *ears!*" Mrs. Derdon screamed.

"I suppose I should have tried to burn the place down while he was still in it!" Hubert shouted. "It was you gave me a fright, clumping in here with your Mother of Mercy face and banging the coal down on the floor so that I dropped the paper. It was you did it, with your spite and your bad temper."

She sat forward in her chair and spoke, but Hubert could not catch her words through the storm of hatred that blinded, deafened, and choked her, and that shook her so that when she leaned forward to fling her accusations more heavily toward him, she tumbled out of her chair and onto her hands and knees on the floor. She dragged herself back up into the chair as though she was dragging herself up onto a rock out of the sea, and then she sent Hubert a look of terrified appeal that vanished at once under a witless, imploring, craven smile.

Hubert saw the smile and knew that she was silenced. "Well, now you've made a proper fool of yourself!" he cried, "falling and flopping all over the room and crying over a few spots on the linoleum. Come on now and cheer up and stop making a show of yourself over nothing."

"Over nothing is it!" she cried. "If John was here, he'd tell you. John would stand up for me. John knew how hard I worked. Working and slaving to keep the place nice and you call it nothing. But what do you care! You never cared about me and you never cared about him and you ended up driving him out of the house." She stopped because Hubert had leaned back in his chair and was smiling at her.

"I'm going to tell you something, Rose," said Hubert. "You won't like it but I think it's time you learned. Do you know who really drove John out of the house?"

Mrs. Derdon said nothing.

"Answer me," said Hubert.

"I thought you did," Mrs. Derdon said.

"You thought what it suited you to think," Hubert said. "No, I

218

didn't drive John out. We never got along, but that was because you made it your business to see that we didn't get along. You drove him out yourself," Hubert said. "It was to get away from you. That was all he wanted. You wouldn't even let him go to school by himself. He couldn't go on the tram by himself like the other boys until the priests told you to leave him alone. And when he went to work you were down there at lunchtime half the time, weren't you? He got so that he was ashamed to be seen with you. A month before he left, he told me he was leaving, but he didn't tell you till the very last minute, because he knew you'd find some way to stop him and he was bound and determined to go. How do you like that? Tell me, how do you like that little piece of information? He told me first."

"If he got ashamed of me he got it from you," Rose said.

"Oh, of course you'd have to say that," said Hubert. "Of course you can't face facts. But I've had to face facts. He was sick of you and I'm sick of you, sick of your long face and your moans and sighs—I wish you'd get out of the room, I wish you'd go, go on, go away. I don't want any tea. All I want is not to have to look at you any more this evening. Will you go?"

"Oh, I will," Mrs. Derdon said. "I'll go. Indeed I will. Only to get away from you, that's all I ask."

She hurried out into the hall. She felt very free. She felt very independent. In that untrammelled moment she surveyed herself in the hall mirror as she adjusted her hat and stuck her two mother-of-pearl hatpins through her thick light-brown hair. For the first time for many years she saw the color of her own eyes. They were a clouded green, and as she stared at them she saw that they were filling up with tears.

Giving the hatpins a final push, buttoning her coat, taking her key to the front door out of her handbag and throwing it on the hall table, she saw that she was in terrible danger. She was in danger of hurling herself back into the room and throwing herself into the chair alongside Hubert and begging him to forgive her and to comfort her. She listened fearfully for the sound of her own running footsteps and for the sound of his voice but there was only silence in the house, no sound at all. She had been in danger, but she had not given way, she had not moved. She turned off the light in the hall and also the light that shone over the front door, to show that she expected no welcome back, because she was not coming back, and she left the house. She was astonished; she felt an indulgent astonishment at her former anguish and helplessness and at the importance she had attached to the house and all its little furnishings, when all the time all she had ever really wanted was to run away as far as she could go. It had taken the awful things Hubert had said to make her see the true facts of the case. He had hunted her out of her own house. He must have been mad for a moment there, to say such things. His face had been very red. He had never been so angry before. But he had ordered her out. She had always felt responsible for the house. She had always thought he needed her there to take care of him. There were a lot of little things she did for him—waiting on him and seeing that things were as he liked them to be. He would miss her. But nobody could ever blame her for going, not after tonight. Nobody could ever accuse her of running away from her duty. And she could not blame herself, after what he had said to her, after the terrible things he had said. It showed the sort of man he was, that he would make up things like that. She would never give him away, she would never let out a word of what he had said, even to John. She would never tell anybody. She would try to forget it herself, but it was going to be difficult to forget a shock like that.

She reached the corner of her own street and began to hurry along Sandford Road. She began to consider what she was about to do. She would have to tell Father Carey that Hubert had driven her out of her home for no reason. She would tell him that she was afraid to go back there. What she had in mind was to borrow enough money from Father Carey to pay her way to where John was. She was sure that when the priest heard her story he would give her the money. She didn't know him well, she had only had the one talk with him, when John went away, but she had often attended his Mass and she was sure he would not refuse her. Once she saw John again and talked with him, she would be on sure ground. She would find some kind of work, maybe even in the seminary. Sewing, cooking, minding children, even ordinary housework, she would do anything, and when you came to think of it, there were a lot of things she could do. She had always wanted to be a nurse, when she was young. There might be some work to be found in a hospital. She would expect very little in the way of pay, only enough to keep body and soul together. She would do her work, she would go to Mass, she would pray, and that is all she would ask in exchange for the chance of seeing John once in a while. She would become friendly with all of John's friends. They would come to her with their troubles and she would be the one who would know best how to talk to them. The priests in charge would wonder how they had ever got along without her. She was surprised that all this had not occurred to her before, and then she remembered that she could never have left the house if Hubert had not thrown her out. Now nobody could attach blame to her. She had done the only thing she could do. Someday she hoped Hubert would be ashamed of himself, but by then it would be too late. It was too late now. As long as she lived she would not be able to forget what he had said, or to remember exactly what it was he had said, only that it was the sort of thing people in their right minds didn't think of.

She was hurrying along Sandford Road in the direction of Eglinton Road, which led to Donnybrook and the church where John had been baptized and where they had all always gone to Mass. Sandford Road was always very busy, a main road out from town. On her side, on the side of the road where she was walking, the noisy trams went by her on their way out from town. The trams were nearly empty; the depot was not far away. The corner of the street where she lived was one of the last stops out from town. On the other side of Sandford Road, the trams passed on their way into town and they, too, were nearly empty. It was dark, except for the light from the street lamps and the occasional dim glare of light from the trams as they passed. It was the time of evening when nearly everybody was at home. A few men passed her, getting home from offices, and a few young girls. Boys and girls whirled by her on bicycles, not in crowds, as they would have been half an hour or an hour earlier, but in ones and twos. It had rained during the afternoon and the air was damp and cold, with a vigorous wind that she was grateful for because it seemed to wash her stiff face. The wind felt clean.

She crossed Sandford Road and stood on the corner where Eglinton Road runs in to Sandford Road. Eglinton Road was very wide, with big stone houses set back from the road and high up with stone steps in front of them. It was a residential road, quite well-to-do. There was no one on Eglinton Road, as far as she could see, and the way looked far and dark that she had to walk. She thought she had better sit down for a minute and collect her thoughts before she saw the priest. She wanted to tell him enough to convince him, but she did not want to tell him too much. She wanted to speak to him clearly and sensibly, so that he would respect her and give her the money. She wanted him to give her the money, but she wanted him to continue to regard her as an upright, dependable woman who had been driven to do what she had done. A few paces from the corner there was a wooden bench set alongside one of the heavy, big-branched trees that marked the length of Eglinton Road. This tree, the one nearest the bench, was so old and secure that some of its root lay coiled and twisted about it above the ground, making a rocky pediment on which John had often climbed when he was small, finding his way around the tree with his small hands against the trunk while she watched him from his bench. Although it could hardly have been the same bench. That was a long time ago.

She sat down and began to try to select and arrange the words that would best describe her plight to Father Carey and win his sympathy. There was what she had to tell him, about Hubert, and what she had to ask him for, the money, and her reason for having to ask for the money, to get to John. She started her appeal to the priest one way, and then she started it another way. She put in more and more details, to make her story more persuasive, and then she took out some of the details. She couldn't make up her mind whether to end by asking for the money or to work the money in as she went along. The more she fumbled with the words, the more she became convinced that her story was lame and sounded suspicious. She hadn't the ability to describe the scene that had just taken place between her and Hubert. A person would have had to be there, to have heard it, to believe it, and if a person had been there the scene would not have occurred. She was going to go to Father Carey and make a show of herself, that was plain. He would never believe. He would think she was making it all up, or that she was making an excuse of some little incident to spite her husband and get to her son. In either case, he would disapprove. He would tell her to go back to her husband. He would say, "Mrs. Derdon, you must return home at once. And you must on no account go near your son. If you interrupt your son's studies now, you may endanger his vocation." She could hear the priest saying the same words over and over again, and she couldn't hear him saying anything else. It was no use. He would never give her the money. She would have to find the money somewhere else, and there was no other place to go. But it would be useless to go to Father Carey. Worse than useless, even. He might get out his car and take her back to Hubert and make her go into the house. He might side with Hubert against her. It was more than likely that he would.

If John had happened along Eglinton Road at that moment he would have seen on his mother's face the fierce, cruel expression that they had both always thought belonged on his father's face. She looked capable of anything. She looked capable of murder, but she was only suffering what murderers suffer before they strike. But she would never strike. She was afraid. She thought it was pride that held her hand, but it was only fear. Fear and longing struggled for supremacy in her soul, but it was not their struggle against one another and against her that troubled her—it was her lifelong denial of herself, bolstered and fed as it was by fear. She longed to be near to someone, but there was no one who wanted her. She was sure of that. Nobody wanted her; it was her only certainty. It was bad that people turned their backs on her, but what was worse, worst of all, was that she saw no reason why they should not turn their backs on her. She was not surprised at the way her life had gone. She sat bewildered by her own judgment against herself, and unaware of it.

She felt cold. It was foolish to stay out in the air this time of year, this time of night. She put her hands inside the sleeves of her coat. She did not want to move just yet. She kept thinking that something

223

wonderful might happen, and that if she stayed patiently where she was, somehow or another she would be able to get to where John was. If she fainted from the cold and from exposure, an ambulance would have to come and take her to the hospital, and if she was in there, sick in the hospital, surely they would see that there was great necessity for John to come home again.

She must have come this way, around this corner, thousands of times, and she looked curiously about, because she had almost never been here at night before. She looked at Sandford Road, where trams and cars and bicycles and people moved steadily, passing one another, and she gazed down Eglinton Road at all the lighted houses, as far as she could see. She seemed to be saluting what she looked at, but she was no longer thinking of where she was. She was thinking of the place where John was, and of the town where she had been brought up, and of the hospital that was not going to admit her, and she was seeing the future that had once lain before her, full of light, reflecting heaven, that was now opaque and blank like fear and reflected nothing.

She got up and started walking. When she got to the corner of her street she saw that the light over the front door was lighted, and the light in the hall was lighted, too, and all the lights in the front sitting room were on. As she unlatched the gate the front door opened and Hubert peered out. He opened the door wide and she walked in past him and began taking off her hat and coat. He closed the door and followed her down to the kitchen.

"Rose, listen to me a minute," Hubert said. "I'm awful sorry about what I said to you. I don't know what got into me. I had no right to say what I said."

"It doesn't matter," she said.

"Oh, it does matter," he said. "Forgive and forget."

"I'll forgive you because that's what John would want me to do. John would never want me to hold a grudge, and that's the reason I'll forgive you. But I didn't come back for his sake. I came back because it's my duty to stay here and keep your house."

She was trying to keep her dignity but her voice trembled, and she was wearing the craven smile, but Hubert could not see that, because she was standing at the stove with her back to him, waiting for the kettle to boil.

"Have it your own way," he said. "Maybe someday your precious John'll have his own parish and you can go and keep house for him. Then you'll have him all to yourself. All to yourself. Maybe then you'll be satisfied."

"The tea is ready now," she said.

They had their tea in silence and when he was finished Hubert left the kitchen and she heard him go along the hall and into the front sitting room. That meant he must have lighted a fire for himself there. She would have two grates to clean in the morning, and the back sitting room to do, if she could do it. She would not look at it until morning. The damage would all be very clear then. She poured herself another cup of tea. It was warm in the kitchen, and there was no hurry about clearing up. She didn't mind the thought of tomorrow as much as she might have. She kept going back to Hubert's remark about her keeping house for John. There was more in that remark than met the eye. Sometimes people said more than they meant to say. She wondered if Hubert had realized what he was saying. He had probably meant it for a sneer at John, at the idea that John would ever be given a parish. But why should John not be given a parish? It was very likely that he would get one, sooner or later. Of course it might be a long time, but she could wait. Her family was long-lived on her mother's side. If anything happened to Hubert, she could sell this house, keeping only enough of the furniture and other things to make John's new home look familiar to him. She would make a new cover for the armchair he always liked, and a new cover for the cushion that had the mysterious stain on it. She would manage his house for him. The first few days would be strange, but after that they would settle down as though they had never been apart. She would become known in his parish as a very holy woman, and everyone would look up to her. His vocation would be her vocation. Everybody would say what a devoted mother she was, an example to all. All the ladies would consider it a privilege to have tea with her, and she would invite some of them. She would wear only black. John and she would have a great deal to say to one another, there would be no end to their conversations. She saw quite clearly now that all this was going to happen. It might be thirty years before John got a parish, but then again it might not take anything like as long as that. Whenever it happened, she would be ready. She would always be ready to go to his side, whenever he needed her. All she had to do was wait. There was no doubt that what she foresaw would happen, and when the day came she would pack up, sell out, and go straight to John, and after that it would be roses for the two of them all the way, roses, roses all the way.

Family Walls

For the fifth day in a row there had been no rain, and in Dublin, even in June, that was unusual. Hubert Derdon, who worked in a men's outfitting shop on Grafton Street, in the center of the city, had brought his raincoat with him when he left home in the morning, but when closing time came and he saw the golden evening he thought he might walk all the way home instead of taking that long ride out in the tram. He was a creature of habit. His daily habits were comfortable, but it would do him no harm to miss his tram for once even if it meant being late for tea. Hubert was always thinking about doing more walking. He knew that for a man in his forties he did not get nearly enough exercise. But there was the raincoat, and having to decide whether to carry it or put it on. If he was going to make a start on walking he did not want to start in his raincoat. And in the back of his mind he had an objection to wasting all that exercise on hard pavements with nothing ahead of him. He thought of mountain paths and tangled woods and narrow roads that ran between green fields. He imagined himself wearing a heavy pullover and walking steadily, but not in the direction of home. All the time he was thinking about walking he was hurrying to get his place on his usual tram, and in the end he turned his own corner and walked past the neighboring houses to his own front door and turned his key in the lock at the same time as always.

Thinking about doing all that walking had given him a sense of energy and well-being. He felt in good health and good humor, and contented to be coming home after his day's work, and he was smiling as he stepped into the hall. There were red glass panels in the side frames of the front door, and he was always aware of the glass, and always closed the door carefully. At the same instant that he was hanging his raincoat on the rack, he looked down the hall and saw the kitchen door close quickly and quietly, but not quickly enough to prevent him from seeing that Rose was down there. Her head was turned away from him as she closed the door.

The entrance hall where Hubert stood was narrow. It was no more than a passage, and the floor was covered with linoleum. At the end of the hall there were stairs going up to the bedrooms and, farther along, the three steps down to the kitchen. The hall was dim although it was still bright outside. The kitchen had been lighted up, the glimpse he had seen of it before the door closed. There had been only a second of time, and hardly more than a line of light that narrowed to a thread and then vanished. He might as well not have seen Rose at all, but he had seen her, and he wondered if it could possibly have been intentional—to shut the door in his face like that. He considered going down to the kitchen and asking some question, saying something, anything at all, but instead he went along the hall and into the back sitting room and walked over to the window, and turned at once from the window and began to stare at the doorway. But of course it was already too late. By this time Rose should have opened the kitchen door and called up, "Is that you, Hubert?" She must have heard him coming down the hall. You could hear everything in this house. He listened, but he could hear no sound at all. That was strange. He should at least have been able to hear some little noise, teacups and saucers or something, the tea being got ready. He might as well have been alone in the house for all the evidence he had of life near him. He felt that he was alone, and he wished there was someone in the room with him who could give him advice, because he wanted to be told to go straight down to the kitchen, or else, not to go down there but to sit down at once and ignore the whole matter.

He wished he had someone to talk to. He wanted the impulse he felt—to go down to the kitchen—to be made impossible by a command that he was bound to obey. But no word came to forbid him, and so although he knew it was impossible for him to go down and speak to Rose, he knew also that it was not forbidden, and he did not know what to do. What he could not do was to sit down. He was too angry to sit down. But he was trembling, and he sat down in his chair, which had its back to the window and was beside the fireplace, where it stayed summer and winter, close to the hearth, with Rose's low chair across the hearthrug from him. The hearthrug was a dull, warm red, and it was fringed at the ends.

Hubert wished he hadn't seen the door close. If he had taken that walk home, he would have been very late, and he wouldn't have seen the door close. But when had he ever walked home from work? Never. Rose had closed the door at the exact moment when she had every right to expect him home, and something in her attitude as she closed the door told him that she had seen him letting himself into the house. The more he thought back, the more he was sure he was right. In the glimpse he had had of her, there had been something hasty, he would even say furtive. Unless he was imagining things. But he knew he wasn't imagining anything. She was down there now, wondering if he had seen the kitchen door close, and she was frightened, and he wondered what she was thinking about him. She had no right to behave like this. It was intolerable. The whole thing was intolerable.

Then he heard the kitchen door open and footsteps on the stairs. When Rose appeared in the doorway Hubert felt such dislike that he smiled. He saw the confusion caused by the smile, and he saw her hand fasten on the doorknob as her hand always fastened on something—the back of a chair, or her other hand—before she spoke.

"The tea is ready," she said.

"I don't want any tea," Hubert said.

"What's the matter?" she asked. "Why don't you want your tea?"

She was standing stiffly and her face was pink. It was clear that she knew she was in the wrong.

"I don't want any tea," Hubert said. "That's simple enough, isn't it? And I can guarantee you this—the next time you shut a door in my face like that I'm going to walk out of this house and I won't come back. I mean what I say."

"Hubert, I don't know what you're talking about," she said.

Hubert said nothing.

"Will you let me bring you up a tray?" she asked.

229

"Never mind about the tray," Hubert said. "I don't want your tray. If you'd only get out of here and leave me alone."

Hubert watched until the door was shut and then he leaned forward and put his elbows on his knees and began to study the red hearthrug. He began to hum softly:

"She is far from the land where her
        young hero sleeps,
And lovers around her are sighing,
But—"

He sighed and lay back in his chair and was silent. He wished he had followed his original plan and walked home. Then he would not have seen the door close. If only he had not seen it close—but he had seen it, and having seen it he had to take a stand. It was partly the fault of the house, which was much too small. Any house would have been too small, but this one was much too small. There wasn't a corner in it where you could hide without causing questions—those silent questions that were not questions at all but reproaches.

There was no possible way for Hubert to ignore what went on in the house. He would have liked to be able to shut his eyes. Then he could control his temper. Rose was not ashamed that she had closed the door against him; she was only frightened because she had been caught closing it.

He wished he had had sense enough to go down to the kitchen and have it out with her the minute he saw the door close. He felt he was walking along a path that was separated from another identical path by a glass wall so high that it went out of sight. The path he was following was full of mistakes that he recognized, because they were all his own, but while every mistake was familiar to him, every mistake came as a shock, because of the different intervals of time that elapsed between one mistake and the next. Just when he felt fine and imagined everything to be all right, there was another blunder. There seemed to be no escaping the contentiousness and disagreeableness in this house. And all the time he was making mistakes and tripping over himself he could see through the glass to that other path that was also his own. On that path there were no mistakes,

and he did only the right thing and did it at the right time, and
he knew how to deal with everything, and he walked like a man who
was in command of himself and his life. Sometimes it seemed that
only a trick of light, nothing at all, stood between Hubert and the
place where he would know how to conduct life in accordance
with its meaning, which he understood perfectly.

Nothing in his life made sense. But once you had said that you had
said it all. Hubert could hardly march out of his house and down
onto the main road and stop some stranger and say, "I understand
nothing." To do a thing like that would be—it would be the ac-
tion of a madman.

If he had been on his own it wouldn't have been so bad, but a wife
makes a man conspicuous, especially if he doesn't amount to much,
and at this moment Hubert felt he amounted to nothing at all. Poor
Rose, he didn't blame her, but by her presence in his life she showed
what he had tried to do and that he had hoped, and by her behavior
she showed what his hopes had come to. He was ashamed of her.
Without her, who knows what he might have done. And then again he
might have gone through life invisible, but anything would have been
better than being held up to ridicule in his own house. Anything in
the world would have been better than being held up to ridicule to himself. He felt uncomfortable in his chair, and angry. It was not that she
was demanding or extravagant. She asked for nothing. The reason he
grew irritable when the time came to hand her the housekeeping money
every week was that she always took it apologetically, and on the few
occasions when he had forgotten it, reminded him timidly. Of course,
he grew irritable once in a while with her pretences, and no one
knew how many times he restrained himself when she irritated him
nearly beyond endurance. He could not stand the way she ate, or to
know the amount of food she ate, which was a good deal more than
he ever felt inclined to take. The word "appetite" embarrassed him,
and the knowledge he had of her appetite, which was so much
greater than his own, made her mysterious to him, but not in a way
that aroused his interest or affection. He thought her appetite was
something to be ashamed of, and he did not want to think about it.
He did not grudge her the food, but he thought she attached too

much importance to it. He dreaded to see her eat, because he could not keep his eyes off her, and there had been times when he saw her turn red and swallow quickly when she caught him watching her. He always had his breakfast by himself, and he had his dinner in town in the middle of the day, so there were only tea times and Sunday dinners to be got through.

Sometimes as they sat at tea Hubert told Rose about incidents that had taken place in the shop during the day. These anecdotes dealt mainly with the customers, and often the point they were working up to was the customer's discomfiture, which Hubert found funny, or the customer's ignorance, which Hubert also found funny. Some of the men who came to the shop were so dense that they did not know they were making fools of themselves or how they were laughed at after they left the place. They were the men who were too tall or too short or too fat or too thin for the patterns they preferred and for the cut and fit they decided upon. Hubert derided the dense customers, not because they looked ridiculous, but because they did not seem to know how ridiculous they were. Hubert could forgive any man for looking like a fool if he played the fool and showed that he could laugh at himself, and take a joke, but he had no mercy on people who believed, or pretended to believe, that they looked just like anybody else. Outside the shop Hubert could call attention to people's shortcomings and so test their sense of humor, but at work he naturally had to restrain himself, and it used to drive him nearly mad to see all those posturing fellows get away without knowing they had been observed by a man who had a sharp and humorous eye and a great gift for cutting people down when they got above themselves.

Hubert had heard Rose returning to the kitchen, but he had not heard the kitchen door close, although he knew she must have closed it. Now there was no sign from the kitchen. "Well, that's all right," Hubert said, "let her do what she likes." But he couldn't go on sitting in his armchair forever, doing nothing. He couldn't concentrate. He couldn't read. He didn't want to read. He didn't want to do anything. He had made up his mind not to give in to her. Sooner or later somebody was going to have to make a move, but Hubert felt that the decision had been taken out of his hands, and that it was now up to Rose to make some gesture. When he first came home and saw her close the door against him, he had had the choice between going down to the kitchen or not going down there. Now that choice was gone. Instead of making the choice he had asserted himself, and any sign he gave now would mean that he had backed down. She would have to come out of the kitchen sometime. She would want to go out to have a last look at her garden. Bedtime would come. It was only a matter of waiting until the normal routine of the house washed him out of the corner he had been forced into. It would be all the same in a hundred years, but Hubert knew that as long as he lived he would never understand why Rose had closed the door against him like that. He no longer wondered why she had closed the door, he only wished he had not seen it close.

The window behind him was a big oblong, almost a square, a sash window, and it faced the end wall of their garden. At the other side of the wall lay the courts of the tennis club. Hubert and Rose considered the members of the tennis club to be a gay and fashionable set, and Hubert said they were a worthless crowd. On Saturday nights they could hear dance music from the large new addition to the club-house. The members called the new addition the Pavilion. The dance music annoyed Hubert, and although Rose had once loved to dance she never protested when he got up and shut the window so that they could have a little peace and quiet in the house. The entrance to the club was on the main road that ran past the end of the terrace of small houses where the Derdons lived. On one side, the club grounds ended at the long end wall that was common to the twenty-six gardens owned by the Derdons and their neighbors all up and down the terrace. The farther boundaries of the club were marked by groves of trees. If Hubert had gone to stand by the window he would have seen the tops of the trees far away beyond the courts, and beyond the trees, coming toward him, the sky. He didn't move. He sat and listened. The window was open at the top and he could hear the quarrelsome old woman next door scolding her middle-aged daughter, who was unmarried and lived at home, doing the housework and cooking and easing her occasional rebellious rages with loud crying fits that could be heard in the Derdon's kitchen and also in the back sitting room. That garden next door was a wilderness of ivy and nettles and neglected cabbage plants. It was a disgraceful household. Hubert hoped the unhappy daughter would not have a crying fit this evening, and he wished both women would be removed to some lunatic asylum and that a single man who was never at home would move in next door. He listened to the old woman's thin, cruel voice, and he thought he heard her daughter's hysterical silence. He heard, faintly, voices from the tennis courts, and he heard the Donovans' big collie crying pitifully as it strained at the chain that held it to the cramped kennel that had been its home from a puppy. The Donovans kept the dog as a protection against burglars. Hubert wished a burglar might climb over the end wall and free the dog, who could then go into the house and kill Tom Donovan and his wife and their three impertinent children, and perhaps have enough to eat for once in its life.

He heard more than he could bear to hear. The back sitting room was filling up with lives he despised and with people he detested, and he had no defense against any of it. He could have closed the window, but he was sure that the minute he appeared there with his arms up, pushing the sash tight, Rose would open the kitchen door, coming out into the garden, and he did not want to see her. He didn't want to see her because he did not care about her. It was the first true thing he had said in a long time, and he was glad it was out in the open at last. He simply didn't care about her. He cared nothing at all about her, and he couldn't understand why he hadn't realized it a long time ago. He couldn't stand the thought of seeing her and having to speak to her and having to go on living in the same house with her. He could not think of her now without seeing the fluttering dishonesty of her expression, and he wondered if it would ever seem worth his while again to try to speak directly to her. What was the use of trying to talk to her? She never said "Yes" or "No." It was always "Whatever you like," or "I don't mind," or "Maybe, if that's what you want." And then the mute resignation that followed his decision, which, of course, was never what she wanted, although wild horses would not have dragged an objection out of her.

No, he wouldn't bother trying to talk to her. It wasn't worth his while, and it would only distress her for nothing. All the same, although Hubert felt that Rose was of no importance, he knew she was better than a good many people—better than the two women next door and better than the Donovans and better than that loud, good for nothing crowd at the tennis club. And he knew she was defenseless, and he felt that his indifference left her exposed, even though she didn't know about it, and he pitied her, because in her own way she did her best, and nobody cared anything at all about her. She was a lost cause, all right, and it was a good thing that only he knew it. It would be terrible for Rose if the rest of the world knew what he knew about her. It was no accident that she had always lagged behind him. She had no sense. She was not able to take care of herself. She had always been the same.

Rose had not always been the same, but there was no one now to tell what she had been or to see her as she had been seen. Once in a while she thought of her father, who died when she was ten. When she remembered him, trying to remember his voice, she looked more than ever like a bird that has found its feet on the ground instead of finding its wings in the air. She looked around her, and wondered. She was tame, but the place was strange. Whatever she might have been, laughing, solemn, hopeful, melancholy, serene, unquiet, ambitious, or whatever she might have become, she was now only tame. She had turned tame when her father died, as she might have turned traitor to a cause she had once been ready to give her life for. She had known her father was dead but not that he was gone, and even when she began to know he was gone she refused to believe that he was gone out of sight, and she put the strength of a lifetime into her struggle to keep him in sight until she was sure he was safe. She had forgotten all that was familiar to her in her struggle to stand by the one who had made it all familiar. She knew he would expect it of her. He had said that she was faithful. He had said that she would never let anyone down. Over and over again he had said she was a good child, and that she had no bad in her. He had always defended her to her mother.

Rose's father had thought the world of her, and he had told her,

235

and told anyone else who would listen, that she was an unusual child who could do anything she set out to do. Once when she was dancing around their kitchen showing off, he said, "One of these days Rose is going to show us how the birds fly." There was no end to their conversations, and they agreed on everything. After he was dead, when she set about remembering him, she found that she had memorized him, and he was so clear in her mind that, as she listened to her mother and the neighbors talking about him, all she had to do was to look above their heads and she could see him—not as he had been but as he was now, above them all and smiling down on them as he listened to the nice things they were saying about him, although none of them had had much opinion of him when he was alive. She hated them all, but the more she hated them the more she feared them, because she knew that if they found out about her dreams they would laugh at her and call her "Miss Importance." Her mother had always said that she had too good an idea of herself, and that she was too fanciful.

Rose knew that she must be a good child, but she never learned that there is more to being a good child than just doing what you are told. She did not know where she was. She wanted to be told what to do, and when she was not told, she imagined she had done something wrong. She had never been able to meet the world on its own terms—she did not measure up—and she had no terms of her own, and had not tried to make any. She had not known she had the power to make terms. She found the world difficult, because, while she knew that life is precious and must be watched night and day or it will vanish without warning, she also knew that in the long run life is of no value at all, because it vanishes without warning. Between these two sharp edges she made her way as well as she could. When Hubert first saw Rose he thought how light and definite her walk was, and that her expression was resolute. He never learned that the courage she showed came not from natural hope or from natural confidence or from any ignorant, natural source, but from her determination to avoid touching the two madnesses as they guided her, pressing too close to her and narrowing her path into a very thin line. She always walked in straight lines. She went from where she was to the place where she was going, and then back again to the place where she had been. She kept close to the house. She might as well have been in a net, for all the freedom she felt.

In the early days of their marriage Hubert and Rose lived in two rooms at the top of a house on Somerville Street, off Stephen's Green. The first evening they walked in there together was the evening of their wedding day. It was also the occasion of Rose's first journey in a train—from the town of Wexford, where she was born and brought up, to Dublin. A friend of Hubert's named Frank Nolan met them at the station to welcome them and to help carry their parcels and suitcases. Rose was carrying a basket of groceries her mother had packed for her at the last minute. It was all she carried, but Hubert and Frank were burdened down. When they reached the top of the tall building they were all breathless from the long flights of stairs. Hubert dropped everything he was carrying on the landing and put his hand against the wall to support himself, until he could catch his breath.

"What made you stop?" Frank said to him. "We'd have been in heaven in another five minutes."

Rose thought Frank was very funny. Frank had found the rooms for them and he had given Hubert the key at the station. Rose had watched Hubert put the key carefully in his waistcoat pocket, and now she watched him take it out again. He was very self-conscious, and in his eagerness to open their door he stumbled over one of the suitcases he had put down, and he nearly fell through the doorway ahead of Rose, but Frank grabbed him and held him back, and Rose went in first.

"Ladies First!" Frank shouted, loud enough to rouse the whole neighborhood. They were all there laughing. Rose put her basket on the shaky round table that stood in the middle of the room and she stood there looking around her while Hubert and Frank brought in the luggage. The scrap of thin carpeting under her feet was faded, and it was so worn that most of it was the same straw color as her basket, with traces of red and pink to show how bright it once had been. When everything had been brought in, Frank made a great display of trying to pick Hubert up and carry him around.

"This is a remarkable parcel, Madam," he said to Rose, while Hubert struggled. "It has delusions of grandeur. It thinks it's alive."

Rose had never laughed so hard in her life. She saw Hubert watching her and admiring her, and she knew they were both showing off for her benefit. Then Frank suddenly got serious and took his watch out of his pocket and looked at it and said he had an important appointment, a matter of life and death, and that he was two days and ten minutes late already. He was outside and closing the door after himself while he was still talking, and he wouldn't listen to Hubert's invitation to stay a minute. Then he vanished and they heard him running down the stairs. Rose looked at Hubert.

"Frank's a great man," Hubert said, "but I'm glad he's gone. Aren't you? Aren't you glad, Rose?"

"Yes," Rose said, and then she turned and went quickly to the window, a small, square window that looked across Somerville Street to the tops of the houses beyond.

"It's a lovely sky," she said.

"Take off that old hat," Hubert said. "You're at home now."

She had lifted the flimsy green net curtains that covered the windows while she was looking out, and as she raised her arms to take the pins out of her hat the curtains fell back to the wall and she saw that they were of unequal lengths.

"Look, one of these is too long," she said. "I'll have to even them up."

She took her hands from her hat and lifted the curtains and stepped back, measuring them together at their hems.

"About an inch," she said. "That should be right."

She let the curtains go, and when they dropped back into place she sighed with satisfaction, as though they had passed a test and carried the whole house to victory with them, and now she knew that the curtains and the walls and the long stairs up would stand fast and keep their appointed positions, all true weights to anchor her so that she would never get lost, because she was held safe where she belonged. She turned to Hubert and smiled at him. Then she remembered her hat and she put up her hands and began searching for the pins again.

238

"I'll do that curtain tomorrow," she said.

"Green curtains for your green eyes," Hubert said, but he knew there was no comparison, because the curtains were a garish green and Rose's eyes were the color of the sea.

When Rose was asleep her face looked solitary, and when she was awake she looked lonely. There was implacability and pride in her solitude, but her loneliness was helpless. Hubert could not reach her solitude, and he could not destroy her loneliness. He thought of the sea, and did not know why. When she woke up suddenly, turning over in bed, that implacable solitude shone triumphantly in her eyes for an instant before loneliness shadowed them. Hubert marvelled at her. He couldn't understand why she had married him, and at the same time he couldn't understand how she had lived until she married him.

"How did you ever get along before you met me?" he asked her.

"I don't know," she said. "I can't remember."

She was always smiling at him. She only stopped smiling in order to smile again.

One evening after tea he asked her if she had mended his socks. They were still sitting at the table—the shaky round table in the room with the green net curtains. They were two months married to the day, and Rose had bought a slice of dark fruit cake to celebrate the anniversary. She had cut the cake into fingers and they had eaten it all except for one small piece which lay on the plate between them. Hubert knew she wanted the cake but that she also wanted him to have it. He intended to give it to her, but he wanted to tease her. When he asked about the socks he was grinning. He still thought it absurd that Rose should do his mending. Rose had her elbows on the table and she was looking at her hands and admiring the one that wore the wedding ring. When she heard his question she looked at him in astonishment, as though he had deliberately said something he knew would hurt her.

"I forgot them," she said. "I forgot to do your socks. Isn't that just like me, to forget the one thing you asked me to do."

"It's not all that important," Hubert said.

He was still smiling, but he was hurt. She looked at him as though he was turning out to be just like her mother—catching her out in a mistake and then bullying her.

"It doesn't matter," he said impatiently. "Here, look, have this nice piece of cake."

"I don't want it now," she said, and "now" told him he had spoiled everything.

"Oh, all right, so," he said, and he took the piece of cake and crammed it into his mouth and got up from the table and went over to stand by the window.

He pushed the green net curtains aside and looked out. He saw the chimneys of the houses on the other side of the street, and the grey streaked sky above. It had been raining on and off all day. As Hubert watched, another shower began, and the raindrops dashed violently against the window. He felt a chill go through him although the windows were closed. Rose still sat at the table where he had left her. He felt ashamed of himself. If he had left her alone she would have eaten the cake and then she would have been happier. He longed to comfort her but the cake was gone and he could think of no other peace offering. He wished he knew what to say to her. He hoped she would soon get up and start clearing the table, because until she gave some sign he could not turn from the window and he was tired of standing there looking out at the rain and blaming himself. Then he turned without intending to, and she was sitting with her head down and her hands in her lap. She looked at him piteously and said, "I'm sorry, Hubert." He said gently, "There's nothing in the world for you to be sorry about."

She gave no sign that she heard him, but she continued to look at him. He felt that she was waiting for him to tell her what to do, and that she would do whatever he said. Her helplessness confounded him. He felt he could deal with *her*—after all, she was Rose, he knew her, she was his wife—but he could not deal with her helplessness. If he had put it into words he might have said, "I married Rose, not her helplessness," as another man might have said: "I married her, not her family." Hubert had seen Rose get that beaten look in her mother's presence, but there was no need for any of that now,

240

and he knew it would be a bad thing to encourage her in these moods. It would be bad for *her*. Her mother had warned him that Rose was inclined to brood over nothing at all. The thing to do was not to take her seriously and not to admit that there was anything wrong. There *was* nothing wrong. Hubert knew that the way to deal with Rose when she was in this frame of mind was not to comfort or coddle her but to distract her, and so instead of putting his arms around her, as he wanted to do, he said, "The shower will be over in a minute. Why don't we forget about all this and go out for a little walk and talk about the nice house we're going to have all to ourselves one of these days?"

The house they found was the one they lived in now. The linoleum on the floor in the back sitting room where Hubert sat had been there when they moved in, and they had paid extra for it. Before they moved into the house, they came out on the tram from Somerville Street one day and walked around the empty rooms they would soon be living in. One tour of the house was enough for Hubert but Rose was reluctant to leave, so he sat down on the floor in the back sitting room, with his back to the wall under the window, and told her to look around to her heart's content.

He was not easy in his mind, but the deed was done now—they had the house. He listened to Rose walking about upstairs. There was linoleum in the back bedroom but none in the front. She walked across the bare boards of the front bedroom and then she stopped. She was at the windows upstairs, looking out and wondering about the neighbors. Now she was coming back, and down the stairs. Her step was dulled by the narrow red carpeting on the stairs, and she was coming slowly and being careful to keep to the center of each step. She continued on down to the kitchen. The floor in the kitchen was covered with red tiles. After a minute she left the kitchen and came into the back sitting room, which they then called the dining room.

"I love looking around like this," she said. "I'll never get tired of this house. I wonder how they came to pick out those colors."

She was looking down at the linoleum, which was beige and brown and maroon in a pattern of large and small feathers.

"It's in very good condition," Hubert said gloomily. "I'm afraid we'll have to get used to it."

"Oh, it's not that I don't *like* it," Rose said.

She looked curiously at the linoleum other people had admired and taken care of. If it hadn't already been in the house she would never have owned it. It was like a gift brought from some foreign place. She would never have chosen that pattern or those colours. They were a part of something strange, from someone else's life, souvenirs of a country she did not know at all and where she did not want to be, because she would find herself timid and ill at ease there, and nothing there would ever be as real to her as the linoleum they had left behind was now under her feet. She walked possessively around on it.

"I never want to leave this house," she said.

Hubert got out of his chair and walked to the door. His mind was made up. He would go upstairs and wash his hands as usual, and change from his suit coat into his woollen cardigan, as usual, and then he would come down and let events take their course. His mind was made up, but even so, he hesitated before opening the door. But once the door was open he was up the stairs like a shot and into the bathroom, where he scrubbed his hands vigorously and splashed cold water on his face. He felt better already, knowing he was going to do the right thing. It was all a lot of nonsense, much better get everything out into the open. Now he would go straight down to the kitchen and have it out with Rose. He would laugh her out of her gloominess. It was only a matter of finding the right thing to say. He would get her to laugh at herself and see what nonsense all this bickering was. He hurried down the stairs and down the three steps that led from the hall to the kitchen as though he was bringing news that could not wait, good news, the best news, but at the kitchen door he hesitated and then, hearing no movement inside although she must have heard him thundering down the stairs, he beat a loud postman's tattoo on the door and burst into the room to find it empty. The door into the garden was open. She had gone out there and he could not follow her. All the neighbors would look out through their back windows and anyone who happened to be out in the neighboring gardens could hear every word he said.

He looked over at the stove to see if by any chance she had left the teapot there, but the top of the stove was as clear as the top of the table and the drainboard by the sink. The kitchen was spotless. She had finished working there. There was to be nothing to eat, then.

He went back up to the sitting room and went in. There on the dining room table which they kept folded against the wall opposite the fireplace she had left a tray. He went over and looked at it. Brown bread and a slice of ham. She had taken the trouble to shape the butter into curly balls. A tomato. Three chocolate biscuits. The teapot was at the fireplace, sitting inside the fender with the cosy over it. He hurried over to the teapot and pulled the cosy off it, and carried it to the table and shakily poured tea into his cup and returned the pot to the hearth. It was too hot to set down on the table. He poured milk into his tea and drank it down quickly. He wanted another cup at once, but this time he carried the cup over to the hearth and filled it there. Then he sat down at the table and began to eat his way through everything on the tray. When everything was gone he felt better, although he thought he could have done without the third chocolate biscuit. He had been hungry, that was all. Famished. He wouldn't mind having his tea from a tray like this every evening. He sat gazing at the ravaged tray and thinking about how she had smuggled it into the room while he was upstairs. It was clever of her. She had wanted him to have his tea but she had not wanted to face him. She had taken a lot of trouble over the tray.

He got up and went to the window. She was there, kneeling sideways to him by the flowerbed that ran along the wall where the laburnum tree was. The laburnum had been there when they moved in, together with a yellow rose that was on the opposite side of the garden. Apart from the laburnum and the rose there had been nothing. The place was a wilderness when they first saw it, but Rose had seen immediately that it had the makings of a good garden. Her work in the garden was wonderful. Hubert did not know where she had got her knowledge of flowers. She was kneeling out there now, settling

243

something, some little plant, into its bed. She was intent on placing the plant in its exact place, and she was as anxious at her work as though she had taken the future of the world between her hands and must set it right once and for all because there would be no second chance—no second chance for her, at least—to prove that if it was left to her, all would be well. For this moment the weight of the world was off her shoulders and in her hands.

She finished and sat back on her heels and rubbed her open hands together to get rid of the earth. Then she put her hand on the handle of the watering can and began to get awkwardly to her feet. Hubert looked away from her and down at his own hands. There was no need for him to watch her, to know how she got up. He had seen her often enough, raising herself after doing out the fireplace, by placing her hand on the edge of the coal scuttle. When he looked out again she was standing with her back to him, looking about her as though she was calculating the effect of some improvement she had in mind. She raised one hand to her hair, to smooth a loose strand up off the back of her neck into the thick bun she wore. She was wearing a white blouse with loose sleeves, and as the sleeve fell back, her upraised arm gleamed. Hubert saw her wrist and her elbow, and in that fragment of her he saw all of Rose, as the crescent moon recalls the full moon to anyone who has watched her at the height of her power. Then Rose stooped and lifted the heavy watering can with both hands and began to move slowly away toward the end wall, watering the plants as she went.

The day was almost worn out. The light was thin—fading light that left everything visible. That evening's light was helpless, the day in extremity, without strength enough left to dissemble with sun and shade, with only strength enough left to touch the world as it withdrew forever from the world. The evening light spoke and what it said was "There is nothing more to be said." There is nothing more to be said because what remains to be said must not be said. It is too late for Rose.

Hubert was silent. He had nothing to say, and in any case there was no one to hear him.